Rogue Magic
World Breaker Book 1
N. R. Hairston

Cover Design by Miblart

Published By

OTHER TITLES BY N. R. Hairston

Magic and Mischief Series
A Magical Reckoning,[1] Book One
A Symptom of Magic,[2] Book Two
A Victim of Magic,[3] Book Three
Sun Cursed
Cursed Magic,[4] Book One
Savage Magic[5], Book Two
Lethal Magic[6], Book Three
World Breaker

---

1.   https://www.amazon.com/Magical-Reckoning-Supernatural-Betrayal-Mischief-ebook/dp/B071P7HQVH/ref=as_li_ss_tl?s=digital-text&ie=UTF8&qid=1495929540&sr=1-1&keywords=a+magical+reckoning&linkCode=sl1&tag=fbp02-20&linkId=53cd93b9dc96241660ae8b41ec2bdefe

2.   https://www.amazon.com/gp/product/B07489BQVL/ref=series_rw_dp_sw

3.   https://www.amazon.com/Victim-Magic-Stories-Supernatural-Mischief-ebook/dp/B07H5FHBFB/ref=sr_1_6?ie=UTF8&qid=1536873999&sr=8-6&keywords=n+r+hairston

4.   https://www.amazon.com/dp/B075YDZZ45/ref=sr_1_3?s=digital-text&ie=UTF8&qid=1506478708&sr=1-3

5.   https://www.amazon.com/Savage-Magic-N-R-Hairston-ebook/dp/B094DXP7J1/ref=sr_1_6?crid=2BGRD37EYPF31&dchild=1&keywords=n+r+hairston&qid=1620470219&s=digital-text&sprefix=n+r+%2Cdigital-text%2C148&sr=1-6

6.   https://www.amazon.com/dp/B094DQ663R/ref=sr_1_10?crid=2BGRD37EYPF31&dchild=1&keywords=n+r+hairston&qid=1620470219&s=digital-text&sprefix=n+r+%2Cdigital-text%2C148&sr=1-10

Rogue Magic,[7] Book One
Bloody Magic,[8] Book Two
Battle Magic,[9] Book Three

World Breaker Beginnings (Novellas set before the events in Rogue Magic, though you don't have to read one to read the other.) Read this series for free when you join my mailing list, here.[10]

Rebel Magic,[11] Book One
Stolen Magic,[12] Book Two
Crooked Magic,[13] Book Three
Dirty Magic,[14] Book Four

---

7.   https://www.amazon.com/dp/B075YGLN4P/ref=sr_1_1?s=digital-text&ie=UTF8&qid=1506478708&sr=1-1

8.   https://www.amazon.com/gp/product/B094DR-RQH7?ref_=dbs_m_mng_rwt_calw_tkin_1&storeType=ebooks

9.   https://www.amazon.com/dp/B094DS7WLQ/ref=sr_1_8?crid=2BGRD37EYPF31&dchild=1&keywords=n+r+hair-ston&qid=1620470219&s=digital-text&sprefix=n+r+%2Cdigital-text%2C148&sr=1-8

10. https://landing.mailerlite.com/webforms/landing/h2l3b2

11. https://www.amazon.com/gp/product/B075YD3B6V?notRedirectToS-DP=1&ref_=dbs_mng_calw_0&storeType=ebooks

12. https://www.amazon.com/gp/product/B075YTLVZK?notRedirectToS-DP=1&ref_=dbs_mng_calw_1&storeType=ebooks

13. https://www.amazon.com/gp/product/B075YF35XX?notRedirectToS-DP=1&ref_=dbs_mng_calw_2&storeType=ebooks

14. https://www.amazon.com/dp/B094DSC8ZX/ref=sr_1_5?crid=2BGRD37EYPF31&dchild=1&keywords=n+r+hair-ston&qid=1620470219&s=digital-text&sprefix=n+r+%2Cdigital-text%2C148&sr=1-5

Feral Magic[15], Book Five
Lawless Magic[16], Book Six

Rise of the Dragons

Fire and Ash,[17] Book One
Smoke and Flame,[18] Book Two
Dust and Cinder,[19] Book Three

Atina and Ridge

We Got Powers Too,[20] Book One
We Wreak Havoc Too[21], Book Two

---

15.   https://www.amazon.com/dp/B094DQHDHY/
ref=sr_1_3?crid=2BGRD37EYPF31&dchild=1&keywords=n+r+hair-
ston&qid=1620470219&s=digital-text&sprefix=n+r+%2Cdigital-
text%2C148&sr=1-3

16.   https://www.amazon.com/Lawless-Magic-World-Breaker-Beginnings-
ebook/dp/B094DPBVHN/
ref=sr_1_11?crid=2BGRD37EYPF31&dchild=1&keywords=n+r+hair-
ston&qid=1620470219&s=digital-text&sprefix=n+r+%2Cdigital-
text%2C148&sr=1-11

17.   https://www.amazon.com/Fire-Rise-Dragons-Trilogy-Book-ebook/dp/
B076VFSGTZ/ref=sr_1_4?s=digital-
text&ie=UTF8&qid=1531259254&sr=1-4&keywords=n+r+hairston

18.   https://www.amazon.com/gp/product/B076V3N5H8/ref=se-
ries_rw_dp_sw

19.   https://www.amazon.com/gp/product/B076V14N8H/ref=se-
ries_rw_dp_sw

20.   https://www.amazon.com/gp/product/B07F8D55LL/
ref=dbs_a_def_rwt_hsch_vapi_taft_p1_i10

21.   https://www.amazon.com/dp/B094DQSMS5/
ref=sr_1_9?crid=2BGRD37EYPF31&dchild=1&keywords=n+r+hair-

We Got Witches Too[22], Book Three

Rebel Writers Anthologies

<u>Street Spells</u>[23]

---

ston&qid=1620470219&s=digital-text&sprefix=n+r+%2Cdigital-text%2C148&sr=1-9

22.   https://www.amazon.com/dp/B094DP9PNQ/ref=sr_1_13?crid=2BGRD37EYPF31&dchild=1&keywords=n+r+hair-ston&qid=1620470219&s=digital-text&sprefix=n+r+%2Cdigital-text%2C148&sr=1-13

23.   https://www.amazon.com/gp/product/B07F6GXSWV/ref=dbs_a_def_rwt_hsch_vapi_taft_p1_i11

Rogue Magic

I've made enemies of the wrong people and they're coming for me.

My name's Rekia and I'm wanted, dead or alive.

A normal day for me is hiding thieves and criminals in alternate universes where their pursuers can't find them.

On my latest assignment, I ran across a plot between two powerful worlds.

If left unchecked, it could destroy all worlds, including my own.

I can't let that happen.

My enemies put a price on my head, but I never go down without a fight.

Now, I'm coming for them. I've gathered a few friends and we're hunting.

If I die, I'm taking a few hundred of them with me.

Chapter 1

"Two billion dollars in your bank account and you're crying over a couple of million? You robbed the Rosent boys blind, then ratted them out to the police. They're going to kill you. You know that, right? If you don't leave town, you'll be dead by this time tomorrow. What are you going to do, Larry?"

Instead of answering me, his eyes roamed around my small home, taking in the modest furniture and simple design. I wasn't really one for coordination, so whenever I saw something I liked, I just bought it. I didn't care much about it matching or fitting in. Which was why my living room held a large deep-seated brown couch, a blue loveseat, and a chocolate recliner.

The walls were a mauve color and the carpet a flush beige. Most didn't understand or like my decorating sense, but to me, it felt like home.

Larry still hadn't answered and I wasn't sure how much longer I would wait. It was his life hanging in the balance, I was only trying to help.

See, no one else could do what I did and we both knew that. I didn't just hide people in a different city or state. No, I took my clients, most on the run from the law, to alternate universes, and they paid me well to do so.

I'd built my business from the ground up, but it was always people like this Larry that were the tough ones. He pushed black-rimmed glasses up his nose, his expression sour and calculating.

He was a tall, medium-built man, with black hair cut close to his head. He looked like the type who'd stick a knife in your back whilst smiling in your face and telling you how sweet you smelled.

He was a hustler, and he'd just been caught in his own trap. The Rosent brothers were going to kill him if he didn't get out of dodge, so I wasn't sure what the stall was.

He looked down at my desk, which happened to be in the middle of my living room, because, that's where my office was. "Look, lady..."

"You can call me Rekia." Lady, woman, girl, those had never been my name.

He swallowed hard, still not telling me if he wanted my help or not.

"What do you want to do?" I needed to get this over with so that I could get on with the rest of my night. I hadn't eaten since this morning and for the last two hours my stomach had been screaming in protest.

I looked at Larry and waited.

When he started to sweat and fumble with the paper in his hand I went ahead and called it. "Look, if you don't want to do this, or if you're having second thoughts..." I let the rest trail off hoping he'd get the point.

He pushed his glasses up his nose again, then ran a hand down the front of his suit coat as if straightening out wrinkles. "Are you sure you can do it?" he asked, as if scared to believe.

I was used to this question, as I'd heard it many times before. I'd found the simplest answer was the best. "Yes," I said, offering nothing more.

He swallowed hard, and I could tell he wanted to believe me but was too afraid to hope. I couldn't help him there. He had to make this decision on his own. I wouldn't take him otherwise.

His eyes darted around the room for a second, then he looked at the paper in his hand again, his fingers crinkling the edges just a bit. "Twenty-five million dollars is a lot of money."

My mouth went dry. The greedy ones always tried this. Especially the ones who'd messed up so bad in their current lives that they really didn't have anywhere else to go.

I could help them, yet the thought of throwing a few million my way bothered them so much that they were willing to risk possible death just to keep from paying me.

It boggled the mind to be honest, because I never broke them. My fee wasn't half their income, nowhere near really, yet they still acted as if I'd robbed them blind when it came time to pay.

Larry's case hadn't been an easy one, as he'd demanded certain things of the alternate universe I was to deliver him to, and I'd had to search to make sure all his specifications were met. I was tired now and just wanted to get myself something to eat and rest.

He stood, staring from me to the paper, not saying a word.

I let out a sigh. This wasn't going any faster and by this point I felt the need to assert myself a bit. "A million dollars extra for every minute you stand here. That's one million. In fifty-nine seconds, we'll add another million so..." I waved my hand through the air letting him know that I would continue until he stopped me.

His eyes popped, as he balled up the paper in his hand. I could see a vein pulsating on the side of his neck as the barely concealed rage he'd kept so carefully hidden under the surface floated to the top.

I'd seen it when we'd first met. Larry was the type who figured everybody around him owed him something. That type of thinking had led to him stealing from the Rosents in the first place. He'd thought himself entitled to whatever he wanted. Except now it was time to pay, and the fee was his life.

Not saying a word, I braced myself for the tirade that was sure to come. I hated this part and was grateful not many of my clients went this route. The ones like Larry always did, though. Somehow, they thought if they yelled loud enough they could make me dance to their tune. I shook my head, because I'd had to prove more than a few wrong.

Larry took a few steps forward, his fist clenched at his side. "You're no different than the Rosents. You all want to shake somebody down, take all their money. Well, I squealed on them, and I'll do the same to you unless you give me all your money right now. Come on, lady, hand it over, because if you think I'm paying you all that money, you obviously don't know me very well."

See, this is where I questioned their intelligence, because the one thing they never seemed to ask themselves is, if I can hide them in an alternate universe, then what else can I do? My eyes stayed on him, as he took another step forward, and I knew what he was about to do.

I took a deep breath and tried to prepare myself. When I'd first started this, my heart would beat out of my chest when this time came. It still sped up some, because I knew what was ready to happen and I didn't like it one bit.

Then, as predictable as a bird who shits, he came at me. Or tried to anyway. By now his face was red, and his eyes held a deep-seated childish rage that was probably the norm when he didn't get his way.

He made it a few inches from my desk before I flicked my wrist and used my telekinesis to send him spiraling across the room. He hit with a loud thump and crumpled against the wall by my living room window.

Plaster fell into his hair and all around him. Dammit. I hadn't meant to hit him that hard, just enough to slow him down and show that I meant business.

He looked around as if trying to figure out how he'd landed where he had, then came shakily to his feet, his eyes searching the room as if there were anyone here, but me.

I kept my focus on him, because from the murderous look on his face, I knew he wasn't done yet. His hair was in disarray, and he'd lost his glasses in the fall.

He stood agape, is if not sure anything he'd witnessed in the last few seconds was real. "I'm going... I'm going to..." He lunged again, and I never even moved from my spot.

I held up my hand and stopped him mid-stride. He tried to move forward, his eyes going wide with panic when he couldn't. He looked at me with that same wild expression as before, and I knew that he still didn't get it, not really. I held him there a little longer, waiting for it to sink in.

I let out a frustrated sigh, because sometimes I wished we could just get on with it, and not have to go through this unnecessary hassle. They always underestimated me, and I thought I knew why.

To some I just looked non-threatening. I was about five feet six, small framed, and my black hair was cut short, only a bit of it falling in my face, which made me look more twenty-three, than twenty-nine. They thought me an inexperienced little girl and I had to prove them wrong every time. I'd hoped to skip that lesson with Larry, but such was not the case.

I could tell the exact moment it all fell into place, because then came the real panic. He licked his lips, and true terror crossed his face. His eyes bored into mine, showing defeat and just enough regret to make me let him go. For now, anyway.

I dropped my hand, and he felt around his chest as if making sure all of him was still there, then he took a tentative step forward.

I braced myself, knowing this could go only one of two ways. Either he'd accept it and move on, or he'd hit back with even more threats.

He picked his glasses up off the floor, then raised a shaky finger at me. "How... how did you do that?" His voice quivered when he spoke, and I steeled myself, because I now knew where this was going.

He swallowed hard and backed up a few steps, still pointing his finger. "It's not natural what you just did. No one should be able to do that." His voice rose to hysteria. "Witch, you're a witch, and you're trying to send me to hell." He shrunk back, holding his hands up as if to protect himself from my voodoo magic.

I shook my head. It had been his greed that caused this situation in the first place, nothing more.

He took a few more steps back, fear the only emotion I saw on him now. I sat up a little straighter in my chair, knowing that this would all soon be over.

He wouldn't try anything else, and he wouldn't tell anyone what had happened here today. Scared men kept their mouths shut, and right now, Larry was as scared as they came. Now I just needed to clinch the deal.

"You can go now," I said, rubbing my temples as a small headache started to form. "Nothing really left for us to discuss." I busied myself at my desk, going over invoices, and thinking about what I wanted for supper.

I watched him out of the corner of my eye pick up the paper he'd dropped. He fumbled with it a bit, then handed it over, refusing to meet my eyes.

I took it from him and looked it over. It was blank except for that one string of bank numbers that would transfer the twenty-five million from his bank account to mine. "Thank you."

He seemed to have calmed down, and I wanted to soothe the tension between us as much as I could.

Flashing him an easy smile, I picked up the phone, called my contact, told him what he needed to know, and waited until he confirmed that the money was safely in my account.

I'd let Larry slide on the extra million I'd demanded, now that we both seemed to be on the same page. At least I hoped we were anyway.

He stood in the same spot, watching me anxiously until I hung up the phone. "Everything okay?"

I looked up from my desk. "Everything's fine. Come back tonight, and we'll go from there."

He put his glasses back on and hurried out the door as if scared I'd change my mind at the last second.

I couldn't help shaking my head as I watched him go. He was a thief and a coward, but I knew he'd be back tonight revving to end this.

I took another sip of water and started to mentally prepare myself for later. It may have seemed like I charged a lot, but, well yeah, there was really no way for me to justify it. It was a lot of money, but I didn't keep it all for myself. I gave a significant amount to my parents, plus my two nieces and three nephews.

I only had three siblings, two older brothers, and one older sister. Kevin, the oldest, was married and had two boys. Chanel, the next to oldest, was divorced and had a daughter. My last brother, Greg, who was a year older than me, was single and had a boy and a girl.

I'd set up trust funds for the kids, much to the chagrin of my brothers and sister. They didn't like how I made my money and didn't mind telling me so every chance they got. They each made a decent living but understood that providing for my nieces and nephews was important to me, so they didn't stand in the way of that.

Sitting up in the chair, I scooted under my desk and pulled up my calendar. I didn't have anyone else for at least two weeks. Which meant I could take care of some of the follow-up duties that came with the job of relocating people to parallel worlds.

My headache still forming, I massaged my temples again, thinking about the man who'd just left. He'd called me a witch. I wasn't a witch, but that hadn't been the first time I'd been called one. What I could do wasn't natural to my home world. I'd inherited a lot from my father, me along with all my siblings.

I went to the kitchen to make myself a cup of tea, hoping that would help settle the ache in my head. My brother Greg could probably just move the headache away but I didn't have that ability.

My father came from a place a little more advanced than our world. He and all the people of his world had the power to form portals and travel from dimension to dimension. My father's world wasn't the only one that could do this, but the numbers were far in between.

My water boiled and I poured it into a small mug, teabag already in place. I took a seat at my kitchen table and dropped two sugar cubes into my cup.

Only a select few knew what I could do. They didn't know how, but they knew I was the person to come to when you no longer had the option of going home.

I stirred the tea and took a small sip. The liquid was bitter and burned my tongue a little, making me ease back in my chair and sigh contently.

Over the years, I'd made quite a name for myself, and I was good at my job. I could hide you where you'd never be found. I figured that was worth a few million. I took another sip of tea, pleased with the taste.

It may have seemed like a dream job, to some, but it was not without its dangers. I never knew what I'd run into, and there was always the possibility of something or someone slipping back through with me. I had to be careful.

I only took people to alternate worlds advanced enough that the people who lived there knew other realities existed and wouldn't look at them strangely when they showed up. I only took them to places where their money could be changed and converted into the money of their new world.

I also, only took them to places, where the dialect was the same as our own, and the worlds similar enough that they didn't feel they were too far removed from all they knew and loved.

They all came with millions, and I always picked a place where the money differences would still allow for them to live a decent life.

Not that they deserved it, but because they'd paid me to, and I tried hard to never go back on my word. It was bad for business and bad for my reputation in general. But Larry? He'd been asking for it. Still, if he came back ready to leave, I'd take him where he needed to go.

IT WAS AFTER EIGHT when he finally showed up. He looked a little more confident and self-assured this time, something that hadn't been there before.

I smiled. He was finally ready. I asked him to take a seat on the couch while I grabbed my things.

I live in a very modest, three-bedroom house. If not for my nieces and nephews, it would have been a one bedroom, but I needed a place for them to sleep when they stayed over. Others might not have thought it was much, but they loved it, which was all that mattered.

I was halfway down the hall when I turned to look back toward the living room. Larry stood in the same spot I'd left him, hands in his pocket, shoulders hunched as if he couldn't believe what was about to happen. Satisfied that he was ok, I walked on.

The smell of lilac hit me as soon as I opened my bedroom door, and I inhaled deeply, enjoying the scent. My room consisted of three-year-old furniture that I'd gotten from the furniture store down the street. My queen-sized bed was in disarray, as I'd gotten up in a rush and hadn't had time to make it. That was often the case, I was starting to suspect I just didn't like making the darn thing.

I had two oak dressers set up on each side of the room that matched the brown headboard of my bed. The carpet was a deep blue and I'd painted the walls orange and yellow, just for the fun of it.

My closet was a huge walk-in and knowing that Larry was waiting, I opened it, and tried to hurry. Tonight, we would be going into uncharted territory. It wasn't often that I took people to a world that I hadn't already visited and set up contacts. I had many associates, in many different dimensions, because it just made my job easier.

But Larry being the greedy little man that he was, had requested a world where his billions would double or even triple. I'd found the place, but I'd never been there, so I knew nothing about it or its people.

It would have been smart of me to do a little run through before now, but I simply hadn't had the time.

Anyway, I was usually able to handle myself pretty well, so while I felt a little apprehension, it was more because I would have to stay for a while, setting him up and making sure he found somewhere to live. Something I didn't normally have to do on worlds where I already had trusted contacts.

I looked in my closet and decided to change into a simple pair of black jeans and a brown sweater. Simple was best when walking into a situation unknown. Usually, I dressed in accordance with the world I was going to, but since I'd never been there, I had no idea how they dressed.

I'd already loaded my backpack when Larry had left earlier, so at least that was done. I'd learned long ago that it was always wise to prepare for, well anything, really. Especially when entering into a world unknown.

I'd had crisis with three of my clients and hadn't had a moment to breathe until now, much less check out a new world.

I pulled my sweater over my head and slipped on my jeans. I never really dropped my clients cold. I always kept an eye on them. I usually gave it about three days, then I'd check to see how they were doing, and make sure they were getting on okay.

After that, I'd wait another two weeks, then another few weeks after that. Then it was only once a year, until I felt safe enough to leave them alone completely. They could always get in touch with me if they needed to though.

I made sure of that, if they couldn't reach me personally, for whatever reason, then one of my contacts, in whatever world they were in, would be able to find me.

Shoes on, and bag ready, it was finally time to go. I walked back into the living room to see Larry in the same spot, waiting. "I'm ready," I said, anxious to get this over with.

Larry jumped upon hearing my voice, and I noticed a few nervous blinks before he could talk. "So how do we do this? Do you just wave your hand or...?"

I fastened on my backpack and made sure the straps were tight. "No. There are certain spots we have to leave from," I lied.

He rubbed sweat-soaked hands down the front of his pants and nodded.

Feeling just a little sorry for him, I walked to the front door and opened it. "After you."

Chapter 2

I n the car beside me, Larry fidgeted and fussed with anything he could get his hands on. I knew he was scared, and unfortunately, there was nothing I could say to make him feel better. I'd been through it enough times to know that my silent support was probably the only thing that would keep him somewhat grounded.

Yeah, he'd been a jerk, but at this point he was my responsibility and I took that seriously.

I kept my eyes on the road, thinking about my chosen profession. I didn't really know why I did what I did, my sister said I was a thrill seeker, always looking for the next rush. I shrugged. Maybe I was, but I loved world hopping and didn't see myself stopping any time soon.

It took forty-five minutes to get where we were going. The spot I'd picked was one I'd used many times before, as it offered privacy and there were enough twists and turns that it made it easy to tell if someone was following me.

No one in this world, my home world, knew what me and my family could do. My clients never knew until they walked into my office. They didn't know about alternate dimensions and thought things like telepathy and telekinesis were just stuff they saw on their favorite TV show every week.

I'd like to keep it that way. The thought of us ending up on lab tables was not a pretty one. We could handle ourselves, so really it was the ones who would try to take us that would be in danger. My sister would then ask why I brought attention on myself, by doing what I did. She believed I got a high out of playing hard and fast with the law. I didn't, at least I didn't think I did, but I was careful enough, that it had never been a problem.

Even if someone did go public with my secret, who in their right mind would believe them?

I pulled up to an open field, with no livable houses for miles. If someone didn't know any better, they'd swear that we were in the desert, instead of a small rural part of the country.

We got out of the car, and I shivered just a little, thankful for the thin sweater I'd decided to throw on. It wasn't exactly cold yet, but as the night wore on, the temperature would steadily drop. Right now, it was okay, and the cool breeze blowing through my hair didn't hurt things one bit.

Taking a moment to think, I turned to look around. People had lived out here once, evident by the empty barns and shacks littered about. I walked to one with a sunken, wooden porch. Half the roof was caved in, and the walls looked like they would soon follow.

Larry seemed skeptical. "This is it?" He took in the rotten smell of mildew and waste, the ramshackle remains of neglect and abandonment, and his shoulders sagged as if all his worst fears had come to life. The look on his face said he'd been right from the start and all of this was just too good to be true.

Not wanting him to see how I opened my portals, I directed him away. "Go to the car and get your things while I get started."

I waited until he'd disappeared before walking to the wall and placing my hand on it. Yeah, I could have done this at home, I could do it anywhere, but the less he knew about my powers, the better. I didn't need him going to this new world of his, able to tell exactly how I did what I did.

I flexed my hands, and concentrated hard on the universe we were about to enter. Focusing my energy, I transported it from my hands and into the wall. It started off slow, almost like a bubble, then the blue glow began to spread and open.

"So, this is it then?" I heard him gulp behind me. I jumped a little, startled, then smiled and nodded. He didn't smile back, his eyes intent on the portal in front of us.

I took a step back and tried to focus. I needed to make sure we could slip in undetected. I just found it easier that way. When people knew you could hop worlds, they often had a million places they wanted you to take them. To avoid all that, I'd started going in incognito.

Not knowing what I was doing, Larry grabbed his roll away cart and waited. I couldn't believe he'd actually brought a whole cart, like the kind you get at Sam's club when you're shopping for the whole year.

I looked down at the monstrous thing and shook my head. It was piled high with all the things he deemed necessary to take with him. Refusing to waste any more time, I grabbed his hand. It was clammy, wet and reminded me of just how scared he really was.

Letting his fear really sink in, my voice took on a softer edge when I spoke. "Hold me tight, okay?" He nodded, then placed his life completely in my hands. Not an easy thing to do. I let out a breath of tension and made sure to keep hold of him as we stepped into the portal and walked through to the other side.

I was used to the sickening feeling of my protons and neutrons being torn apart and put back together again, but Larry wasn't. He looked like he'd spun around in a bunch of circles until he was too dizzy to stand up. Expecting this, I waited for him to get his bearings.

The new world I'd brought him to was called Sentra and it was ice-cold here. The wind whipped around us furiously, and suddenly I regretted not bringing a jacket. I turned from Larry, aiming to offer him some privacy while he got himself together and stopped short at what I saw.

I'm sure my mouth hung open a little as I took in the sight before me. What even was this? I mean, I'd been to some pretty strange places before. Some even felt like hallucinogenic dreams. But this right here, well this was something else entirely.

I took a few steps forward, as the wind picked up hollering and screaming. The streets were lined with gold. No seriously, the streets were lined in what looked like pure freaking gold.

I looked around a little more. The sidewalks sparkled and shined every color of the rainbow with what looked like rubies, diamonds, and who knew what else.

Diamond-laced sidewalks. This place had diamonds in their sidewalks. At a loss for words, I just stared on, wondering why the expense, the extravagance?

I would have pulled out my phone and started snapping pictures if it wasn't so unprofessional. The buildings were tall, majestic even, and felt almost magical in their appearance. They too had diamonds and rubies down the side of them and many looked to be platinum plated.

My eyes lit up like a small child's first time at Disney world. Everything looked so beautiful, so unreal. I'd never seen anything like it in my life, and the effect of having so many sparkling jewels staring up at me made me feel like I was trapped in a diamond Rubik's Cube. My eyes started to cross and I blinked them, not sure if I could stay here long. The effect was a bit staggering.

This place was full of money. It gave me hope. If I could make a few contacts, set up an office, get to know the lay of the land, maybe I could start bringing more clients here. I would have to be in constant contact with this place for at least a year before that could happen, though.

Larry, apparently having gotten ahold of himself, walked to where I stood and looked around. His eyes bulged as he turned in a small circle taking it all in. "This is, wow. Never did I imagine it could be like this." The greedy look in his eyes shined and sparkled, and suddenly I was sure he'd fit right in.

Deciding to get down to business, I scanned the area, trying to find the best place to scout out directions. I settled on walking straight ahead and motioned for Larry to follow.

He grabbed the handle of his cart and pushed his glasses up his nose. "So, what do we do now?"

I saw a few people walk by, and a few cars on the street. As I said, I tried to take people to worlds that were not much different from our own and spoke the same language. Each world was unique to itself, but the people here looked the same as you would find on my world and so did the cars, the ones I'd seen anyway. That wasn't always the case in the worlds *I* visited strictly for fun, but I always wanted my clients to feel as at home as they could, so here we were.

I stopped a lady with diamond high heels, diamonds also on all fingers, neck, and wrist. It wasn't dark here, like it had been when we'd left home. It looked to be midday, and though there was no sun in sight, the lady's jewelry still blinded me.

Larry licked his lips as he watched her. He raised his hand, and I could literally see him itching to touch one of the sparkling stones. I gave him what I hoped was a stern stare and he at least had the nerve to look sheepish.

Ignoring him, I turned to the woman. "We're from off world, and we're looking for the place where we can convert our money and set up lodging."

Standing tall, with black hair, and brown eyes, she looked me over, seemingly unimpressed. I looked down at myself, seeing what she saw. I had no jewelry on. I'd bought my pants and sweater at the local Wal-Mart, and my shoes were from there as well.

I wasn't as done up as she was, but I figured I looked decent enough. Plus, I was comfortable, which was always the deciding factor when buying clothes.

Her face twisted as if the sight of me physically pained her, and her gaze shifted to Larry.

Her eyes raked over his designer suit and his fifteen-hundred-dollar shoes, and she probably figured he was okay to talk to. I don't know what did it, but where I'd gotten a frown, he got a smile so bright, that it almost put her jewelry to shame. He smiled back, and I felt the stirrings of another headache coming on.

They began a conversation, and I walked off to the side, thinking he'd get more from her if I wasn't around. A small flash of red caught my attention, and I moved to my right to investigate. I thought I saw a red shirt disappear down a gold-lined gutter drain, but I couldn't be sure.

I rubbed my eyes as the light from all the jewelry played havoc on my sight. How did these people ever see anything around here? Probably they were used to the constant glare from the jewels, but for me, it only made it that much more difficult to see.

I waited a few more minutes, hands shielding my eyes before he finished his conversation and walked to where I stood.

The lady had moved on, yet Larry practically beamed. He had a small piece of paper in his hand that he waved back and forward. I took it from him and shook my head. The borders of the paper were white platinum, with diamond horses embroidered all around. Insane.

I waited outside the large diamond-studded exchange building while Larry went inside to convert his money. My stomach let out a small growl as the sweet smell of pies and desserts fluttered past my nose. World hopping took a lot out of me, and I was always hungry afterward. Extremely hungry, which is why I usually kept snacks in my bag, in case I didn't have time to stop and get food.

I looked around until I noticed we were a few doors away from a bakery. So, they did have normal things here, like restaurants, maybe even movie theaters and such. Somehow, I found a bit of comfort in that. Larry was still my client, and I did want some parts of home here with him to make the transition a little better.

Still, after today he needed to learn how to make his own connections. My job was to get him here. To hide him where no one could find him and that was it. I'd help as much as I deemed necessary, but I needed him to show me he could be self-sufficient.

Looking around at the glamor and what I assumed was a fast lifestyle, I was kind of on the fence now about bringing more people here. Thinking back on the rude woman from earlier, I realized that it didn't seem all that friendly a place.

As if to prove my point, more than a few people walked by while I waited for Larry, but none of them would talk to me. They all had the same 'I'm better than you, so I can't even spare a glance your way' air about them.

I guessed I would have to cancel this place off my list because it was becoming increasingly obvious that there were no contacts to be had here, especially if I couldn't even get a hello.

IT TOOK ABOUT THREE hours to find Larry a house and get him set up. These people worshiped money, and as long as you had it, everything ran smoothly. Good for Larry that he was practically swimming in the stuff now. I thought about what I'd learned of this world so far, and wondered what would happen to him if he ever ran out of cash. I shuddered just thinking about it.

Closing the door on Larry's new house and turning around, the sparkle and shine from the streets, sidewalks, and buildings nearly stopped me in my tracks. The contrast in colors and shapes were simply breathtaking. Imagine hundreds of diamonds and jewels all laid out, glimmering and shining in the light of day.

The effect was startling, dazzling even. Throwing professionalism out the window, I took out my phone and snapped a few pictures for memory sake. I'd never seen anything like it in my life and doubted I ever would again. It was electrifying.

I started down the street but turned back after a few steps to take another look at Larry's new house. It stood tall, made completely of platinum. Diamonds covered the whole three-story structure and the sidewalk leading up to the front porch.

Looking around the neighborhood, I saw that all the houses were like this to varying degrees so I figured that Larry would fit right in. Add to that, the fact that he seemed pretty pleased with his purchase and my work here was done.

It was a strange place, yet I found myself kind of sorry to be leaving. Oh well, I'd be back in three days to check on him at any rate.

I decided that it was best for me to leave the way I'd come, as it seemed like a less populated area.

Another flash of red caught my eye for just a second, giving me pause. Maybe it was nothing, but I didn't plan on sticking around to find out. That old saying that, 'curiosity killed the cat' had never felt truer.

I checked my surroundings, making sure I was completely alone before I did anything. Some may say I was overly cautious, but after some of the things I'd seen, I knew a little precaution was always a smart move. Looking over my shoulder one last time, just to be sure I was alone, I opened a portal and stepped through.

The contrast from there, to back home was wicked. To go from a light, bright, and sparkling place, to one that was dull and dark, had me rooted to the spot for a minute. The difference was almost depressing, yet I'd never been so happy to be home in my life.

I turned in the direction of my car, thinking about what I wanted for dinner, and that's when I saw it. Red. Again. On this side of the portal. In my world, not on the other side where I'd been sure I'd left it. Something cold and hard settled in the pit of my stomach as I looked on.

This time it took shape in the form of one man and one woman, both sporting the color red. Unlike Larry they weren't stumbling around in circles, which spoke to frequent portal use, though maybe they hadn't been through one in a while because they did seem a bit disoriented.

I flexed my hands getting myself ready for anything. I'd brought them into my world, so it was my job to deal with them.

Chapter 3

I watched the two figures in front of me, and silently cursed under my breath. I'd been on the lookout for any trespassers, so how had I allowed them to slip through? I ran a hand down my face and wondered if it was just those two or if more had joined. I hoped not, but I couldn't be sure of anything at the moment.

I waited until the two interlopers found their footing, before asking any questions. "What the hell do you mean by hijacking my portal?" I kept my hands at the ready, in case they tried anything. I hadn't taken the time to learn about the world they'd come from, or if they had any powers, a costly mistake that I didn't plan on making again.

Holding onto each other for balance, they finally looked at me. Both stood about six feet and had jet-black hair. The woman's stopped at her waist. The man's, at his shoulders. On both of them, it hung in dry, matted, useless clumps. From their features and coloring, had they been from my world, I would think them originally from overseas, China maybe.

They both had deep-set eyes, the color of sandstorms, yet their clothing was ragged, torn, and disheveled. They looked like they'd stepped into a sewer, snatched up whatever they could find, and put it on.

I scratched my head. Had they really just come from the rich land I'd just left behind?

The woman stepped forward, head held high and back straight as an arrow. "I'm Nico, and this is my brother Toma."

Try as I might, I couldn't bring myself to care about their names. I didn't even try to hide my irritation when I spoke. "Rekia. Now, you've been following me all day, and I want to know why."

Toma looked to his sister, and I assumed a silent conversation took place between them, because when he turned back around, he began to speak.

His voice was a deep baritone that kind of sent a chill up my spine. Not enough for me to forgive what they'd done though. "Look, we saw you when you came in. We could tell from the way you were dressed that you weren't from our world."

He stopped talking and looked around, taking in the scenery probably. "I know we were wrong to follow you, but there are only a handful of people in all the known universes who can do what you do."

Yeah, well, tell that to my father's people, I thought.

He shrugged, hands in his pockets. "We may have never gotten another chance."

I walked over to my car with them following closely behind. Nico turned back toward the house. Her eyes took in the sunken roof, the broken steps, and every other misfortune that had befallen this place over the last hundred years or so.

She looked horrified when she grabbed her brother's arm and pointed to the deserted house that clearly no one lived in. "Maybe we should have stayed where we were." Her face held the same disdain as the diamond lady, like she seriously thought this was where I lived.

She'd figure it out in her own time. I took a seat on the hood of my car, spreading my hands out behind me for balance.

They stood in front of me, not saying anything, as if they expected me to make the first move. Fine with me, because I had more than a few questions. "Why do you two look like you slept with the garbage last night?" Not the most eloquent way to start, but it'd break the ice.

They flinched as if I'd slapped them. I sat up straighter on my car. This to me was interesting, because what the heck did they think they looked like? Was this surprising information? Did they think themselves to be fresh and clean?

That they were proud went without saying. Something told me that this pair had just recently fallen on hard times and was still adjusting to the change. Something was going on here, and damn me to hell if I didn't want to find out what it was.

Nico stepped forward and swiped a small strand of hair out of her face. Her eyes were hard, voice toxic and warning. "We've not had a decent meal in months. We eat what scraps we can find. Drink out of discarded bottles. We dress like this because we have nothing left to wear. What's your excuse? Why do you look the way you do?" Bitch. I'd give her that though. Coming from the world she did, I guess she expected everyone to walk around looking like they'd just stepped off the runway. Me in my battered sneakers and torn jeans, must have looked quite the sight.

I wondered if her brother felt the same, yet his face remained blank so I couldn't tell. Maybe he did and was just better at keeping his emotions in check. "That still doesn't explain why you followed me. Why are you here?" Maybe I could have been more sympathetic, but she wasn't exactly dripping with niceness either.

She took another step forward, arm raised, face in an ill-gotten sneer. Whether she was ready to attack or not, I'd never know, as her brother's booming voice stopped her cold. "Nico, stop. We need her help, remember. It's not her fault we're in this situation. It's ours."

Deciding I'd had enough of this little show I got off the hood of my car and went to the driver's door. "Talk fast. Got a million other places I could be right now." I'd done two portal hops with no food, and my body would start to breakdown if I didn't eat soon. Besides, who knew what they were really up to anyway, or why I was even wasting time trying to figure it out.

Toma looked at Nico, but she kept her head down, refusing to meet either of our eyes. He turned to me, a slight grimace on his face as if to apologize for his sister's rude behavior. "Can you put us up for the night?" His voice was pleading, yet his eyes looked shamed that he even had to ask.

I kept my face neutral, not ready to decide until I'd heard all they had to say.

He pointed toward my car. "Come on, what's one night? Here we have a chance." He looked to where the portal had now closed. "Back there, we'll die, no way around it."

They both hit me with those swirling brown sandstorm eyes of theirs, waiting for my response. Well, shit. Now, who in the world could resist that? Probably anyone with good sense, and that apparently didn't include me.

I felt my shoulders slump and knew that they had me. My sister was right, maybe I was just a thrill seeker, searching for my next great adventure. I was too nosey for my own good, too curious to just leave things the way they were. Plus, I couldn't just abandon them here.

Settling people into new worlds was what I did best. It was my job, after all. So, I figured I'd help them until they gave me a reason not to.

Also, I really wanted to know what had brought them to this point. Why, in a world filled with richness and glamor, did these two look like they'd been living in a trash compacter? I bit my bottom lip. The urge to know the truth gnawed at me, and I knew without a doubt, that they were coming home with me.

I used my telekinesis to fly my car doors open, to let them know that I could do more than open a portal. Above all else, I would protect myself, and I wanted to make sure I sent that message loud and clear.

"Get in," I growled. "Before I change my mind."

Nico got in the front, and her brother hopped in the back, his seat right behind hers. Her voice sounded surprised as she stared at the broken-down shack. "So, that's not your home. You don't live in there?" Was she even serious right now?

I gestured toward the broken-down pile of wood. "Who could live in there? Tell me." She raised one finger and pointed it at me. I guess indicating that she would expect me to live in such a place. I let out a slight chuckle and started the car. This was going to be interesting.

WE MADE IT TO MY HOUSE a couple of hours later, and I'd never been so happy to be home in my life. I plopped down in the first chair I saw, simply exhausted from dealing with the two of them and everything that had come earlier. Plus, the only thing I'd eaten was three Slim Jims and a candy bar.

Nico and Toma both took their new bags and headed to the back. I took a few moments to show them where everything was, then I left them to it.

I figured I'd order us something to eat while they took baths and got themselves cleaned up. I probably should have been scared, but instead my heart pounded with excitement waiting to see what would happened next.

We'd stopped at the mall on our way home, where I'd bought them six outfits a piece, three pairs of shoes, and an assortment of other things they might need while here.

Probably I was being played for a fool, but so what. This had turned fun, and my interest was now fully engaged. I wanted to know their story. Like I'd said many times before, my curiosity would be the death of me someday.

The food came just as they were finishing up. I set the table and sat down, waiting for them to join me. Nico walked in first and took a seat.

I'll admit that my mouth hung open just a little. This was not the same woman who'd followed me through the portal.

The soiled and dirty rags from earlier had been replaced with a blue pantsuit and black sturdy shoes.

Her hair too had undergone a transformation. No doubt it would take a while for it to get back to its former glow, but at least now it was clean, had a little shine to it, and from what I could tell, she'd even fluffed it out a bit.

When Toma walked in a few minutes later, I almost stopped breathing. His black sweater and slacks hid the food deprived body I'd seen earlier, showered and cleaned, he carried himself a little straighter. Even on the verge of starvation, he was an attractive man.

His hair, like his sister's, was bone straight, and it looked like he'd done his best to put a little shine to it. An hour ago, these two had looked like street bums. Now they looked like productive, wage-earning members of society.

I'd ordered three large pizzas with the works along with a tossed salad and breadsticks. I had a couple of leftover beers in the fridge, and I took those out along with three bottles of water, which I was sure they needed more than the beer.

I picked up a slice of pizza. The cheese began to drip and fall off, so I hurried it to my mouth not wanting to waste one bit of it. It slid down my throat hot and delicious, and I licked my lips, loving every bit of it.

Before picking up another slice, I looked at the pair sitting in front of me and cleared my throat. "Now, I did what you wanted. So, I want the truth. Nobody looked like you two on your home world. Everyone I met today was covered from head to toe in diamonds and jewels. By the way, why the hell do you guys have diamond sidewalks and gold streets? It's such a waste."

I wanted an answer, but they were too busy throwing food in their mouths. I hadn't finished one slice, and they'd already gone through two and had started on the salad and breadsticks. I got them each another water, as they'd drained the first ones.

Nico wiped her mouth with her napkin. "We have no money and no way to make any. I mean we can't even get a decent drink of water." She stopped for a minute, put a breadstick in her mouth and angrily bit a piece off. "They left us to starve to death!" Her voice held passion and fire.

Toma placed his hand on her arm and picked up the conversation. "They took everything we owned, our cars, houses, planes, all our money, everything."

"Why?" I asked, my eyes lighting up with excitement. Now we were getting somewhere.

He picked a tomato slice out of his salad, poured some salt on it, and popped it in his mouth. "What do you know of crime and punishment?"

I shrugged. "If you commit a crime you go to jail."

Nico gave off a sarcastic chuckle. "No jail. We don't have jails, but we've heard people from other worlds talk of them. They sound like a nice concept." Wonderment lit her voice. "I wish we had them."

Toma took a swig of his beer and wiped his mouth with the back of his hand. "I think anything would be better than what we have."

That he and his sister wanted to be locked up, left an empty feeling in the pit of my gut. What the hell kind of place had they come from, where prison was the most desired option?

The more I thought about it though, the more things started to click into place. "So you two are criminals on the run?"

They both shook their head, but it was Toma who spoke. "We're not on the run. As I said, we have no jails. When someone commits a crime in our world, they're stripped of everything they own. No one's allowed to help you in any way. You're left to struggle alone on the streets until you finally die of starvation, exposure, or a number of other things."

My mind flashed to Larry. Somehow, I believed he'd fit right in there. Such a cruel world. "So, what did you do?"

Toma turned to Nico, and the two stared at each other, neither saying a word, yet neither looking too happy either. "We were in business together, my sister and I," Toma finally answered, yet every word he spoke held resentment.

Nico's fist clinched from its spot on the table, and her face went hard as stone. She seemed to want to say something, but for some reason held herself back. Interesting. I took a swig of my beer, eager to see where this was going.

She turned hurt, angry eyes on her brother, who stared back at her unflinching. I couldn't really decipher what any of it meant, but the whole situation was intriguing.

Not wanting to add fuel to the fire, but because I really wanted to know, I asked again. "So, what did you do?"

Without a word, Nico pushed back her chair and stood. Not looking at Toma or me, she walked down the hall slowly, as if each step, was hard and painful.

I waited until I heard a door shut, then turned to her brother.

"It's a touchy subject," was all he said.

That still didn't answer my question, and I could tell from the way he dropped his head to his pizza that he knew that.

Deciding to keep my hands busy, I got up to clear away the dishes, but something in me just wouldn't let the subject drop. "Are you going to tell me what happened or just keep beating around the bush?"

He looked confused for a minute, then understanding flowed across his face. "That means stop messing around, right?"

I nodded. He still didn't answer, and so I stopped what I was doing and waited.

Ignoring me, he got up and cleared the rest of the stuff off the table.

Either one of them told me what I was dealing with, or they had to leave. I wouldn't go into this thing blind, and they had to understand that.

After a minute, his hands stilled, and he turned to look at me. His eyes blazed into mine, daring me to judge or take offense. "They called her a murderer. Accused her of killing one of our top senator's brothers." I blinked at him, not sure I'd heard right, but his face stayed stony and hard.

A little too stunned to speak, I walked into the living room and took off my shoes, because I needed to do something with my hands. I was speechless to be honest, because for some reason that had been the last thing I'd expected him to say. I sat on my couch and pulled my legs up under me while I pondered my next move.

Toma came in slowly and took a seat opposite me. He didn't say anything, just waited for me to get my thoughts together.

I looked down the hall where I'd last seen Nico go. I'd thought maybe she'd swindled a few people out of their money, perhaps made a few back-alley deals, but murder had never entered my mind. There was still one question I hadn't asked yet. I looked to Toma who'd just taken his shoes off and sat them in his lap. "Is it true?"

His gaze shifted to the floor. Until now he'd had no problem looking me in the eye, and this bothered me a bit. "She's not a murderer," he finally mumbled.

I shook my head. Something about this just didn't sound right. I found it hard to believe that he wouldn't know more than that. They seemed so close. "So why are you on the run?"

He blinked. "We already told you, we are not on the run."

I felt like screaming, just to relieve some of the stress, because we were just dealing in semantics now, and he was being more than a little shady. "Okay," I said, my voice as patient as I could make it under the circumstances. "You're not on the run. You were just stripped of all your riches?"

He nodded.

"What were you accused of? Did they think you helped her?"

He laughed without humor. "Apparently because I was her business partner and her brother, I knew what she was up to and didn't stop her, which made me as guilty as she was."

"That's ridiculous."

"Hey, that's our world. What can I say, guilt by association? Now everything we own has reverted to the state. That's what happens when you're found guilty of a crime. Hence our very low crime rate."

"And your diamond-lined sidewalks. Look, I don't know what really went on, but what do you want from me? What do you expect me to do?"

He gripped his shoes tightly in his hands, still not meeting my eyes. "We're just looking for a new start, and one day clearing our name. Out on the streets like that," he shook his head, "We would have died eventually. Anyone caught helping us, would be forced to join us. So, nobody did." He swallowed hard and looked away as if thinking about the one person he'd expected help from and didn't get it.

I nodded my head and yawned. He'd given me some things to think about, but right now I was too tired to process them.

"So, I guess you're tired." He said it like it was a question.

I stood. "And I'm going to bed."

He came to his feet, his shoes still clutched tightly in his hand. "Good of you to let us stay. We appreciate it."

I yawned again and did a little stretch. "Yeah, well, it's been a long day." I didn't have anything more to say. All I wanted was my bed.

I started down the hall, and he followed right behind me. I quickly turned around, making him halt, a startled look on his face. "My bedroom door locks and I can do more than open portals. Something to think about, and tell your sister."

He laughed, and I saw a flash of something in his eyes. I didn't know him well enough to know what it meant, and I didn't care. The only thing I wanted now was deep and uninterrupted sleep. I should have known it wouldn't be that easy. Such is my luck, I guess.

Chapter 4

They attacked me while I slept. I awoke to a wet, meaty, hand covering my mouth and nose. I blinked, but couldn't see who was holding me down, but I did note they smelled like garlic and sweat.

My flight-or-fight response must have kicked in at some point because I didn't have time to think before I'd mentally hurled my attacker across the room and levitated myself in the air, hands up, ready for a fight.

I tried to make my eyes adjust to the darkness, realized how stupid that was, and TK'd the lights on. I didn't see anybody. Cautiously I lowered to the floor, thinking they could be hiding under the bed or in the closet.

As soon as I landed, a hard fist to my jaw knocked me backward. It hurt like hell, and I grabbed my jaw as pain exploded across that whole side of my face.

Why? That's all I wanted to know. Was this how Toma and Nico planned to reward my generosity? A sneak attack when they thought me unable to defend myself.

The intruder came at me again, and this time I could clearly see him. He was a big healthy man, who looked a lot like Hercules on steroids. I blinked for a minute because that hadn't been what I'd expected to see. I also felt relieved that

Nico and Toma hadn't turned on me, but I still didn't understand what was going on.

I had no idea who he was or where he'd come from. All I knew was, if I didn't get control of the situation this could mean the end for me. Throwing out my hand, I got a mental hold on him that made it impossible for him to move.

His face first registered shock, then rage took over as he undoubtedly found that no matter how much he struggled his body was now mine to control.

All I wanted was answers, and I had about a million questions. "Who sent you?" Before he could say anything, a loud crash from the next room made me jump and almost lose my hold on his body. Almost.

I did release his head though, as I needed him to answer my questions.

His facial muscles now his own again, the first thing he did was treat me to a nasty grin. "Why do you protect killers?" His voice came out in a hiss, his eyes reminding me of small cannons.

I furrowed my brows and tried to think, because he really could be talking about any one of my clients. "Can you be a little more specific?" I asked, keeping my hold on him.

He grunted, then answered. "You hold Toma and Nico from Sentra. You helped them escape. You will be punished with them. You are surrounded." Well, he was blunt if nothing else, I reasoned.

Before I could respond properly, another loud thump had me jerking my head toward the hallway. What the hell was going on out there? Still keeping a hold on my new friend, I slung my door open and took cautious steps backward making sure Hercules followed.

I stopped in the living room and looked around.

I didn't really see anything before a solid punch from my right, sent my head spinning, and had me bend over and gasping for air. The pain was excruciating and I put a hand to the injured part of my face and tried to breathe through it.

I didn't know what was going on, but I still hadn't recovered from the earlier blow, so this one only made it a hundred times worse. I pushed down the ache and tried to think.

What was up with these people and hitting me in my jaw? Did they not have another body part they favored?

My hold on him now broken, Hercules and his new friend both came at me. I mustered what strength I could, and floated to the ceiling, out of the line of fire.

Still gasping for air and trying to ease away the pain, I looked down at the two men below me. They looked like twins, except one had red hair and the other brown.

I could feel my face starting to swell, and that only pissed me off more. Killing them would be easy now that I was the one with the advantage. Lucky for them I wasn't in the habit of taking lives, no matter how good a reason I had.

The two men grinned at each other, and something hard settled in my chest as I realized that this was just the beginning. In the time it took me to ponder that, the room was flooded with people, and I remembered too late, that he'd said we were surrounded.

I swallowed hard as something cold and wet wrapped around my neck.

Tight and brutal, it cut off my air supply and caused involuntary tears to spring from my eyes. I hated this, hated to show this weakness, hated being so helpless that I couldn't even move, couldn't breathe. I didn't even have the strength to summon the mental energy to remove whatever gripped my neck.

The big Hercules came at me again, and I closed my eyes, thinking only of my family and how this would crush them. The most messed up part being that they would never even know why. Hell, I didn't even know why. All I knew for sure was that it had something to do with Toma, Nico, and a murder they claimed to know nothing about.

"Release her and come get what you came for," Nico said. She and Toma had entered the living room. They both had marks and small cuts on their faces and arms, and I assumed it had been them I'd heard earlier. Hercules grinned sadistically and ran for them. Nico opened her mouth and, a firestorm flew out, causing Hercules to burst into flames.

Toma turned to whoever held me. He pointed his fingers, and a line of white sand shot out.

I could hear choking and gagging from behind me, then the sound of someone hitting the floor reached my ears. In less than a second the pressure let up and my neck was free. I slowly massaged it, knowing there would be a bruise there, but too happy to still be alive to care.

Once I caught my breath, I turned in the direction of the person who'd been choking me, but all I saw was a man lying on the floor, sand coming out of his mouth, as if he'd suffocated on the stuff. The sight of it sent chills down my spine, and I turned to Toma and Nico, wondering if they were ele-menters or something else.

A loud boom made me jump, and before my eyes, the room was once again filled with intruders. I didn't know where they'd come from, or how they'd gotten here, but this time I saw the cold, wet thing before it got me.

It was a woman, and the thing was blue, slimy, and com-ing out of the palm of her hand. I focused my mind and ripped her whole hand off. It didn't seem to faze her. She simply held up the other hand, so I ripped that one off too.

She still came at me, and so I had no choice. I put my hands together, then pulled them apart, mentally tearing her to shreds. I opened my eyes in time to see her body fall into small pieces all over my living room floor.

I tasted bile, becaue I hated when it came to this. It wasn't the first time I'd had to kill to protect myself, but that didn't make it any easier. Still, I knew had I not killed her, she would have definitely killed me.

I looked to Toma and Nico and saw that they were hold-ing their own. While I'd been having my mini freak-out, they'd left ten bodies on my floor, all dead.

I nervously bit my bottom of my lip, trying to calm my-self, but this was horrifying. This was the same living room where my nieces and nephews sat on the floor watching TV, and playing board games.

Now everything was covered in blood, guts, and body parts. My stomach lurched, and I knew what I had to do.

I mentally picked up every one of my intruders, every speck of blood, and all the human tissue that I could find. I even sent out feelers to the other rooms in my house where

Toma and Nico had fought before they'd entered the living room.

Trying not to look too hard at the bloody mess before me, I opened a portal and sent it hurling through to a world that I knew to be a wasteland.

That done, I turned back to the siblings. "Will there be more?" They didn't answer. Trying to keep my temper under control, I asked again. Perhaps this was normal for them, but dozens of dead bodies polluting my living room floor was not my idea of a good time.

They'd shown me what they could do, perhaps now it was my turn. I floated midair, held out my hands, and threw them both against the wall, not at all caring about the thump their backs made when they hit the plaster, nor about the two dent marks they would leave.

Surprise sharpened their features, as they struggled to get free. Nico shot me a look of pure rage, while Toma's eyes held nothing but surrender.

I focused on him since he was the only one likely to talk. "Are you ready to answer me now?"

He nodded. "When we left they must have followed our scent."

That was not what I'd expected to hear, and I didn't understand what he meant. "What scent? Do you have a scent? I don't smell it."

Toma looked to where I still floated midair. "Come down here and talk to us."

Nico was still pissed. "You dare attack us? After we saved your life!"

Ignoring her, and coming to the ground, I turned back to Toma. "Give me one reason why I shouldn't open a wormhole and send you both flying through?"

"Look, every family has a very distinct smell. Only certain people in our world can sense it, and they usually work for the senators. Just like there's only one known person who can open a wormhole. He too, worked for the senators."

"He doesn't anymore?" I eased them both slowly to the ground, figuring I'd made my point. Nico's hard stare didn't waver, but Toma just seemed glad to be on solid ground again.

He pointed to the spot I'd opened the portal and sent the dead bodies hurling through. "He's dead. It'll take a while for them to find a replacement, so that'll buy us a little time."

"If he was so important then why would they send him here?"

Nico rubbed a bruised spot on her arm. "How else would they get back? Anyway, he's not irreplaceable, it'll just take a few days."

I really didn't like those odds. "So basically, they followed your scent here. Okay, now what can we do so that doesn't happen again?" While I waited for one of them to answer me, I flopped down on the couch, exhausted. It had been a most eventful night so far.

Toma sat down as well, looking as tired as I felt. Nico's gaze traveled from me to her brother. "We could try to hide our scent."

Toma gave his sister an appreciative nod. "We could try to mask it from the time we entered your world."

I rubbed a hand over my still sore throat, surprised I hadn't gone hoarse yet. "You think you could have tried to mask it earlier?" It sure would have saved us a lot of trouble if they had.

Toma shook his head. "We were too weak. No food, no water, but at least now we can try."

My head started to ache again, and I realized I couldn't be in the room with them a second longer. I knew it'd been my choice to bring them home, and I'd stand by that. Whatever they had to say still didn't explain why they hadn't at least told me what we were up against.

Disgusted, I got up to go to the bathroom. Halfway down the hall, I turned back. Right now, I didn't trust either of them, and I needed to get some stuff off my chest. "Do whatever you need to, because this can't happen again."

If it did, I was done with them. I wouldn't send them back to their world to starve though. I'd find somewhere nice for them to go. I'd even set them up with a job and some money if they were willing to take it. I figured that's all I really owed them, if that.

The thing was, I didn't believe they wanted to go to another world and call it their home. They were used to a certain lifestyle on their home world, and if they could find a way to prove their innocence and get it back, I believed they would.

The golden streets and diamond sidewalks, came off to me as a power play, letting anybody who entered that world know who the top dog was. It was a dominance act, perpetrated by a world that thought if you didn't walk around looking like a million dollars you were nothing.

Closing the bathroom door behind me, I leaned over the sink and splashed handfuls of cool water on my face. It felt good, and maybe I just needed to take a moment for myself. This whole situation was like trying to find water in the desert, and I still wasn't sure what the outcome would be.

I sat on the edge of the bathtub and tried to figure out my next move. The obvious answer was staring me in the face. I could just open a portal and send them away, but that wouldn't help anyone, and the guilt would probably eat me alive.

No, this was my problem now, because I was making it so. I wanted to know more about what was happening, wanted to help them if they were truly innocent, so for now I'd ride it out. My heart gave a leap of excitement at the prospect and I sighed, thinking that maybe my sister had been right all along. Maybe I was a thrill seeker. I just hoped that we'd all be left standing when the dust cleared.

Chapter 5

We finally decided that Toma would stay up and keep watch, while Nico and I got some sleep. All I wanted was my bed. The rest could wait until morning.

I awoke to the smell of coffee, bacon, and eggs. Hmm. I licked my lips in anticipation as my stomach led me to the kitchen. The smell of Clorox and pine cleaner hit me on the way and I figured Toma must have spent most of the night cleaning up. I'd have to thank him for that later.

He stood in the kitchen, wearing a white shirt and blue jeans. He had a dish towel in his hand and was steadily putting food on the table.

Grateful to have someone else doing the cooking for a change, I sat down and waited.

He took a seat across from me and raised a mug of coffee to his lips. "I hope you don't mind. I figured it was the least I could do."

I nodded my approval, not yet ready to talk. Toma walked to the stove and came back with two plates heaped high with cheese eggs, crisp bacon, and jelly toast. He placed one in front of me and sat down with the other.

I didn't bother to tell him that I preferred my toast with a little butter or plain. He was making an effort, so I'd do the same. "Please explain to me what happened last night, because I'm starting to really wonder what I've gotten myself into here." I was trying to be nice, but my words still held a little bite, letting him know that I had no patience for games.

Toma put down the piece of bacon he'd been about to bite and turned to me. His eyes seemed to be searching mine for something, maybe compassion or possibly understanding.

Hell, for all I knew he was trying to decide whether he could trust me or not. Finally, he spoke. "We weren't thinking. We saw you enter our world and knew this could be our last chance. I'm sorry if you think we used you, but we would have died without your help."

Well, that didn't answer my question, but I guessed it would have to do for now. A few minutes later Nico joined us, and the rest of the meal was eaten in a strained silence.

"ONE WAY TO MASK OUR scent is to throw them off. You know, put a little confusion into the game," Toma said, finishing up the dishes and coming into the living room. Nico, who'd been drying, came in behind him.

I'd been lying on the couch watching TV, but this made me sit up. Finally, some pro-action on our part. "How can we do it?"

Nico shrugged. "We go out and walk. Go to as many places as we can. You know, spread our scent around."

Marvelous. Maybe it would work. With a newfound vigor, I came to my feet. "Let me get my stuff." My number one rule was always be prepared, and it was a lesson I was determined to teach these two.

I walked into my room and noticed my bag still packed from the night before. With all the confusion, I hadn't even had time to unpack. Thinking about the events that had led up to this point, I swung it over my shoulder, hoping I wouldn't live to regret this decision.

Not knowing if they knew what to pack, I went ahead and filled up bags with bottled waters, canned foods, flashlights, etc. For Toma and Nico, as well. They were standing by the door when I walked back into the living room, and I handed the bags over, explaining the importance of always being prepared. In my line of work, you never knew what was going to happen next.

Toma gave me a grateful look and Nico a small nod.

I thought our first stop should be downtown on Main Street. There were a million little shops there and ducking in and out of each and every one of them was enough to run anybody in circles.

We'd walked for an hour before we reached Ripples shop, and I felt the strangest sensation. My whole body started to hum, and I had the overwhelming urge to go right. Something was pulling me there against my will.

It was almost magnetic. I tried to fight it, but somehow my body involuntarily turned in that direction. I could feel the tension start in my shoulders, because if they'd found us already, then they were better than I'd originally thought.

I tried to get the attention of my companions, but their bodies seemed to be reacting in the same way

"Don't try to fight it," Nico said, through strained teeth. "We need to check this out."

We stopped in the alleyway between Ripples and Comcast Cable.

A man with close shaven red hair, stood there with his hand outstretched, a shit-eating grin on his face.

Of medium height and weight, he was dressed in a pair of black jeans and shirt, with a small red jacket for warmth. Once we were in front of him, he dropped his hand and the feeling of being pulled instantly disappeared.

Nico was the first to react. With an impetuous fury that I was rapidly beginning to associate with just being a part of her personality, she slammed him against the wall and held her arm under his throat. "Talk," was the only word she uttered.

Toma put a hand on her arm as if they'd been through this a million times before. "How can he talk if he can't breathe?" He turned to the man, a hard look on his face. "You heard my sister, talk."

The man knocked her hand away, then wiped his shirt down. He stood unblinking and confident as he looked at the two siblings. "I can sense power in others. Sense it and bring it to me. But that's not my only talent. If your power's down, and by down, I mean if you're missing at least twenty-five percent of it, I can read it and tell everything about you. As it relates to you two, you've lost a lot, and I know why." He didn't sound mocking, but I didn't think he was ready to be very helpful either.

He seemed pretty proud of what he'd just done, so I thought it was my turn to speak. "I'm not impressed. What do you want?"

He held his hands up in front of him and backed away in faux surrender mode. "Only to help. You know." He flicked his hand in the air. "You help me, I help you. That's how it goes."

Nico eyed the stranger with well-founded skepticism. "What do you want?" she finally asked.

He stared back at her, a smug grin on his pale face, and my shoulders started a slow slump because I got the feeling that whatever he said, wasn't something we'd be able to walk away from. "My boyfriend is a creator. As long as we're in the place that it happened, he can recreate anything."

Toma took a few steps forward. "And supposing you're able to offer his services without asking him first, this helps us how?"

The man looked from me to Nico as if he expected one of us to answer. When we didn't, he clicked his tongue and went on. "Did you hear what I said? I can sense what happened to you. You were both convicted of murder. If you're innocent, as I'm sure you are." He stopped to grin. "Then this will prove it."

Toma and Nico both turned to me as if they were seriously giving this guy's offer some thought. Time to nip this in the bud and move on. "We don't know anything about him." I tried to explain. "What if he's leading us into a trap?" It came out a little harsher than I'd intended, but seriously.

These two were too smart to fall for that. The fact that they were even considering it meant they were a lot more desperate than I'd originally thought. Not a good sign.

Desperate people did stupid things that they later regretted but couldn't take back. This had the potential to go very bad. I was willing to help, but my life wasn't up for forfeit and they needed to understand that.

For now, I just wanted to prove them innocent and hop off to my next adventure, my conscience clear that I'd done the right thing.

The man turned to me, a victorious grin on his face that said he knew he'd won. "Where shall we begin?"

I licked my lips to stall and think of a reason to say no. Tying in with this guy seemed like a terrible idea, and could only lead to more trouble. "How can we trust you if we don't know your name?" It sounded weak to my own ears, but it was the best I had at the moment.

The man did a mini bow, then held out his hand. "Chaz Dean at your service, Ma'am."

Toma waited until Chaz was done before he said anything, but when he did speak, his voice came out hard and demanding. "Where's your boyfriend and what do we have to do in return for your help?"

Chaz looked toward the ground, his shoulders taking on a small slumping motion. It was probably the first piece of true emotion he'd shown since we'd met him. This time when he spoke, his voice was barely above a whisper. "Well, he's in the blocker, what you here call jail. So is my brother, who also needs to be rescued by the way."

Well, shit. I shook my head as all the resistance I'd had shed away. Something about the way he said it, or maybe it was the air of despair when he spoke of his brother and boyfriend, whatever it was, it resonated with me.

He'd piqued my interest, and I could feel my blood rushing at the thought of a prison break. Could I pull it off? I really wanted to know. I blinked and shook my head, wondering what was wrong with me.

Pushing those thoughts away, I turned to Chaz. "Why aren't you in jail too?" I asked. I didn't know if he'd ever done anything to ward going to jail, but this was a good way to find out.

He looked sheepish and turned away. "Because I can run faster than them?" He said it as a question rather than a statement.

Great, so he was a criminal too. My own little gang of outlaws, just what mother always wanted for me. I took a moment to collect my thoughts, then turned back to Chaz. "What did you three do?" I wasn't really sure I wanted to know, but I needed to understand what we were dealing with before I fully committed. I didn't think I could deal with too many more murder charges.

He straightened his shoulders and looked at me without an ounce of shame on his face. "All the time, we like to steal, it's just something we like to do. What? Don't look at me like that. It's better than murder. Besides if we didn't steal, we'd actually have to work. And seriously, who wants to do that?"

Well, it's not like I worked a regular nine-to-five, but this dude was ridiculous. Still, if he could clear Toma and Nico's names then we at least needed to listen to what he had to say. "What do you want?"

He hung his head low. "Okay, you got me. Maybe I wasn't completely honest before. I can't run faster than them. It's just that I've been caught ten times. My brother five and my boyfriend only three."

I took in the crestfallen looks on Toma and Nico's faces. Apparently, we all agreed that we were dealing with a fool.

He kept talking as if oblivious to the subtle change in atmosphere. "They don't have the funds to keep habitual offenders like myself clothed, fed, and sheltered. So, they send us away, where we can't be a drain on society and their pocketbooks."

Nico tilted her head to the side, a curious expression on her face. "If you don't work how do you eat here? How do you live?"

He held up his hand and wiggled it. "Five-finger discount, love. Haven't you ever heard of the five-finger discount?" He grinned again. That seemed to be his favorite facial expression, and I almost told him that if he didn't stop it'd get stuck that way. At least that's what my grandma used to say anyway.

I walked down the alley, a good distance away from him, then called for Nico and Toma to join me. It was their lives at stake. I felt that they should make the final decision. I wanted to do it. I knew I did, and I now thought that my sister was probably right. I did have a problem chasing after that fast rush of adrenaline. Something I'd have to work on in the future.

"What do you guys think? Do you want to put in with this yo-yo?"

Nico nodded, then shrugged, her voice so matter-of-fact that it was almost scary. "He reneges I'll kill him. I think he should know that." She turned around and started to open her mouth.

I put my hand on her arm to stop her. "I don't think maiming him is in our best interest. Here, let me."

I held out my hand and lifted him in the air. He looked shocked for a moment, then curious. "Betray us, and I'll let her loose on you." I turned to Nico, and she opened her mouth sending fire flying past his head.

His voice came out strained. "Okay, okay, I get it." I let him go, and he fell back against the wall. He took a moment to catch his breath, then turned to us. "Like I said before, you help me, and I'll help you. Calm down. You twos have no reason to go all native on me. All's I'm asking for is an honest bargain. You all get me my brother and my honey, and I'll help you clear your names."

To my surprise and relief, Toma and Nico, both gave reluctant nods of the head. That now decided, I turned back to Chaz. "I guess we'll have to go to your home world to get 'em. Do you have anything you want to take with you?"

He walked down a little way and retrieved a bag from under a pile of grown out bushes. "Never leave home without it," he smiled, holding it up.

I tried to concentrate on him. "Tell me about your world." I reached for his hand in order to get a deeper connection.

Thankfully it only took a couple of seconds for me to form a clear picture in my head and open a portal big enough for us all to fit through.

Chapter 6

Stepping into Chaz's world, the first thing I noticed was varying shades of red, from cherry to sangria. Everything was this color. The streets, the square shaped buildings, the round shaped houses, even the cars, everything.

What a strange place to be from, I thought looking at the large grin on Chaz's face. He seemed pretty steady on his feet, which told me he'd told me hopped more than one portal in his time.

Nico and Toma wore twin looks of displeasure. I guess coming from a world full of glittering diamonds and sapphires this must have been like stepping through a field of shit. "How can you stand to live here?" Nico asked, her eyes roaming over the contrasting shades of red that covered, well, everything.

The air itself smelled of red hots and sausages from a nearby street vendor. My stomach jumped at the smell, and I promised myself our next stop would be for food. I had snacks in my bag in case it got too bad, but that never took the place of a real meal. My body always needed the energy after a portal hop.

Chaz motioned for us to follow him, taking a sharp right turn at the end of the street. "Come on, this is probably the best way to get there without being seen." He led us across a candy-apple-colored street and onto a deeper-red sidewalk.

When we'd only walked a few paces down the road, a loud shrill voice stopped us cold. "Hey! What are you doing here?" A small redheaded man stood pointing at Chaz and screaming to the top of his lungs. "Thief! Thief! Come get him. He's not supposed to be here. He raided my safe and stole all my red coins! I'm starving because of him!"

Shit. This was exactly what we didn't need right now. Rooted to the spot, we watched in horror as more people ran over, blowing whistles, pointing, and accusing Chaz of various crimes. Not willing to join in his own denunciation, Chaz took off running, yelling over his shoulder for us to follow.

We wasted no time doing exactly that. Toma and I ran neck and neck. "Why didn't we see this coming?" He tapped his temple. "Common sense. I guess none of us have it." I had to agree. Common sense said we should have not only suspected this but been prepared for it. Well, no use worrying about it now, I reasoned.

We ran until we came to a big field of red grass. "Hey, over here," Chaz shouted. I looked back, and while I couldn't see anyone yet, I could hear footsteps pounding on the sidewalk, their whistles blowing louder and louder.

We ended up by a big red tree, whose leaves were red and orange. It looked beautiful and reminded me of autumn back home. Nico squared her shoulders. "I'll fight if I have to."

I grabbed her by the arm and swung her around. "Kill or hurt innocent people to protect a thief, I don't think so." I turned to Chaz. "Whatever you're going to do you'd better do it now."

He lined himself against the tree and held up a single finger. "You worry too much. Now watch this." He walked about ten paces in a straight line, then dropped to his knees.

Chaz yanked on the grass, and to our surprise, it opened to reveal a small man-sized rabbit hole. There was no dust or weeds accumulated on it, which spoke of frequent use. There was even a ladder so that you wouldn't fall or hurt yourself on the way down.

Nico and I went first, with the other two right behind us. Once we were safely inside, Chaz pulled on a latch and closed the hole up.

"Nifty little trick you have there," Nico said. She looked impressed.

Toma nodded his agreement. "We can use something like this at home. For the outcast. A place where we can at least live without fear. It's an idea."

It seemed like we were in a network of tunnels that twisted and turned in every direction. But it didn't smell musty or dirty like one would expect from a tunnel. The delicious smell of hot sausages and cabbage filled the air, almost making me dizzy with anticipation. I was very hungry, but the last thing I needed was to stop and try to eat, not while we were still on the run anyway.

As we walked on, I noticed that the walls were different shades of red, orange, and burgundy. Weaving in and out from one tunnel to the next were an array of different people. Chaz led us through the tunnel until we came to an open room on our right.

Inside a few medium-sized beds lined one wall. On the opposite side of the room, two men and a woman played a game of dice. From the guys' jeers and accusations, it seemed like the woman was winning.

We walked to a corner where a man with red hair and a small goatee, sat eating a plate of cabbage and sausages and reading a book. The spine looked worn, and the cover was almost gone, which made me wonder how many times he'd read it before, as he seemed completely engrossed. Maybe it was a really good book, or maybe he had nothing else to read. Who knew the ins and outs of this underground hangout?

When he saw us, he put the book down and stood slowly. Shoulders tight, and face hard, one word came to mind as I looked at him, dangerous. His assessing gaze traveled from Chaz, to Toma, and lastly to Nico, and myself, a look of extreme displeasure on his face.

Going to stand in front of Chaz, he made a show of looking over the other man's shoulder. "You're back. I see that." His eyes turned toward Toma, Nico, and myself, then back to Chaz. "No Clink, No Kirk, and who the fuck are they?" He pointed to us.

For the first time since we'd met him, Chaz looked worried. He wiped a sweaty hand down his face, and tried to placate the man standing in front of him. "They're here to help is all."

The man didn't look convinced, and his eyes turned hard as granite, making him look even more treacherous and unpredictable.

I made an attempt to smooth things over as best I could. "Look, we don't want trouble. We're not here to rat out your hideout or anything. Chaz asked for our help, and so we're giving it. That's it." I made a slicing motion through the air, hoping that I'd come off a little menacing, but pretty sure that I hadn't.

The man tilted his head to the side as he looked at me. "Because you're so kind and generous that way?" He made the mistake of reaching toward me as he spoke.

Not knowing what he planned to do, I snatched his hand and bent his forefinger back until I heard it crack. "Don't ever try to touch me again, or next time I'll rip your whole freaking hand off." I'm not a violent person, but touching me without my permission was a surefire way to draw my ire.

Undaunted, he reached inside his boot and pulled out a long blade. The look on his face said he had every intention of cutting me into little pieces and spreading my body parts throughout the various tunnels. Either that or my imagination had gotten away from me for a bit. "You wanna try that again, bitch?" His voice came out low and gritty, and before I'd had a chance to respond, he'd leaped my way.

Reacting as quickly as I could, I took a step back and held out my hand trapping him in place. The rage on his face was almost comical, but this was anything but a joke.

Out of the corner of my eye, I saw Toma and Nico advancing from the left. I held up my other hand, stopping them in their tracks and letting them know that I didn't need their help at the moment. I then dropped both hands, hoping to cool tempers down.

The man wasted no time. As soon as he realized he was free, he came at me again. Which in my book made him either the dumbest or bravest motherfucker alive. Without a second thought, I squeezed my hand, closing his esophagus, cutting off his air supply.

Pain contorted his features and his eyes bulged. With no air coming, he fell to the floor, clutching his throat and trying desperately to breathe. A line of fire flew past his head, missing him by mere inches.

I turned to Nico. "We don't want to kill him. He attacked us, that means defending ourselves not committing murder. I'm really starting to wonder," I stopped talking before I said something I shouldn't.

Which was that I was really starting to wonder if she had killed the senator's brother after all. Her first impulse always seemed to be, hurt first and ask questions afterward. It was something for me to think about later.

I turned back to the man who had now stopped moving and lay helpless on the floor, wheezing and gasping for air. Toma grabbed my arm and whispered furiously in my ear. "What do you want to do, Rekia? Want to kill him, keep squeezing. Want us to make it out of here alive, then let him go and we'll at least have a fighting chance?"

Realizing he was right, I let the man go. He jumped up immediately, stumbling and trying to regain his balance.

He pointed a single finger at me and tried to talk, but no words came out. I looked around and noticed that the room had suddenly filled with a bunch of shady looking characters with red bats and brass knuckles. "Get' em," he finally croaked out, and they obeyed, coming at us from all directions.

"Run!" I yelled, working my mind and hands together to throw them all against the wall.

"This way," Chaz shouted. We followed him without question.

"I can't hold it at this distance for much longer," I bellowed out between gasps of air. It didn't matter though, those who hadn't been in the room were making a run for us. Nico turned around and a hail of blazing hot fire shot out of her mouth. It hit on one of the walls and sent those chasing us scrambling to put it out. It wouldn't last long.

We came to what looked like a regular part of the floor that proved to be an escape hatch when Chaz yanked it open and motioned for us to follow him down. "Nobody else knows about this. Something Clink found a long time ago."

The room we stepped into looked dingy and dusted over. Half-eaten food and bottles of what I assumed were beer lay tossed all over the place. Disgusted, I put a hand to my mouth to cover the atrocious smell. It didn't work, as the scent of mold and rot still permeated my nose.

Nico looked horrified. "Why live like this if you don't have to? I don't understand. There is nothing stopping you from being a productive member of society. But this is what you prefer?"

Chaz, who'd been peeking around a corner, walked back to us, fist clenched at his side. "Do you know that we just pissed off 'the man', the most important person down here? He doesn't hit women, ever. That's the only reason we got away, because he let us, but now it'll be me who has to pay. There is no explaining, no apologies. He hates me anyway, and this is a perfect excuse. If you," he swung around and pointed at me, "hadn't been so quick to attack then maybe I could have worked something out. No outsiders are allowed. You have to pay your dues."

He stopped for a moment and shook his head. "I can't come back here, and now I have to tell Kirk and Clink that they can't either," his voice lowered as if he couldn't believe this was happening. "Come on, there's a way out over—," before he could finish his sentence a door on the other side of the room burst open and the redheaded man from earlier entered, followed closely by a few of his friends.

Chaz held up his hands in a very non-threatening manner. "Glone, come on, these people are here to help. We didn't mean no harm."

While Chaz was pleading for our lives, I was busy with my hands behind my back opening a portal. My only thought was; perfect getaway.

Toma saw what I was doing and tapped Nico on the shoulder, as he slowly moved closer. Nico grabbed Chaz, who was still begging for mercy, and together we all dove through.

Chapter 7

I watched until the portal closed, making sure no one else slid through. "Well, wow," I said turning around. We were on a big beautiful beach, with clear blue water, white sand, and hundreds of people. I squinted my eyes as the rays from the sun blinded me.

Figuring we were severely overdressed, I took off my sweater and stuffed it in my backpack. Everywhere we looked people were having a good time. Bodies moved all around us, dancing, drinking, smoking, eating, and swimming. One couple had a small round music ball beside them and seemed to be in their own world as they slow danced through the sand.

Ah, I thought, remembering my words. I'd opened the portal for a perfect getaway. So apparently a perfect getaway is what we got. If I didn't concentrate on the exact world, then it was basically a crap shoot.

If I was to think of 'jungle world' then the portal would open to anything from a rainforest, to a world so out of control and steeped in chaos that one would call it a jungle. That's why it was usually best to know the name of the world you were going to and focus on that.

The smell of seasoned meat and fresh roasted vegetables led me to one of the many buffet tables lining the beach. This was the kind of place I could get used to. If we didn't have more pressing matters to attend to, I would go about setting up contacts.

I needed some food to replenish my energy from the two portal hops, so we'd stay here long enough for me to do that. I grabbed a beer from the cooler beside me, stuck a hot dog in my mouth, and took a seat on one of the many picnic tables and thought about it. Maybe I could expand my business. Sometimes people just wanted a nice vacation without going through customs or any of the other million things that plagued you when you're trying to just get away.

Coming back to reality, I finished off my hot dog, and shook my head to expel such foolish thoughts. The last thing I needed was more people knowing what I could do. It was one thing to take escaping criminals who were never coming back again. It was a whole other to take happy little families who had to come back after a couple of days and expect them to keep their mouths shut. Wasn't going to happen.

The others also grabbed drinks and a small bite of food, then joined me at the table. We'd just hopped two portals back to back and the calories and energy it took to do that, meant our bodies needed the fuel.

"So, all of this is free?" Nico finally asked, looking around. No money had changed hands since we'd arrived, and no one had charged us for our food and drink. "They just give it away? How do they live?" I guess coming from the world she and Toma lived in, giving something away for free, must have seemed incomprehensible.

I did my best to explain. "Not every society is based on money. Some work on the barter system. Then you have others where everyone puts in their fair share, and they all work together for the common good. This must be that type of place."

The couple beside us turned up their little music device. Instead of round like the other couples, this one was a small square thing with white and gold stripes. It turned out such a nice rhythmical tune, that I found myself involuntarily tapping my foot.

They smiled at us, then stood and begin to dance closely together. I smiled back and took a swig of beer as I addressed Toma, Nico, and Chaz. "I'll say we made a good getaway." It was meant as a joke, but fell flat on its face, as no one laughed.

Toma ignored me altogether, choosing instead to take in the scene before us. "This is too easy. I can't believe all this stuff is just free. Don't you guys think so?"

Chaz, who still looked nervous, took a long swallow of his beer. "I don't care about all that, bud. All I want to know is, can they follow us here? I keep watching my back waiting for Glone and his thugs to attack."

Nico tapped the top of her beer against her lip, a thoughtful look on her face. "That's the one thing I can't for the life of me figure out." She put her drink to the side and leaned over until she was just inches away from Chaz's face. "You had to know what the situation with Glone was, so why did you take us there when you knew there would be problems?"

He looked surprised at her question. "It was that or the blockers, love, now which would you prefer? We can go back you know, give the blockers their fair shot at us."

Far be it for me to take up for Nico, but I was curious about this myself. "Don't get cute. She asked you an honest question. Was there nowhere else we could have gone? Now you can't go back to your home world. Is that what you really wanted?"

He didn't bother to answer, and so I turned to Toma, and all thought went out of my head as I took in the bottle of Potomac Bomb in his hand. "Uh, where'd you get that?"

Potomac Bomb wasn't something they made on my home world. It was about five times more powerful than moonshine, and deadly too.

He took a sip, then passed it to his sister. "This guy," he pointed to the dancing couple who had now sat back down and were busy drinking their own glass. "Said it was good stuff. I've had it before. So has Nico. We know how to drink it."

Nico downed some then passed it to Chaz, who took a good swallow and tried to pass it to me.

I shook my head. "No, one of us has to be clearheaded," I snapped.

Chaz snorted. "Chill the fuck out, princess."

I gave him a cold stare, but didn't say anything more.

Toma placed his hand on top of mine. I looked down at it, then up into his questioning eyes. "Everything okay? Do you want to stop for a while?"

My heart softened just a little. Hey, I'm human, so yes, I was grateful that at least somebody had concern for my well-being. "I'm good. Just wondering how we're going to be able to break his friends out of prison without getting caught is all."

Chaz took another swig. "I can do more than just sense power you know." He burped the last part out.

Nico's eyes flamed to life. Her black hair was pinned back from her head, giving her an almost severe look. "See, we can't trust him! All he does is lie. As we sit here, he probably has a thousand different tales bouncing around in that thick head of his."

Chaz tried to make a show of looking sheepish but failed miserably. If anything, it made him look even shadier than he had before. I could see now that those two would get along great.

All around us, music blasted, and voices rang out in joy and cheer. Seemed like we were the only pessimistic people around. I didn't know about the others, but breaking people out of jail wasn't something I did on a daily basis, especially not when they really deserved to be there.

Which was beyond hypocritical of me, I realized, as I usually hid them away before they even reached a jail cell. I placed my elbows on the table and rubbed at my temples. "Let's get this over with."

"Can I at least get another beer?" Chaz asked, reaching for the barrel.

"No," Toma and I said in unison. Startled we looked at each other for a moment before quickly looking away.

"I think there's a deserted spot over there," Nico said, pointing to a less populated area of the beach.

Once we made it to the designated area and was sure no one else was around, I turned to Chaz. "Can you give me the address of the jail? I'm sure you know it, many times as you've been there," I said it as a joke, wanting to make him smile.

He gave me a pretend sour look, which was probably more real than he wanted me to believe. "Eight hundred eighteen Winslow RD," he finally said.

I placed my hand on the bright yellow building that housed the public restrooms, and opened a portal to take us there.

MOONLIGHT LIT OUR PATH as we entered back into Chaz's world. We exited the portal only a few feet away from the prison, which sat back about fifty feet from the road. Nothing else was around, no houses or buildings, only trees that hung long, managing to give the whole area a creepy feel.

The place itself was a large red building with steel fencing all around it. I cracked my knuckles, my heart doing a little leap. It looked formidable, forbidding even, and I could easily see it housing about three thousand Chaz like criminals.

"So, what's your plan, love?" Chaz asked, smacking his hands together.

I looked at the large structure in front of me, not having a clue how to break into it, but knowing that was part of the fun. I tilted my head to the side. Steel black bars covered all the windows, and there was no way we could just stroll through the front door. "I guess I could levitate up and then get inside one of the windows, but I wish I knew which side they were on."

He pointed around to the other side of the building. "In my lengthy experience of dealing with this place, I'm willing to wager a bet they'll be over there on the fourth floor."

"Together?"

He shrugged. "Who knows? I haven't talked to either of them. Remember? I got banished away. Not supposed to be here. So, could we please hurry?"

I was hoping for a little more information than that, but I'd take what I could get. I grabbed him by the hand and pulled him along. "Come on. I guess I need you since I don't know where I'm going and I have no idea what they look like."

Nico's eyes scanned the building. "You may need back-up."

Too many people meant a greater chance of getting caught. "Nah, I need you and your brother to keep lookout here."

Her brows scrunched together in a way that said she wasn't happy with my decision but would respect it. "Just be careful and hurry out. You two are the only ones who can help us clear our names."

I nodded and let Chaz lead the way. We silently crept around to the south side of the prison. "Here," he said, finally coming to a stop.

I looked up to the windows on the fourth floor. The problem would be floating up that far without someone seeing us, maintaining both of us in midair, plus getting the window open.

I rolled my shoulders and gave myself a small pep talk. I could do this. Of course, I could. I flexed my hands and squared my back. "Come on," I said, grabbing him by the hand. It was wet with sweat which spoke to his nervousness.

"Ah, do try not to drop me, love," he said, squeezing me a little tighter than I would have liked.

"I can't do much good with a broken hand," I hissed. He loosened his grip immediately. Thankful to have my blood circulating again, I focused on the challenge before me.

Putting all my attention on the task at hand, I tried to build up my courage. I'd been to so many places, been on so many adventures, but I'd be lying if I said I didn't still get scared each and every time I faced a new challenge.

I could do this. With Chaz holding on to me for dear life, I lifted us both off the ground. Making sure to stay in the middle of the building, and being as careful as I could, I floated us to the fourth floor.

I held Chaz's right hand in my left. In order to give the window my full power, I was going to have to use both hands. "I'll hold you steady. I just need you to grab me around the waist."

He looked horrified at the thought of letting go, if only for a few seconds. "No thanks. I'm fine like this."

I wasn't about to argue with him. Instead, I simply moved his arms around my sides. His sharp intake of breath let me know that I'd just scared the crap out of him. I tried to placate as best I could. "Try to relax. I have a lot of experience with hands around my waist." The last thing we needed was one of us panicking and making a mistake.

Holding my hands out, and squinting my eyes, I used my telekinesis to bend the bars back. They creaked, then swung against the side of the building with a bang. Chaz and I both startled, before taking a second to control ourselves.

Not wanting to waste any more time, I mentally slung the now unprotected window open.

"Hands of dynamite, girl you're good," Chaz said, a little bit of awe mixed into his words. I'm glad somebody found value in this bullshit.

For my part, realizing we'd just broken into a prison, sent ripples of fear and adrenaline racing through me. On the one hand, I couldn't believe I'd actually done it, on the other hand, *holy shit*, I'd actually done it!

I turned to Chaz, hoping he couldn't see the excitement in my eyes. "Show me where to go."

The room we landed in was the laundry area. The strong smell of starch and lemon tickled our noses as we walked past the industrial sized washers and dryers.

"Which way?" I asked Chaz.

He put a single finger to his lips, motioning for me to be quiet. Walking on tiptoes and checking all sides, we walked to the door that led to the hallway. Guards lined the halls. There seemed to be one for every five cells.

I ran a nervous hand through my hair and tried not to be rattled. Feeling my confidence fail, I let out a sigh. How the hell were we supposed to get around all them? I looked to Chaz. "Where should we start?"

He shrugged and waved his hand up and down the hall. "Take your pick, love. I have no idea which cell. Only what floor." He looked dejectedly up and down the hallway at the multiple guards. "Is there nothing you can do to even the odds, love?"

I thought about it for a moment. There was no easy way around this. The option of getting in and out quietly was lost.

Standing beside me, I could hear Chaz impatiently moving around. I started to close my eyes to better think. Hmm. Something tickled my brain. Closed eyes... eyes closed or covered. Maybe it would work.

Closing my mind to everything else, and focusing only on the fourth floor and only on those outside the cell, I heard the first screams of confusion as the guards' hands involuntarily flew to their faces and covered their eyes. "Come on," I said, grabbing Chaz and running down the hallway.

While the guards were busy bumping into walls and falling all over each other, we ran from cell to cell, checking for his people. Near the next-to-last cell, I heard an excited shout. "Here! Right here, love."

Keeping the guards' hands on their faces, I wrenched the doors to the cell open. A tall guy, with skin the same dark brown as my brother Greg, stepped out. He had beautiful reddish-orange dreadlocks that went a little past his butt, and a big smile on his face as he stared at Chaz. He was of muscular build, and I had no problem imagining him working out every day.

His eyes held knowledge and intelligence and I wondered how he and Chaz had ever gotten together.

"Clink," Chaz said, suddenly out of breath.

The man wrapped Chaz up in his arms and squeezed. The two shared a few quick kisses and, still holding hands, Chaz asked where his brother was.

A dark look came over Clink's face as he pointed down. "In the hole. Knocked five of them out before they stopped him. You know Kirk, fist first, questions later."

"Uggg," I said, falling against the wall, my body drained. My arm tingled and my fingers cramped. I wasn't used to using this much power at one time, or for so long. And the fact that I was operating on minimum food and rest didn't help any.

"Hey what the fuck do you think you're doing?" We heard one of the guards yell from down the hall, their hands now removed from their faces due to my weakened state.

"We still have to get Kirk," Chaz yelled, as we took off down the hall.

My legs turned to rubber when I started to run, and I fell back against the wall. I couldn't make it. I was just too weak. I took a moment to breathe, then tried it again, only to start a slow descent to the floor. I was almost there when strong arms wrapped around me and lifted me up. I looked beside me to see Clink holding me tight. "I got you," he said.

I nodded and lay my head on his chest, grateful for a chance to rest.

Chaz stopped to look at us, his breath coming in heavy gasps. "Oh, love, I know you're weak, but all the doors to the steps are locked on every level. Is there any way you could get us out a window?"

"I'll try," I said, not moving from the comfort of my savior's arms.

Running down the hall, with an alarm sounding loudly in our ears, we stopped at the first window we saw. I raised my hand, and the window started to shake and rumble. The guards were only five feet from us now and coming fast. Sweat dripped from my brow, as I let my mind go free, lifting us in the air.

We wobbled and shook, but still stayed afloat. I reached out and put my hand on the bars. The contact strengthened my hold, and I was able to throw them back freeing the window behind them.

I opened it as far as I could and flew us out of there. We fell the four stories to the ground, my guidance making it a somewhat soft landing.

"This way," Chaz said, running around the right side of the building.

Clink scooped me back up, and we took off behind him. Halfway there, we ran into Toma and Nico.

"What happened to her?" Toma asked, carefully removing me from Clink's arms and cradling me in his.

"Over here," Chaz said. We walked to a door marked private, on the lower end of the building.

I shook my head. "This one's on you guys. I still need enough juice to get us out of here."

Clink held his hands up. "Here take this off." I looked at the power stripping bracelets on his wrist, wondering how I was just seeing them. They were used to hold power in, and stop your abilities from working. I'd been to many worlds where prisons and jails used them to keep powerful criminals from escaping. I used my telekinesis to fly them off, and he nodded me a thanks.

"Just one second," he said, hanging his head and going completely still.

"He can astral project," Chaz explained. "He's letting Kirk know we're coming."

Clink was back in a second. "He's ready to go. Can anyone open this door?" In the background, we heard heavy footsteps coming our way.

"Hurry," Chaz said, looking from me, to Toma, to Nico, probably trying to figure out which of us could better save his brother.

As natural as anything in the world, Toma opened his mouth and shot a stream of bullet shaped sand at the door. Each one hit hard and loud, but served their purpose of taking the hinges off. Nico and Chaz rushed inside, Nico already breathing out fire.

"I need to open a portal," I whispered to Toma's chest. He put me down, and I held my hands up. We could hear the guards getting closer with each passing second, and I hoped like hell I still had enough energy to do this.

Coughing as my lungs filled with the smoke from Nico's attack, I put my hand on the brick, trying desperately to make something happen. My eyes burning from the smoke, I now had to squint to see anything. Nico was definitely out of control. I raised a weak head to look at Toma. "Is she trying to burn us alive?"

He let out a huff, then turned to where fire was rolling and smoke billowing. "Sometimes she overreacts."

"Here they come," Clink called. I had no idea if he was talking about the guards or Nico, Chaz, and Kirk.

It didn't matter because a small portal had started to form beneath my fingers. Hoping the rest would followed, I jumped through and landed on a king-sized feather bed. Oh, heaven.

It only took a second for the rest to come tumbling in. With them was a tall, pale, bald man, who had to be Kirk, Chaz's brother. Like Clink, he stood about six feet three. He looked angry, and bothered, so much so that I shivered at the thought of meeting him in a dark alley late at night. Before he had a chance to ask, I waved my hand, and removed the power stripping cuffs from his arms.

He looked shocked for a moment, then nodded at me.

"Where are we?" Nico asked. Her eyes lit up as she took in the size of my bed, the quality of my sheets, the plush carpet, and everything else that spoke of wealth and prosperity.

I pulled a pillow under me and sunk deeper in the covers. "One of my other houses," I said only half awake.

Her voice was incredulous when she asked. "How many houses do you have?"

I really just wanted her to leave me alone. "None of your business. I keep a few scattered throughout different worlds in case of emergencies and such things." Those few words cost me, and I found myself fighting to keep my eyes open.

I turned to see them all lined up by my bed, looking lost and unsure of what to do next. "You all help yourself. I keep staff here, and there's plenty of room. Eat good and rest up. We move out in a few days," I said between gasps. "Just go ahead and—." That was it. I couldn't take it a moment longer and was more than happy to surrender to the darkness as it took me under.

I awoke to the smell of fresh fruit, bacon, and eggs. I sat up in the bed to see my housekeeper, Anna staring at me with concerned eyes. "You slept all night, Rekia, I was so worried about you." I was usually up every three hours or so, so I understood her concern.

I tried to sit up a little higher, just to let her know I was okay. "Have the guests been taken care of?" I asked.

She nodded and continued rubbing the cloth across my head. I didn't tell her to stop. It felt too good, and I was still too out of it to do anything else. "I smell bacon." I looked down to the tray in front of me piled high with some of my favorite breakfast foods.

I tried to pick up a piece of bacon, but my hand shook so bad that I dropped it. Shit. I really had overdone it this time.

Anna picked it up and put it to my mouth. "Thanks," I said, after taking a small bite. I looked at her and smiled, grateful to have such a kind woman taking care of me. I made a mental note to raise her salary. This was certainly going above and beyond her job duties.

A shadow loomed nearby, and I looked up to see Toma standing in the doorway, watching. "I'll take it from here." Well, at least he looked relaxed and happy. The smell of my fruit-scented bath soap drifted toward me as he walked into the room. I looked him over, realizing that he'd changed clothes and washed his hair. He looked clean and refreshed.

"Rekia?" Anna asked, not sure if she should leave me alone with this stranger.

I sunk my head deeper into the pillow and waved her on. "Everything's fine."

This seemed to reassure her a little, and after one more quick look at Toma, she shuffled out of the room.

He sat in the chair she'd just abandoned. "You going to be okay?"

"Not if you don't feed me," I mumbled.

"Sorry." He picked up a forkful of eggs and gently led them to my mouth. Hmm. They had cheese and green onions in them just the way I liked.

"Have you eaten?" I didn't want his food to get cold trying to play nursemaid to me.

He picked up a slice of strawberry and brought it to my lips. I took it in my mouth and chewed slowly. "Yeah, what's her name, Anna, she saw to it that we had a good dinner last night, clean sheets and a hot bath. Then, this morning, there was a hot buffet of breakfast waiting for us. It's been a long time since I lived in such luxury. You better be careful, or you'll spoil us," he laughed.

Good, after that many portal hops they needed to recharge their energy from the food as much as I did.

After more eggs and one more slice of bacon, I asked the question I'd been wondering about all morning. "Where is everybody? It seems so quiet here." We really did need to come up with a plan to clear their names, so that we could all go our separate ways.

He brought some freshly squeezed orange juice to my lips and answered while I lapped up as much as I could. "They're around. I think most are eating, resting, or getting cleaned up. Don't worry, we're not going anywhere, especially since none of us know where we are."

Nor will you ever. I didn't say that though. Instead I tried for something neutral. "Just a peaceful little world that I go to when I want to get away from it all, there's not much stress here."

He let me lap a little more juice into my mouth. "I think you need a couple more days of rest. I'm sorry that helping us has brought you so much trouble."

"It's been an adventure," I said dryly.

"I'll say," he said, wiping my mouth again. "Would you like something else to eat?"

I looked down, startled to see that I'd cleaned my plate. Portal hopping did that to you, and I hadn't eaten in a while. "No, I'm satisfied. Wake me up at dinnertime." I sunk back into my pillows and barely remembered him picking up my tray and leaving the room.

When I woke again, it was dark outside, and I felt a little better. Not one hundred percent by a long shot, but good enough to walk around. I vaguely recalled Anna getting me up and taking me to the bathroom a couple of times, but by the way my bladder was protesting, it was like I hadn't been in days.

Once that was taken care of, I walked in the direction of my dining room. Wonderful smells were coming from there.

"Ah, you're up then, Rekia," Chaz said as soon as I walked into the room.

I nodded at him and took a seat beside Kirk. They all had a plate in front of them, and the conversation seemed to be flowing freely.

I looked at the feast before me and shook my head. Anna had really outdone herself this time. Food lay on platters and in bowls from one end of the table to the other.

Toma stood and grabbed a plate. "What would you like?" he asked me.

I waved my hand to let him know that it didn't matter. I had complete confidence in Anna and knew that she only ever fixed things that she knew I absolutely loved. The little meal from this morning hadn't been enough to build my energy back up, not after I'd wasted so much of it the night before. I needed food, and lots of it.

Nico got up and poured me a glass of water. The shock of that alone could have knocked me to the floor. I looked at her to get a clue where her head was, but her expression was unreadable. "Do you want something different?" she asked.

Talk about twilight zone. "No. The water is fine. Thank you." She nodded and sat back down.

From the corner of my eye, I noticed that Kirk watched her every move. Oh boy. I didn't even want to know what that was about.

The scent of sliced ham, baked macaroni and cheese, turnip greens, and cornbread filled my nose as Toma placed my plate in front of me. I didn't want to be a pig, but seriously, my body was craving this, and I saw no way to be polite about it.

"So," I said, looking from Toma and Nico, as I crammed food into my mouth. "The plan in the morning is to go to your world, and do what?

Nico finished the food in her mouth. "Three senators rule Sentra. All laws go through them. If Clink can show them that we didn't do it, then they'll have no choice but to declare us innocent and reinstate our rights as full Sentra citizens. Since Chaz said Clink has to be in the place the event happened to do the reacted, we'll have to go to Kolo's house when we get there. He was killed at home, in the bedroom."

I nodded, "So, Clink will show them who murdered the senator's brother and they'll just set you free?"

Toma and Nico shared a look that I couldn't decipher. Then Toma spoke. "Once they see who the guilty party is, they'll be brought to justice. No way around it"

I accepted that, satisfied. If all went as planned, tomorrow would be the end of our little rogue's adventure and we'd all go back to our separate lives. Fine with me. I'd had my fun and was now ready for this to end.

Shoveling food into my mouth and not using any of the manners I was brought up with, I didn't look up until I heard Kirk clear his throat.

He looked over to Nico. "Hey, girl. How 'bout some fun? It's been a hell of a long time since I had a good row, even before I went in the blocker."

I held my breath waiting for her to jump across the table. "The blocker? You mean jail, right?" I asked, wanting to divert the conversation and keep her from strangling him. Not that I would blame her if she did. The fucking nerve.

He spared me a glance. "Right," he turned his attention back to Nico.

To my surprise, she seemed to be thinking it over. Well, this was surprising and utterly unexpected.

Finally, she nodded, mind apparently made up. "It's been a while for me too, so yeah, I'll do you. Come into my room later." She sent a scathing look to Chaz and Clink. "I mean, why should your brother have all the fun."

Chaz dropped his fork in mock horror. "Hey, how do you know?"

She picked up a piece of ham and took a bite. "You guys sleep in the room next to mine. All night, all I wanted, was for you two to shut up." Her voice rose a little on that last part.

Chaz laughed and pulled Clink over for a kiss. "Don't worry, babe, she's just jealous."

Clink kissed him back, then turned to Nico. "Sorry, but can't promise it won't be just as noisy tonight."

Nico smiled, it wasn't pleasant. "Don't worry, I'll show you the same courtesy you've shown me."

I'd had enough. Listening to them sitting around discussing their sex lives was not my idea of a good time. Time to make my exit. I pushed my plate away and stood. "Be prepared to move out tomorrow."

THE NEXT MORNING, AFTER we'd had our breakfast, I found backpacks for our three new friends and refilled mine, Toma's and Nico's. I noticed Kirk sticking a little closer to Nico and assumed they'd had their night together. None of my business I decided, turning back around.

Toma walked up to me while I was saying my goodbyes to Anna. She kind of gave him the side-eye, then turned her attention back to me. I held her hand in mine to better convey my feelings. "You did good. Thanks for not walking out on me. I left a bonus in your room, and you can expect a little more in your pay from now on."

She smiled at me, gave Toma another fleeting look, then hurried out of the room.

I watched her go, just a little baffled at her reaction. "She's shy," I joked.

Toma burst out laughing. "Everyone's ready," he said.

"Then so am I, let's go clear your name." I brushed past him and walked into the living room where the others had gathered. I was rested, well fed, and feeling one hundred percent myself again.

"Ah, love, I have a question for you," Chaz said, coming to stand in front of me. "As you well know, us going back home is not an option." He paused for a moment and shifted his eyes to where Kirk and Clink stood off to the side. "Think you could shoot us back here when this is all done."

"No." There was no hesitation in my words. Chaz had to be out of his mind to even ask such a thing. "This is a peaceful place with good hard-working people. I won't bring you here to rob and steal from them. You can come back to my world with me." I looked at Chaz. "It is where I found you after all." That way I'd be able to keep an eye on them. Besides, there were a lot worse criminals in my world than these three.

I was on my way across the room when I caught sight of Nico bouncing from side to side, an uncertain look on her face. I bit my lip hard, because something told me my day was ready to get a lot more complicated.

Her gaze shifted unsurely to her brother.

I narrowed my eyes. "What?"

Nico took off her backpack and adjusted the straps. "We can't just go there like that. You don't get an audience with the senators just because you want it. You have to bring them gifts."

I looked at Toma, and he nodded.

I flexed my hands, trying not to choke them both. "What kind of gifts and how much are they going to cost me?" I didn't like them pulling this shit on me at the last minute, and I wouldn't let them forget about it easily. If I started to feel like I was being used, there were going to be some problems.

Deciding to let it go for now, I looked from brother to sister. "What do you suggest?"

Nico put her backpack on and held her head high as if she had nothing to be ashamed of. "There are three high senators, a hundred lesser senators, and then eight hundred under them. They are the ruling party of all of Sentra. The man they accused me of killing was one of the high senator's brothers, one of the top three."

I could give two shits around a turkey's ass. This beating around the bush nonsense didn't fit her character. "What do they want?" Maybe my voice was a little sharper than it needed to be, but she was seriously starting to piss me off.

Nico squared her shoulders as if ready for an attack, like she knew her words would piss me off. "As a regular citizen of Sentra, it's not something I had to worry about. It was their duty to see to all of our concerns. As an outsider though, well, you have to pay to meet with the three great ones."

I felt a vein pop. What part of how much would it cost me did she not understand? Part of me just wanted to throw my hands up and walk away, but another part of me was filled with curiosity at what came next.

Also, if they really were innocent, then I had to help them. I wouldn't be able to live with myself if I didn't. "How many dollars will I be throwing down today, because I'm only willing to go so far. You should have told me."

I turn to Toma to include him as well. "And you should have told me too. Come on, guys, you know you should have told me this shit before now. Fuck it, we'll figure it out when we get there."

Vein still popping over their unexpected deception, I placed my hand on the wall, opening a doorway to a world rich with money and greed. I took a second to brace myself for the unknown, then stepped inside, the others right behind me.

Chaz's eyes lit up like he'd just been given the keys to a gold mine. "Red men who swim in the sea, what kind of wonderful rich world are you from?"

Kirk walked to one of the golden mailboxes on the street corner. His brows furrowed as he checked all around it, even bending down to get a look on the underside. Inspection finished, he stood and looked at Nico. "How do you keep looters from chipping off little pieces here and there?" He seemed genuinely curious.

Clink ran his hands up and down the sidewalk, a look of complete awe on his face. His eyes took in the golden streets, the jewel-laced buildings and the diamond-studded cars riding by. "Do the blockers here have bars made of gold?" he asked Toma.

Toma, who was busy checking the street and peeking around corners, wiped sweat from his brow and shook his head. "There are no jails here. You break the law, and you're left on the street to die of starvation or exposure, whichever gets you first."

Nico's eyes searched up and down the street, her voice low and urgent. "This way. His home was still locked up last I checked. He'd willed everything to me, so now there's a big debate over who gets what."

Toma waved for us to follow him as he ducked into an alleyway. "Come on, we need to hurry before they catch our scent."

We walked a while, ducking in alleys and hiding out behind buildings until we reached a house, excuse me, mansion, castle, whatever, with a front yard so big it looked like the size of three football fields.

Chaz looked upon Nico and Toma as if seeing them for the first time. "You had all this? You walked away from all of this?"

Nico gave him a narrowed eyed look. "It's not like we had a choice," she said dryly. "Come on."

We crept around the back of the house where Nico removed a key from the bottom of one of the trees. "We'll go in this way," she said, opening a door on the side.

Inside, the place held all the amenities that one would expect in a mansion of its size. The extent of their luxury was sickening and obscene. Who needed diamond walls and golden floors, TV's made of pure platinum, with diamond coat hangers and ruby dishes? It was a play at power and dominance, kind of like, 'If you have fifty gold dishes, then

I'll have a hundred.' The one with the most golden dishes wins. I shook my head, it was all too much, and for some strange reason, it made me long for my small house back home.

"Could feed my family for years," Chaz said, rubbing his hands across every shiny surface he saw.

Kirk picked up a pair of gold and diamond sunshades. "So this is how you like to live then, girl? Nothing but the best for you, hey?"

Nico, who was busy ushering us toward the steps, stopped when she heard this, her eyes raking in the sheer magnitude of the place. "It was all I'd ever known," she said in a voice that suddenly sounded lost and unsure. "Come on, he died in the bedroom."

We walked through the living room and down a long hallway. A large portrait of an older man with black hair combed carefully to the side, covered a good 50 inches of one wall.

"Is this him, then?" Kirk asked. "He looks like a man who's used to getting what he wants. Is that the case with you then, girl? What kind of brother would allow such a thing?" He looked at Toma.

Well, this was news, I blinked, but wondered how I'd missed that Nico and the murdered man had been romantically involved. Apparently, she'd told Kirk though.

Toma stared holes at a smaller picture on the wall, taking on a glassy wounded look. In it was a picture of two men and a woman. "These are the three high senators." He pointed to a female of medium height, with black hair and skin. She looked cunning and intelligent, like she had multiple plots in her head, and was ready to execute them at a moment's notice. "This is Saylor."

He pointed to a man with skin the same tone as his and Nico's. "Beside her, the man to her left, this is Remus." The man had a bald head, and a hard look in his eyes. He looked like he'd knife you just for the fun of watching you bleed to death, all the while eating popcorn and laughing.

A shiver ran over me, as Toma pointed to the last man. "This is the murdered man's brother, his name is Welvina and he's the most ruthless of them all." He had pale skin and brown hair. If I thought the first two senators were scary, this one looked like the type to stick a knife in your back, at the same time he sung you a sweet lullaby, telling you everything would be okay.

Another shiver ran through me and I wondered if proving their innocence would be enough for these three to let them come home, unharmed. Only one way to find out, I guessed.

Toma ran a hand down his face as if he couldn't believe what was about to happen. "We need to get a message to them. So, they can meet us here and put an end to this once and for all. Once we show them we're innocent, that should be the end of it."

I blinked at his words, a layer of uncertainty finally lifting. This was the first time I'd actually heard him say without doubt that he thought his sister to be innocent and it was more of a relief than I'd realized.

He turned to her. "Do it."

Nico picked the phone up, dialing as slowly as she possibly could. "Ursha, yes, I know you have resident identifier." She put the phone back down. "They'll be here in a minute."

Clink shook his arms out and cracked his neck from side to side. "Practice run." He walked farther into the bedroom and inhaled deeply. His brows furrowed as he turned back to look at us. "Wait in the hall."

We stepped back, and he closed his eyes, crouched down, and spread his hands out, walking the length of the room.

Chaz watched him in awe, a look of pride and adoration on his face. "He's focusing on that one event," he let us know. "That helps bring it out faster, and then we don't see nothing we don't want to."

We heard a rippling sound and thick white smoke filled the air. Clink stepped back into the hallway with us. When the smoke cleared, there were four people now standing in the bedroom. They looked as solid as the five people I had standing beside me.

The look of shock on Nico's face crept into her voice as she spoke. "What is this? Why are the senators here?" she asked.

Toma placed a calming hand on her arm. "Just look."

"Kolo," she said, looking in the room at the man who'd once been her lover. "What did they do to you?" she whispered.

Inside the room, the action continued. We watched in awe as Saylor walked in a small circle, her diamond heels clicking loudly against the platinum floor. "This deal with the Clamorers could bring in an extra two hundred billion a year. More than enough for us to split four ways. But we can't do it without your cooperation. Your bank is the deciding factor. Without it, there is no deal."

Kolo shook his head and tried not to look intimidated. A crooked smile crossed his lips. "I can't see a way to make this right. Say what you will. Beg if you must. He cocked his head to the side. "I kind of like the idea of you on your knees."

If he meant to hurt her, he'd failed, the pleasurable smirk on her face said as much. She pointed to Welvina and sat down.

He walked over to Kolo and placed a hand on his shoulder. "Brother, think about what it'll mean. Think about what we could do. Don't grow a conscience now, not when we need you as cold and heartless as you've always been. Think about this brother, what would Nico say if she knew you'd passed on a deal with this much money? Do you think she'd still spread those pretty legs for you every night?"

Kolo looked unsure. He turned to a picture of Nico on the nightstand. His eyes went soft for just a second before he shook his head, which seemed to strengthen his resolve. "Look, I'm not doing it. We're not doing it, so just stop with the nonsense and let's focus on something else."

"He's right you know," Nico said, a tear falling down her cheek. "That much money slipping through our fingers, there's no way I would have turned a blind eye to that."

I left her in her misery and turned back around. I wanted to hurry this along, before those three got here for real.

Remus, who was behind Kolo, pulled a rope out of his pocket and held it straight between his hands. Welvina and Saylor exchanged predatory glances.

Welvina went to a chair and sat down. "Won't you change your mind, brother?"

Kolo watched the other man, a sad look on his face. "No, brother. I will not."

Saylor quickly came to her feet. "So be it," she said, pulling a long knife from inside her hair.

"Now wait a minute," Kolo said. He tried to stand, but, before he could make it halfway out of the chair, Remus wrapped the rope around his neck and squeezed him back down to a sitting position.

Small desperate gurgling noises came from Kolo's mouth as he fought and struggled to break free. His eyes turned to his brother, pleading with him for help. He reached out his hand trying to call the other man to his side.

Welvina looked from Saylor to Remus. "I'm sorry brother, but you should have taken the deal." He walked up to him and sunk to his knees. "I'm sorry," he whispered again before holding up his hand and blasting him with thick red energy. "May you rest in peace." Kolo's body went limp, but he still wasn't dead.

Small pathetic noises still sounded from his half-moving lips. Saylor put the knife away and walked over to him. She placed her hand over his nose and kept it there until he took his last breath.

"So now you know all?" A loud thunderous voice sounded from behind us. Startled we whipped around to see that the three murderers had joined us without our knowledge.

"You," Nico yelled, making a move to lunge forward.

Welvina held up his hand and released a thick line of red energy that knocked her back. A loud thumping sound echoed through the house as she hit against the wall, then crumpled to the floor.

Toma immediately took up the fight, his face full of rage and vengeance. He shot bullet-shaped sand out of his fingertips, seemingly aiming at no one and everyone in equal measures. Saylor's hands glowed with blue energy, which she used to block every one of his attacks.

From other parts of the mansion, we heard voices and footsteps. We couldn't fight them all. "Let's go," I said, running for the safety of the bedroom.

I turned for just a second to make sure the others followed, then opened a portal and jumped inside. Once it closed, I turned to make sure the others had made it through.

Everyone was accounted for, except, I stepped back with a gasp. A shaken Kirk stood holding a bleeding and wounded Nico in his arms. Her face was pale, and her eyes closed tightly. She wasn't moving and I felt my heart jump to my throat. She was losing blood fast, herself and Kirk both covered in it.

Chapter 8

Kirk's voice sounded frantic and scared when he spoke. "We have to get help, or she's not going to make it."

I looked to Toma, but he stood stock still, cold, and unapproachable. His eyes were widened and staring unflinchingly at his sister. His whole body radiated furious anger and rage. Not knowing how to approach, I stepped back a few steps to give him space.

Another look at Nico showed her even more pale and trembling. Kirk held her tight in his arms, his fear palpable as he mumbled soft words into her ear. I ran a nervous hand down my face, and tried to think.

We didn't have a moment to spare. I knew that. Picking up a phone that worked no matter my location, I punched in the number that would call my sister. "I need your help."

Never one to waste time, Chanel got straight to the point. "Where are you and what do you need?"

"I'm at my place on the world Yello, and I need some healing." I hung up the phone and walked over to Kirk. "Bring her this way."

Chaz looked around. "So just how many houses do you own?" he asked.

Ignoring him, I made my way to one of the empty bedrooms. Kirk placed her down gently, never taking his hands off her completely.

Toma stood beside her bed, fists clenched, eyes hard and dangerous. "What happens now?" I didn't know what to tell him, so I focused on her instead. This was all happening too fast, and I needed more than a moment to get my thoughts together.

I sat down as easy as I could on the bed beside her and ran soft fingers through her hair, offering what comfort I could. Her whole body was cold and wet with sweat. She went completely still for a moment, and my eyes went wide, fearing the worst. I looked to Kirk, and he nodded, letting me know that she was still all right for now.

Chaz watched closely, a strange look on his face. His voice cracked when he spoke. "When's your sister getting here?" He laid his head back on Clink's chest, and the other man wrapped his arms around him.

Two minutes later, the wall in front of us rippled, and a portal opened. "Here she is now," I said getting up and walking over.

"Who's hurt?" She asked as soon as she entered the room. A little taller than me, she wore her hair in black twisted curls, that flowed all around her face.

I pointed to the bed. She raised a brow, and I'm sure she had a lot of questions, but to her credit, she knew now wasn't the time.

She went straight to the bed and placed a hand on Nico's chest, then let out a sad sigh. "This woman is too far gone. I need blood from a relative or someone who loves her."

Toma stepped up and held out his arm. "I'm her brother. Where do you need it from?"

Chanel looked at me, and I could tell that time was quickly running out. She took off her backpack and pulled out a large blade.

"You give this blood freely for the life of your sister do you not?"

Toma nodded. "Yes, I give it freely."

"Good, because it won't work if you don't want it to. The blood cannot lie." She slashed him across the face with the knife. He fell back, stumbling to his knees. She went down with him. Sucking the blood out of his open wound as fast as she could.

Quickly she ran back to the bed and jumped on top of Nico. Leaning over the other woman, she shot blood out of her mouth at an unearthly rate. It carried with it a blue healing light. It raised my sister off the bed until she was lying horizontally in the air above the wound, blood and light shooting from her mouth so fast you could barely see it.

Blood remedy, used only when the person was two steps away from death. It was too powerful to try any other time. I looked at my sister as she floated back to the ground. I never ceased to be amazed at the power she held, yet never once had she tried to use it for personal gain. Oh well, to each their own, I guessed. At least Nico was looking better.

The first thing she did was rub her hand across her chest where the hole had been a minute ago. "It's gone," she said in genuine surprise. "The pain is gone as well." She jumped off the bed looking even better than she had before. "How?"

She looked around the room until her eyes landed on Chanel. "Did you do this?"

Chanel stared back at her a moment, then pointed to me. "At my sister's request."

Nico looked from her to me. "Thank you, thank you both." She ran to her brother, who was smiling brighter than a thousand-watt bulb. He picked her up and spun her around. "Scare me like that again, and I'll break every bone in your body. I'll boil your skin in toxic water. I'll—"

Nico held up her hand, cutting him off. "Enough." Her eyes went soft for just a second. "I love you too," she said.

My sister watched them for a bit, then pulled me to the side. "What else do you need? Because I need to get back." I gave her a hug. Not something I normally did, but perhaps it was hug your sister to death day. She pushed me off her, claiming I was taking her breath away, then turned serious in an instant. "Are you okay?"

I looked at the other members of the room. They all looked like criminals. The thing was, I wasn't so out of place with them. My entire income came from hiding crooks in places our laws couldn't find them. "I'm fine. Go home to your family." I kissed her on the cheek and waved as she opened another portal and slipped through.

I watched until she was gone, then turned to the others. "To the living room," I said.

"Well, this house is a lot smaller." Chaz sat on the love seat with a flop. Clink sat beside him. Toma, Nico, and Kirk took the couch while I sat in the recliner.

Chaz ran a hand over his closely shaven head. "Can I have a sandwich or something? Do you have a helper here as well?"

I shook my head. We'd just hopped two portals in quick succession, so I was sure the others needed food to recharge as well. I know I did. "No, this is a small four-bedroom house. I'll order us something from the pizza place down the street."

I picked up the phone and ordered six fully loaded pizzas with hot wings on the side. Remembering that my favorite pizza place here on Yello also kept beverages on hand, I called back and ordered some twelve packs of water, beer, and cola.

Chaz sat back and placed his hands behind his head. "So how long are we held up here then, love?"

"We leave tomorrow." I reached into the side table by my chair and pulled out some bills. It was Yello money. I had houses on many worlds, and I kept them all stacked with readymade cash, for when I visited. "Give this to the pizza man when he comes. I'm going to take a bath." The events of today had left me feeling dirty all over.

EMPTY PIZZA PLATES and cans of beer lined my living room table. It would be a mess to clean up, but no one had wanted to sit in the stiff-back chairs in my dining room.

Clink picked up a gooey slice, letting the cheese slide into his mouth. "Man do you know what they feed us in the blocker? Powdered eggs and runny potatoes. Once every two weeks or so we may get a dried-up lump of meat, but nothing like this."

Chaz took a long swig of beer. "Only the best for you, babe. Only the best for you." He leaned over and gave the other man a quick kiss on the cheek.

Kirk, who'd finished his meal, turned all his attention to Nico. "Are you feeling well enough for a roll then, girl?"

She looked up at him, her face as unreadable as ever. "Yeah, come to me later. I feel the need to prove myself alive." She rounded her shoulders when she said it, as if making the point that life was still flowing through her.

Painfully I bit my tongue, having learned a long time ago to keep my mouth shut when dealing with people from different worlds. Their customs were their own, and I'd let stuff like a man constantly calling a grown woman "girl" roll off my shoulders for some time now. None of my business how others chose to conduct themselves.

Once everyone had finished, I got a trash bag from the kitchen and started to clean up the mess. "So who are the Clamorers?"

Toma got up to help me. Picking up fallen napkins and empty cans off the floor, he answered my question. "They are a self-titled superior race from Clamor. I know we have some dealings with them, but it's nothing to kill over. At least I didn't think it was anyway."

Putting the last paper plate in the trash bag and closing it tightly, I opened the door in the dining room and placed the bag outside. "What kind of people are they?"

Toma must have gone to get a wet cloth while I was taking out the trash, because now he was busy wiping down the table.

I took a seat and waited until he'd taken the rag back into the kitchen.

He sat beside his sister. "They're a lot like us actually. I'm sure in your travels you've come across a couple of worlds similar to your own."

"Plenty," I said, waving my hand for him to continue.

"While physically we look very different, they do seem to share the same love of money as us."

For now, I was bored. Did I really need to deal with another group of people as greedy as the Sentra's? I thought not. "How are you different? Physically, I mean?"

Toma took a small minute to think before he answered. "To them being ten feet is kind of tall."

"To me being ten feet is kind of tall and I didn't see any giants walking around in your world so what the hell are you talking about?"

A small chuckle before he continued. "What I mean is, ten feet to them is like six feet to us. To them six feet is really short. Eight is pretty average. And nine and ten are sort of on the tall side."

Okay, now we were getting somewhere, but I'd been to worlds with shorter people, taller people, oddly shaped people, and so many other things that would shock the normal person. So, no, still wasn't interested. "Continue."

"They have great big heads, like the size of a large watermelon, and their arms are so long..." he stopped for a minute to look around the room, his eyes landing on Chaz. "Yeah, him, one of their arms can be easily the size of his whole body."

A rush of adrenaline flowed through me at the prospect. Giants, we were dealing with a world filled with giants. My heart began to beat out of my chest at all that lay before us. I felt both giddy at the unknown, but also a little cautious at all that could go wrong.

I stood, ready to refill my cup when something familiar caught my eye. I turned just in time to see the right side of my living room wall ripple and shake in the way that said a portal was opening. I figured it was probably my sister checking that we were okay.

Chaz and Clink were sitting on the love seat that lined the wall where the portal was forming. I frowned. Chanel wouldn't open a portal this close to where people sat. No. This was someone else. "Get out of the way!" I screamed at them.

Chaz moved in time. Clink did not. Before we could react, a tall muscular man with a bald head, stepped out of the portal and held out his palm. A thick line of red energy shot out and lifted Clink off the ground. It wrapped around his neck, and began to squeeze as he clawed at it, feet dangling as he struggled to get free.

Chaz acted immediately. "Let him go you swelled up piece of dog shit off the left tit of a gutter whore," He leaped forward, with Kirk right behind him.

Throwing my hand up, I tried to use my TK to remove the energy from Clink's neck, but it was like I'd come up against a brick wall, it wasn't working, nothing was happening.

What a hell of a time for my powers to fail me. I flexed my hand and looked to Toma and Nico who were spitting bullets and fire respectively. That wasn't working either, and I felt my heart sputter, as everything we threw at the man bounced off him like a ping pong.

I swallowed hard as fear spread through me. What was going on? Did this dude have some kind of magical shield protecting him? If so, it meant that my powers hadn't failed, they'd just been blocked.

Which didn't help, because without our powers, we were at his mercy. He could do anything he liked to us, and there wasn't a damn thing we could do to stop it.

Behind him, two more men rushed through the portal. One had black hair the other brown, but both looked like they worked out at the same gym as the first guy.

Red energy shot out of their palms too, and soon all of us were caught in the red grip of death. It latched onto my throat and would itself around. Tight unbearable pressure cut off my air supply and no matter how much I kicked and struggled I couldn't break free. In fact, fighting only made it worse. I told myself not to panic, but it was hard. Unless one of us thought of something, we'd all be dead soon. My vision darkened and I wondered if this was the end.

Closing my eyes, I tried desperately to decide before it was too late. Mentally I could call out to my sister, brothers, and even my father if need be. There were only three men, each of them holding two of us. Still, I didn't really want to involve them in this, but I didn't want to die either.

Soon it wouldn't matter because my strength was steadily declining. Still trying to fight, but not able to hold my arms up any longer, they flapped to my sides while my eyes started to droop.

Then something strange happened. Chaz, who was being held in the air by the same man who choked Clink, let out a bloodcurdling scream that snapped us all to attention. Not able to do anything but watch through hooded lids, I fought the urge to scream myself, as the red light filtered through him until he himself was red.

Then I was falling. Released from the grip of death, I hit the floor with a loud thump. Coughing and massaging my now sore throat, I looked around and saw the others had been released too.

Toma and Nico looked as confused as I felt. Kirk and Clink for their part were both watching Chaz with intense scrutiny. Slowly, and with the red light seemingly acting as some type of fuel, Chaz lifted himself off the ground and into the air.

Our three new guests, who did at least seem shocked at this new development, must have had a plan B ready, because without missing a beat, they pulled tiny, pointy, weapons out of their pockets.

They looked like small guns, but buzzed and hummed with the same red energy that came from their hands. I didn't have time to run or jump before one hit me dead in my shoulder and sent me rolling.

"Uggg." My upper arm burned hot and painful, making me feel like I'd bathed in fire for a week.

Off in the distance, the far, distance, I heard someone calling my name. It sounded almost like Toma. I could sense footsteps coming my way, then nothing, until I heard another body hit the floor.

Sweat covered my face, dropping into my eyes and down my back. Every part of my body felt gutted and felled. This was the worst pain I'd ever felt in my life. My body felt like it was shutting down and fear gripped me like a cobra that just wouldn't let go. What if this was the end of the line for me?

I started to close my eyes, then popped them back open, refusing to give up. I wouldn't go down like this, wouldn't let my family find my body like this. I couldn't do that to them.

Taking a deep breath, I tried to focus. I needed to know what we were dealing with. From my spot on the floor I tried to take stock of what was going on around me. I craned my neck to the side, trying to get a better view of my surroundings. The first thing I saw was Chaz.

He still had the power he'd stolen earlier. He held up his hands and sent red energy into the first guy who'd entered the living room. The man let out an ear blasting scream then exploded into a million pieces.

With no time to react, one of the other intruders shot his pointed weapon directly into Kirk's eye, throwing him into the wall where he fell to a helpless heap in the corner. More pain rippled through me, as I tried to cry out, hoping Kirk was okay, then everything went black.

WHEN I CAME TO, I WAS still lying on the floor, and I was still in a shitload of pain. I tried to move, but the best I could do was crawl. Something wet and sticky kept making me slip. Slowly a familiar smell found its way to my nostrils. Blood. I'd been laying in a puddle of my own blood. My chest filled with fear and disgust.

Still on my knees, I crawled until I could maneuver myself against the nearest wall, and use that as a sort of back brace to hold me up. Once in a somewhat better position, I took a moment to breathe through the ache in my shoulder and upper body.

How the hell had we ended up here? How had shit gone so wrong? Tears slid from my eyes, and I used my hand to angrily wipe them away. This was... I went numb for a second, and tried to will the image of blood and dead bodies away. No one was left standing. No one.

Beside me lay Toma, his face slack, his body not moving. He was covered in bruises, and just looked battered and discarded. More tears slipped out of my eyes as I looked upon his lifeless form. Maybe he was dead. Everything in me froze, as my heart beat out of my chest, my whole body rejecting that as a reality.

Off on the other side of the room was Kirk and Clink. They too were covered in marks and cuts, while each bled profusely. In front of them were Nico and Chaz. It looked as though these two had fought to the end, as they were mere inches from where the last two assailants had been standing. Strangely though, there was no blood around Chaz, only what seemed to have flowed over from Nico's body.

Nico's body. I put a fist to my mouth to hold in a sob. Oh no. Fuck. No. Just... No. I screamed, louder and harder than I'd ever screamed in my life. It came out like a roar, and it exhausted me so much that I fell over again landing in blood that mixed with the tears running down my face.

Family. I needed my family here. Where were they? I couldn't do this alone. I needed them, needed their help and their comfort, more than I'd ever needed anything before.

Breathing hard, but still not able to move more than a few inches, I sent out a very weak signal. Maybe it would be enough, maybe it wouldn't, maybe I'd never know because maybe I'd never wake up again. Darkness.

This time when I came to, I was in a soft bed with nice warm blankets pulled all around me. I snuggled down in the covers, determined to enjoy this good feeling just a little bit longer. The pain from earlier had trickled down to a slow ache, and I was clean and comfortable.

I would have loved to stay like this forever, but I needed explanations. The last thing I remembered was bleeding out on the floor, so how the hell had I gotten here? Careful of the dull pain in my shoulder, I eased myself up to a sitting position.

Everything looked familiar. The bed, red curtains, small TV in the corner, red and black walls, all of it was mine. I was home. Not home home, but one of the houses I kept scattered about.

Now how had I gotten here, and where were the others? I ran a hand down my face, as I looked around. Surely, I hadn't been able to open a portal in my previous condition.

Voices outside my room caught my ear, and I shut off my own thoughts in order to listen. Chanel. I heard my sister's voice. So at least someone in my family had heard my call. My movements were slow as I scooted closer to the edge of the bed.

I could probably walk now, but I wouldn't know until I tried it. I stood up and immediately exhaled. My knees and arms wobbled as if in competition to see which could shake the fastest. I took another calming breath, and the sound of other voices drifted to my ears.

They all sounded familiar. They were talking urgently among themselves, but I knew my brothers when I heard them. Kevin and Greg were here. Great. Now we had some backup.

I followed the sounds, holding on to the wall and pausing between each step. "Hey guys," I said, stumbling into the living room and falling into Kevin's arms.

"You know you still need to be in bed, right?" he asked me, as he placed me on my cherry-colored love seat. I didn't give a damn about any of that. What I wanted to know was what the heck had happened.

Looking around the room, I noticed that none of my new friends were anywhere in sight. "Are we alone?" I asked, trying to listen out for any sounds that would tell me where they were.

Chanel cocked a thumb down the hall. "They're still recovering. You realize you've been in and out for a week?"

My eyes widened. "A week?" Great. I was hoping to be through with all this within a week and back to my business. I hoped it hadn't suffered too much in my absence. "Where are Toma and the others recovering? I mean they are here right? You haven't flung them off to some distant universe, have you?"

Greg shook his head. He didn't look mad, just irritated. Strangely he put me in mind of a constipated bull. "Yes, your friends are here resting. You know dad just went home yesterday after he was sure you were okay. You scared the hell out of us. Now here we are, away from our families, babysitting you and your ragtag friends."

Though his words sometimes stung me, I'd learned a long time ago to shrug them off by coming back with a sarcastic remark of my own. "Oh, come on Greg," I teased. "We're not ragtag, I prefer to think of us as a respectable gang of individuals. I'm thinking about getting us little buttons to go on our shirts."

I tried to suppress a smirk as Chanel and Kevin laughed, and Greg rolled his eyes and looked away, letting me know that we were fine.

Chanel picked up some mail that'd accumulated since my last stay here and put it in a little drawer on one of my side tables. "I think... well now that you're up and walking around, all of us don't need to be here. We've left you with plenty of food in the fridge, plenty to drink. You were already pretty well stocked with your toiletries and stuff, so I'll say you're all set. We're going home."

Wow, but when was the last time all four of us were together like this? I didn't want them to go, especially since I was just now joining the party.

Greg stood and shook his head at me. "Oh, just wipe that look off your face, Rekia. We do have families you know? Remember your nieces and nephews? Our jobs? We can't all make money swinging from one adventure to the next."

Yes, you really could if you wanted to. You can open new worlds just as easily as I can. Of course, I didn't say that to any of them. Instead, I smiled and thanked them for coming. But then something occurred to me. "The Sentras that attacked, how did they lose our scent?" I looked around the room, wondering if someone was ready to come crashing through the wall.

Chanel was the first to speak. "We each, dad included, spread out, but none of the worlds you have houses on, or deal with on a regular basis. We took a piece of your clothing, something from each of you and spread it out to many different worlds. In those worlds, many different towns, cities, and countries. It'll take them forever to figure it out and try to sniff you out here, by then your scent will be lost." Smart move. I nodded my head at her to show my approval.

Kevin gave my leg a little squeeze and stood. "Are you really going to be alright? Chanel told us about the other day. I don't like it. You've always worked solo before, so what gives?"

"Kevin, I—," I stopped when I heard footsteps coming up the hall.

Toma stood in the doorway, a confused expression on his face. His eyes darted from me to my siblings, and back again. "So it's not a dream then?" When no one answered, he walked fully into the room.

Still looking like he was in some sort of hallucinogenic haze, he shook hands with both my brothers and gave my sister a light, casual hug. "I vaguely remember being fed and taken to the bathroom repeatedly. I appreciate that, but where's my sister?"

Chanel took a moment to check the bandages on the right side of his stomach. "She's fine. She looked bad when we first got here, but was one of the first to recover. Her and Chaz have actually been up helping take care of the rest of you. She's the one who warned us they could track you by scent."

Oh, well that explained that. "What about Kirk and Clink?" I was almost afraid to ask. Chaz needed both these people in his life and I would hate to see his reaction if one of them suddenly wasn't. I didn't know if I was equipped enough to deal with the emotional fallout that would come from him losing either his brother or his boyfriend.

Greg let out an impatient hiss of air and begin to massage his left palm, a clear sign that he was itching to open a portal. He did have a job and a family to get back to.

I let out a sigh. They didn't deserve this, and suddenly the only thing I wanted was for them to be gone. Back to their families and a life that didn't indulge in murder and mayhem.

Chanel finished up with Toma, then turned her attention to me. "Well, I've healed you all as much as I can. No blood remedy was needed, but you were hit with some powerful stuff."

She frowned and I knew whatever she said next, I wasn't going to like. "You better know what the fuck you're doing because I'm not ready to lose a sister, and this shit right here... Rekia what are you doing? How could you put yourself in danger like that?" She stopped for a moment and closed her eyes. "And us, every time you call, you..." She stopped talking, seemingly unable to continue, but I got the gist of it.

She thought I was endangering them and maybe I was, but it still cut like ragged glass across my neck. Even more so because I knew she was right, and I also knew that hurting me was the last thing she wanted to do. "So I won't call you anymore." Shit. I didn't mean for my voice to break, had tried real hard to keep it in check, but my emotions were real and raw and right now, I hurt like hell.

She shook her head. "You better call. That's not what I mean, and you know it."

I backed up a couple of steps. I couldn't do this now. Not right now. Chaz and the others had put their lives in my hands. I couldn't let them down. I had to stay focused. "So, everyone's okay?" I asked, which was my way of diverting from this unpleasant conversation.

She stared at me for a hard moment before she answered. "Yeah." Her voice spelled her disappointment, but to her credit, she tried not to show it. "Look, you do realize that your friend, Chaz, has some pretty amazing powers, right? If he hadn't done what he did." She looked off in the distance, a few tears slipping from her eyes.

Crap, now tears were rolling down my face as well. She wiped her eyes, and exhaled swiftly. "He saved your lives. His power is... He can steal power. I think it's a last resort as it weakens him too much otherwise."

"He was knocked out with the rest of us. I saw him."

"It weakens him," she said again.

Greg's fingers still caressed his palm. "Takes too much out of him, his body is not used to holding power at such a level. We had to go to the store five times in one day, just to keep him fed and hydrated, but after day three he was able to start helping us with you all."

"What about Kirk? He was hit in the eye."

"Yeah, that'll take a little longer to heal. But it will heal, give it about two more weeks. For now, we have a patch over it, just trust me when I say you don't want to see it."

I'd certainly take her word on that. "And Clink?"

"He just took a light hit to the arm, been up a few times. He's actually doing okay."

Sitting in my chair had allowed me to recharge a bit and get used to the dull ache in my shoulder. Standing up, I noticed that my legs didn't shake quite as bad as they had before.

Limping over to my sister, I gave her a hug. "Thank you, I'll try not to call again if I can help it." She gave me a kiss on my right cheek. I squeezed her hand, then moved on to Kevin and Greg. "Now go," I said, sitting back down. "Tell my nieces and nephews that I love them, and don't forget to tell dad that I'm fine."

I waved until they disappeared, then turned my attention to Toma. "Are you okay?"

He pointed to his wounded shoulder and smiled. "You mean this. This is nothing. Living on the streets of Sentra I've faced much worse."

"Well I haven't, and I still need time to rest. I feel all disoriented. I think I need to gain a little control back," I said stiffly.

He chuckled softly. "I think I rather like seeing you with your guard down. To me it's beautiful."

Not really liking where this conversation was going, I tried to make light of the matter. "Me pouring with sweat and dripping blood, that's what you find appealing? You need to get out more."

He raised a curious brow then shrugged. "Maybe so." He looked down the hall toward the rooms that held our sleeping friends. "So, what do you think of Chaz's new power? Makes you wonder what else he's been keeping from us doesn't it."

No, not really. I tried to put my feelings into words that he'd understand. "He didn't really lie about it. He doesn't know us from little red riding hood. I don't blame him for not putting all his eggs in one basket. It doesn't make him sneaky, just smart." I tipped my finger to my chin. "And it also makes him someone I want to know more about."

Toma walked toward the kitchen. "Guess he'll be sticking around for a while then, huh?"

Well, yeah. With power like that, we'd be stupid to get rid of him now. That, and the fact that I'd grown somewhat fond of his offbeat sense of humor.

I didn't say any of that to Toma though, as it struck me as strange that he would even make such a comment in the first place. Didn't he know what we were trying to do here?

I pondered on that until he came back into the living room, gripping a checkers board game in his left hand. He set it on the couch, made a quick dash down the hall, and came back with a fold up table.

"Wanna play?" He set the game up, eyebrows raised in my direction.

I picked up a red chip and turned it over in my hand. "Tell me about the guys that attacked us?" I shook my head to hide my irritation. Shit like this couldn't happen again. We got fucked up this time, next time could spell the end. They should have known better. Brother and sister had messed up big time, and I had to let him know. We could have freaking died and all because of their carelessness. I put the chip down and looked him dead in the eye. "Neither you nor Nico were thinking. You should have known they would follow our trail. The rest of us, we're not used to people finding us through scent alone."

He sniffed and held his head up. "Yeah, but it's not like we really had time to think. Everything happened so fast. And we did go there with the intention that we would be cleared. Remember? "

Unfortunately, I did, which left me with one question. "How will you clear yourself now, and how much of my time will you and your sister be taking up?" I tried to say it light-heartedly, but I was serious and that's how it came out.

He moved a game piece across the board and shrugged. "We'll think of something, won't we? I mean, we always do."

I tried not to sigh as the ache in my shoulder came back with full force. I couldn't deal with this, not now. I stood up and braced myself against the wall. My legs felt a little better, but they still weren't a hundred percent, and so I figured it was better to be safe than sorry. "I'm going back to bed. You can fill your sister and the others in. Be ready to pull out in three days."

He nodded, and I walked on. I'd made it two-thirds of the way down the hall when I heard Nico shout: "Hold still while I clean your eye, you damn idiot!" Shaking my head, I went in my room and closed the door.

Chapter 9

We'd been there two days when I started to itch to get home. My home, in Virginia, to my little three-bedroom house. Being away from one's business for too long was never a good thing.

To be honest, I was starting to wonder what little treats awaited me. Taking Chaz and my other new friends back to my place was not something that filled me with joy, but I needed to check in, and I didn't really trust them here on their own.

I was feeling better now and for the past day had been able to walk without limping. Also, my shoulder no longer felt like someone had poured hot grease on it, so there was that. I sent a silent, thank you to my sister as I knew this was the work of her healing powers in full effect.

ONCE ALL THE BAGS WERE packed, and everyone stood in my hallway ready to go, I made the announcement.

"I'm going to stop by my main house for a bit, just to make sure things are still tidy there. Any objections? No? Good, let's go." It's not like I gave them time to form an opinion. Hey, they were the ones hitching a ride with me. If they didn't like it, I didn't know what to tell them. I needed to do this.

We landed in my living room, and to my surprise, the place looked just as we'd left it. No superhuman crazy psychos had come in and ripped it to shreds, which put me in a better mood than I'd been in for days. Until I opened my front door that is.

I had the intention of checking my mailbox, but when I cracked my screen door, I saw a lady and three kids. From the tired look on the woman's face and the way her head hung a little to the side, I could tell they'd been there for a while. She was slim of build and her brown hair was in disarray. Her clothes looked dirty and worn, like she'd had them on too many days without changing and I wondered how long she'd been there.

She raised her head and looked at me as I stepped a little closer. "Hi," she said, her voice coming out in a croak. I looked at the black ring around her eye, her swollen jaw, and the look of hopelessness on her face, and knew exactly why she'd come.

Her kids too wore that same tired expression. The oldest, a girl, looked to be about fifteen, another girl looked about twelve, and the boy was probably around eight or nine. "Come on inside," I said, holding my door open for them.

Here's the thing. Do I believe in karma? Why yes, I do. Is that why I helped people like this lady and her children. Who knows, I certainly hoped not.

It made me feel good, and in reality, it made all this worthwhile. They never know what I can do. These battered and abused women and men who come to me seeking help from the spouse or lover who would do them harm.

The one thing they did know, was that I could hide them where their pursuers would never find them. Of course, that meant cutting ties with everyone they loved. So, it wasn't an easy decision.

I mean let's face it, I can't have a bunch of people jumping from this universe to another, then coming back to this one and expecting them to keep it a secret. So no, when they go, it's with the understanding that they will never come back again. Never see any of their family again.

Some can't handle it, and so they don't go. That's fine. I still give them enough money and enough leverage to make sure that the one person stalking them never finds them again. Even if it means finding said person and showing them a little of what I can do.

So what if they tell? Who in their right mind is going to believe them? And it's not like they know my name, or where I'm from anyway. Luckily, I'd only had a few of those. Time had yet to tell which category this lady would fall into.

I asked Nico and the others to excuse us, and waited until they were safely down the hall before taking a seat and asking my new friend to do the same. She dropped wearily onto the couch with her three kids falling right beside her.

"So, tell me what's going on?" I said, hoping to get the conversation flowing.

A few angry tears fell down her cheeks, then she cleared her throat, and sat up a little straighter in the chair.

When she looked up at me, I saw a grit and determination in her eyes that hadn't been there a second ago. This woman still had some fight in her. Good, because for what happened next, she was going to need it.

"I was told you could help me, I was told you can make me disappear," she said. Yeah, but she didn't know how. They never knew how until they got here. I had a name in certain circles. I was called the taker. I could hide you where no one would ever find you. I sometimes wondered about those who whispered my name into the ears of others.

I suspected my money man, the guy that confirmed my cash had cleared the bank, was giving me a lot of free advertisement. I'd had him send a few people my way when I'd first started, and from there it'd just rolled on.

I thought about the group in the back and where we would go next. Clearly, we couldn't leave things the way they were. Thinking about it, I figured I could do a two for one with this lady.

Find a nice place for her to go and a good place for us to recuperate and learn as much as we could about the Clamors. But, first I had to make sure she understood exactly what she was getting herself into.

"Can I use the bathroom?" I looked up and noticed that the little boy had stood and was hopping from foot to foot. Distractions can lead to very bad things. My manners must have got left in a dumpster somewhere. Pointing down the hall, I told him to take the first door on the left, then motioned for his mom and sisters to follow me out the room.

I led them to my pantry where I kept clothes and supplies for occasions just like this one. "Go ahead and find your sizes so that you can get cleaned up and I'll fix you something to eat. How does spaghetti with meatballs sound?"

Instead of answering the mother held out her hand for me to shake. "Hi, I'm Sharon." She pointed to the oldest girl. "Tonya is sixteen, Julie fourteen, and that little jumping bean is my baby, Cayden, he's twelve."

"I'm Rekia," I said, taking her outstretched hand into mine. "Now the thing I need you to understand is, that you can never come back. You have to be absolutely sure that this is what you want, because once you leave, there is no returning."

"I'm sure," she said, looking at the two girls.

"What about you?" I asked Tonya. "Are you ready to leave all your friends, your boyfriend, everybody?"

Tears spilled from her eyes and down her face, but she nodded a slow yes.

I looked to Sharon. "Your mom? Dad? Brothers and sisters? You will never see them again, for as long as you live. Do you understand that? We can let them know that you're all right and that you're doing well, but you can never see them again."

She Looked at her kids then back to me, and showed some of the grit I'd seen earlier. "I'm ready."

I left them to get themselves together while I ordered spaghetti from the Italian restaurant down the street. Besides, my other house guests were being a little too quiet for my liking, which made me want to check on them right away.

WHILE EVERYONE ATE and got acquainted, I sat in my bedroom trying to figure out my next move. Taking Sharon and her children to a world that I knew well, and was a lot like ours, seemed like my safest option. Craning my head to the side, I called for Toma.

"What's on your mind?" he asked, coming into my bedroom.

I laid back on the bed and looked up at my solid white ceiling as if that was an adequate answer to the question.

Toma sat down beside me and grabbed my hand, starting a slow and eyebrow-raising massage. "I assume you're not going to charge your usual asking price?"

Even though I told myself that I wished he'd stop, the massage did feel good, so I closed my eyes and let him continue. "Hmm. No, no charge, do a lot of pro bono when I can."

Then as quickly as it started, the hand rubbing stopped. Opening my eyes, I looked into the deepest brown eyes I'd ever seen, and almost gagged on my own cheesiness. Really, when had I started thinking like a lovesick teen? Without a doubt, this had to stop.

Eyes still deadlocked with mine, Toma leaned over top of me and held himself up with his elbow. He pushed a few strands of hair out of my face. "Why did you really call me in here, Rekia?" he asked, voice filled with an emotion that I couldn't name, face inches from my own.

"Well it wasn't for that, buddy." I jumped up, clumsily, and probably with more swiftness than needed, but as long as he got the point, I didn't care. "Be ready to pull out in the morning, we must take this woman and her children to safety, now go forth and tell the others or something." Just please get out and stay the hell away from me.

THE NEXT MORNING SAW all ten of us packed and ready to go. Damn, how had I gone from being completely alone to having two, then three, then five, and now nine companions? Things had certainly gotten more interesting lately, and like it or not, I was locked into this until the end.

Sharon looked nervous but determined. Her kids stood beside her, damn near clinging to her. I took a deep breath before I began to speak. So much went into the delivery. My words, the way I spoke them, the tone of voice I used, the twitch, or non-twitch of an eyebrow, everything affected her decision to stay or go.

It was best to get on with it, but I always found myself asking the same question. Would she think me crazy and run screaming from my house? Quite possibly. But it was the price I was willing to pay to keep her and her children safe.

I'd had a friend growing up whose dad used to beat her mom. He never cared if we were there or not and one day he went too far. I wiped a hand down my face as I blinked back tears. My friend went to stay with her aunt in North Carolina after that, and I'd never seen her again. So, yeah, stuff like this, I took very personally.

I watched Sharon closely. "Do you think you can handle it?" I asked, after I'd laid it all bare to her.

Her lips trembled, and her eyes took on a haunted look. "Get me the hell out of here," she finally said, head held high, eyes full of determination.

I gave her a slight nod. I knew how hard this was for her and I wished I could offer more comfort. Instead, I simply gave her a reassuring smile, as I opened a portal and we all stepped through.

While our new members took a moment to adjust, I looked around. We were in Shinow. Not much different from my own world, meaning it wasn't behind us in technology, but it wasn't that much farther advanced either.

It took a moment for Sharon to catch her bearings. The kids seemed pretty shook up as well, so it was a while before everyone was themselves again. I went in my bag and passed around protein bars, knowing they needed to regain their energy.

When they finished eating, Sharon took in the sights around her, her eyes wide in disbelief. "I can't believe it, can't believe, how..."

I stopped her before she could go further down that rabbit hole. "Yeah, well some questions are better left unanswered, come on, let's get you hooked up with one of my good friends."

I led them down the road and across two streets to one of my contact's office. "You guys wait outside while I see what's what."

I walked into the red office building and there he sat, curly black hair, and crooked teeth, looking as edible as a pudding pop. He stood about six feet, with a broad chest, and clearly defined muscles. Tattoos covered his neck, chest, arms and back, making my fingers tingle with the memory of touching them. Hell, my heart sped up just from the sight of him.

The office looked small up front, but most of his employees were hidden behind the wooden door in the back. Preferring to do most of the grunt work himself, he had no receptionist, so the first person you came upon was him.

His office consisted of three file cabinets, three desks, with computers on them, and an office water cooler. On the wall hung pictures and posters of his favorite bands, along with a list of labor rules and employee rights.

I licked my lips and inhaled briefly, before reminding myself the reason I'd come here in the first place. "Trent." It came out a little more breathless than I would have liked, but oh well.

A pleased smile crossed his face as he watched me walk closer. "Been a long time. Where you been?" His voice came out lazy and nonchalant, but I knew him better than that.

I leaned over his desk and ran my fingers lightly through his hair, soft on top and brittle at the ends. It was the familiarity that had me sucking in a breath. "Might not have been with you Trent, but sure as hell've been thinking about you." Which was probably truer than even I wanted to admit.

The right side of his mouth quirked into a playful smirk. "Well, that's original." He pulled me onto his lap and wrapped his hands around my waist.

Hard, chapped lips met mine in a kiss that tasted vaguely like whiskey and cheese. "I can be ready in two hours," he whispered, placing small feather light kisses up and down my neck. Something he knew I loved.

I needed to end this now, so as hard as it was, I pushed him away. "Yeah, well I'm not here for that." I stood and took in his confused expression.

I hastened to explain myself. "I have one of my ladies. She has three kids, and she is definitely in need of a job."

Rubbing a slow, deliberate hand, across his chin, he sneaked a peek outside. "When are we going to talk? Hmm? When are we going to get together again? That's what I want to know. We'll get to her," he pointed out the window, "later."

I made sure to give my head a firm shake, just to let him know that I meant what I said. "Got a lot going on here, Trent. Let's talk business. She needs housing, school schedules, and someone to show her the ropes. She needs help adjusting to this new world, you know the drill."

"Okay," he said, but his eyes had a "you owe me look" in them. Good, I liked owing him favors, it always came out pleasurable on my side. "Does she have any skills, what does she do?" He began pushing keys on the computer while I walked to the door.

"Sharon, could you step in here for a moment, please." She turned to her kids, but having been through this before I already knew what to say to set her mind at ease. "They'll be fine. Nico will look after them, and we have a clear view from inside the office.

"This way," I said, as I led her inside. I could tell right away that something was wrong. Trent's expression was no longer warm and inviting, now it just looked worried and maybe even a little angry.

I didn't know what had happened in the short time I'd went to get Sharon and walked back in, but whatever it was, it would have to wait. Right now, this lady and her family were my top priority.

Trent gave me a 'we'll talk later' look, then held his hand out to Sharon. "Nice to meet you. I'm Trent, and I run an agency tailored to people who are trying to start over. What type of job are you looking for? Do you already have something in mind, or would you like to go through training?"

She looked out the window, saw that her kids were okay, and turned back around. "I had my Real Estate license. I liked that until he..."

"Stopped you from doing it," Trent finished for her. "Well don't worry about him. He can't stop you from doing anything here, let's get started."

IT TOOK FIVE HOURS to get her set up with housing, food, work, and school for the kids. I paid the first six months of her rent, bought her a decent secondhand car, and made sure she and her kids had more than enough cash to last until her first paycheck. After that, she was on her own, unless she really, needed me. Regardless, I'd be back to check on them regularly.

See, I may have charged criminals like Larry twenty-five million, but I liked to think that I put it to good use when I helped people like Sharon.

"Call Trent if you need anything." I said to her. "The woman he set you up with is named Rhonda, and she'll help you get adjusted. Trent knows how to get in touch with me if it's really an emergency, but only if, okay?"

Her eyes became wet with moisture, and I put a gentle hand on her shoulder and turned her away from her kids. She needed to remain strong in front of them.

It always came down to this at the end. Giving up one's whole life was never easy, and I applauded her for making it this far without breaking down. "I know it's hard, but look at it like this, he can't find you here, can't hurt you or the children. You're safe. Try to keep that in mind when all this gets to be too much." She nodded like she understood, then squeezed my hand and said a soft goodbye before she closed the door.

My mind immediately switched to Trent, and the look he'd had on his face when I'd last seen him. Something was seriously wrong, and the quicker I found out what that was, the better.

Toma, ever perceptive, walked up beside me. "There's something you're not telling us. You've been acting different since you came out of that office. Talk about it?"

I stopped in front of Trent's office building and shook my head. "Later, right now I need to talk to him."

Trent sat with his fingers tapping on the desk, brows furrowed, and face unreadable. I swallowed hard, as I knew that was not a good sign.

Trent was a pretty easygoing guy, so to see him like this meant shit had somehow gotten fucked up. A sinking feeling told me that it had nothing to do with him, and everything to do with me and my band of merry little criminals.

Now was not the time for pussyfooting around. I sat in the chair in front of him and got straight to the point. "What's going on?"

He turned sad, worried eyes my way, and I felt a cold chill go through me.

He grabbed my hand and held on to it. "You know I love you, right?" I nodded, and he continued. "I think you know what you mean to me. You're my buddy, my friend, a good person, and one hell of a lay."

This felt like goodbye. This sounded like he never expected to see me again. I tried to keep my expression neutral, as my eyes became wet with moisture. I wanted to crawl into his lap and have him tell me that everything was going to be okay. I wanted to lay my head on his shoulder and have him gently run his fingers through my hair.

I wanted to stay right here with him as long as I could, but I had people depending on me. Now was not the time for a breakdown. So, I pushed my personal feelings aside and tried to focus on the task at hand. "I feel the same, now get to the point. People are waiting for me, remember?"

"I know." His voice came out soft, almost placatingly so. Which did nothing to assuage my doubts. I gave a small inpatient head tilt, causing him to nod and finally turn his computer screen around to face me. "This is what I saw, while I was looking for a job for your lady."

It was an interworld email with me as the subject. It only took a few seconds to read, but what I saw made my blood run cold. This was not good. This was bad, very bad, and I had no clue what we were going to do about it.

It basically said that they knew Trent was an associate of mine and if in contact with me, there would be a handsome award for my capture, dead or alive. It was the dead or alive part that got me.

The sheer danger in that statement alone was enough to set my teeth on edge. I now had literally no one I could reasonably trust. It would be beyond foolish at this point. "How do you think they knew about you?" I asked him.

He shrugged as if to say my guess was as good as his. "How many worlds do you visit? How many people do you see? How many contacts do you have? Not that hard to find you if you've never had to hide before." True. I may have kept a low profile on my own world, but every other place I traveled knew about alternate dimensions.

I looked up at him and frowned, my face probably asking what my mouth could not.

He scoffed and shook his head. "Do you even have to ask? Because if you do—" I leaned over and placed a soft sweet kiss on his lips before he could finish the sentence. I knew he'd never betray me.

At least I hoped he wouldn't anyway. He gripped the back of my head tight, as our kiss turned almost desperate with the fear that this would be the last time we saw each other.

I stood, but before I could leave he grabbed me by the arm, coming to his feet as well. Our eyes locked, and I fought against the burning sensation behind mine.

The look on his face was naked and raw and told me everything I needed to know. "I'll be careful," I rested my forehead against his and we stood, breathing in each other's air before I finally pulled away and walked out the door, not sure if I'd ever see him again.

"It's about time," Nico started on me immediately. "Fuck your boyfriend on your own time, we have shit going on, remember?"

All of this is my time, I resisted the urge to tell her, not wanting to start an unnecessary fight. "He's been offered money to sell me out. So we have to assume everyone in his office has. I can trust him. I don't know about them." I shook my head as the realization of our situation hit me dead in the chest. "We can't trust anybody." It was a sobering thought, and I allowed it to rock me for a moment before squaring my shoulders. "From this point on we're going to have to make moves like everyone we meet is a potential traitor."

"Weren't we doing that anyway?" Kirk asked as he put an arm around Nico's waist, his eye patch still firmly in place.

Toma focused his attention on me. "What do you want to do?"

I thought about it for a second. "We need to regroup and think this thing through. I keep a little cottage on my father's home world. No one knows about it. Good place to lay low for a while."

Nico knocked Kirk's arm off her and walked over. "Wouldn't that be the first place they'd look? Your father's home world?"

"I've never told anyone about my split-heritage. I'm Earth-born, and that's all they need to know." I also made sure that my father and his home world stayed private, no matter the world I was on. No one knew about him, or his world, I felt more than confident that we'd be safe there.

But just to be sure, I wouldn't let my father's people know that I was there.

We walked into the alleyway between Trent's building and another. I made sure no one was around, then opened the portal to take us to my father's home world.

We arrived in my living room. The floor plan, a simple four-bedroom, kitchen, bath, and living room, nothing more and nothing less.

I had a lot of family here, but I thought it best to not alert them to my presence. I didn't want any more people mixed up in this then needed to be.

Two portals so closely together, meant that our bodies would start to breakdown soon, if we didn't recharge. I looked in the fridge and noticed that it was empty. Picking up the phone on the wall, I ordered a shitload of groceries, then got down to business.

"Okay, what do we know?" I sat down at the kitchen table and waited for the others to do the same. The dead or alive buzzed through my head and I knew if I thought too hard about what that meant I'd lose it. I'd messed up, big time.

None of us really knew what we were doing. We were not a coordinated team working together. We didn't even know each other. Maybe if we did and had worked together for a while, we'd have a better shot. As it stood now, we were just a bunch of people, stuck together, trying not to get killed.

"We're in deep shit," Chaz said, once everyone was seated.

Ignoring him, I looked from Toma to Nico, but it was Clink who spoke first. "What we should be asking ourselves is, if it's just you they're looking for. Maybe they've contacted people from all of our lives. Maybe none of us can go home until this is over."

"None of you can go home anyway, remember?"

Confused, Clink turned to his boyfriend, who quickly looked at the floor. The damn coward. I guess he hadn't told him about our little misstep with Glone and company. A conversation best saved for another time. "Chaz will explain all that to you later, for now," I waved my hand to let them know the floor was open to anybody who had a suggestion.

Clink's eyes ricocheted from Kirk to Chaz until finally landing squarely on his boyfriend in a piercing 'there'll be hell to pay later' sort of gaze. He turned back around to face the rest of us, a heavy sigh on his lips. "Then if none of us can go home, I say we go for broke, what do we have to lose?"

Absolutely nothing. We had absolutely nothing to lose, which made this all the scarier. "So I guess we go for broke then, huh?" I asked at the same time a knock sounded at the door. My groceries had arrived.

Toma jumped up, looking relieved to be able to step away for a second. "I'll get it," he said, catching the bills I threw at him and hurriedly walking away. He came back arms fit to bursting.

Clink stood to help, talking as he did so. "We are each extraordinary in our own way. Very powerful, the lot of us, if we can't figure this out, then who can?"

Kirk moved from the table and went to lean against the counter, a thoughtful look on his face. "So what you're saying, Clink, is that you think there's a lot more going on than what we see? Maybe we're not looking at this the right way, but what are we missing? There has to be something, right?"

I reached into the bags they'd set on the table until I had ham, cheese, mayonnaise, and bread in front of me. "Anybody else want one of these?" I received three "yeses", one "What do you think", and a blank stare.

I put mayonnaise on the bread and started to assemble the sandwiches on a plate. Toma got the chips out, while

Nico filled each glass with ice. Guess she was back to being nice again. I got the feeling I would need a roadmap to keep up with her mood swings. I stopped working for a second and turned away from the food. "What do we know? That's what we need to be asking ourselves."

"Wrong." Nico looked up from pouring the drinks. "Hope soda is all right with everyone. Now, what we need to ask ourselves, if we really need to be asking ourselves anything that is, but what we need to try to figure out is, what don't we know? We know what we know, but what is it that we don't know?"

"What is it that we don't know, but we probably should?" Clink piped in.

I put the food in the middle of the table while Kirk put a stack of plates and napkins down. We all dug in, recharging our bodies, while still considering the problem at hand.

I popped a chip in my mouth and looked at each person sitting around my table. Clink was right. We each held special skills, powers if that's what you wanted to call them.

This shouldn't be that hard to figure out, but maybe we just needed a new perspective. I took a bite of my sandwich and had to stop for a minute to enjoy the taste. Hmm, the cheese, we didn't have this type of cheese anywhere on my home world.

I put my sandwich down, my finger tapping lightly on my chin. "We don't know anything about the plan the Clamors have. What is it exactly they want from Sentra? Why was Kolo so against it? Someone as greedy as the people from your world, it had to be something pretty bad for him to turn down that much money, but what could it be?" I looked from Toma to Nico waiting for an answer.

They wore twin blank expressions. Good grief, were they really that much in love with money?

"Kill a million people; kidnap a bunch of kids and puppies? Something?" Both shook their heads. This was ridiculous, we were getting nowhere.

I pushed away from the table irritated at the whole situation. "I'm going to bed. Your sleeping arrangements are your own. Just try to think, write it down if you have to. Something has to break through with one of us."

"WHAT YOU MUST THINK of me and my sister, my whole world really," Toma walked into my room, uninvited, and closed the door behind him.

I looked up from where I'd been brainstorming and tried to force a smile. From the look on his face, I could tell it must have looked like I'd pasted it on with sticky glue. I really didn't feel like having this conversation, but Toma hadn't really done anything wrong, so I tried to not take my frustrations out on him. "I visit a lot of worlds. I'm used to different points of views. What's on your mind?"

Taking a seat on the bed, he looked like he was bracing himself for something he didn't really want to say. Either that, or he just wasn't sure of my reaction. "You can always back out, you know."

His shoulders drooped, and he looked down at his hands, twiddling one thumb over the other. "There's nothing stopping you from dropping us all on some inconspicuous world and going back to your normal life."

Fire coiled in my blood at the unfairness of the whole situation. "What the fuck do I have to go back to?" He flinched as if I'd struck him, but I was too far gone to care, my anger having been building for some time now.

I slammed the notebook I'd been writing in down and stared at him. My voice came out gravelly and low. "My photo, by now, has probably been plastered on every world I've ever visited and then some. So please tell me how am I supposed to go on with my life when I'm wanted everywhere?" I'd been trying real hard not to be angry, but damnit, this shit was really starting to take a toll on me. It was my fault, I knew that, so it wasn't really him I was angry at, it was myself.

I couldn't just walk away, ever, though I really wished that I could sometimes. The need to know more about Toma and Nico, the excitement of carrying out my first prison break with Chaz, the thrill I got every time we hopped to a new world not knowing what to expect, had all led me to this point and I had no one to blame but myself.

Toma sighed sadly, and after a few false starts, finally put to word what he wanted to say. "I'm sorry that we brought you into this, but to be fair, you made the choice to help us. You could have sent us on our way, but you didn't." Yeah, well, let my sister tell it, I was like a pig in mud right now, loving every minute of the chase and the hunt. I ran a hand down my face, because I wasn't feeling too excited about anything at the moment.

When I didn't answer, he kept talking. "And I have to say, if I had to do it all over again, I wouldn't do anything different. Me and Nico, we've done nothing wrong, and we deserve a chance to clear our names.

"In return, we'll do everything we can to help you clear your reputation and keep your good name intact." That said, he got up and walked out the door without a backward glance.

I was pretty sure that clearing our names would be a lot harder than any of us thought. What we needed was a game changer, something to tip the odds in our favor, but what?

By the time my eyes shut for the night, I'd gone over it a million times and was still no closer to a solution.

"I THINK WE NEED TO break into Clamor," Chaz said, feet stretched out in front of him, looking a lot more relaxed then I thought he should.

My head snapped in his direction, not sure if he was serious. "What?"

He sat up a little straighter, then flashed me a bright smile. "'Bout time you started taking me seriously around here." He made sure all eyes were on him before he began to speak. "Toma, and Nico, you want to clear your names and go home, right?"

They both gave him heated looks because he already knew that's what they wanted. He ignored them and continued. "The way things went down in that house with Kolo, bad business that. It seems obvious that the Clamors and your people," he pointed to Toma and Nico, "are up to some bad stank. Since we can't go back to Sentra... well, what do you think? How else are we going to find out anything?"

He was right of course. Though I loathed to tell him so, I knew that I must. "We can't just barge into Clamor with no plan." I turned to Toma and Nico. "From your earlier days, do you know any of the people there? Someone we can make contact with. Got anyone you trust there?"

Toma spoke to me as if I were a two-year-old child who had no knowledge of how the world worked. "The main reason business between Clamor and Sentra is so great is because we're both the same. Any one person who knows us would sell us for less than one of those little round brown things you sometimes have."

Little brown things? I couldn't keep the exasperation out of my voice. "A penny? You're talking about a penny, right?"

"Yes! Anyone we know would sell us out for less than one of your pennies."

I found myself at a loss for words. Good grief, what a lovely group of people they were. I didn't like this. Didn't like it one bit. I wasn't used to going in blind, and I realized that was about all I'd been doing lately.

Man, how I longed for the days when I could take a client to a world already set up with contacts, get them settled, and go on my merry way. Where had my nice, peaceful little world gone to?

"Let's take a vote," I said, standing up, and looking around at the others.

Nico shook her head. "What are we, five? We're going to Clamor. No voting needed, because that's the only way to put an end to this. Anybody got a problem with that?" Her voice came out intimidating and more than a little threatening.

After no one said anything for a couple of seconds, she turned to me. "How soon can we leave?"

Chapter 10

The next morning, we started for Clamor. Not sure if this was the right move or not, nervous energy attached itself to my stomach and simply wouldn't let go.

I tried steadying breaths to ground myself, but the real truth was, that I was scared we'd used up our last bit of life, and this was the end of the road for us.

According to the reasoning of Toma and Nico, we were on our way to a hostile place, with hostile people, where everyone hated us and wanted us dead. I'd be nuts not to feel at least a little apprehensive. Yet here we all stood in my living room, bags packed, breakfast ate, spirits high. Maybe we were all nutballs.

Toma stuffed the last of the supplies in his bag and slung it over his shoulder. "Try for Bown, that's the main producing city of Clamor and where all the decisions are made. Nico can take you all to a spot to lay low while I search through the city records."

Clink nodded, his orange-red dreadlocks moving up and down, and I was once again taken aback by how beautiful they were. "Using powers will only draw attention. We need to get in, find what we need, and then poof." He flicked his hand, then looked around, eyebrows raised, as though asking if anyone had a problem with that.

I agreed with everything he said. Only... "We can't just pop up in the middle of the city. It would be to obvious, especially if the Sentras are already looking for us. Surely they'd share that with the Clamor." I wrangled my hands, because it just seemed to damn risky.

Toma shrugged. "It's what we have to do. We're not going to find out anything any other way."

I chewed on my lip, guessing that would have to be enough. With shaky breath and unsteady hands, I focused on the world Clamor, then breached opened the gap and stepped through.

THE FIRST THING I NOTICED about Clamor was that it looked almost identical to Sentra, and at first, I thought I'd goofed. Then I took a good look around and realized no way was this Sentra.

The diamond plated sidewalks and golden streets were the same, except everything here was longer, taller.

"The average height here is eight feet, with nine and ten being a little tall and six being rather short," Toma reminded us.

My mouth hung open a little as I took it all in. I'd been to worlds with taller than average people before, but the effect the diamonds and jewels had on this place made it dazzling.

I stood in awe of diamond-studded doorways that seemed to stretch for at least twelve feet in the air. Platinum cars and buses whose height seemed to rival their length.

Cold whipped around us, as diamonds and jewels stared at us from every angle. It was... amazing.

"Is that Yan-Yan?" Nico asked. She pointed to a woman of about five feet, who walked with a Clamor man and woman. The three seemed to be in serious conversation.

"That's Kolo's sister," Nico said, voice raw. "She's next in line to take over the bank from him. What's she doing here?"

"Maybe she took the deal," I offered, softly.

Nico looked at me hard for a minute, rage contorting her features, then she started toward the other woman. Kirk stopped her before she'd made it two feet. Grabbing her by the arm, he yanked her around to face him. "Just where do you think you're going, girl? You're not going to find out anything that way."

"You don't know that," she snapped, snatching her arm back.

Toma stepped into the tight space between the two of them and faced his sister. "Let's follow from a distance, see what clues we can pick up. She may not have taken the deal. She could be here on normal Sentra business," he reasoned.

Another man, tall, with black hair, came out of the building and caught up with the other three.

"Mach," both Nico and Toma said in unison.

"Judging from the fact that he looks to be about five-feet-six, I'll take a guess that he's from Sentra as well?" I asked.

Toma nodded. "He was Kolo's second-in-command at the bank. Strange that he and Yan-Yan would both leave the bank to come here. That's not how it usually works."

"What do you think it means?" I asked.

"Perhaps I can be of some assistance," a voice behind us said.

We all snapped around, and I wondered how the hell we'd let someone sneak up on us like this.

"Saylor," Nico said, taking a step forth. Toma put his hand on her arm to slow her down.

It took me a couple of seconds before I remembered where I'd seen this woman before. She'd been the female senator who'd helped kill Kolo, and had attacked us when we'd found out.

"I don't want to fight," she raised her hands in front of her and took a few steps back. "I know you don't trust me and I don't blame you, but believe me when I say all is not as it seems. I want to help you."

Nico sneered, and I agreed. This lady was crazy if she thought we'd ever consider putting our lives in her hands.

"What you see is a deal going down that will rob every Sentra and Clamor of billions of dollars, all the whilst making the few at the top richer."

"Is this what Kolo was killed for? Because he refused to go along with it?" Clink asked.

Saylor nodded. "All money goes through his bank. If they could take out ten dollars a week, from every single citizen, that would be billions. They needed Kolo to give access to the Sentra accounts, because the Clamor banker was already on board. The Clamors and Sentras have technology they made together, to keep the citizens of both worlds from finding out, even from the most ruthless of audits."

Toma cursed under his breath, and Saylor turned to him. They held each other's gaze until it became uncomfortable for the rest of us. Which intrigued me. There was definitely something going on there. I watched a little closer.

"You helped them do it," Nico accused.

Saylor wore a black designer pantsuit. Her black hair hung loosely around her shoulders, framing her face perfectly. Her skin tone was a beautiful dark brown, reminding me of my cousin Robin from my father's home world. "Why do you think I'm here? To do what I can to put a stop to it. Welvina and Remus have gone too far this time. I only want to help," she said.

I'd say they'd gone too far when they'd killed Kolo, but that was just me. I thought back on what we knew. Kolo died because his brother, who already had billions, wanted even more money in his pockets. I looked from Saylor to Toma, to Nico, figuring I'd never understand any of them.

Nico looked ill, as she let everything sink in. "So, what are you going to do about- -hey, where the hell did she go?"

I'd been so focused on Nico, that I hadn't even noticed Saylor slip away. I turned to the others. Five blank faces stared back at me.

Then I felt it. Tension, danger, without even having to turn around, I knew we'd been discovered. It seemed that a group of Clamors had quietly snuck up on us. A band of elite spies we were not.

"Guess we're going to have to break that little thing about not using our powers," I said, levitating a few feet off the ground and going into a defensive position.

"You think?" Chaz asked. He focused on the tall man to his right, and the man fell to the floor, his power drained. After that, all hell broke loose.

Now, usually, when I levitate, it gives me an advantage. This time all it served to do was put me on equal footing with my attacker. Before I could blink, I felt a boot slam into my face and knock me back.

I hit the ground hard, and rolled to my side, as the impact of the diamond sidewalk knocked the air out of me. Pain shot through my body tearing me up inside, and I took a few gulps of air, trying to talk myself through it.

My whole face was on fire. I felt like I'd been stabbed by a thousand burning needles, as the diamonds on the sidewalk cut into me. I tried to rise up, to rejoin the fight, but somebody kicked me in the face again, this time hard enough to make me lose my vision for a minute.

This was too much. Blood shot out of my mouth, and a metallic, salty taste assaulted my tongue. The fact that my face felt like chopped liver was probably beside the point. That shit hurt. It hurt like hell, but I couldn't, no wouldn't, let my team down.

I had to get up. Off to the side, I could have sworn I saw about five different Clinks. Then I remembered his power of astral projection and figured he was using it to throw the Clamors off-balance.

Kirk hit the ground with a large fist and it rumbled and shook beneath us, throwing us all off guard, not just the Clamors. Realizing that wasn't a good line of attack at the moment, he simply put that power into his fist and hit the Clamor man closest to him, dropping him with one punch.

Nico threw fire at everyone close to her, but the Clamors were as quick as they were tall and in the end, it only took three of them to disable her completely. I watched in horror as they placed a muzzle on her mouth and bound her hands. That was it. I'd seen enough.

I tried to stand, but doubled over, as pain ripped through my lower right jaw and the arm I'd used to break my fall. I didn't want to panic, but damn, this was not going as planned.

I tried to sit up again and watched in horror as more Clamors came. Tall, hunkering figures, they were more intimidating than a child's worst nightmare. They spread out, large gangs of them, turning the odds significantly in their favor.

Toma released sand shaped bullets from his mouth and hand, but each was deflected by the taller, quicker, Clamors. Soon he too was down for the count as four Clamors climbed on top of him and hog-tied him on the ground.

I held up my hand aiming to use my TK to undo the ropes. The same Clamor that had picked on me before must have stood waiting for me to make a move because as soon as my hands went up, his leg went up as well. This time the kick was to my stomach, followed up by a punch to my face.

Brother and sister were out. I guessed they were considered the two most dangerous. Blood rolled down my face and into my eyes, but I still saw when three jumped on Chaz. They hit him in his face, chest, and stomach, dropping him in an instant. Once Chaz fell, all the fight went out of Clink.

What once was five Clink's became one. And that was his downfall. In his haste to get to Chaz, he'd forgotten all about the fight going on around him. Four jumped on him at once, and I watched in horror as they beat him to a bloody pulp before he'd made it anywhere near the other man.

My eyes searched for Kirk. As tall as he was it was hard to tell him apart from some of the shorter Clamors, especially since his eye had healed and he'd removed the patch. He used this to his advantage. As Clink, Toma, Nico, and Chaz were being loaded into a gold-plated van, he'd carefully and slowly, snuck up beside me.

Soon I felt the comfort of his hand around my waist as he lifted me off the ground. I gladly put most of my weight on him, never had I been more thankful to have someone holding me up.

"We have to get out of here. We can come back for the others later." He whispered in my ear. I agreed. I didn't think I could take too many more kicks to the face. Already I was starting to feel dizzy and disoriented.

"Un, un, un," my number one tormentor laughed, wagging his finger. Damn what was with this guy? I looked up at him and committed him face to memory, brown curly hair, pale, big ears that stuck out, and of slim build.

He'd see me again one day, I vowed, anger making my hands clench. This was not over.

"We can't win," I whispered to Kirk, who still had his arms around me, holding me up. "Let's surrender for now. We need to save our strength. We'll get another shot." I looked at the number of angry Clamors around us.

I counted eighteen before giving up. "We can't win against these odds," I whispered furiously. "No need to get ourselves any more bruised than we have to." I hoped he was listening because I wasn't entirely sure he understood the severity of our situation.

Kirk threw both his hands in the air, causing me to almost fall over when he removed his arms from around my waist. As it was, I only stumbled a few steps. "We'll walk to the van ourselves," he said, to the Clamor right in front of us. He tried to lend me his arm again, but my tormenter pushed me to the ground before he made contact.

I hit the diamond sidewalk face first and curled into a fetal position as pain danced a wicked waltz over my body. After that, everything went black.

Chapter 11

The first thing I noticed upon waking was pain. Lots of pain, shooting from my head to the rest of my body. The second was how bright the light was. It shined directly in my face, causing me to put a weak hand over my eyes to try and block it out a bit, though it didn't really help much.

I blinked and looked around, as the light faded just a little. What greeted me was dingy beige walls, two long narrow beds on either side of the room, and a dirty white bucket and sink.

I looked at the bucket with particular disdain. There was a nastier than life scent emitting from that thing. What smelled like weeks' worth of blood, shit, and urine, filled my nostrils making me want to black out all over again.

I sat up on the side of my bed, raging pain making the task that much harder. At the foot of my bed sat a chair. At the foot of the other bed also sat a chair, except this one had one very pissed off Nico sitting in it, shooting daggers my way.

"How long?" I tried to croak out. My hand instantly went to my throat, which was dry and itchy from non-use and thirst. I tried to massage it, but it didn't really do any good.

Nico looked about how I felt, dirty, grimy, and tired. Her hair hung in useless clumps around her face and her clothes were filthy, ripped, and torn. Believe it or not, she looked even worse than when I'd first found her on Sentra. "Three days." She got up and walked to the long glass door that stood between us and the rest of the world.

"Have you tried—"

"Everything," She cut me off. She turned away from the glass and focused her attention my way. "I knew it would be useless, though. Clamor jails are fitted with power blockers."

"So, we can't get out?" I asked, all hope draining from my face.

Her dark eyes roamed over the dirty walls of our cell. "Any power you try to use will bounce back on you with three times the strength. Hardly worth the effort, especially in your condition."

Instinctually, I put my hand to my own swollen face. I had no doubt I was black and blue everywhere. She had a point, best to heal from these bruises before I added any more to the bunch.

Nico moved at a snail's pace as she walked back to her bed, which alerted me to how much pain she must have been in. She sat down gingerly on it, then slowly scooted until her back was up against the wall.

She took a moment to center herself, then drew her feet up in front of her, giving me a sad look in the process. "They're going to come for you now." She took a few quick breaths, and I assumed she was trying to work through the pain.

That didn't sound good, at all. "What do they want?" I asked, barely able to get the words out.

"Information."

I tried to speak again, but the only thing that came out was a croak. My throat was drier than a deserts rear end. "Do they feed us?" I finally managed to ask.

Nico nodded, though it looked like it hurt to do even that. "Just enough to keep us alive. I had more food than this when I lived on the streets."

It made sense. Less food kept us weak and easier to control. "So, I've not eaten in three days?"

She put a hand to her side, a small grimace on her face. "I woke you up for every meal. Gave you half my food and drink." It was said in such a matter-of-fact manner that I knew she didn't expect any gushing thank yous or weird pseudo-bonding moments. She'd done what she had to, to keep me alive, case closed.

I nodded her an acknowledgment, because I at least had to do that, right? She could have left me here to starve, but she hadn't, and I would forever be grateful for that.

"The fellows?" I asked, voice still scratchy as hell. I ran another hand over my throat, looking at the sink and wondering what the odds were that it was safe to drink the water.

Nico shrugged. "They're on the other side. Don't know if any of them are together. Not too high a crime rate here on Clamor, but I do know that men are kept on one side, and women on the other."

I started a slow massage of my neck muscles. "You been in this jail before?" She seemed to know a lot about the place.

She swallowed hard before answering. "Came here once. Business. Saylor and Toma got into it with a couple of Clamors. All parties ended up here. All except Saylor of course. Being a Senator meant that she was right and everyone else was wrong. The two Clamor's were fined heavily and ended up with a ten-day stay here."

Yikes, talk about knowing when to keep your mouth shut. "And Toma?" I asked.

"We got him out right away."

"Who?"

She stretched her legs out in front of her, then brought them back to their previous position, grunting in pain as she did so. "Kolo, Saylor, and I," she said, as if it hurt just to speak.

"All four of you were here together?"

"I've only been to this jail once. To pay the fine for Toma and get him out. We've been to Clamor plenty of times. It's the world we're friendliest with."

I blinked hard. Who knew what really went on between the Clamors and the Sentra? Their definition of friendship left me reeling.

Embarrassed at the idea of falling flat on my face, but not able to keep the pressure off my bladder any longer, I tried to stand. There were only a few steps between me and the bucket, but it may as well had been a mile. Slow was not an option. I had to go now!

Nico, noticing my dilemma, wordlessly stood up. She put a hand around my waist and practically carried me. Sweat dripped from her to me, and I could hear her taking in small breaths, trying to push through the pain.

Thankful for her help, I was able to pull my clothes down and sit just in time. I looked at her out of the corner of my eye, so grateful that they'd put us in a cell together. Without her here right now, I would have been lost.

"Not dead then?" a voice from the other side of the glass-like door asked.

I stood as quickly as I could, yanking my clothes up in the process. I paid for it immediately as pain shot through my body, rocking me back.

This dude was as tall as the other Clamors, with a wide waist and face. He sent Nico a tray of food through an opening that hadn't been there a second ago, which meant he must have put in a code or something to make it appear.

The smell assaulted my nostrils, but I couldn't place it.

I decided to give it a closer look. The tray carried one bowl, a piece of bread, which I was sure could put out a window, and a clear cup, with some thick orange goop in it. The bowl held what looked like mashed potatoes, squirted heavily with equal parts mustard and ketchup.

My stomach rumbled just looking at the disgusting mess, and I couldn't wait to get a hold of some. Hell, I was willing to eat my bedspread, if I thought it would digest properly.

"Not for you," the huge man said, looking straight at me. "You have to talk to Clerry first, and then you can eat." He turned to Nico. "Finish up, and I'll be back for that later." He turned back to me. "You follow me."

He pushed some buttons, and the door slid back just enough for me to exit, then slammed back the moment I was on the other side. Still in pain, my movements were slow as I followed him wordlessly down a long hallway.

The walls were pure white diamond, as were the floors, and the only smell in the air was disinfectant. Which a huge relief after smelling the disgusting odor from the bucket in my room.

We walked until we came to a large gold-plated door. The guard ushered me inside. Sitting behind a massive desk was another man, who looked an awful lot like the one who'd brought me here.

He turned his chair around when he saw us enter and looked at the guard. "Thank you, Jerry, has she eaten?"

"Brought her straight to you."

"Then go get her a tray. She can eat in here while we get acquainted." Jerry left without another word.

The man's smile reminded me of a leopard as he gestured to the chair at my left. "Sit. My name's Clerry, and I think we're going to be great friends."

I took a seat at the table in the corner. My first thought was that I needed a booster seat, but if I sat on my knees, I could just about make it work.

While waiting, I took the time to size up the room. Platinum and gold. Even in prison, the place was filled with sparkling jewels. No doubt, if Sentra had prisons, they'd look marginally the same. The table in front of me was solid gold, with diamond trimmings. The chair I sat in, pure platinum. Letting everybody know who the big man was here.

Clerry's office was huge. It had soft plum carpet on the floor with gold trimmings, two deep-seated couches covered in rubies, a diamond studded chaise, and a platinum footstool. It was a room fit for comfort and luxury, and Clerry seemed to revel in it.

Neither he nor I spoke a word until Jerry came back with my food. He placed it in front of me, and I wolfed it down in two minutes flat. I couldn't taste it, which was probably a good thing. The thick orange liquid, I drunk so fast that I ended up choking.

Clerry's eyes glistened with faux sympathy as he watched me eat. He sat up a little straighter in his chair, rubbing and patting his desk as one would a small animal. His voice sounded as if he'd done nothing but suck on sweet honeysuckles all day. "There, there, Rekia, there's no need for that. There's plenty more where that came from. Jerry, go get her another helping."

I watched as the other man left the room. Jerry and Clerry. Were they related? They did look a lot alike.

Clerry nodded, as if I'd correctly answered some imaginary question. "Ah, I can see the wheels turning in your head. I've been asked this before. Yes, we are brothers. Running the prisons and jails are a family business. No one leaves here without having to throw a few million our way. Best not to end up here in the first place. Lucky for me if you do, though." He smiled, and revealed an even row of perfect white teeth. Bastard. I'd kill for teeth like that.

Jerry came back, and once again, I dug into my food, not stopping until my entire plate was licked clean. I then ran a quick tongue over my lips, trying to catch any errant crumbs, before sitting back with a sigh. Man, had that hit the spot.

Jerry removed my mess, then left without another word.

Clerry waited until the door closed, then turned to me. "I want to show you something." He manipulated a few buttons on his desk and four widescreen TV's lit up. One on each wall in the room. Of course, they were crusted in diamonds. I wasn't even surprised at this point.

As the screens came into focus, my eyes widened, and I had to bite my bottom lip to keep from screaming. Toma, Chaz, Kirk, and Clink all sat in different cells. My newly eaten food settled in my stomach like cold lead and I had to put a hand over my mouth to keep from bringing it back up. These people were vile.

My head swiveled as I looked from one screen to the next. What I saw sickened me and my eyes stung from the pressure of unshed tears.

Toma lay on his bed, his face bloodied and swollen. The white bucket in his room overflowed with feces to the point that it covered a small part of the floor surrounding it. My hands started to tremble as I looked on, and I figured the smell alone had to be torture.

Chaz lay on his side, his eyes darting to the right constantly, a look of fear and concern playing across his broken and scratched up face. I could only assume he figured Clink or Kirk to be in that direction, and I wished I had a way to put his mind at ease.

Clink looked broken. Utterly and completely broken. What the fuck had they done to him? Curled in a ball, I could barely recognize him, he was so covered in marks and wounds.

Rage built in me like an inferno, so much so that I could taste it on my tongue like an elusive taunt. I turned my heated gaze back on Clerry, only to see an evil, amused glint in his eyes as he carefully watched my reaction.

Last was Kirk. He sat up on the side of his bed, looking like a large ball of barely contained fury. He had a gash across his forehead, and his arms had so many cuts and scrapes on them, they almost looked to be a part of his skin.

My thoughts turned back to Nico. It didn't seem as if she'd been beaten daily and from what I could tell, neither had I. So my only question was, why the big difference in how they treated us? Were the guards on the men's side just that more vicious?

"I know what you're thinking," Clerry chuckled from behind his big desk. "Well, there's a reason for everything we do."

Something told me I wouldn't like his reason very much.

He chuckled again. "You have one of two choices. Tell us why you're here? Who sent you and why you also visited Sentra?" He smiled again before continuing. "If you do that, you can each pay a simple fine of about... oh, I don't know, let's say about five million apiece, and then you'll be free to go. What do you think?"

Did I really need to say anything? This guy lived in a dream world, and I didn't believe a word he said. "If we don't talk?" I asked, testing the waters.

His face darkened, and his eyes became hard as granite. Ah, there it was, I thought. The true man behind the facade.

His voice was low and dangerous when he spoke, enough to send goose pimples down my arm. "Then you will be forced to breed." His eyes raked over me, a lecherous grin on his face. "Your ability to jump dimensions is priceless." He ran a diamond-studded hand down his face, his eyes telling me what his mouth didn't.

As he watched me, it hit me like a ton of bricks. They were never letting us go, no matter what we did. Our value was priceless, as he'd said, and they planned on capitalizing on every bit of it.

At least this explained why Nico and I hadn't been beaten and starved. They needed us in good shape to produce all these babies they had planned for our future. I shook my head, disgusted.

This man and his family made my skin crawl. I let my eyes wander around the room looking for a way out. That's what we needed. Not being able to tap into our abilities made the task almost impossible.

A feeling of complete helplessness threatened to take me over, but it wasn't just my life at stake here. I needed to focus. Something had to give, no way in hell was this how it ended for us. Every single member of my crew deserved better, and I'd be damned if I let them down at the eleventh hour.

I had to think. Nico'd said the cells were power-proofed, but what about other parts of the building? I wondered... Trying to be slick by hiding my hands under the table, I tried to put the death squeeze on Clerry's heart.

A force like frozen wind slammed hard into me and sent me spiraling across the room. I curled into a fetal position, as sweat covered my face. Something was happening to me and panic set in immediately. Unbearable pain crippled my chest and my vision blurred as my head became light and woozy.

Then, just as quick as it had started, it stopped. Sweat dripped down my face, and I took a few gulps of air, happy to still be alive. I came to my knees and wiped away more sweat, my heart pounding out of my chest.

Clerry gave off a good-hearted chuckle. "That was dumb. Look." He queued up another TV, and the pictured moved backward in slow motion. It stopped on Nico and I talking.

"Any power you try to use will bounce back on you with three times the strength. Hardly worth the effort, especially in your condition."

"Did you think she was lying?" he asked, with a sarcastic smirk.

Sitting there, heart racing, looking at the victorious grin on his face, I decided to live. No way would I let this guy be the one to take me out.

Slowly I came to my feet. A little shaky, but I still stood on my own. Determined to show as little weakness as I could, I gritted my teeth at him. "I'm going to kill you." My voice quivered, and my whole body shook, but I meant every word. I was wet and sticky, but I stood my ground, though it took everything in me not to collapse on the floor.

He didn't seem fazed by my words at all. "I know you'll try your best," he said as if talking to a five-year-old child. He pressed another button on his desk. "Jerry get her out of here."

"Do you know what they have planned for us?" I asked Nico as soon as Jerry walked away and I was safely back in my cell.

She shrugged. "Take 'em three years with the birth control I used to use."

Oh yeah, birth control. That lovely little thing they shot in my arm every five years. How had I forgotten about that? I'd just had it done six months ago. Still... though, just the thought of what they wanted to do sent shivers down my spine.

Nico looked up and down the hall, making sure no one was around, then lowered her voice. "Got a land dispute coming up." She said it like I had any idea what she was talking about. That short trip to Clerry's office had exhausted me, and I sat with my back to the wall, trying to get myself under control.

When Nico still hadn't said anything after a couple of seconds, I looked at her and waved my hand. "What's this about a land dispute?"

She looked out the cell, checking again before she spoke. I didn't know how to convey to her, that they heard every word we said and settled for tapping my ear and looking up so that she would get the point.

She nodded, like it didn't matter one way or the other. "A land dispute is a dispute about land. Whoever wins gets the land. The loser has the right to call victory. Calling victory means the two fight to the death unless one side pays the council. Basically, whoever pays the most gets the land. If no one pays, they have to fight it out."

I was confused. "Why wouldn't they just pay?" They could earn more money. They couldn't earn another life, but I guessed they didn't see things that way.

Now she just sounded exasperated. "I don't think you understand how important money is around here. Even if they were to take the coward's way out and pay, their husband or wife would never forgive them for giving away so much cash." She swallowed hard before continuing. "You lose respect, you lose business, it's better to just fight and get it over with."

I gaped at her unable to process what I was hearing. "So, it's better to lose your life?" These people really were crazy.

She sounded tired of me and this conversation. "You'd never understand. We're from two different worlds, in more ways than one."

She was right about that. "What difference does that make to us?" I asked, not even sure why she'd brought it up.

She gave me a small calculating smile. "They'll take us."

No, they wouldn't. "Why?"

"To show their power. Their superiority. Or you know, because not one of those depraved motherfuckers are willing to miss it, and they're not confident enough to just leave the prison empty of guards. Anyone could portal in and save us. They don't know you, Clink, Kirk, and Chaz. They have no idea what type of world you're from or how powerful your people are. They're not going to risk the chance of one of them portaling in to save us."

Point taken. I still didn't get her excitement, though. "How does that help us?"

"It's outside."

"So... ah, but will our powers be blocked?"

She shook her head. "No, but we'll be under heavy guard, and you have to remember these people are powerful too. We were no match for them before. Now?" She looked over at my bruised face and seemed to grip her side a little tighter. "It's really a gamble."

It was a gamble, but we had to try. We couldn't let this opportunity pass us by. I did have one question though. "How do you know all this?"

She gave me a blank look.

"Not how do you know about the match, but how do you know one's coming up."

"Heard the guards whispering about it earlier."

My thoughts went to the images I'd seen on the screen back in Clerry's office. This would be a lot harder than we thought. "Have you seen Toma and the other guys? They can't help us." My voice broke a little as I spoke. "They can't even help themselves."

Her only response was, "We have to do something."

Chapter 12

On the day of the land dispute, Nico and I were loaded into a platinum van by two armed guards. I didn't know where Toma and the rest of the guys were, but understood they probably didn't want to take the chance of putting us all together.

"One of your men will be fighting today." Clerry smiled at Nico and me from the front of the van.

My heart sunk to my chest and I looked at Nico. "Do you have land here? Does Toma?"

She shook her head, a slightly disturbed look on her face. "No, but you can always pay someone to fight for you if you're scared, sick, or absent."

"Why would you be absent?"

"Business. Business always comes first here. Anyway, you can have someone fight for you, if the money is right."

I sat back and watched the tall buildings sweep by at a rapid-fire pace. It had to be Toma, only he would even know to do this. Still, why would he? Was it for the money, or something else?

I looked back at Nico, but the scowl on her face only made me more nervous. Could it be that he'd bargained for our freedom? Or maybe just that of his and his sister?

I put a little steel in my spine and tried to prepare myself for what was to come. Whatever it was, it wasn't good, I just knew it. This would not end well.

As we rode along, I tried to keep an eye out for anything that could possibly help us. Nothing stood out, and before long the van pulled into the largest, most elaborate stadium I'd ever seen.

My mouth hung open in awe as I took in blue and yellow benches crusted in diamonds and pearls. Each row had a comfortable plush seat, and a cushioned back rest.

Food vendors set up around every part of the circular design. I smelled everything from baked chicken, to hot dogs, to steak. My mouth watered at the prospect, but I was pretty sure that feeding wasn't on the agenda.

Sat in the middle of the stadium, and visible from all sides, was a large golden platform crusted in diamonds. It was lit up and raised about six inches off the ground. It looked magnificent, majestic even. I guessed that was what they'd be fighting on.

I looked to Nico to see if she was taking this all in. Then I remembered that none of this was new to her, and she'd probably seen it all before. I'd tried talking to her on the way over, but it was like conversing with a brick wall, and after only a few minutes I'd given up, figuring like me, she was worried about Toma.

Far and near I saw way more Clamors than I'd ever imagined. A giddy excitement seemed to bubble through the air and into each one of them. The place overflowed with Clamor men and women. They must have really loved the gore here, because every seat in the stadium seemed to be filled.

Today was special. This event was special. Someone would die today, and the Clamors acted as butchers watching the slaughter.

I sat in the seat appointed to me, with Nico on my left and Clerry directly behind us. He seemed to be infected with the same giddy anticipation as the others.

I felt myself lose a little hope, as I looked at the numerous Clamors surrounding us. Sweat soaked my skin and fear filled my chest. I was scared. A fact I was finding harder and harder to hide as my hands seemed to be shaking nonstop. The last I'd seen of Toma, he'd been sick, beaten, and barely able to move. So, what the hell made him think this was a good idea?

Nico put her hands over mine, stopping them midshake. "He wouldn't do this unless he knew he could win."

I nodded and, cut my eyes to where Clerry sat engaged in conversation with the Clamor woman on his left. Good, the better for us to talk without fear. "So you're not worried at all?"

She removed her hand. "Why should I be? He's a grown man. His decisions are his own."

I blinked, not sure I'd heard her right. "Nothing like brotherly love, huh?" Hard to believe she wasn't at least mildly concerned. Had it been one of my brothers... but maybe that was it. Maybe she had that much confidence in Toma and his abilities. Maybe fear for him was something foreign and not easily recognized. Whatever the reason, the only silver lining I could see was that he'd be able to use his powers.

The thought clicked in my mind like a thunderbolt. I could use my powers, and so could the rest of us. Was it possible? Could we really leave this place today? I looked at the massive number of Clamors still filing into the arena.

Then I thought of how easily we'd been overpowered before and deflated in an instant. We didn't stand a chance in hell. We'd be disabled in a matter of minutes. So much for that plan.

After about ten more minutes of sitting, a tall bald Clamor finally appeared in the middle of the platform. I didn't see a mic, but I was sure one was hiding somewhere because when he talked, his voice seemed to be magnified by a thousand. "Today we are here in a land dispute against C. J. Elmore the second, and Walter T. Griffins the third." His voice sang out with pleased excitement. "C. J. Elmore has taken ill and cannot fight today. In his place, there will be Clink." His voice said that last part as if he was announcing a royal rumble.

But wait. What? Had I heard right? Clink? Did he actually say Clink? I looked to my left and saw the tiniest hint of a smile on Nico's face. What the fuck was so funny? I was horrified. Clink would fight? Could he even astral project in his condition? Still, even if he could, would that skill really do him any good against the power of a Clamor?

Both men came out onto the platform. Clink, limping and stumbling, his orange-red dreadlocks pulled into a ponytail that hung well past his butt.

I watched on in horror. He didn't look good. This would be a slaughter. The man he was up against, Walter, was every bit as strong and powerful looking as I'd imagined he would be.

"Why would he do this?" I whispered to Nico.

"Because he's a fucking genius. Think about it." She tapped her temple.

I didn't have time to figure out what she meant, before a horn sounded and the whole stadium went completely quiet.

Fear coursed through me and caused my palms to become clammy and wet. I couldn't watch this. I had to watch this. Fuck that, I had to help. There was no way I would sit by while Clink was ripped to pieces in front of me. Nope. Wasn't going to happen.

Something must have shown in my body language, because Clerry leveled me a death stare. "You have two guards on you each. Don't even think about getting cute, okay?" I turned around to see a man in a blue and gray uniform sitting behind me, and another sitting in front of me. I noticed two on Nico as well. As helpless as it was, I still had to try.

I couldn't just sit back and watch as someone I'd rescued and brought here died for the pure enjoyment of the Clamors. I had to do something. What, I had no idea.

I looked around until I finally found Chaz, Toma, and Kirk, sitting just a few benches down. I couldn't get a clear look at their faces, but even from the side, I could see the tension radiating from each of them. They had two guards a piece on them as well.

I looked to the stage, and where once there'd been one Clink, suddenly there were three. It was an unnecessary drain on his powers. The two fake images flicked in and out at rapid speed. He couldn't hold it together. He just wasn't strong enough. That power would have been better used defending his life for a few seconds longer.

The boom dropped, the crowd screamed, and the fighting began. Walter wasted no time yanking up the huge stick he'd been handed. Clink reached for his as well. While Walter looked big and powerful, Clink looked like a gnat trying to hold onto a long tree branch.

I held my breath as Walter went straight for the knees, knocking Clink down with a single massive swing. Before Clink could move a muscle, Walter was on him, this time he went for the face. My chest heaved as I tried to fight down the scream starting in my throat.

Clink managed to get a kick in, but the effect only cost Walter a small stumble before he charged again. This time Walter went wild, hitting and pulping Clink with unrestrained abandonment.

Then I heard it. A bloodcurdling scream that caused the whole stadium to quiet in a second. Chaz. There it was again. A cry filled with anguish, pain, and uncontrollable rage.

The wind changed, and the air itself shook. Oh fuck, I knew what was coming now, and it was nothing good. I thought back to before and the small amount of power, Chaz had had to draw upon. Compared to this, that had been peanuts. This was massive and all encompassing.

I looked to Nico and saw the sly smile back on her lips. She'd known, of course she had. I cursed myself for being so stupid. No way would Chaz sit by while Clink was beaten to a pulp. The air around us twisted and stirred, even causing Walter to stop his murderous assault.

We had to protect ourselves. An out of control Chaz was a very dangerous Chaz, and he didn't really have too great a handle on his power when he got like this. I grabbed Nico by the shoulder and pulled her with me under the bleachers, as others around us began to slide from their seats.

We watched from our protected shelter as numerous Clamors were raised in the air and thrown from one end of the stadium to the other. One man was clawing desperately at the air, a look of utter terror on his face, but it did no good, as he was tossed aside like the rest. It was all we could do to hold on. Then light turned to dark, and everything went up in flames.

From my hiding space, I saw Chaz, standing on the stage in front of Clink, protecting him. He looked wild, his shirt was ripped open, and he stood four feet off the ground, blue and yellow energy crackling up and down his skin. He had his hands outstretched, as his eyes blazed red. I was scared to even move. He looked absolutely terrifying.

I turned to Nico wondering if she saw this as well, but as I did, the bench that stood as protection was ripped away with violent efficiency. Dammit, Chaz, not us too. I tried to fight it, tried to reach out to Nico as she and I were both lifted into the air and slung with such force that I feared I'd never open my eyes again.

I DID OPEN MY EYES again, and when I did, I wished I'd just kept them closed. All I felt was pain. Something from above me dripped down and hit me square in the face. Not sure what was going on, I opened my eyes a little wider and realized I was in some type of cave.

"Good to see you moving around," I heard a voice off in the distance say. I tried to sit up, but the pain kept me grounded in one spot. "You're not ready for all of that." This time the voice moved closer, and I recognized Saylor.

What the...? I didn't even have the energy to fight her, nor to ponder what her agenda was. Had I escaped one prison only to end up in another? "How long?" I croaked out. My throat was as dry as sandpaper and hurt like fire. The musty damp smell of the cave didn't really help.

She moved a little closer and asked me to repeat myself. Try as I might, my voice still came out in a tiny whisper. "How long have I been here?"

Comprehension dawned, and she answered me in the most nonchalant voice I'd ever heard. "Three weeks." Alarm shot through me as I tried unsuccessfully to sit up again. "I told you to stop that," she said, gently pushing me back down. "Everyone's okay, they're just in the other room." She pointed to the left, and I saw a small opening that seemed to lead to another part of the cave.

"Are they really okay?" I managed to ask. I realized I was laying on a sleeping roll, with a heavy blanket thrown over top of me.

She nodded. "Everyone's pretty much been in and out. Chaz and Clink are the worst. If not for the severity of their injuries, I would have moved you long before now. Staying in one place for too long is not a good idea." She took a seat on a big rock in front of me.

"I need to sit up. I can't keep talking to you like this. I feel like a lopsided fool." She walked over and helped me until my back rested easily against the cold hard cave wall.

"You hungry?'

I nodded, as my stomach jumped to attention at the mere mention of food. She walked away giving me time to focus on the situation. This lady Saylor made me nervous. Was she really on our side? I couldn't tell. I thought of the others. The last thing I remembered was Nico and I flying through the air.

Saylor walked back in carrying a tray, which she set over my legs. Just the smell alone was enough to make me cry. It held clear broth, a chunk of bread and a mug filled with tea. I sipped the hot broth and instantly felt warm all over. I looked up at her and smiled. "Thanks, for this. Where are we?"

"Underground, hiding from your enemies." She sat back down on her rock.

"How did we end up here?" I dipped a piece of the bread in the broth to soften it, then folded it into my mouth. It tasted like heaven, and I hurried to repeat the action. "How come we're not still in that stadium?"

She smiled and shook her head. "I came in after Chaz's little display. I gathered you all up, with help, and brought you here."

"What about the Clamors?" I sipped more broth and washed it down with a little tea.

"They're recovering. Some were hurt really bad. Some killed. I knew if Clink were hurt then Chaz would step up."

Her smile was smug, but the fact that she knew that much about us ran my blood cold.

I tried to stop my head from spinning as realization dawned on me, and I looked at the enigma before me. She still had that same smug look on her face, and for a moment I wanted nothing more than to wipe it off. "How did you set this up? Do the Clamors still trust you?" She seemed to be walking on a tightly wound rope, just a tug here or a pull there, and she'd be down for the count.

She shook her head. "The Clamors trust no one, but I am on the high council of Sentra, so they could hardly tell me no if I asked for a little visit to the cells."

"How did you know that this Elmore dude would suddenly fall ill?" It took a lot of planning. I looked at her with a newfound fear and awe. She was as cunning as they came. Willing to knock out anyone and anything that got in her way. I wondered where my friends and I fit into that equation.

She shrugged. "I made sure he was poisoned."

"You killed him?" I gaped. Maybe she was crazy *and* deadly.

"No, I poisoned him. He didn't die, just took ill for a while. Then I went to see Clink. Made sure we were not being recorded, and told him about the fight and the rules."

Comprehension dawned on me like sun on a rainy day. "I'm sure you stressed what a shame it would be for Chaz to have to sit by and watch as he was beaten to death." I soaked the rest of my bread into the broth and lapped it up greedily. It was the best thing I'd ever eaten, and I didn't want it to be gone just yet. I looked back to Saylor.

She smiled. It wasn't friendly. "I guess I did something like that."

"Clerry? Jerry?" Just the thought of my two jailers sent a shiver down my spine. I could go forever without seeing either man again.

"Both dead. You have Chaz to thank for that. Maybe his out of control attacks are not that out of control after all."

Before I could answer, the wall to the right shimmered and changed, indicating a portal opening. I looked to Saylor.

"I had to have help to get you here," She blinked. "This person came to me. I didn't approach them."

Another person brought into this mess? Didn't we already have enough people to keep track of?

"You look like shit." The woman in front of me had short black hair and a pair of red eyes that I hadn't seen in ages. In her hands, she carried two huge bags. My cousin Robin, from my father's home world. What the hell was she doing here? I asked as much.

She smiled and took a seat on the floor in front of me. "I watch your house, Cuz. You don't come around often, and in your line of work you never know when you'll need to drop in to hide away, I mean visit."

I took a sip of tea. "That explains nothing." What did she mean she watches my house?

She chuckled again. "You know you really should feel lucky to have family looking out for you. I set up alarms to let me know when, and if, someone ever enters your house. I hate the thought of you walking into an ambush. If someone came, Rusty, Blake, and I would deal with them before they ever had a chance to hurt you. Family sticks with family. You know how we roll."

I couldn't resist the urge to smile. Rusty and Blake were brothers and our cousins as well. My father's family were close. We looked out for each other no matter the consequences. "So, the alarms went off and what?"

"I saw it was just you, but still something seemed off. So, I gathered Rusty and Blake, and we watched you until you left."

That was a little creepy, but okay, I'd go with it. "So how did you find us again?"

She shook her head and felt my forehead with the back of her hand. "Are you sure you feel better? I followed you through, of course. Piggybacking off your portal, opening my own a good way away from yours."

I leveled her with a stare. "So, you watched me get beat up?"

She sighed heavily, "Would you had rather we all ended up in jail? I was alone, Rekia. I did what I had to."

"She came to me," Saylor said, speaking up for the first time. "She saw us talking. After that, it was simply a matter of manipulating some land records, whispering in a few ears, and here we are." She spread her hands out in front of her.

I drunk down the rest of my tea before I answered. "You could have been killed," I hissed at Robin. "How'd you know you could trust her? She could have killed you."

Robin looked at Saylor with a challenge in her eyes. "I mean, she could have tried. But we both know how hard a task that is, so..."

I shook my head, not at all pleased with her answer. "Even still."

She looked annoyed, and her voice told the same story. "Look, I hung back, I mean look at her. Obviously she wasn't one of them. I followed her to Sentra, gathered up Rusty and Blake, and waited until she was alone to corner her."

I moved the tray away and made a move to stand. Robin assisted me immediately. Once solidly on my feet, I used the cave wall for support. "Where are they now? Rusty and Blake?"

"Home. We took turns coming back here. They did help get you and your friends out of that stadium though."

"My sister?"

She shook her head. "I told no one. That's your funeral. I want no part of it."

"Well, I don't appreciate being kept away from my friends. I'm not special, and I won't have you treating them as if they're lesser or something." This separation thing reeked of Robin.

She had the nerve to blink at me. "Well, aren't they?" she deadpanned.

I blinked back. "Excuse me?"

"Well, can they open a portal? Can they manipulate time? Do they know about blood healing? What can they do to help you that your own family can't?"

Unwilling to have this stupid discussion with her, I slowly made my way into the other room of the cave. It was a huge, open space, littered with rocks both big and small. Water dripped from above, giving the place a musty, mildew smell. It was dark in here, but either Saylor or Robin had set up a large overhead light, and that made it easier to see.

Clink and Chaz lay on the only mattress in the room. Scattered about were Toma, Nico, and Kirk, each on a bedroll with a heavy blanket like my own. The less to carry the better.

The fact that Robin saw fit for Chaz and Clink to be more comfortable than practical let me know just how serious their conditions must have been.

"They're out of the woods now," she said, when she noticed the strained look on my face. "I gave them sedatives to help them sleep. You needed to wake up, and you seemed to be healing faster, so I haven't given you any in a while." She held up her bags. "That's why I'm here, to change bandages, and check that everyone's okay."

I eased onto a rock up against the wall. It would be a while before I felt one hundred percent again. "Don't give them any more medicine. I need them clearheaded and alert."

Her eyes went upward. "Well, you can help me feed them and change their bandages."

After they'd all awakened and been fed and rebandaged we got down to business. I was so glad they were okay, and it took a moment for me to process it all.

Clink looked much better with fewer bruises and no open scars.

I looked at my cousin and knew she'd done double-time making sure he was properly cared for. I owed her. As much as she grated on my nerves, she was still family, and even though she didn't know them, she knew they were important to me, and that's all that had mattered.

Chaz seemed better, but the haggard look on his face told me just how bad it had been. He and Clink sat together on the mattress, holding hands, and leaning on each other for support.

We needed to leave. Three weeks was much too long to be in one place. Robin meant well, but leaving us all in a doped-up state with only one person to guard us showed just how inexperienced she was in dealing with something like this. Even more so than us.

We could have been attacked at any moment, with no way to defend ourselves. And why in the hell had she trusted Saylor? Still, so far, it seemed to be paying off. For now, anyway.

I looked at my cousin and sighed. "Robin, look, I appreciate everything you've done."

She stopped me cold. "I've been away from my job too long. Trust and believe I don't want to interrupt you and your little band of renegades anymore than I have to. But I will make sure you have the supplies you need. I will watch where you go next, and you will keep in touch with me daily." She reached into her pocket and pulled out a universal phone, replacing the one I'd lost some time ago.

"Thank you." I looked over at the others who just seemed anxious for her to go.

"No thanks needed. We're family. Your backpacks are home with Blake and Rusty."

"I hope they're filling them with supplies."

"Why else would they have them? Stay here. I'll go see if they're finished."

I waited until she left before I addressed the others in the room. "I have a place on Lark. It's kind of underground, and when I bought it, I took steps to ensure its privacy. It's not on any maps, you can't search land records to find it, it's hidden from everything. That little prize cost me a whole months salary. So..."

Toma nodded understanding. "So, you bought it in case you were ever caught doing your job."

I smiled. If the government ever found out just how many criminals had just poof and disappeared with my help, I'd be in a world of shit. Still, my world didn't even come close to the technology of some of the other worlds I'd visited, so it hadn't been my own government I'd had in mind when I'd built the damn thing.

Nico got up and stretched her legs. "So, if it's anything like the rest of your places I'll assume you have food and comfort. So why is it we have to wait for your cousin again?"

Kirk, who stood behind her, reached out to rub her shoulders. "Oh, come on, girl. Stop being argumentative. We have to make it there first. Never know when extra supplies can come in handy." She didn't say anything, but she did lean into his touch a bit.

I looked over to Chaz. He'd saved us all, more than once. I'm not above gratitude, and I'm not above admitting when I'm wrong. Time and time again Chaz had proven himself. No matter his crimes, deep down he was a good person who loved his family and loved his friends. Loyalty, the one thing you couldn't buy or steal, and Chaz had it in spades.

He caught me staring and nodded. "You can't keep me down for the count, love." He smiled, though it came out more like a grimace.

I sat down on the rock in front of him, glad for the chance to let my legs rest. "You saved us again. You deserve far more than a simple thank you, but at the moment it's all I have to offer."

He shrugged as if it was nothing. "You could give me a million dollars. You know how much I love money." His voice sounded dry and rough.

"Let me get you something to drink."

I walked back into the other part of the cave just as Robin popped back in. "Where's Saylor?" I asked, looking around the otherwise empty space.

"Got rid of her."

"You mean you took her home, right?"

She leveled me with a death stare. "Well, what else what I do with her, Rekia? I'm not the criminal here, remember?"

"Well..." I said, cocking my head to the side in a good-natured sort of way.

She held up an index finger and tried not to grin. "Don't you even... we, we promised never to talk about that again." And now she did smile.

Relief flowed through me as I realized we were still on the same page after all. I laughed, then walked over and engulfed her in a big hug. "Thanks, for this, but from here on out, I don't want you involved."

She detangled herself from me and nodded. "That'd be my cue to leave." She pulled me into another hug. "You take care of yourself, Cuz, no excuses."

I waved until she disappeared, then called the others in to pick up their bags. "We won't leave from here. I don't want my cousin coming back and piggybacking off my portal."

Chapter 13

It wasn't where I wanted to be, but it was clean, comfortable, and private. We arrived in the middle of the day, directly into my underground living room.

The first thing we did was get Chaz and Clink set up in a bedroom of their own. When I'd first bought it, I'd made sure the house was fully stocked with things like toilet paper, soap, washing powders, and any other such amenities.

I had canned food, a lot of it still good, as I'd tried to buy as fresh as I could. Things like milk, eggs, and cheese, we would have to do without, because it wasn't worth the risk.

The water here was fresh and safe to drink, but I'd still made sure to get some bottled cases of the stuff, along with cases of orange pop, Coke, Pepsi, juice, and other such things I knew my family loved to drink. Hey, they might've had to hide out too. Who knew?

Nico nodded her approval as she took the place in. "Well, this is certainly a step up," she said, looking at the plush carpet, deep-brown colored walls, and deep-seated furniture. "Much better than your main house."

I'd spared no expense with this place because if my family ever needed to be here with me, I wanted them to at least be comfortable.

Kirk smiled in her direction. "This more up ya alley, aye, girl?"

I left them to it and turned my attention to Toma. "Pick whatever rooms you want. I'm going in for a hot bath and a sit down."

Toma looked at the blue underwater sea life painted on the hallway walls. Something I was sure only me, my nieces, and nephews would enjoy.

It was the perfect escape. It was underground, it was hidden away, it had more than a few secret passages and quick getaway routes, and it already had everything we needed. So, I saw no reason to make it cold and unwelcoming. I figured if I had to use it, either I was in deep shit, or would be soon, might as well feel good while I could, right?

It was almost like I could sense my bedroom calling out to me. I started down the hall, turning around to face the others before I'd completely walked away. "I'm going to my room. You guys set up wherever you see fit."

My bedroom was huge, because hey, why not, right? My plush triple-king-sized bed sat in the middle of the floor. My bathroom was a room in and of itself, with hot tub and Jacuzzi. Looking at it, though, I found myself missing my small, simple, three-bedroom home more than ever.

Sitting on the side of the tub, I turned on the water. I wanted it as hot as I could stand it, because the thought of Sentra, Clamor, and everything else we'd been through had my skin crawling. So, I'd take this time for myself and focus on me, and only me.

I emerged from my room three hours later, refreshed, rested, and feeling better than I'd felt in days. The others were in the living room eating spam and crackers to recharge their bodies after the portal hop.

Toma got up and came back with a plate for me. The spam was cut up and fried with the crackers crumbled in. It looked disgusting, but it was spam, and I loved spam, so I gave it a try.

Looking around I took note that I wasn't the only one who'd taken advantage of running water and hygiene products. Everyone looked fresh and newly scrubbed. Which would hopefully prove to be a good morale boost. We needed that.

Clink sat off in a corner by himself. He was propping his head up with one hand, his expression downtrodden and severe. Maybe he was just worried about Chaz, or maybe he needed someone to talk to.

"How is he?" I asked, taking a seat beside him.

Clink's face had healed, and he was definitely getting around a lot better, but his spirit seemed distracted and detached. He sighed heavily before he answered my question. "I did what I had to. Not sure he'll understand that, but I hope that he does."

It took a minute for me to realize what he was talking about. Then I remembered the fight, the stadium, and the sacrificial choice he'd made.

My voice, when I spoke, was as soft and reassuring as I dared. "If you hadn't done what you did, we'd still be in that hellhole. You realize that don't you?"

He didn't seem impressed, and his facial expression still held that same stoic look as before. "I still did what I did. No denying that. Lots of things can be changed, facts ain't one of 'em."

"Fact is, that we're here, and not there. Can't you see the benefit in that?"

He shrugged and got up to fix him and Chaz a plate of food. I didn't say anything, just watched him walk away, shoulders drooped and head low.

I looked up to see Toma watching me, a curious expression on his face. "We can't stay here forever," he said, stating the obvious.

My voice was thick when I spoke. "No, we can't. But we do need time to recuperate though. So for now, we hide, we rest, and we let Chaz heal."

LATER THAT NIGHT IN my room, I tried to figure out our next move. I had many favors I could call in. I just wasn't sure now was the time to do it. What I needed was contact with someone on the outside, someone I could trust. Only one person came to mind.

I didn't really want the others to know what I was doing, so I waited until well after midnight before I opened the portal and stepped through.

I walked into a bare bedroom where a figure lay under a pile of covers. I'd only taken two steps when it jumped up, wrapped me in black lasso rope and hurled me close, until I was only inches from his face. "Move and I'll—oh, hey Rekia, give a guy a little warning next time, huh?" Trent said.

He let the rope go, and I waited until it had completely unraveled before moving. It would have shocked me otherwise. It had been given to him by a man from Saluton. Saluton was a world filled with magic, and this had been Trent's gift for helping the man and his family start over in Shinow. "I wasn't really expecting a warm welcome, Trent, but this is ridiculous."

"You knew what you were doing," he said, as he dropped the lasso to the floor. It hit with a thump, and I gave it a guarded look. I couldn't command the damn thing. No one could. It answered to Trent alone. I couldn't even use my telekinesis to break free from it. Which made for some fun nights when we were in the mood.

He looked me over. "You alright? I've been worried. Had some pretty shady characters come around looking for your whereabouts. Didn't tell them shit." He narrowed his eyes. "What the hell have you gotten yourself into, Re?"

I put my head on his chest and wrapped my arms tightly around him. "Just let me stay like this for a second. I take my comfort in sneak and steal mode these days." He leaned over and kissed me on the forehead, lightly running his fingers through my hair, before leading me over to the bed.

I sat down with a huff. "So what's been going on?"

Trent sat down directly behind me and started a slow and pleasurable massage of my shoulders. "They talked to everyone who works for me. I don't know about some of them, you need to watch yourself."

I let out a soft sigh, and rejoiced in the feeling of his touch a second longer before answering. "I need information. I need a way out of this mess. I'm tired of it all. Tired of hiding, tired of looking over my shoulders, tired of being in prison."

His hands stilled on my shoulders. "Prison? What the hell, Re?"

I turned and flipped him on his backside, straddling his hips. I leaned over and placed a long sensual kiss on his lips. He tasted like garlic, hmm. I loved garlic. "Later," I said abandoning my shirt and everything else.

He flipped me over and kissed me hard. "Later then."

Some time afterward, we lay snuggled down in his bed discussing what had happened. I told him everything except about Lark. It wouldn't be much of a secret hideout if I did that.

He took it all in, then looked at me, fire in his eyes. "What'd you need me to do?"

I sat up and braced my back against the headboard. "Keep your eyes and ears open. The smallest thing can mean something. I need all the help I can get. This thing, I thought I knew what I was doing, but things have gotten so far out of my control, that I just don't know anymore."

He ran his hand up and down my arm. "I'll do what I can on this end, Re, but I'm not optimistic."

Well that made two of us. "How's Sharon?"

He laced his hand in mine and kissed my fingertips. "She's doing fine. The kids are adjusting okay. My employee, Rhonda is keeping an eye on them."

I couldn't put it off any longer. "So, tell me about the dudes who showed up looking for me."

"Two guys, one girl. Offered one million dollars for any information leading to your arrest."

"I've already been arrested, remember? Were they tall?"

He blinked twice before comprehension dawned. "No, from what you described of the Clamors, I don't think this was them. Doesn't mean they weren't working for them, though."

"True."

"Re?"

"Yeah?"

He held my face between his hands, then slowly kissed the tip of my nose, under my chin, then my lips. I shivered, wishing I could crawl up inside him and stay there forever. "Be careful. You're wanted dead or alive. You and all your friends have a kill first order. A million for each of you. That's a lot of money."

My breath stopped for a full ten seconds. A million for each of us. Were we really that much of a threat? Six million dollars was a lot of money. Any number of people would turn us in for that tidy sum.

I tried to get my thoughts together, but it wasn't easy. They'd just put a target on our backs, and our task had just gotten that much harder. I looked to Trent. "I need to end this. I want my life back."

He kissed my hand, then stood, and wrapped a towel around his waist. "I need a shower."

"Me too," I got up as well and led the way to his bathroom.

"Your sister came by," he said casually, like he was asking me to take out the trash or something.

I stopped dead in my tracks, causing him to bump into me. "When?"

He charged on in front of me. "'Bout two weeks ago. I told her I hadn't seen you, but, she's worried, you know."

I put that thought away for later, then turned on the shower and pulled him in with me. "Enough about my sister. I don't want her dragged into this." I grabbed his washcloth and began to wash his back, his strong muscles smooth under my touch. "If she comes again, tell her the same thing."

I'D JUST PUT MY SHOES on and kissed him goodbye when the front door banged open. Instinct and foolishness made me jump in front of him. Pride and stubbornness made him push me behind him.

All thoughts of his lasso out of my mind, I hissed at him. "Trent, don't be stupid, you can't fight them, I can."

He sounded very offended. "I don't need you to protect me. Go. I'll be all right."

Rhonda rounded the corner, and both of our shoulders sagged in relief. "I didn't realize you had company. I can come back." She looked from me to Trent. Yet she made no move to leave, and she had a key to the front door, interesting.

Trent pointed up the hall. "In a minute, alright." She looked me over once more, then turned, and walked away.

I felt a headache coming on. "Can we trust her to keep her mouth shut?"

He gave a measured look up the hall before he answered. "Not sure. That amount of money can make people do crazy things. I'll try to keep an eye on her, but I don't think you should come back until this blows over."

I couldn't agree more. I gave him another quick peck on the cheek before I walked into the closet and disappeared.

"YOU KNOW I WAS REALLY starting to worry about you," a voice said as soon as I materialized in my bedroom.

I think I may have jumped about three feet. "Toma, what the hell are you doing in here?"

He came to stand in front of me, arms folded across his chest, his entire air said that he was pissed, yet I had no idea why. "Checking on you, same as I do every night."

I blinked, not sure I'd heard him right. "You check on me every night?"

He said it as if it was nothing. "Have since that first night at your place. Can I ask where you've been?"

I blinked again at his boldness. "Can I get a cold beer first?" I walked up the hallway with him following closely behind.

He opened the fridge and took out two beers, popping the top on both and handing me one. I needed time to figure out how much I wanted to tell him. I walked into the living room and took a seat on the couch, gulping down half my beer in the process.

"I needed information, found out a couple of things."

He sat beside me and took a swig of his drink. "You should have woken me, let me know you were leaving." He rubbed his hands through his hair. "When I saw your room was empty, when I couldn't find you, it took me a minute to remember you can open a portal anytime you want. So, I settled down to wait for you."

I remembered that attack in my bedroom that first night he and Nico had stayed with me, so I wasn't really opposed to him making sure I was all right. The thing was though, it made me feel suffocated, tied down. Like I was punching a clock and had to be at a certain place, at a certain time, every night, and that wasn't something I could ever get used to.

"I appreciate the concern," I said slowly so as not to offend. "But I'm not used to being checked on." I took another swallow, then drained the whole beer.

"Here, let me." He picked up the bottle and put it in the trash. Then grabbed me another, popping the top on that one as well. "What do we do now?"

"Well, we're wanted dead or alive. I did find that out."

His face never changed expressions. "Are you surprised? Especially with what happened on Clamor?"

"I guess not. Did I tell you that Clerry and Jerry are both dead as a result of Chaz's little attack?"

He nodded, took a swallow of beer. "You mentioned that at dinner."

Right. Just lately I didn't know whether I was coming or going. My nerves seemed permanently balanced on the tip top of a very small needle. "We can't do anything until Chaz heals. But after that, I say we need to confront this thing head on. I want my life back. I want to spend time with my family. My nieces and nephews. Fuck!" My voice rose to a shout, and without thinking, I slammed my bottle down on the table causing it to drop to the floor.

Toma moved immediately. "I'll get it."

I stood, wanting nothing more than for this night to be over. Toma reached for me, tried to pull me into a hug.

I sidestepped him and picked up my bottle before he got the chance. "I did it. I'll get it up. You can go to bed if you want. I'm not going anywhere else tonight."

I waited until he was down the hall before I collapsed completely.

ONCE CHAZ FULLY RECOVERED, which took another three weeks, I decided we needed to move again. Getting an update from Trent seemed like our best option. I hadn't talked to him since I'd snuck in that first night, so I was sure something new had come to light.

Standing in the living room, waiting for me to open a portal, Chaz let his bag fall to the floor. "Oh, come on, love, do we have to go back to that place again? It reminds me of your world, all plain, and simple and prehistoric. How do you stand it there?"

While once I would have rolled my eyes, this time I just smiled. Damn, but it felt good to have the old Chaz back again. "How did you survive it? Your time of exile in my world?"

He picked his bag up and chuckled. "Lots and lots of alcohol."

I shuddered. "A drunk Chaz has to be a scary thing."

"Very," he agreed.

I laughed again, then turned to open the portal. I'd originally thought to pop up in the alleyway of Trent's office building, but figured that would be too dangerous. Walking straight into his home, gave us privacy and kept him out of it, in case someone else came by to ask questions.

We entered into a dark quiet living room. I knew he was at work, so that didn't surprise me. What did surprise me, was the female figure sitting off in the corner. Saylor. What the fuck? This damn lady was everywhere. What the hell was she doing in Trent's house?

Suddenly a sick feeling hit me right in the gut. "Where is he?" I asked, through gritted teeth.

She rose in an elegant manner befitting a queen. "Do you know how long I've been here waiting for you?"

She had a hell of a nerve. I walked up to her, got in her face. "I won't ask you again. Where the fuck is Trent?"

She frowned, a sad smile forming on her lips. "They took him."

Before I could stop myself, I'd wrapped my hand around her throat and began to squeeze. "Who has him? And what do you have to do with it?"

Toma put his hand on my arm. "She can't answer you if she can't breathe. Let her go now, Rekia." His voice was a little harsher than I thought necessary.

I shook his hand off me but released her nonetheless. I had to fold my arms in front of me to keep from lashing out at her again. "Talk."

She rubbed her throat, then sat back down, clasping her hands in front of her. "We know you came to see him a couple of weeks ago."

"So, you waited for me to come again?"

She nodded. "But you never did, so we took him instead."

"Who took him?"

She threw her head back and laughed as if any of this was funny. "The Clamors and the Sentras, of course."

Nico came to stand in front of Saylor. Her body popped and hummed with energy, and I knew it took everything in her not the rip the other lady's head off.

I too needed to focus. Saylor had played a part in Kolo's death. I couldn't forget that.

Saylor looked her up and down then stood up. "Get out of my face, Nico. You won't win, but you already know that."

Nico held her hands up, and I held my head down. We didn't have time for this.

Luckily, Kirk came to the rescue. He wrapped his arms around Nico and pulled her back. "Oh, come on, girl. We got work to do now. We'll deal with her later, okay?" He tried to walk her backward, but she pushed him away and went to sit down on her own, shooting both him and Saylor death rays.

"Got you a red-hot firecracker there," Chaz laughed, slapping his brother on the shoulder. "Don't see how you're ever gonna get that one trained." He laughed again before he sat down.

Toma looked from Saylor, to Nico, to Chaz. "She's not a dog to be trained by your brother or anyone else. You'd do well to remember that." He looked back to Nico. "Your attitude's not helping. Calm down." Finally, he turned back to Saylor. "You're lying, telling half-truths, and you're hiding something. Now, what's going on, spill it?"

Saylor reached out to touch his hand, giving him a sly look from under her eyelashes. She now cooed when she talked, her voice both condescending and saccharine.

"Come now, is that any way to speak to your wife? I've told you what I could, but I'm still talking. I haven't gotten up to leave yet."

My world tilted sideways. Wife? Toma was married? To Saylor? This made no sense at all. Why hadn't they told me? Why keep it a secret?

He shook his head. "We're not married anymore. You left me a long time ago, remember?"

She smiled as if reminiscing. "Good thing too, or I might have ended up in the gutter with you."

Toma smiled, it wasn't friendly. "I'm sure you would have killed me the first chance you got."

She nodded her agreement. "And your sister too." She looked to Nico to drive her point home. "Debates still out on you."

I couldn't take anymore. They could have their family re-union later, for now, we needed to focus. "Trent!" I yelled, causing the whole room to go silent. "Remember him? My buddy. My friend! He's missing." I turned to Saylor. "Now where the fuck is he?"

She tsked at me. "Your blood pressure can't sustain emotions at such a high level. Sit down and calm yourself. I'll tell you what I know."

I glared at her, but knew yelling and fussing would do no good. We needed to hear what she had to say.

She cleared her throat. "Okay then. We know that you came to see him a couple of weeks ago. Rhonda, his employee, told us."

"She wouldn't do that," I interrupted.

Saylor looked at me as if I was the dumbest person alive. "She would if we paid her well, and promised he wouldn't be hurt."

I counted to five, my breath ragged and raw. I sat still, digging my nails into my palms to keep from lunging. "Has he been hurt?" I asked, my voice pained and low.

She shook her head. "No more than normal. I won't let them kill him, don't worry about that."

Clink wasn't convinced. "But you're here, now."

Saylor smiled at him. "Nice of you to speak up, Clink. We've not finished questioning him yet." She turned to me. "He hasn't told us anything either. He denies you were even here. We now know that's a lie though."

What was her game? Whose side was she really on? I just couldn't tell anymore. "What will you say when you go back?" I asked her.

She cocked her head to the side and stared at me. "You mean will I call him a liar? No. It doesn't suit my purpose. I'm trying to help you, remember? I'll sacrifice him if I have to, but for now, he's safe, at least from me anyway."

I thought about him being tortured and beaten and could feel myself physically shudder. Saylor tried to give me a sympathetic look, but it came out more cocky than reassuring. "He's a grown man, Rekia. He'll be alright."

I tried to keep the skepticism out of my voice. "If it's all the same to you, I'd still like to know where he is. Clamor or Sentra?"

"He's here, under Clamor and Sentra guard. The Shinow won't allow us to take him off-world. Which is good for him, because I can protect him better this way. I'm on the ruling council. No lowly Clamor or Sentra guard dare defy me."

"But you can't order him released?"

She pursed her lips together. "That would be ridiculous. Why would I do that? What reason would I give? I love myself a lot more than I love him, or you, so don't expect too many heroics where either of you are concerned."

Fair enough. "What are you going to do now?" I asked.

She stood and brushed her clothes off. I'd forgotten she was from the same world as Toma and Nico. To her Trent's humble little house probably looked about one step up from the gutter. "I'm going home." She looked around and frowned. "I've been here long enough."

I wasn't satisfied. "Hey, lady." I moved closer. "You don't really expect us to trust you, do you?"

She cocked an eyebrow. "I helped you escape Clamor."

"Because it suited you and whatever plan you've got cooked up. What is it that you want? I can't help but feel like we're all chess pieces being moved around at your will."

She had the nerve to look pleased. Hell, she even beamed at me. "So nice of you to think so highly of me, Rekia. I like you as well. Now I must go. Toma, Nico, until we meet again."

Chaz waited until she'd closed the front door, then stood, pulling Clink up with him. He turned to me. "Aye, love, they probably sent her here as bait."

I didn't know about that. She seemed to have her own agenda. Still, maybe she wouldn't turn us in, but we couldn't take that chance. I raised my hand. Yet, I couldn't do it. Something prevented me from opening that portal. I didn't want to leave Trent. She'd said he was okay and possibly he was. I didn't trust her, though. Not where his life was concerned.

I needed a moment to think. This was my deal. I needed to do it alone. One person could be a lot stealthier than six. They needed to go. I needed to stay. It was as simple as that. I opened the portal, then stepped to the side, and waited for each one to go through. Hopefully, by the time they noticed I wasn't with them, it would be too late.

I waited a few seconds before turning around, and the first thing I saw was Clink, standing in front of me, arms folded, eyebrow raised. "So, what's the plan, Rekia?"

I sat down and glared at him. "It doesn't include you, so why are you here?"

He said down beside me, a bemused look on his face. "Where did you send them? Back to Lark?"

I nodded. "They'll be safe there. Why didn't you go with them and how did you know what I was planning? Are you psychic?"

He gave me a blank stare then shook his head. "It was written all over your face. Not sure how the others missed it. Besides, you need me. I can watch your back. Make sure you're okay. Two is always better than one."

I looked him over. He stared back unblinking. "I want him safe," I finally said.

Clink sat back and threw an arm over the couch. "And I want to help you. But I need to know what you're planning. We can't just walk in there half-cocked."

"You have no defensive powers," I pointed out.

He seemed nonplussed. "Doesn't mean I can't help you with the powers I do have. You'd be surprised."

Okay then. "I know this place pretty well. I come here a lot, for business, sometimes for pleasure." I stood and paced in a small circle. It was comforting, and helped to focus my thoughts. "There's only one jail in this city. Unless they've taken him to another town, I know where he is. The problem is getting to him."

Clink tapped a finger to his lips, looking deep in thought. A small smile slowly formed. "I'm not invisible," he said.

I tried not to groan. If this was the level of help I could expect from him, then he should have just gone back with the others. "Yes, I can see that. I'm looking dead at you." My voice shook with impatience.

He chuckled and dismissed my sarcasm with the wave of a hand. "I can be invisible when I astral project. If I want to, if I need to."

"And you're just telling me this now?"

"It's unpredictable, I can't always hold it, and I'd hate to be caught with my pants down, so to speak."

My pulse quickened as the possibilities rumbled through my mind. This could work. "You remember what he looks like?"

"Never forget a face."

I stopped pacing and sat down, a little dizzy from all the back and forth. "But you don't know where he's at or how to get there. How long can you stay invisible?"

He thought about it for a minute. "Sometimes seconds, sometimes minutes, it all depends on how I'm feeling. Right now, I couldn't tell you with any certainty."

It was better than nothing, and about the best we had right now. We talked for a few more hours going over details and exit strategies. I could only imagine what was being done to Trent, how he was being treated. It made something fierce and protective rise in me as I counted down the hours to nightfall.

I knew where Trent kept his lasso, and I wondered if he'd used it on them, or been completely caught off guard. I went into his bedroom, pushed a few buttons, then stood back as the wall opened for me.

I let out a sigh of relief, as I saw the black rope curled up in its little box, awaiting Trent's command. I put my hand on it and bit my lip to keep from crying out from the burning pain it sent rippling through my arm. "This is for Trent," I whispered to it like he'd taught me so long ago, for occasions just like this one. "Let me take you to him." We'd practiced this enough that it recognized my voice and knew that it could trust me. The burning sensation stopped, and I wasted no time gathering it up.

MOONLIGHT LIT UP THE sky, making it hard to be incognito. Trent lived about two miles from the town jail. Clink and I had no choice but to hoof it. The sidewalk crunched loudly under our feet, making me cringe with every step we took.

"I don't think anyone will notice us as long as we keep our heads down, and avoid eye contact," Clink offered.

Well, that was easier said than done. Still, we made it to the alleyway behind the jail with no problem. Here the grass was cut down, and there was no trash or litter to be found. Also, the air smelled clean and fresh. It's where officers of the court took their coffee breaks, so I guessed they kept it as neat and tidy as they could.

I looked at Clink, who busily looked up and down the alleyway. "Are you ready?"

He rotated his neck and flexed his hands backward. "Be back in a minute,"

But he didn't go anywhere. "You're still standing right here."

Irritation marred his face. "No, I'm in there. Don't you know how this works? I need to concentrate."

I snapped my mouth shut immediately. I didn't want to do anything to mess this up. I leaned up against the wall and waited for him to come back.

After about ten minutes, he straightened and looked at me. "He's in a room in the basement. His people are standing guard with the Clamors and the Sentras. It doesn't look like they're letting them touch him. He looks good. I think the Clamor and Sentra are here at a very thin courtesy. They can't get to him like they want. His people won't allow it."

That wasn't really good news. "How long do you think they're going to put up with that? The Sentra and Clamors are a proud people. They have diamond sidewalks and platinum buildings just to show who has the biggest stick. They'll only hold off for so long." Shinow had dealings with some pretty powerful worlds, and were invaluable to open market trading, which was probably why they hadn't already made a move.

"There were two guards for each world," Clink said.

Did I really expect them to make this easy? I tried not to groan. "He has six people guarding him? Is that what you're telling me?"

Clink nodded. "Don't worry about it. I have a plan. Can you create a portal that gets us inside, right where he's at?"

I shook my head. "We can leave now, go to another world, and then when I create the portal, I'll make it right inside the jail."

"Good enough, just follow my lead."

Right. This didn't feel right to me. "How am I supposed to know what to do?" I knew my voice sounded dubious, but walking into a situation with no known course of action just seemed, stupid really.

Clink didn't seem fazed by my skepticism. He shrugged as nonchalantly as ever, then stared at the side of the building that led to the jail house as if waiting for me to open the damn portal.

"Fine you want me to trust you I will, but you better not make me regret it."

We stepped through the portal to a world full of sunshine and light.

"Where are we?" Clink asked, looking around at the endless trees and forest full of grass.

"Away from civilization. We don't need the trouble."

I held my hand out, ready to open another gateway. "Are you sure you know what you're doing?" I asked.

He gave me the side eye. "I like living as much as you do, Rekia. Trust me, I've thought this through."

I sighed. These guys had proven themselves to be trustworthy time and time again. For me, it was just hard to go from working alone and depending only on myself, to suddenly having a group of people working with me.

It felt jarring, almost as if my whole little private world was being taken away from me and there was nothing I could do about it. On the other hand, though, it felt good to have people to lean on, to help out, and to have my back.

I looked at Clink and nodded. "I'll follow your lead, but just remember if we get caught, I can send you to places where they'll never find your body." The last part was delivered deadpan.

He laughed heartily, then beamed at me. "You know, Rekia, I like your style."

Well, flattery will get you everywhere Mr. Clink. "I like your style too. Just don't make me regret trusting you."

I opened the portal into a utility closet, praying no janitor was there picking out a broom or something. It was small, crowded, and had the nauseating smell of pine cleaner, bleach, and dried up dirt and mold. Talk about your bad combinations.

I pulled the collar of my shirt over my nose, then slowly opened the door. It was the basement, so for now it was empty, as I imagined not many people came down here. "What now?" I asked Clink in a whisper.

He peeked his head out and looked around. "I think it's that way," he said, pointing up the hall.

We slowly walked out of the closet, mindful of our surroundings, knowing the smallest thing could give us away. We'd taken about five steps before he stopped at a brown door on the right. "He's in there. When I tell you to open the door, do it."

I nodded and focused my telekinesis on the door handles. As soon as he gave the word, I flew the door off its hinges and stepped back. At first, the only thing I saw were the six shocked faces of the guards. Then, the guards faded away, and I saw two different guards in a fight with what looked like three inmates trying to escape.

It only took me a second to realize that Clink had used his skill to recreate, in order to cause a diversion.

I wasted no time taking out the Clamor and Sentra guards. They were the ones with the power and the biggest threat to me. I held my hands together, then pulled them apart, causing all four men to bang into the wall repeatedly until they fell. The two Shinow guards I simply shackled with their own handcuffs, and took their keys.

Meanwhile, Clink created three of himself to further throw them off. While he stayed busy with his antics, I ran to the cell door. Trent stood slack-jawed at the scene in front of him, his eyes jumping from the conjured-up guards fighting to the six laying on the floor.

With the wave of a hand, I wrench the cell open. He was in my arms in seconds. "Later," I said raising my hand. I knew we needed to move fast. "Clink!" I yelled, before opening the gateway and jumping through.

We skidded through ten different worlds before I felt safe enough to go to our desired destination. I'd stopped on the fifth world to recharge with protein and carbs, then again on the tenth, before finally taking us where we needed to go.

My living room on my father's home world was dark and closed up when we portaled in. I checked to make sure both men were with me, before collapsing on the sofa, out of breath and sweating. "Well that was interesting," I chuckled halfheartedly.

Trent sat down beside me, then reached over to place a quick kiss on my lips. "Thank you, Rekia."

I kissed him back and savored the flavor of onions, from the last world we'd recharged on. "My pleasure." My voice came out tired and exasperated as I handed him his lasso.

He nodded me thanks and sat it to the side. "Guess you've finally succeeded in turning me into an outlaw, huh?"

I laughed and laced my hand with his. "Didn't your mamma tell you to stay away from girls like me?" I teased.

He kissed me again. "My mamma ain't never met no girls like you. You're one of a kind, and you know that, you just like hearing me say it."

That I did. I started to reach out to him, but my phone rang, bringing me back to the present. "It's me, Robin, is everything okay?" my cousin asked as soon as I put the phone to my ear.

I stood and walked into the kitchen. "Everything's fine. Trent's here, though. I need you to pick him up some groceries, and anything else he might need."

She gave an exaggerated sigh, but I knew that she'd do it. "How long will he be here?"

"Until this thing blows over. You just make sure you check on him every day." I opened the fridge and pulled out a bottle of water. "Also make sure you keep a close eye on this place. I don't want him hurt, got it?"

I could practically see her rolling her eyes through the phone. "Yeah, I got it. Are you okay?"

"Fine, just get over here as soon as you can. If I don't make it." I paused, not wanting to say what I had to, but knowing I needed to. "You make sure he gets back to his home world. I'm counting on you, okay? Just keep him safe if I'm not able." I hated to say those words to her, probably as much as she hated to hear them, but burying our heads in the sand wouldn't make the situation go away. "Tell them I kidnapped him if you have to. I don't want him to lose everything because of me."

I wasn't sure if that would work, but I wanted to shield him as much as I could. He hadn't asked for any of this, and his only crime was trying to protect me, willing to lay down his life so I didn't have to lay down mine. It warmed my chest that he would do anything to shield me, but also made my heart ache that he had to.

Robin let out a long exhale of air. "Anything else, oh great one?"

I counted to five before I spoke. "Just don't let anything happen to him, Robin. He means a lot. He's a good friend to me, okay."

Her voice sounded annoyed, but not really. "Oh, I'll take care of the man." She hung up the phone.

I walked back into the living room where Clink and Trent were deep in conversation. Both men stood when I entered. "Robin's coming over as soon as she can. You have plenty here, but she'll bring you more."

I went to Trent and took both his hands in mine. "She's going to check on you every day." I squeezed his fingers, then sighed because I knew he wouldn't like this next part. "You were kidnapped. You didn't escape. I kidnapped you and held you hostage. If I don't come back, she'll see you home."

He pulled me into a hug. "What'd you mean if you don't come back, Re? Why can't we figure this out together? I don't like you going off like this."

I pushed him away, then folded my arms in front of me. "You know me well enough to know that I'm going to do what I have to."

He pointed his finger at me. "That ain't nothing but stubbornness making you act this way. Just try to be careful. I don't think I can do this world without you."

I tried to lighten my voice. "Well technically we live in different worlds so..."

He raised his brow, and I gave him one last kiss, then turned to Clink. "You ready, cowboy?"

He nodded, and I opened the portal to take us to three different worlds, stopping quickly on a fourth for food so that we could recharge, then on to Lark.

"It's about fucking time," Chaz said as soon as Clink and I appeared.

He sat in the living room with the others, all looking worried and weary.

Clink reached out and pulled Chaz into a long intimate kiss. "We're okay. We didn't get hurt, and all is well with Trent. So let's focus on more important things." He kissed him again, then touched their foreheads together. "You can ream me out later, okay." They smiled at each other as if sharing some private joke.

I addressed the others. "While we were rescuing Trent, I had an idea."

I sat down beside Toma and got straight to it. "I think we need to kidnap Saylor."

Toma vetoed me outright. "You need to get that out of your head. She's on the high council of Sentra. Not going to happen." His voice sounded normal, but I could clearly hear an undercurrent of anger there.

I looked at him. Was he trying to protect her, or us? "It's not like you're Sentrans in good standing." I reminded him.

Nico shook her head. "Nor will we ever be if we follow this foolish scheme of yours. What'd you want to kidnap her for anyway? She's not going to tell us anything unless she wants to."

I felt helpless and alone. Somehow, I had to get through to them. No one would make eye contact with me, which meant they all thought it was a bad idea. "She's in the middle of all of this! She's playing both sides to fit her own agenda. Doesn't that make you curious?"

Blank stares all around. I looked at each of them, willing somebody to speak up on my behalf. If they didn't like my plan and had a better one, then I was all ears.

Finally, Toma found his voice. "She's not as easy to handle as you may think." He chuckled softly to himself and shook his head as if reaching out to some distant memory from long ago.

I gave him a hard look. That was not the response I'd hoped for. We couldn't just sit around and wait for the next attack. I didn't know about the others, but I wanted my life back, dammit! "So, what should we do then?" I asked no one in particular.

Toma steepled his hands together. "I don't like the Clamors having such a large impact on Sentra business. Damn Welvina and his money-making schemes." His voice rose a few octaves toward the end.

Chaz whispered in Clink's ear and listened while the other man whispered back. "We have an idea." He looked from Nico to Toma. "If we could prove to the people of your world who the real killers are, will it make a difference?"

Toma nodded. "If we can be falsely accused and lose everything then so can they. If we can prove that the senators were behind Kolo's murder that's even better. It gives us our standing back, plus removes them from power."

Nico's face held the doubt she must have felt. "How are we supposed to do that?"

This time Clink answered. "I can recreate the same scene I did before. The one where all three of them killed Kolo. With help, I can make it so that every citizen of Sentra sees it. It would be good to get as many of them in the same spot as possible. I can try to focus the same image as many places as I can, but I'm not strong enough to do it alone."

If he could make all, or even most, hell I'd settle for just a few Sentra, see what happened, then we might be able to end at least some of this.

"How do we expose the other part though?" Kirk asked. "I mean we can show them the killing, but what about the scheme to take Sentra and Clamor money from its citizens? Clink?"

The other man shrugged. "Don't see why not. I've seen it firsthand so it shouldn't be too hard to call an image up. But will that work on the Clamors? They seem the most dangerous of the two."

Kirk got a thoughtful look on his face, then held up his hand. "I remember when I was there, hearing a few of the guards talk about suspicious activity on their bank accounts."

I pondered this for a second. "So maybe Welvina and the others haven't covered their tracks as well as they thought?"

"That's one explanation," Kirk allowed. "If we could get Clink to prove it, we may be able to bring down both worlds."

Clink shook his head and let out a small sigh. "I can't do it alone, though. I need help."

"What do you need?" I asked.

"Glone."

I almost choked on my own spit, "Why do you need Glone?"

"He can do what I do, except he doesn't have to be in the exact spot, and he wouldn't turn me into the cops if I go back home."

Was he serious? Hadn't Chaz told him everything? "No. Why tell the police, when he can just, you know, kill you?"

He actually laughed. "That's ridiculous, Glone would never hurt me."

I blinked hard, wondering if this was a joke. "We barely escaped last time," I shuddered when I thought about Glone and his minions chasing us through the underworld of Chaz's home.

Chaz shrugged. "What do we have to lose? After all we've been through, are we really going to let Glone keep us from achieving our goals?

"You're not scared of him?" I asked.

Before he could answer, Nico's cold, hard voice cut in. "If we need him, then let's go get him. If we bring him here, he won't have his friends to back him up, and we'd have the advantage."

Clink's voice was so loud it boomed. "We'll ask him for his help. If he says no, then that's the end of it."

Chaz shot him a death glare. His voice was like ice when it came out. "Figures. I guess I shouldn't be surprised."

Clink reached out to touch his shoulder, but Chaz moved his hand away. I think we all might've gasped as we'd never seen either of them as mad as they seemed right now, certainly not at each other, anyway.

Clink sighed heavily. "Clear your mind of the clutter, Chaz, and you'll see that kidnapping Glone is the dumbest way to get his help."

Chaz glared, and Kirk came to stand beside him, putting a comforting hand on his shoulder, then both men gave Clink a look that would skin a cat.

Clink tilted his head to the side, but he didn't look in the least intimidated. He almost looked amused as his gaze shifted from one brother to the other, like he wished they would try him. "I'm not changing my mind. You wanna kidnap Glone? You do it without my help. I don't want no part of that bullshit."

Kirk looked to his brother. "Chaz, let me—"

Chaz cut him off with a shake of the head. He sounded sadder and more resigned than I'd ever heard him, when he said, "No, Clink is right. We'll just do it Clink's way, and hope for the best." He reached back and patted his brother on the hand. "It's okay. Everything's fine. Leave Clink alone. His plan could work."

With that Chaz turned and walked slowly down the hall. He looked, if I had to pick a word, heartbroken. Clearly, I had no clue what was going on, but something told me before we left Crimson a second time, I'd know way more about Clink, Chaz, and Kirk then I ever wanted to.

Chapter 14

The next morning, we all stood, backpacks on our shoulders, and determination in our hearts.

"Can we go straight underground this time?" Chaz asked. "I'd hate for the red men to get us before we even get started." He seemed a little better than he had the night before, but not by much. Shoulders downcast, expression wary, I suddenly wondered just what we were walking into if it elicited this type of reaction from Chaz.

I made sure I had everything I thought we might need. Starting above ground had never even been a consideration anyway, and there was no use standing around wondering.

If there was one thing I was confident in, it was that we could take on anything thrown our way. Still, I felt a pinch of reserve as I opened the portal that would take us to the underworld of Crimson.

We arrived in the same room we had, the very first time we'd visited. Glone stood in the corner talking to another man of similar height. The way he pointed and gestured led me to believe he was giving orders of some sort. All that stopped the moment he noticed our presence in the room.

He turned to us with a glare. His gaze on one man. "I see stupidity is still your number one skill, Chaz." He put two fingers in his mouth and whistled loud enough to make my ears squeak.

In seconds, about fifty hostile-looking men and women surrounded us. Some had sticks, and bats, where others looked powerful enough to break our necks with one hand. "We didn't come to fight," I yelled, throwing my hands up in the air.

Glone walked up to me, his face so close to mine I could smell the taters and onions he must have eaten for breakfast. "That was a neat little trick you pulled last time. I could use something like that around here. Gives the phrase 'world-wide trading' a whole new meaning."

"You mean worldwide stealing, don't you?" I sneered, pushing him out of my personal space.

He held his hands out in front of him. Though he smiled, his eyes never lost their hard granite look. "Look around you, babe. What the fuck makes you think you have a choice here?"

Clink scoffed, and stepped in front of me, causing Glone to take a few steps back. Huh? Well that was... interesting. "Stop the bullshit, Glone. We need your help." His voice softened. "*I* need your help."

Glone just stared at Clink, giving no indication of what he really thought, so I decided to try and sweeten the deal. "I can pay you, a lot." I'd hoped the lure of money would some-how make him drop his defenses.

Hearing Chaz groan, let me know just how off my cal-culations were. This wasn't Clamor, or Sentra, I'd have to re-member that.

Glone's face took on an even harder look as he tore his gaze away from Clink to look back at me. He waved a hand around the cave. "What exactly do you think we need money for, down here? You think we want to go up there?" He pointed toward the ceiling. "Get a little red house, find a little wife, and live happily ever after?"

His voice rose in its mockery. "Fuck that shit! We're criminals, and we're down here because we want to be. I like stealing. I like making my own rules and answering only to myself. So, let me ask you, what the fuck can you do for me?"

He got back in my space. This time it was Toma who pushed him away. "Don't." His voice was low, lethal, and actually sent chills up my spine. This was not good, and I could see it all going south real soon. I just didn't know what to do to defuse the situation.

I looked to Clink. He nodded, then turned back to Glone. "You gonna make me beg? Is that what you want, Glone? Me on my knees in front of you begging for it?"

Glone honest to goodness flushed. Maybe we were on to something here, as Clink seemed to have a certain way with the other man. I didn't understand it, but, hey if it worked...

I looked to Chaz, lips tight, fists clenched, he stared at the two men before, him jaws locked with attention.

Glone started to reach out, thought better of it and dropped his hands to his side. He walked over to Clink, got in his personal space. "Now why would I want you to beg, Cli? You ain't never gotta beg me for nothing."

Clink moved a step closer. "Don't play games with me, Glone. I didn't come here for your shit."

Glone took a step back. He glanced around the room as if making sure there were more of his people here than ours. "Why you here, then Clink? What else do I have that you want?"

Clink shook his head. "Glone."

Glone clicked his tongue, then looked at me. "I want her to take me where I want, when I want, no questions asked."

Chaz shook his head. "She won't do that."

Glone glared. "Did I ask you?"

Chaz struck out, but Clink stopped him before his fist could make contact. "We didn't come here for that," he hissed at the other man.

Chaz shook Clink off him, his face red with anger. Kirk came to stand by his brother's side. He glared at Clink. "Don't do that again."

Clink and Glone both came to attention at this. Glone was the first to speak. "The fuck you gonna do if he does?"

Kirk cracked his neck from side to side. He looked at Glone. "Wanna find out?"

Oh, good grief. Were they serious? When the hell had things shifted this bad? What did they know that we didn't, because somehow, it'd become Chaz and Kirk against Clink and Glone and that made no damn sense at all.

I cleared my voice, causing all four pair of eyes to turn my way. "I won't be your toy soldier, Glone," I said, putting that ludicrous idea to rest. "We need your help. I'm asking here."

He rubbed an irritated hand down his face. "You're asking alright, but what're you offering? I told you what I wanted. Now how you gonna make it happen?"

I looked to Toma and Nico letting them know they were free to jump in at any moment. Nico sighed heavily then spoke up. "All you want to do is steal and be an outlaw. So how can we help you? What do we have that you can't just steal for yourself?"

Glone looked around the room at all his friends, then to Nico and Toma. "Give me unlimited access to your world." He turned to me. "And to yours, and I'll do what you want me to."

He was crazy if he thought I'd ever let him loose in my world. I shook my head. "You don't even know what we want from you, and you don't know anything about our worlds. For all you know, Toma, Nico and I are all from the same place."

He gave me a look that said he'd expected so much more from me. "Nothing about you." He pointed to me. "And them." He pointed to Toma and Nico. "Are the same. Your powers are completely different and that itself tells me that your worlds are different. You're the only one that can open a portal, I know that."

I rolled my shoulders and stood up a little straighter. I wanted him to see that I wasn't backing down from this. "I'm not giving you my world. Name something else."

He thought about it for a second. "What I want is for you to owe me a favor, anything I ask."

I crossed my arms in front of me. "Within reason. I won't do just anything. We want your help, but we'll do without it if we have to."

He tilted his head. "Four favors then. You give me four favors and I'll give you anything you want within my power.

That's why you're here, right? You need my power." He looked at Clink. "Why else would you be here?"

Not wanting him to get lost in Clink's eyes again, I spoke louder to bring his attention back my way. "Four favors within reason."

He pulled a small, red, universal phone out of his pocket and handed it to me. "Put your number in. I'd hate for us to not be connected, you know."

I programmed the number to my universal phone and handed it back to him. He called immediately causing my side to jingle and ring.

I raised an eyebrow. "You don't trust me?"

"Don't trust nobody, now what do you want?" He waved his hand, and the others disappeared as quickly as they'd appeared.

As we told him about Toma and Nico's world and what we needed from him, his face went from disinterested, to amused, to downright predatory. "If your world is really made of diamonds and jewels, then how did you stop this lot from coming home with the gold?" He pointed to Clink, Chaz, and Kirk.

I snapped my fingers. "Four favors, remember? I need you to focus."

He looked out the doorway, and for the first time, I saw his face take on a vulnerable look. "I'll take one of those favors now."

If that would move things along and cement his help, then why not? "What do you want?"

He walked out of the room. "Follow me," he said, pointing down the hallway.

The longer we walked, the more I had to fight down the urge to hurl. The scent was horrifying and smelled like death itself. The stench of open sores, vomit, sweat, and blood, assaulted my nostrils relentlessly.

The room he led us to was large and filled wall to wall with small sleeping cots. Buckets sat by each bed. Some filled with throw up, some empty, some even had water in them. Man-made IV's hung from a couple of beds, some had what looked like thinly held together feeding tubes. Many beds had what I assumed were family members beside them.

There was one man and one woman walking around, asking questions, writing on clipboards, and checking each patient. The room held about twenty of these cots, and every one of them was filled.

There were no vacancies here, and I wondered what would happen if someone else suddenly got sick. Where would they put them, because there was no way this room could fit another cot in here.

There were two desks at the front of the room, which I guessed belonged to the man and woman who seemed to be doing rounds. In the corner stood three red filing cabinets that I assumed housed medical records, which was a good thing, as at least they were keeping detailed notes.

Glone walked straight over to a cot where a woman with bright red hair lay holding a blood-soaked shirt to her side. "This here is my sister, Cherry," he said.

Clink' s eyes took on a wide horrified look. He walked over to the bed and placed his hand in hers. "What the hell happened, love?" He seemed so concerned. Watching the terrified look on his face, I figured the two must be close.

Glone gently pushed a few errant hair strands of hair out of her face. "She took one to the side last night trying to get bandages and more food."

Clink's head whipped around to Glone, his eyes filled with fear. "Fina?"

An almost wounded expression passed Glone's face and he nodded. "I'll keep her safe. Always." He pointed toward the ceiling. "She's up top, protected."

Cherry grunted, a grimace on her face. "We love her too, Clink. Never let anything happen to her."

I wondered who Fina was, but figured now wasn't the time to ask. Instead I took a good look around. Some of the patients were kids and teenagers. Were they here because of their deeds or those of their parents? Either way, I didn't like what I saw. "These people need serious help, Glone, what the hell?"

He nodded. "I agree. That's where you come in. My first favor is for you to zip out, leaving the others here of course, and come back with enough medical supplies, food, and clothes to last at least another year."

I would have done that without him asking. I'd planned to do that the moment I stepped into this room. I looked around, taking in the despair and hopelessness of the place. "I can't carry it on my own. It'll take several trips. If they have to stay here, then you'll have to come with me. Just to help out, of course."

He looked down at his sister, a fond smile taking over his features, then bent and placed a small kiss on her forehead. He stood after that, that cold hard look back on his face in an instant. "Ready when you are."

Toma started to interrupt, but I shook my head. This was not something up for debate. Could it be a trap? Sure, but it was a risk I was willing to take, and frankly, after witnessing the love and concern Glone had for his sister, I didn't think he'd pass up the chance to get her some help just to play out some petty revenge scheme.

I looked to Glone. He was busy watching Clink. What the hell? Something odd was going on with those two, but now was not the time to address it. "We're going to be bringing a lot of stuff back through. Do you have a good place to put it?" I asked him.

He nodded. "We have three rooms we use for storage, but only one has stuff in it, and that's not much, as it is."

"Show me."

We walked to two large empty rooms, then one with a few crates scattered here and there. I thought back to the faces of those kids and felt my heart clench. This was all they had to live on, and all because their parents chose to take the easy way out. It wasn't right, it wasn't fair, and there wasn't a damn thing I could do about it.

I swallowed down my despair. Sometimes, on some of the worlds I visited, I wished I had the power to make it better. To end the suffering, to bring about some sort of peace. It never ended well, though, and I'd learned a few hard lessons about keeping my head down and minding my own business.

We walked back to the hospital room, and said goodbye to the others before I opened a portal, pulling Glone through with me.

I transported us outside a Sam's club on a world very much like my own. Glone seemed steady on his feet, which told me this wasn't his first portal hop, something I found interesting. I put it away to think about later.

Walking over to the side of the building, I manipulated a few keys on the wall. A brick moved out of place, revealing my Sam's card, money, and a few other items for this world.

Glone looked at me sideways, causing me to laugh a little.

"Always be prepared, right?" I asked.

He nodded. "Right."

Glone's eyes lit up the minute we entered the store. That old predatory look came back full force as if he was plotting how to rob the whole damn place without anyone noticing.

I grabbed him by the arm and pulled him over to the shopping carts. "We are not here to steal," I whispered. "Everything we get will be paid for by me. Now grab this." I handed him one of the large rollaway carts that could hold just about anything. "Fill it high with everything you need. I'll get one, and you can fill that up as well. Then we'll repeat. Once done we'll take them to a far corner of the parking lot, away from any cameras, and pushed them through the portal, you got that?"

With a good amount of condescension in his voice and a small twinkle in his eye, he said, "After you, then."

I moved past him and showed my card to the lady at the door that allowed us entrance inside. The first two carts he piled high with bandages, towels, soap, deodorant, toothpaste, toothbrushes, alcohol, peroxide, dishwashing liquid and washing powders.

I pushed my cart, straining from the weight of it. "You have washing machines down there?" I asked.

He came behind me, pushing his cart with no effort at all. "You'd be surprised what we got, girl."

I turned toward the woman behind the desk. "We're donating supplies. Is it okay for us to leave these here until we finish?"

She nodded her approval, and we both snatched up two more carts. These two he piled high with toilet tissue, napkins, plates, silverware, and books.

The next two and the four after that were filled with packages of bottled water, along with a few other choice beverages. From there it was strictly food, clothes, and new beds to go in the sick room, along with bed linen.

It took about two hours to pay for it all. I stayed at the register loading everything up as Glone took the paid-for carts out of the store. Finally, we were done. The last two carts we took out together.

Glone had found a dark corner in the back of the store parking lot. "First, we shove the supplies through, then we continue on," he said.

One by one, we pushed them inside the portal. I left the heavy lifting to Glone as he didn't seem to have a problem with it. Once done, I closed the portal and looked at Glone. "I've got a friend on another world, runs a medical supply company. We can probably get antibiotics and the like, but it's a risk." On my world, you couldn't just sell antibiotics on the street, you had to have a prescription, on Percipco, where my friend lived, not so much.

He didn't even blink. "And after that?"

"Well, for now, we hit a few more stores like Sam's Club. I assume you have electricity down there?"

He nodded. "You'd be surprised the skills and previous employment some of us held before going rogue."

I took a minute to think. "So how about we get a little more of what we already have, plus some freezers, refrigerators, and stoves? Maybe some grills. Then we'll get the medical supplies."

Suspicion narrowed his eyes. "That's way more than we agreed upon. This still counts as only one of my favors. I'm not letting you off that easy."

"And I'm not doing this for you, there were kids down there!"

"They have parents."

"How many are yours?

He didn't laugh. "You're not funny, though I can see that you think you are. Let's just hurry. The sooner we finish with this the better."

"Well at least we agree on one thing," I mumbled, not sure if I wanted him to hear me or not.

The lift of an eyebrow told me that he'd heard me just fine.

The last I knew, Rin's business had been shrinking quite a bit, so he would probably be thrilled with the amount of money I was ready to spend.

I pulled out my phone to give him a head's up that we were coming his way and he needed to get as many supplies together as he could.

In the meantime, we went to a couple of my hangouts, picking up the money I needed for the different worlds we were about to enter. Then we hit six other stores, and two more medical supply companies, before finally stepping into Rin's world.

We were assaulted the moment our feet hit the floor. Four Clamors stood ready. The look of shock on Glone's face would have been hilarious any other time, but not now, not when we were literally fighting for our lives.

"Attack!" I yelled, letting him know that these men weren't to be trifled with.

He nodded, and just like that, the fight was on. I'd learned my lesson on Clamor. I couldn't overpower them, but I could rip them apart. They stood in front of me, big hunkering forms, so secure in their superiority. The one on my right raised his leg, but I'd been through that before and already knew where it was headed. I leaned back and dropped to my knees, sliding across the floor.

The look on their faces said I was just preventing the inevitable. Good. Let them think that, they'd never really witnessed the true extent of my power. Now was the perfect time to show them what they'd been missing.

Two of them came at me, and I let them get as close as I dared, before using my telekinesis. Once they were a few inches away, I put my hands together, then pulled them apart, watching as chunks of them fell around us like rain.

I looked to Glone. The speed and strength he displayed left me staggering. So, this was why Chaz and the others feared him. The two Clamors probably didn't know what hit them. Punch after punch, he alternated between the two men in front of him, breaking them down to their knees, then going in relentlessly until it was clear that neither man would move again.

A part of me wondered where he'd been when we'd been fighting the Clamors earlier. Another part told me to shut the hell up and focus.

Glone and I stood back to back, both our shoulders rising and falling from the strength of our fight. My breath came in heavy spurts as I looked down at the dead bodies surrounding us. Then my eyes landed on a trembling figure trying desperately to stay hidden under a turned over table.

"Fucking traitor," I hissed, anger making my fists curl. "Come out Rin, before I rip your ass to shreds." Why had he betrayed me? Surely the lure of a few extra dollars couldn't have been that appealing to him. Certainly not worth my life. We'd been friends for a long time, and this, I just didn't understand.

Shaking like a windstorm, and clutching a brown money bag in his hand, he stood, yet his eyes seemed unable to meet my own.

Something in me died in that moment because I knew beyond a doubt that he'd sold me out for a few measly coins. Anger rose in me like a hurricane. My fingers flexed back and forth, and I had to stop myself from doing something I knew I'd regret later.

"Look at me," I said, my voice hard as stone. I wanted to hurt him. To hurt him bad, because just the thought of going back to that prison left me shaking. How could he do this? Didn't our years of friendship mean anything?

"I'm sorry." His voice was barely above a whisper.

I shook my head in disgust. "I was bringing you money, helping your business, helping you out. Why did you turn me over to the Clamors?"

Still not able to look me in the eyes, he answered. "Because I wanted more."

Because he wanted more? The greedy bastard. Before I could form a proper reply, I felt a shift of wind and when it cleared Rin was on the floor, his head hanging at a very odd angle. Glone stood over top of him, righteous indignation all over his face. "Fucking snitch," he sneered, spitting on the other man.

Did he just... A revolt started in my gut and worked its way up. I dropped to my knees and cradle Rin's head in my lap, tears making my eyes bleary and tight. Rin was one of my oldest friends, and yeah, he'd betrayed me, but I never would have killed him for it. Never.

I turned my heated gaze on the one who'd started all of this. He stood in the same spot, still sneering down at the man he'd just killed.

I wanted to hurt him bad. He was a snake without conscience. Rin had been unarmed, yet Glone had killed him as if he held a thirty-ton nuke.

I let my anger take complete control, and before I knew it, I'd lifted him in the air and flung him across the room. His body made a loud thumping sound as it hit the wall and crumpled to the floor.

He didn't stay down for long. He came at me quicker than lightening and before I could defend myself, his hands wrapped around my throat. "He was a dirty traitor. What would you have me do? Kill the pig before it squeals."

He let me go, and I rubbed my hand repeatedly over my neck trying to lessen the pain. "What?" I asked, my voice hollow and scratchy. I turned back to Rin. Backstabber or not, he didn't deserve this. "Glone come on, man. This shit here was wrong. You have to see that."

Gathering up supplies, he spared me a disgusted look, before continuing with his task. "It's done, so help me get this shit, so I can take it back to people who really need it."

Now was not the time. But later... "This isn't over."

He grunted and kept right on with his task. I wanted to push it, to rage. Yet I understood the clock was pressing down on us and now was not the time for a lesson in morality. But later, later I'd make sure to bring it up again.

Chapter 15

We arrived back in the room with the supplies. A small group had formed and seemed to be working together to stock and arrange everything. Walking into the next two store rooms, we saw the exact same thing.

These people moved like a well-oiled machine. It was almost disconcerting how organized they were. They were all criminals. One would expect at least a little fighting and disorder. Of course, it could just all be a front, and they'd be back at each other's throats the moment we made our exit.

I shrugged, deciding it wasn't important enough for me to keep thinking about. We walked to the sick room, and I was shocked at the difference. Someone must have sprayed some serious odor ban in here because, though not completely gone, the stench was much more tolerable now.

The beds we'd bought had all been arranged and put together, the new bedspreads and sheets covering them, making the people in them look more comfortable.

Cherry was one of them. She was now all patched up, cleaned, and resting peacefully.

Apparently, someone had been in here playing doctor because everyone seemed to be sporting new bandages and cleaned wounds. The place had been cleaned too, and the smell of Pine Sol and Clorox were much more prevalent now.

The shock must have registered on my face because Glone took one look at me and smiled, nodding at the changes around us. "Like I told you before, Rekia, we have all types of professions down here. A few doctors and nurses have gotten themselves into trouble over the years. They can't go back up there, so..."

Believe it or not, this actually made me feel a little better. Not just that we'd gotten the supplies they needed, but also, because there were people here who could take care of the children and truly knew how to do it.

That made it easier for me to walk away. Not that it excused what that fucker Glone had done, but for now, I guess we'd keep that as our little secret. I locked eyes with him, but the careless lift of his shoulder told me he didn't care one way or another.

He looked around taking in the difference again, and though his face still held a frown, I could tell from the light in his eyes, and the small smile fighting to survive on his lips, that he was pleased.

His gaze landed on Clink and held. Maybe it was the way his eyes immediately went vulnerable, or the small nod of Clink's head, or maybe it was the rage I saw coming from Chaz, or the insecure way he suddenly grabbed Clink's hand, but in that moment, I knew that one of the reasons Glone had agreed to help, had everything to do with the tall, dread-locked man before me.

There was a story there because they were still staring at each other and Chaz's eyes were now black, while Glone had a look of yearning on his face like nothing I'd ever seen.

This was bad, could turn even worse in an instant. I hurried to clear my throat, hoping to break the spell and bring temperaments back to a somewhat normal level.

Glone looked at me, his eyes never losing that soft, vulnerable look. His struggle to not look Clink's way was palpable. "Thank you." This time he did steal a glance at Clink, but then quickly looked away again.

Focusing his attention back on me, Glone closed his eyes for a few seconds before speaking again. "I'm man enough to realize that you went far and above what I asked of you. I may be a thief, but I keep my word, and I honor my debts. I'll help you deal with your problems." He rubbed a hand over his goatee and looked around. "Matter of fact, once I tell the others what you did, how you paid for all of this out of pocket, they'll be willing to help as well."

I looked to Clink and blinked hard at his expression. The look of awe and adoration his face held as he looked at Glone, said more than words ever could.

Glone came to stand in front of Clink, the electricity crackling between the two had me grinding my teeth because we didn't have time for this.

As swift as fire, Glone grabbed Clink by the hips, pulling the other man to him, lifting his face for a kiss.

Chaz reacted immediately. He hit Glone with a quickness and a power that he'd no doubt borrowed from the man himself. Glone was up in a second. Blood pouring from his lips, he wiped it away then kicked Chaz in the face, following it up with a punch to the jaw.

Chaz made a move to bulldoze Glone but the other man flipped it around and pinned Chaz to the ground sitting on top of him. All the fight seemed to have gone out of Chaz, and now he just lay there glowering.

Kirk flew across the room. His long legs meant that it only took him a few seconds to reach them. He stared down at his brother and the other man, fists clenched at his side, his voice hard and angry. "Get the fuck off him, Glone. This shit ended a long time ago."

Clink was in front of him before he had a chance to do more. "Interfering will only make things worse. I'm telling you, don't." His voice was deadly serious, and even I took a step back at the lethal undertones.

Still, this shit had to end. I looked to Clink. "Then you need to handle it." I stared at him for a second, incredulous at the passive role he seemed to be taking in all of this.

It's not that I didn't understand the urge to fight for the one you loved, but we were in the middle of a war, and Glone and Chaz wanted to argue over who got to pull Clink's dreadlocks the longest. Get the fuck outta here. This shit had to end immediately.

But by now Glone had Chaz by the neck, choking the life out of him, and finally, Clink reacted. Knocking Glone back, Clink snatched Chaz up and pulled the other man to him. He shook his head at Glone and together he and Chaz walked out of the room. Glone sneered, but instead of following, he used the opposite door to exit.

I turned to Kirk. "What was that about?

"Not that hard to figure out." He went out the same door as Clink and Chaz but turned left instead of right as they had.

I threw my hands in the air, figuring it was none of my business anyway.

WE DECIDED TO STAY on Crimson a few more days until we could come up with some type of game plan. Something I hadn't considered was just how grateful everyone would be.

Everywhere we went, we were greeted with smiles, thank yous, and looks of awe. People moved out of the way when we walked by, and I didn't want that at all. It was like we were rock stars now, but to me, we'd only done what anyone would have. There were kids here. I would have helped, favor or not.

One thing did strike me, though. Glone could have asked for anything, something personal, and only for himself. Yeah, he'd made comments about me taking him to my world, but I believed it'd all been leading up to him asking for help for the sick and wounded. That's what he'd really wanted. That his first concern was getting medical supplies and food was very telling. Though he was still an asshole, he certainly wasn't the all-out evil madman I'd first thought him to be.

As the day wound down, Nico and I were shown to a room we would share with a few other women. It was small and filled with twins-sized beds. I expected some sort of upset from Nico, but the only thing she did was silently drop her backpack to the floor.

I sat down and looked around. Six beds, three dressers, and one nightstand took up all the space in the room. No doors, so anybody walking by could see inside. The fact that Nico hadn't sneered or made some biting complaint had me curious. "Nothing to say?" I finally asked her.

She lay on her back, one hand flung over her face. When she started to speak, she came up on one elbow. "It's clean, dry, and there's plenty of food. What do you want me to say, Rekia?"

I held up my hands. "Nothing. Hey, I'm just glad we're not arguing right now."

She rolled her eyes, turned over, and that was the end of it.

THE OUTSIDE OF THE hideout was sheltered with guards placed at every entry point. One thing I noticed was a play area for the kids. Complete with swing sets, and guards on all sides. Once again, I took note that this place was a lot more organized than I'd first believed.

There was an outside eating area. Some of the grills had already been here, but Glone and I had pushed about twenty through, and I counted five turned on and smoking. Food was being prepared. Hot sausages, red hots, and hamburgers were some of the smells that assaulted my nostrils. My stomach raged with hunger and I was pleased with how well this was going so far.

I waited until everyone was busy eating dinner before I slipped away. Pulling out my phone, I called Robin and told her to meet me at the house.

She was there when I arrived, in the kitchen, scowl on her face. Trent sat on the couch, body tense, as if waiting for me to arrive.

Robin stood with her hands on her hips. "What do you want, Rekia? I was at work. I need to get back."

Robin owned her own advertising company. I knew how important her career was to her, so I tried to move things along as quickly as I could. "Piggyback off my portal." She opened a small gateway in the exact spot as mine, then reached her hand in and nodded. She looked at me curiously. "Got it. What was that about?"

"Need you to know exactly where I am. In case you need me, or I need you. I'm going to be staying on Crimson for a few days."

She gave me an exasperated look. "Do I even want to know?"

I chuckled good-naturedly. "Probably not. Just keep in touch." I thought about what would happen if Robin just popped up on Crimson without notice. I shook my head. Not good. "They don't like strangers there. They take it very seriously. Only come if it's an emergency, okay?"

She nodded. "Anything else?"

I leaned over and gave Trent a quick kiss on the lips. He tasted like baloney, ham, and cheese. Hmm, couldn't ask for better. I kissed him again, then sat down beside him.

He stared at me. "What are you up to? I can see those wheels turning, Rekia."

I put a small pillow on my lap and began to pull on a loose string. "We've got some help now, and I think we've figured out a way to finally bring both worlds down."

Robin took a seat on the arm of the couch. "What do we do?"

I shook my head. I knew she just wanted to help, but I couldn't put her in danger. If something happened to her as a result of this shit... my shit, I'd never forgive myself. "I need you to stay here, to stay safe, and if anything happens to me, get him home." I pointed to Trent.

He didn't look pleased. "I don't like it, Re. You fighting alone."

"I'm not alone."

"You don't know these people. Not really."

I rubbed small circles into the back of his hand. "I don't blame you for feeling that way, Trent. If the situations were reversed, I'd feel the exact same." I would too, but I didn't really like being told what to do. So yeah, I was being a little hypocritical, but if it kept him safe then it was worth it.

He looked at me for a good fifteen seconds before he answered. "I trust you. If that's what you're trying to ask me. I know I'm not your man and I don't really get a say either way, but still..." He stopped for a moment, then closed his eyes. I could almost hear his heart beating as he opened them again and looked at me, open and honest. "I care about you, Rekia. Just please tell me you'll at least try to be careful. Don't try to be a fucking hero, let the others pull their weight too."

I knew he meant well and that it was hard for him to understand the dynamics of our little group without actually being a part of it. So, I went for patience instead of annoyance when answering him. "They've saved my butt many times, Trent. I trust them, every one of them. They've got my back. I wouldn't go into this with them if I didn't think so." I was surprised, when I said it to realize how true it was.

He nodded. "That's good enough for me."

He sounded genuine, which caused a warm toasty feeling to wash over me. I put both my hands on the side of his face, and brought our heads together. Rubbing noses, kissing lips, I held on to him with the knowledge that I may never see him again. It was a very sobering thought that caused me more than a little disquiet.

In that moment, that second, I needed to feel him, touch him, assure myself that I was still alive, heart still beating. I wanted him to wrap his arms around me and never let go. I wanted to feel something, anything.

From the other side of the room, Robin cleared her throat. "So, I'm going to go now." She pointed two fingers toward the door.

I jumped up and pulled her into a hug. "My mom dad, I don't want them worrying. If I don't come back from this..."

Half-formed tears clouded her eyes. She nodded and pulled me into another hug. "I'll take care of it, cuzzo." She pulled back and squeezed my hand. "I got your back here. You go ahead and do what you have to. This here be one less thing you have to worry about."

I locked the door behind her, then held out my hand to Trent. "Show me what you've done with the bedroom."

WHEN I ARRIVED BACK, Nico was sitting at one of the tables cutting up an apple. She didn't look up.

I held out my hand, and she unceremoniously dumped a piece of the fruit into it.

It was small, red, and sweet and I ate it all in one bite. "Can't sleep?" I asked as I could tell that something was bothering her.

She cut up another piece and shook her head. "It's not that." Her voice was low and I didn't think I'd ever seen her look so vulnerable.

It took a moment for realization to sink in. "If this doesn't work..." I let the last part trail off because we both knew that if this didn't go the way she wanted, she and Toma would both be lost to Sentra forever. Not that it made any difference if we all ended up dead anyway, but I didn't think now was the best time to bring that up.

She gave a slight nod.

I tried to think of something positive. "What about Kirk?" Not sure why I thought that was it, but oh well.

She cut her eye my way, then popped another piece of apple into her mouth. "What about him?"

"You going to see him again?" Provided we didn't all end up dead, of course.

"You going to see Toma?"

The question kind of took me aback because to be honest, I hadn't really given much thought to what happens next. "Why should I?"

From the look on her face, I could tell that was the exact answer she'd expected. She put the last of the apple into her mouth and stood. I watched her go. She was probably on the way to find Kirk, and a small part of me couldn't help but wonder if he meant anything to her at all.

WE NEEDED TO LEARN to work together. There was no way in hell we were going to be able to walk into Sentra, expose the council for the ruthless shits they were, and walk back out alive. No. We would have to fight, and fight hard.

The next morning saw us all on Glone's training field. I did wonder what a group of underground criminals needed with such a thing, but then I decided it was probably best if I didn't know.

Some of his people joined us, pledging their help freely for the supplies we'd given them. Two things, though. The supplies bought Glone's help, and so they were not in fact given freely. Number two was that I didn't want anyone else getting hurt.

We were thirty minutes into our first practice when my phone rang.

Robin.

"Everything all right?" I knew this wasn't a social call.

Her voice was low and slightly worried. "I just got a phone call from Saylor. She wants to meet." I heard what she said, but one part stood out.

"Why does Saylor have your number?" I asked.

She let out an irritated huff. "Do you not remember being sick and barely able to move?"

"Still doesn't explain why she has your number."

"How else was I supposed to keep in contact with her when you were in the cave? Did you think we communicated through pigeons or something?"

I decided to ignore her little jab. "When and where?"

WE MET ON A NEUTRAL world of my choosing. Robin was kind enough to bring Saylor along. I hated this. Hated that she only seemed to be getting more and more tangled up in this thing.

Glone was with us. As he was now involved, I felt it only right to keep him in the loop. He needed to know what we were facing. Chaz stood off to the side, a big scowl on his face. He didn't like it, but he'd just have to deal.

Once everyone was gathered, I cut right to the chase. "What do you want, Saylor? Why are we here?"

"What are you up to?" she asked as if I would ever actually tell her.

I shook my head. Did she really expect us to just up and trust her? "Why?" I asked before Nico had a chance to mistakenly set her on fire.

She set her sights on me as if she wondered at my audacity. "Do you see anyone else here?" She made a show of looking around, driving home her point that she'd yet to betray us. "Nope. No one. So, a little gratitude then?"

I let my nonverbal stare do all the talking.

She smiled as if my irritation made no difference at all. I'm sure it didn't. "I can tell you fighting styles, strategies. I know their next move. I'm in on all the plans. Do you really think you don't need my help?"

I bit my bottom lip and looked out at the ducks making their way across the water, the sunlight shining down on them and highlighting their every move. "No. What we don't need is your betrayal."

Glone ran a hand down his face, smoothing out the hairs on his goatee. "Can't hurt to listen to what she has to say. Take what we like, leave what we don't."

Nico began a careful walk around the other lady, slow and deliberate. I'd never seen her look so dangerous, and I really hoped she wasn't ready to explode. "Why should we let her leave here unharmed? Hmm? She came here unprotected, unarmed, and without a soul in her world knowing where she is. Let's say we send her back in a box or twenty?"

Saylor looked so amused you'd think she was watching a show at the circus or something. She stood stock-still as Nico made her rounds. She raised a diamond encrusted fingernail to her lips, and it was only then that I noticed the deadly look in her eyes. One small movement of her hand had Toma screaming her name.

"Saylor, no. She's my sister!"

I blinked at him confused. Was I missing something, because I was pretty sure that Nico was one of the strongest fighters I knew. I didn't doubt that she could handle herself.

Saylor turned to Toma with a smile. "My silly boy. My Toma, my love. I'm not going to hurt the girl. I only wish to teach her a less—" She turned, and as quick as lightning had Nico strapped to the side of a building, holding her up with one hand while blue energy surrounded her whole body.

She looked to Toma. "Make a move and I'll turn her inside out." She cocked her head to the side. "Then I'll do the same to you, my love." She all but spat that last part out.

Toma's eyes went wide, but I noticed he didn't move one step closer. "You killed Kolo." he said, as if in excuse for Nico's actions.

Saylor tightened her grip on a now almost limp Nico, yet her eyes never left Toma. She tsked, as if to say he'd failed every lesson she'd ever tried to teach him. "Did I now? Did I kill him, or did I show him the sweet mercy of a quick release? He was dead either way."

Toma's eyes strayed to Nico's now lifeless form. "Let her go," he said, his voice low and pleading as he looked at his sister.

Saylor released her immediately. Nico coughed and choked, running a hand up and down her throat, then found the nearest bench to sit on.

Saylor walked up to Toma. Their faces mere inches apart. She flicked her tongue and pretended to lick him from his jawline to his lips. "For you, my love." She sounded sarcastic as hell, but before he could form a reply, a scream off in the distance had us all whipping our heads around.

The ground rumbled when they walked. Not like the ground of their home world, which was meant to hold such weight. Clamors, six of them it seemed. No. Six in front and six behind them, then six behind them, and so on.

My mouth hung open. A whole fucking army. How had they found—? I turned around and wasn't even surprised to see that Saylor had disappeared without a trace.

Chapter 16

That bitch! She'd led them to us. She had to have. I turned to look at the others. "We fight. I won't go back there. We fight to the death if we have to."

Glone shook his head. "Don't plan on dying here today, love." He looked to Clink, who nodded. Something passed between them, a light, a brain thought, I didn't know, but suddenly everything changed.

The loud thunderous sound of bombs lit up the air around us. I dropped to my knees as multiple buildings exploded one after the other. The water rose to fight us, oceans of sea life headed our way, snapping turtles, great white sharks, animals I didn't even have a name for, all came at us.

This gave the Clamors pause. Their long legs stopped their murderous stride as they ducked and looked around.

Over the noise, and the bombing, and the yelling, I heard Clink's voice call out to me. "We have them distracted. Get us out of here now, Rekia."

"They're distracted but still racing forward. I don't have time..."

Two Clamors fell upon me ready to attack. I was ready too, but instead of trying to fight them off, I opened a portal to a desolate reptilian world and sent their asses through.

Robin had the ability to take on the shape of any innate object she touched. Standing next to a tree and rock, she became the rock. Entire body now composed of granite, she still moved with speed and grace. The power of the stone inside her, she punched a Clamor square in the face, knocking him to the ground.

Clink produced two projections of himself, and all three fought the Clamors. He and Glone both used their combined powers to project the image of fake fighting Clamors in front of the real Clamors. A strategy that proved useful, as it allowed Clink and Glone to get the upper hand and go in for the kill shot.

Chaz with his power-stealing abilities was now covered from head to toe with little metal tips. He used it in a spinning body motion, tearing Clamors apart the moment he touched them.

Nico set ablaze any Clamor that even looked to be coming her way. She set up a defensive stance, her and Kirk back to back fighting as a team and holding their own.

Kirk put both his hands together, and hit the ground with power punches, rocking the Clamor off their feet and splitting the ground open around them.

Toma and I stood back to back as well, he shot sand from his hands and mouth at a rapid-fire rate, filling the Clamors' mouth and throat with the stuff, causing them to choke and gag until they finally hit the ground unmoving.

This had been too easy, and we should have been on our guard, but being too caught up in our faux victory, we didn't even see the portal until it was too late. Until it was sucking us into a world that none of us knew anything about.

Not willing to stay there, I immediately tried to open another portal but was knocked back by a force like a hurricane. It lifted me in the air and slung me hard to the ground. I landed on my side, rocks and dirt biting into me.

As soon as I caught my bearings, I jumped to my feet, ready to fight, and saw that we were surrounded by men and women of all sizes and skin tones. They didn't look so much hostile, as curious, and I noticed that every single one of them were dressed as if on their way to a fashion shoot.

I looked to my crew and was grateful to see that we were all still standing. Relief washed over me, as I tried to figure out our next move.

"I would like to be kind," a voice said, somewhere deep in the crowd. "Peeling the skin from your bones is not an attractive option, and it's all so very messy, tell me, what should I do with you now that you've landed in my domain?"

"You can let us go home," I shouted, not sure who or what I was talking to.

Then he stepped forward. He had pale skin and blond hair that hung down his back in curls. He was of medium height and had steel-blue eyes that watched us carefully. He looked to be about thirty. Small in frame, he wore a gold shirt that came down to his thighs, with gold pants and gold bands around his arms, legs, and feet.

I took a good look around. Buildings, tall buildings sparkled and shined down on us. Roads jumped and turned, some on ground, some above it. Chairs of all shapes and sizes lined the street as people got in and out of them. The streets moved, taking the people along for the ride.

This was a futuristic world. I'd been to some before, and I was always amazed at the leaps and bounds in not just technology, but the way of life in general.

He made a show of looking each of us up and down before he bothered to speak again. "Why are you here?" he asked. His voice sounded curious, but there was no mistaking the steel underneath. This man was dangerous.

"We could leave," I said, my hand already itching to open a portal that would take us away from this place.

He looked at his long gold-painted fingernails as if bored. "Well, that's not ready to happen." He sounded so matter-of-fact when he spoke, like he was used to being in control.

The tension in the air was damn near choking me with its viscosity. My crew was tense and with good reason. We'd been through so much lately, and right now we were all tired and worn down from the fight we'd just had. Plus, we had just done two portal hops, without proteins or carbs to keep our bodies going. This was not a good time to start a fight. So, we'd be civil, for now.

I turned to the others, trying to convey that this was a losing battle and it was best to weigh our options before we did anything rash.

The blond one waved his hand, and everyone disappeared except for my group and another man. He stepped beside the first guy. This one was tall, small of frame, and had skin a beautiful ebony color that reminded me somewhat of my brother Kevin. He too looked to be about thirty.

He wore all silver, even his eyes, eyebrows, and hair were silver. I looked at his nails to see that they were as long and as beautiful as his friend's. Only, where the other mans were gold, his were silver. They had little jewels and designs drawn into them. I looked to the golden one and saw that his nails were identical.

The silver one grabbed the gold one by the back of the neck and pulled him close, long fingers curled possessively as he kissed the other man's throat. "Do we have new friends to play with, Kalem, is that what this is?"

Kalem turned in the other man's embrace. He snatched the silver one's head back then kissed his way up his neck. "What shall we do with them, my love?"

Toma had had enough. "Look we just want to go home, okay? We don't mean you or your people any harm."

Kalem smirked slightly. He let go of the silver one and went back to looking at his hands. His face and voice read bored, and he seemed uninterested in anything but his nails. "You couldn't hurt us if you tried. Don't be ridiculous."

The silver one shook his head, as he began a slow walk around us. "I don't know, Kalem, I sense something here." He stopped walking and looked at his friend. "They have power, of that I am sure. The question is, what do we do with them now?"

Kalem smiled, and I felt something inside me shiver. Something about that smile made me want to retch. "You got to pick with the last one. Tell me, Tieden, do I love you enough to let you pick with this one as well? It is my turn after all."

I looked to my crew and shook my head. What the hell were they even talking about? They couldn't really stop me, not if I was fast enough. I gave a nod to the others, so they'd know to be ready, then widened my hands to make a portal.

The silver one, Tieden, while still turned to the side in conversation with Kalem, made a simple turning motion with his hand and my portal disappeared as soon as it had opened.

I let out an involuntary gasp, which caused Tieden to smirk. "When has life ever been that easy, my dear. Don't do that again. You won't like my reaction if you do." He sounded as bored as his friend. What the fuck was wrong with them?

I looked to Nico, and from her defensive stance, I could tell she was itching for a fight. I felt it was best to try and diffuse the situation without violence, though, because soon our bodies would start to breakdown without some type of substance and I hoped my eyes conveyed that to her.

Glone wiped a hand down his face. He hadn't been traveling with us long, so this was all new to him. "Name your price," he said, his voice gravelly and low. "What do you want from us?"

Kalem shrugged. "Who knows?" he said, as if someone had asked him what shirt he would like to wear today.

Tieden, with hands behind his back, turned interested eyes on us. "What can you do?"

Toma shook his head. "We won't perform tricks like a dog."

Tieden rolled his eyes in a way that said there were so many other things he'd rather be doing right now. Even the way he waved his hand to attack was as if he was bored out of his mind.

Gold and silver ropes suddenly wrapped around us. They squeezed my body tightly, cutting off my oxygen and making it hard to breathe.

I levitated in the air, then used my telekinesis to throw them off. The others had used their powers to break free as well, which was exactly what they'd wanted, I realized.

Kalem smiled. "Now that wasn't so hard, was it? Do try not to bring out the beast in my poor Tieden. I have the most horrid time calming him down afterward."

I stared in open bewilderment at the two men before me. Were they insane? They sure seemed to be. His poor little Tieden was over six feet tall and had just rendered all eight of us motionless without breaking a sweat. What were they on, because I'd say my whole crew needed some of that shit.

Tieden nodded. "I'm impressed," he said as if he'd just told us to take out the garbage or something. He certainly didn't sound impressed. He sounded as if he wouldn't know a true feeling or emotion even if it rose up and struck him upside his silver lined head. "Tell me, my dear, Kalem what shall we do with them now, my love?"

Kalem, who was once again giving his nails his full attention, raised a brow as he looked at his friend, lover, whatever. "You love me. I know that you love me because you're letting me choose. Tell me, Tieden, what is it that you love most about me, dear?"

He pulled the other man close and just stared into his eyes. "Is it my eyes? Are they still beautiful to you? Can you still see your whole life when you look into them? Come Tieden, tell me why do you love me so?"

Tieden ran possessive fingers through the other man's hair, letting gold ringlets slide out of his hands and back to Kalem's shoulder. "I love the gold of your eyes and the beauty of your stare." He lifted the other man's hand. "I love your nails, each different and unique but still the same nonetheless. I love—"

A loud groan from Nico stopped him short and had both men turning deadly eyes our way. Kalem tsked. "Seems like someone needs to be taught a lesson, my dear."

Tieden nodded his agreement. "Kalem, tell me, my love, why do they send the most uncouth beast our way?"

Kalem looked at us, disappointed. "It is a bit of a problem is it not, love? Tell me, my dear, Tieden, what shall we do with those who interrupted our lovemaking right when we were ready to climax?"

"Our glorious climax."

Kalem put a single fingertip to Tieden's lips. "It's always glorious with you, my love."

Glone, who probably like the rest of us, was at his wits end with this nonsense scoffed. "How you gonna come just from talking? She didn't interrupt nothing."

Two razor-sharp pairs of eyes turned his way as they both glided to stand on either side of him. Kalem shook his head as if this was the saddest thing he'd heard all day. "Oh dear, Tieden, should we tell him? What do you think, love?"

They boxed him in until they were standing only an inch away. "Tell me what?" Glone asked, arms folded in front of him, voice tight and hard.

Tieden ran a hand through Glone's red hair while sniffing his neck and under his chin. "That a true lover can make you come from a single look. That if it takes more than that, then maybe you're not doing it right. Maybe we should teach you. What do you say Kalem? Shall we teach the dog new tricks?"

Kalem ran a hand over Glone's shoulder and biceps. "I'll say it's been a long time since he's been properly made love to. Let's ask his permission, dear. Let's see if he'll let us make him see stars."

"Until the colors start to blur."

"Until he loses all sense of space and time."

"Until he forgets his name."

"Until he knows only how to scream."

I stood horrified as they went on and on about the things they would do to Glone. Then I saw Clink making his way forth and fuck! Anything he did would just set off a very bad chain of events, between him and Chaz, between these two weirdos, between Kirk and anyone who messed with Chaz.

He stopped in front of them and took measure of Glone's face. "What do you want to do?" His voice could barely contain the anger and undeniable rage he must have felt.

Gold and silver eyes turned on him like fire. Kalem was the first to speak. "We don't touch those who don't want to be touched."

Tieden backed him up. "We don't take what's not given freely." He turned to Glone. "It's been such a long time, hasn't it? No lover to take care of you."

Kalem cooed right on cue. "No one to rub your ears and wash your feet."

Tieden's turn now. "No one to brush your hair and clean your nails."

Back to Kalem, and I could swear these two were getting more turned on by the minute. "No one to lick your sacs and make you sweat."

"Hmm. No one to kiss your eyelids and rub your tongue red?"

Kalem now stood in front of Glone. His body pressing dangerously close to the other man. He dropped his voice and all but purred out the next words. "No one to rub your tummy while massaging your cock."

Tieden took up where Kalem left off. "While I come from behind and make you come until you spit."

Oh, good grief, I'd had enough of this shit. "Glone?" I said, trying to get a sense of the other man's emotions.

He looked irritated with me but detangled himself from the other two men nonetheless. "Sorry, you lot, not today." He looked at me. "Do save this place for later, though." He looked to Clink as he spoke his next words. "A night of fun can do wonders for the mind, wouldn't you say Clink?"

Clink ignored him, and stepped back until he was beside Chaz and laced the other man's hand with his own.

Kalem and Tieden both straightened at the rejection. "Oh, dear we've gone too far, Tieden. He doesn't want us after all."

Tieden lifted Kalem's right hand and kissed his fingertips one by one. "Oh, my love, he wants us just fine, it's the big one over there." He pointed to Clink. "Until his heart no longer beats for him, he could never allow himself the pleasures we can bring."

Kalem shook his head. "We can make him feel so good, love, so good."

Tieden nodded. "We can make him whole again."

Kalem looked at his fingernails. "What must we do to punish ourselves for our miscalculations?"

Tieden let out a displeased sigh. "Oh, my dear, I think you know that we must let them go now. We can't keep them here any longer. What a horrible disappointment this is."

Kalem sighed too. "Very well then, that shall be our punishment." He turned to us, throwing golden hair off his shoulder, and behind his ears. "If you ever want to come back..."

Tieden looked at Glone. "We would be ever so kind."

Kalem. "We'll wash your feet and feed you grapes from our own special vine."

"If you ever come back."

Glone shrugged and looked at me. "Think I might have a grand ole time here. I can wash my own damn feet, but as for the rest, well..." He looked at Clink. "It's been a while."

I didn't care. I just wanted to get away from this creepy ass place as quickly as I could. I turned to gold and silver. "So, we can leave now? You won't stop us?"

Twin nods of the head, but Kalem was the one to speak. "Come back as our guest, and we'll treat you right. We won't attack, as you'd be our honored friends."

Kalem laced his hand with Tieden's, their fingers intertwining. "We'll break bread with you." He pointed to Glone. "Just make sure you bring him too."

Best to be civil while they were in a cordial mood. "I'll see what we can do. Nice to meet you and goodbye." I opened a portal so fast that I was sure my hand would suffer from whiplash. What a freaky little place to be. Who knew when they'd change their mind? We needed to get out while the getting was good.

Robin saluted and opened a portal of her own. I waved her away, then stepped through a doorway to a world where we could recharge on food before taking us back to Crimson.

I landed us in the secret hideaway that Chaz'd shown us when we'd been trying to get away from Glone that first time.

I had to look around for a minute just to make sure I was in the right place. The difference was astounding. Not a bit of trash in the whole place. No empty plates or crushed beer cans lay in sight.

I sniffed the air. It even smelled fresher. The only difference was Saylor sitting up in a chair, legs crossed, eyebrow raised as if to ask us what took so long.

"I'm here for a reason." She said, standing like we hadn't already figured that part out.

Chaz walked over to the small refrigerator and pulled out a beer. "Honestly I'm not even surprised."

Me either. At this point, it was almost expected. I made a move to sit down, then noticed food and other things stuck to the chair. No thank you. Guess they missed that one. "What are you doing here, Saylor?" I asked tiredly.

She held her hands out in front of her as if to say the answer to that question should be obvious by now. "I'm here to help."

Nico snatched up a chair and turned it around, sitting backward in it. "Tell me, sister-in-law," she said that last word as if it was the dirtiest thing she'd ever spoken. "Why is it that every time we're attacked, you're there? Amazing how you always manage to disappear at the right moment."

Saylor chuckled lightly. When she spoke, her words were directed at Toma instead of his sister. "She never was that bright, was she? She's your sister, and I know you like to boost her self-esteem or whatever, but come on. What in her mind would make her think I'd actually risk my life for any of you?"

She walked closer to him, circling him like a vulture stalking its prey. "We always said she should have stayed in learning class for that extra year, didn't we, hon?"

"Saylor," Toma said, voice tight. He stood stock-still as if afraid to move.

Saylor came to stand in front of him, their faces inches apart. He trembled slightly and sucked in a breath. His fists clenching and unclenching. He looked like he could barely contain himself from doing something. What, I had no idea, but it was interesting to see. "Silly boy, pillow talk was made for telling. There are no secrets among friends." She waved her hand around the room as if we were all involved in some after-school special together.

"What do you want?" I asked, irritated with her little display of power.

She broke her gaze from Toma and turned eyes on me. "You're not going to like it."

The matter-of-fact way she said it instantly put me on guard. "What is it?"

She started a slow walk, weaving through each of us as she spoke. "At this very moment Sentra and Clamor are rampaging every world suspected of having the capability of opening portals."

My heart choked in my throat. I tried to talk, only nothing came out but a croak. Heat rushed me. I felt sick and clammy and this could not be happening. It had to be a joke, a trick. I stood up a little straighter, my mind following that line of thought to the end.

What if this was a trap? Saylor played her own game, always. She did nothing without reason and so maybe her reasoning here was leading the Clamor and Sentra straight to my father's home world.

I tried not to show it on my face, but that actually made a lot of sense. Saylor got here through unknown means. What if she'd brought a few fellow Sentra and Clamors along with her? What if they were off to the side, waiting for me to go rushing off so that they could follow and attack?

What if they were waiting for me to lead them to a world full of people with the ability to portal hop? It was enough to give me pause. It was enough to make me look Saylor dead in her eyes and shrug. "Let them do their worst." Already though, my mind was coming up with multiple ways to hit this head-on.

She barely reacted, just a raise of an eyebrow and a look that said maybe she'd underestimated me after all. "Words to live by." She nodded at me, blew a kiss at Toma, then walked out the door.

Kirk stood closest to the exit. "Follow her." I pointed to Saylor's quickly disappearing back, my voice betraying the urgency I felt.

He was back a second later shaking his head. Why was I not surprised? That lady was as slippery as an eel, and how had she known we'd portal into this room anyway. I was starting to think she possessed some psychic power as well.

Toma seemed to relax a little now that Saylor was gone, but the guilty look on his face gave me pause. I watched him with interest. He held my gaze for a few seconds then looked away. Dammit. He was hiding something, something about Saylor.

Something he knew about her that the rest of us didn't. We were in this thing largely because of him and his sister. Keeping secrets at this point just seemed ridiculous, especially since Saylor was one of the reasons we were in this situation to begin with.

Killing Kolo and framing Nico is what set this whole thing off. Was he protecting her? From us? I shook my head. No. That didn't sound right.

Still, there was something he was hiding, and it did have to do with Saylor. So, the only thing I could do was watch him a little closer, and hope to grab a clue.

Later, sitting alone at one of the picnic tables, I turned my phone over in my hand, as I tried to piece together everything in my head. If Saylor was telling the truth, and I called Robin, then that itself would be all the confirmation the Clamor needed.

Calling my sister though, and getting her to call and check back in with me, would be different. They didn't know Chanel, had no way of knowing where she was from and what she could do.

I hated to drag Chanel into this, but we both loved our family and if this was real, if our grandmother and other relatives were actually in danger, and I knew about it and did nothing, then she'd never forgive me. With good reason. I made the phone call.

It took three hours for her to call me back. I sat in the same spot the entire time, flipping my phone over and waiting. When it finally rung, I snatched it up immediately. "Are they safe?"

"*They* are." The way she said it made it clear that somebody wasn't.

"So..." Her reluctance gave me chills.

She sighed heavily, as if she knew her next words would hurt me and was bracing herself for the fallout. "They attacked your clients. Are holding them hostage, and if you don't appear, they'll start killing them."

Something sour ran through me straight to my chest. It was hard, but I tried to force myself to remain calm, for the moment anyway. "How many?"

"At least ten."

What? "There is no way for them to know that many of my clients." Fear shot through me and something deep inside, told me that Sharon was one of the ones taken.

Sharon, who'd come to me for help, trying to get away from an abusive partner. Sharon, who had three kids depending on her. Sharon, whom I'd promised a better life if she'd just let me help her. Sharon, who had no clue what was going on and was probably scared shitless right now. Where were the kids? Had they taken them too?

I started to speak but had to stop to clear my throat. It felt scratchy and dry, making me long for a bottle of water to clear it up. "Where are they?"

"They're being held on Synex." It made sense, from their perspective anyway. Synex was a peaceful place. Its people were not fighters, and often did everything they could to avoid confrontation. Sentras and Clamors descending on their world would surely make the natives run and hide, leaving the intruders to do as they pleased.

I gritted my teeth. I wanted to end this once and for all. I'd had enough. "I'm going to get them back," I let her know.

She sighed, signaling she didn't like it but knew there was nothing she could do to stop me. "Not by yourself, right?"

"No. I'm taking my crew with me."

WE ARRIVED ON SYNEX at the height of the day. Synex was a world filled with ice and snow all year long. I'd had to make a run to the store to get us clothing more appropriate to the weather. Now we stood dressed in thick winter coats, hats, scarves, gloves, and boots.

I pulled my coat tighter around me and shivered. The wind was so fierce that it was painful. This had to be strategy on the Clamor's part, but to what end? I glanced at Toma and Nico who were from the cold world of Sentra, but they too seemed to be suffering just as much as the rest of us.

The Clamor's had made sure to pick a world that would put us all at a disadvantage, which made me even more wary about what they had planned.

We knew this to be a trap going in. It was the reason I'd brought us into one of the least populated areas of this world. We needed time for our bodies to adjust to the temperature. We also needed to find a way to get as much mobility as we could get inside our thick clothing.

As we walked, I used my telekinesis to clear piles of snow from our path. It hit me then, like a brick smacking my face at full speed.

I now knew exactly why they'd chosen this world and the answer made me want to rip them apart piece by piece. These truly were some of the cruelest people I'd ever met. I prayed that I was wrong, but everything in me said I was right.

"Didn't know I'd be freezing my love knobs off, love? When we gonna find some heat?" Behind his face mask, Chaz's voice came through in a clatter. I was sure we all felt the same. I wished there was something we could do to better our situation, but at the moment, I had nothing.

"I could," Nico opened her mouth, and a small flame of fire came out.

"No!" I said, letting the urgency in my voice seep through. "I've been here plenty of times before. The whole ecosystem, their whole-body makeup is in line with the cold. Think of the phrase, 'Ice veins' I'm not saying they have ice veins, no way for me to know that. What I am saying is, I wouldn't be surprised if they did. You get it?"

She looked at the empty land covered in snow. "There's no one around. You brought us into the middle of nowhere."

Nodding, Glone came to stand beside her. "Thought we were just suffering until we came upon some warm heat, or a nice fire. You saying that's not happening?"

I'd told them it would be cold and had made sure they'd dressed accordingly. I'd thought I'd made that part clear but, apparently not. I should have told them that there'd be no relief from the cold.

"I'm sorry," I said, my voice tight. We'd all had small delays that took us away from our set task of proving Toma and Nico's innocence. Now it was my turn.

Chaz had his arm linked through Clink's, the two taking comfort in each other from the cold. "Oh, love, I can't walk another step. Can't we sit down and rest for a bit?" Chaz asked.

There was literally nowhere to sit. "We'll have to take out our bedrolls." I undid my backpack and unrolled the small mat. It was thin because we needed them to be light enough to carry. There was no way to keep ourselves from getting wet. The snow was steady, hard, and most surely mixed with ice.

We did need to rest though. We'd been going nonstop for an hour, and I could feel my muscles cramping for a reprieve. I sat down slowly, knowing we couldn't stay in the same spot too long.

We were out in the open, exposed. If something were to happen, we had no way to defend ourselves. We'd at least been able to generate a little heat when we'd been moving, now we were just getting colder by the second.

We'd each packed jerky and the like and now was the perfect time to replenish on that while we rested.

Kirk held Nico close to him, his arm slung around her shoulder as she glared at me. "You could have gotten us a little closer. You know you could have."

She was right, but I just couldn't take the chance of an ambush. We knew it was a trap, but that didn't mean we had to walk straight into it. I tried to blow air into my gloved hand, which had no effect. "I made a judgment call. Did what I thought was right."

"And we're all suffering for it."

Couldn't argue with the truth and I didn't really want to, so I turned away and focused on getting myself as warm as I could.

Toma had set his bedroll beside mine. "How long before we reach our target?" He was covered from head to toe, even his eyes were hidden behind a thick pair of goggles. We all had protective gear on our faces, yet still, the wind cut straight to the bone.

I shrugged and shook my head. I didn't know the answer. I thought we would have run into something by now. I honestly hadn't intended for us to be exposed this long.

I was seriously thinking about opening a portal to some neutral world, then reopening one a little closer, when I saw flames out of the corner of my eyes.

"Nico, no," I shouted. She'd started a small fire on the ground in front of her bedroll, and I feared what would happen if it got too far out of control.

I stood immediately, intent on stomping it out.

She stared back at me defiantly. "I'm not going to—." The ground shook and rumbled, cutting off whatever she was about to say.

"Hold on," I shouted, trying desperately to create a portal and keep my balance at the same time. The ground underneath me shifted, and I fell down hard. I reached out, trying to grab ahold of something, but it did no good. We were sinking, the fire had melted the snow, which had caused some kind of shift in the ground.

Clink and Chaz held onto each other, both wobbling and struggling not to fall. "We have to move fast," Chaz shouted, but it was too late. The bottom fell out from under them. Chaz reached out to his brother, who was on his feet instantly trying to help. Glone made a grab for Clink's hand, but didn't reach it in time.

We all watched in horror as they fell, holding on to each other and screaming for the rest of us to run. Then the ground rumbled again, and we were all falling and sinking, and I'd never been so scared in my life.

Chapter 17

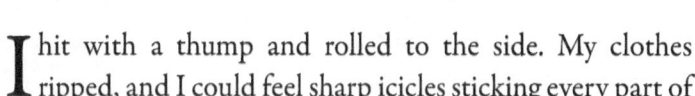

I hit with a thump and rolled to the side. My clothes ripped, and I could feel sharp icicles sticking every part of my body that was exposed.

It hurt to even breathe, and I felt like I'd landed in a bed of pointed needles, instead of ice. "Everyone okay?" I asked. No one answered, and I tried not to panic. Figuring I could see more if I wasn't laying down, I tried to come to a sitting position, but the pain in my shoulder and side fought me the whole way.

I looked around. It was pitch black, but I could tell that snow and ice surrounded us. I'd held on tight to my bag as I fell, but of course, my bedroll had been lost. I fumbled through my supplies until I found a flashlight.

I tried to click it on, but my hands shook so bad that I ended up dropping it. Shit. My gloves had gotten torn in the fall, and my fingers burned each time I reached out.

My hand closed around something long and hard, but it was entirely too cold to be my flashlight. It took a little more searching, but finally I found it. Saying a silent thank you, I clicked it on, praying that it still worked.

It did, but the only person I saw was Kirk. He was laid up against a wall, face pale. I took a closer look and was horrified when I saw the rush of blood coming from his upper arm.

His hand clutched at the spot, trying to stop the flow, but it was doing no good. Survival instincts kicked in immediately, and I was up and moving before I knew it.

On my knees in front of him, I tore off a piece of his coat that was already ripped and used it to tie-off his arm. "Kirk, can you hear me." He didn't answer, but the look on his face broke my heart.

It was the look of a man who knew he was ready to die and had accepted that there was nothing that could save him. I defied that look. Fuck that look.

Tears spilled from my eyes as I talked to him. I tried to keep the tremble out of my voice, but it came through anyway. "Dammit, Kirk. Don't you dare die on me. Chaz will kill me. Nico will resurrect me only to kill me again, repeatedly."

His breathing became ragged and his eyes began to fix. No! Dammit! I would not watch this man die in front of me. I would not. Tears flowed freely now, and I tried to speak, but my tongue felt thick and heavy in my mouth. "I'm going to get you out of here. I'm not going to leave them. I'm coming back, but I have to get you out of here."

I reached out my hand to open a portal to Crimson. Kirk needed the blood of a family member, and I had no clue where Chaz was, or if he was even still alive. I pulled out my phone, calling Chanel and Robin as I went.

"What happen to him?" Cherry asked, as soon as we came through. She was looking a lot better than when I'd last seen her, and was clearly up and moving around. "Get help.

A sister, brother, somebody that loves him. Find them and get them here." I said to everyone I saw.

Robin appeared, and I pointed to one of the girls in the room. "Kirk's family, find them and portal them down here." Robin nodded, grabbed the girl, then disappeared. They'd have to go to another world, then portal back to Crimson where Chaz's family was, then to another world to portal back down here, and I prayed they made it in time.

We were in the hospital room of the cave, and there were a few more empty spaces than there had been last time, which meant that the medical supplies had come in handy.

They got him on a bed, and I could tell it was taking everything in them not to ask me what happened.

Cherry's eyes went wide with fear. "Glone? Clink?"

My throat closed up because I hadn't really allowed myself to think of the others. Hadn't allowed myself to flirt with the idea that they could all be dead. The thought that I'd never see them again knocked the wind out of me, and I had to hold on to a bedrail to stay upright.

Had I led them all to their deaths? Were they all dead now because of me? I gasped as my knees buckled under me and I crumpled to the floor.

"Rekia!" The anguish in my sister's voice had me reacting immediately. "I'm fine," I said, but the pain in my voice, the fact that I couldn't move, and the amount of blood covering me probably told a different story.

She dropped down beside me and held my face in her hands, forcing me to look at her. "Are you hurt? Don't you dare lie to me. Are you hurt?" She took off her backpack and brought out three protein shakes. One for me, one for herself, and one for Robin no doubt.

I drunk it down greedily as Kirk's breath started to rattle. I pointed to the bed not able to do much else.

Chanel jumped up, as Robin appeared with a redheaded woman in tow. "This is Rowan, Chaz and Kirk's sister." She was of medium height and build, and her eyes were frantic as she stared at her brother.

I handed Robin her shake. She'd just hopped a lot of portals in a short amount of time and I hoped it would be enough to sustain her. She drunk it in three seconds flat.

"I need backup," Chanel said. She downed her shake and went to Kirk's side to start the process.

I didn't know if they could save him, didn't know if it was too late, but at least now there was a chance. Shakily I came to my feet. "I have to go. I have to find the others."

"Glone?" Cherry asked again, her voice filled with emotion. She held Kirk's hand looking about as pale as he did.

Tears prickled my eyes. "I'm going to bring your brother home. No... no matter what." I wiped a hand across my face. "I'm gonna bring them all back. Every one of them. I won't stop searching. I promise."

Her eyes went wide. "Searching. Searching? You don't know where they are?"

Before I could answer, Rowan, broke in, her voice filled with fear. "So you don't know if Chaz or Clink are alive? Is that what you're telling me?"

Off to the side, Chanel had started to work on Kirk. I nodded. "I have to go."

Robin came to stand in front of me. "I'm coming with you."

I shook my head. "The weather's freezing and I can't wait for you to get dressed. I have to go."

A woman who'd been in the room when I'd first arrived with Kirk, walked over and handed me two bags. "Had the guys put together some supplies. For when you find them." Her voice went hard. "You will find them." She stared straight at me, eyes unflinching. "You hear me? You will find them." She sounded so sure and confident that I couldn't help reaching out and pulling her into a hug, hoping that some of her strength would rub off on me.

I nodded, and she gave me a sad smile. I gripped the bags tightly in my hands, then opened a portal and stepped through. I needed to land in the exact spot I'd left from because that way I knew I was close to them.

The change in the weather hit me like a train. I'd already had my backpack, now with the two new bags, I could barely move. I couldn't stay in one spot, though. I needed to make some headway. Walking as fast as I could with the bulk, something caught my eye.

I turned my flashlight that way, and almost shrunk back. It was blood, Kirk's blood. I swallowed hard and tried to tell myself he would be okay. Now wasn't the time for breakdowns. I still needed to make it to the others.

I waved my light around to get a better look at my surroundings. I was in a tunnel, an ice tunnel. Icicles lined the ceiling and snow covered everything else.

"Is anyone here?" I yelled out.

Silence.

With the amount of snow and ice, I probably shouldn't have expected an answer, but I'd had to try anyway.

I took a careful step forward, but too much ice was blocking my way. Everywhere I turned, I ran into a wall of ice. I shuddered involuntarily and tried to focus.

I had to break the ice without letting it collapse on me, or sink me even further. I rose in the air and used my mental telekinesis.

Slowly the wall of snow pulled apart, opening a small, snowy pathway. I walked through, mindful that one slip in concentration could cause a cave-in.

It didn't take long before I saw two figures huddled together, using each other to generate what heat they could.

Relief flowed through me, and I almost lost my hold on the parted snow. I was so happy to see them alive that at first, I couldn't even speak. "Chaz? Clink? Can you hear me?" The sound of their chattering teeth made my breath hitch, but it also meant they were still breathing.

I got down on my knees in front of them, thankful I'd gotten to them in time.

"Oh... love... please... tell me... you're ready... to open... a portal... and get us... out of here." Chaz said through chattering teeth.

I rubbed my gloved hand over his. "We have to find Nico, Toma, and Glone. I can't do it alone. I need your help."

Chaz's movements were slow, but his head snapped up as much as it could. "My... brother," he croaked out.

I tried to find the courage, because I couldn't lie to him, I never would. Yet I didn't know what to say. I had no clue if Chanel and Rowan had been able to save him. I closed my eyes and tried to find the words.

Chaz grabbed Clink's arm tighter and made a move to sit up a little straighter. The stricken look on his face told me he already thought the worst. I didn't have good news for him. I didn't really know what to say.

I looked away trying to gather my thoughts.

Chaz's eyes stayed on me. "My brother, Rekia. Where... is he?" I'd never heard him sound so serious and it only made the reality of the situation that much worse.

"Chaz..."

"Where is he? Take me to him, Rekia."

I shook my head. "He's home, Chaz. Your sister Rowan is with him."

With the help of each other, Chaz and Clink both came to their feet. Clink placed his hand on the small of Chaz's back as if to offer what support he could. "Is he alive?"

I swallowed hard and forced my attention on the wall in front of us. We still had to find Nico, Toma, and Glone.

I looked back at Chaz. It would have been convenient to keep looking away, but I couldn't do it. Something this important deserved eye contact. Besides, I had too much respect for both men not to look them in the face when I told them.

"He was... He was hurt bad. I called my sister. He needed blood remedy. She's there, so are Robin and Rowan. They're working on him. I don't know anything beyond that. I still don't know where Toma, Nico, and Glone are," I said, slowly. "Or if they're still alive."

Clink kissed the side of Chaz's head. "You go check on your brother. Rekia will open a portal for you, won't you, Rekia?"

Chaz looked at me and I nodded. Clink turned all his attention to the other man. "I can't leave Rekia alone. I've got to help her, okay?"

Chaz nodded and pulled the other man into a hug. "Come back to me," he said, as he kissed Clink on the cheek.

I waited until I was sure he was ready then opened a portal and watched him step through.

Once gone, I turned to Clink. "If it... If Kirk doesn't... He's going to need you more than ever."

"He has me."

Even though I knew it was hidden behind my face gear, I still raised an eyebrow. "Does he? You and Glone seem..." I let my words trail off.

"He has me." He repeated, as if there was nothing left to be said on the matter.

I nodded. Now was not the time, especially when we still had three team members missing. I cleared away more snow, and we trudged along, careful to keep our eyes and ears open.

I'd assumed we'd all fallen somewhere in the same vicinity and so far I'd been right. We'd only gone a small way when a loud, angry roar stopped us in our tracks.

We were headed left, but the sound seemed to come from the right. Eyes wide, I turned to Clink. "You hear that too, right?"

Clink nodded. "We're going the wrong way."

Another roar and I couldn't tell if it was a lion, tiger, or some other type of animal. Knowing that our teammates could be hurt, we went toward the sound.

In my haste to get there, I lost a little control, which caused icicles and snow to rain down on us. They bounced off our coats, and around our heads, but we still kept walking.

Then we heard it, an anguished shout that sounded a lot like Toma. Panic ran through me, and Clink and I both hurried our steps, not sure of what we would find once we got to him.

It took a couple more minutes before we reached the right spot. Two ice beasts, stood before Toma and Glone, roaring and beating their chests. The creatures looked bigger than the Yeti, and Bigfoot combined.

Toma and Glone were up against a wall, large sword-like icicles in their hands. So far, they seemed successful at keeping the beasts back.

I didn't want to talk and alert the animals to our presence. At the same time, I had no idea how to fight them. The space was too close, our surroundings too confined.

Clink stepped back the way we'd come, motioning for me to follow. "I'm going to stay back here, but make multiples of myself to confuse them. You use your telekinesis to give Toma and Glone time to escape. We need to open a portal and get the hell out of here. We'll gather weapons and come back for Nico as soon as we can."

It made sense, but I still didn't like it. I didn't want to leave her. "We'll see how it goes," I said flatly.

He nodded and suddenly the room was filled with ten different Clinks. The beasts turned around and let off loud screams. Then one began to talk, his voice filled with anger and rage. "Those tricks don't work on me! I see through all!" And quicker than my eye could track, he had the real Clink by the neck. He lifted him in the air and sneered. "Amateurs."

The beast's hands were the size of bricks, his nails like long white claws. Clink struggled nonstop as his legs dangled, and blood spilled from his neck, and over the beast's huge hand.

Toma and Glone used their swords and charged the second creature.

The first creature roared loudly, and Clink trembled as the animal shook him from side to side.

I watched from one scene to the other, horror filling my every glance. I had to do something. Clink. I had to help Clink. No way was he dying down here today.

Directing my telekinesis, I ripped the animal's hands off with one quick motion. He dropped Clink and turned toward me screaming. Blood spurted from his arms, splattering against the white of the cave.

I ran to Clink and helped him to his feet. "Let's get out of here!"

The beast wasn't having it. Handless now, he still came for us. I slung him back, then Clink and I ran to where Glone and Toma were locked in battle with the other one. He'd broken their weapons and had both men pinned against the wall.

Toma shot sand out of his mouth and hand, but it didn't seem to faze the creature. Glone used his strength to bust a hole in the wall behind him and Toma. I used my telekinesis to throw the beast into his injured friend, then we all took off through the opening that Glone had made, he and I both clearing away the snow and ice as we went.

The beasts followed closely behind us, making it impossible for me to open a portal. Instead, I did what I could to slow them down, dropping snow and ice in their way as we went. We ran until we came to a small opening. Here the snow was cleared, which spoke of frequent use.

The creatures were still coming, and I just couldn't chance opening a portal and releasing them on an unsuspecting world. So, we went on, until we heard movement a few feet in front of us.

We slowed our steps and tried to listen. We could still hear the roars and screams of the beasts behind us, and they set my blood to ice.

Another noise sounded in front of us, and this time we took a peek. I froze as I saw three more beasts standing in an ice room, but behind them was a small opening. I swallowed hard and looked at my companions.

We were cornered. Trapped. The only way out was through the room with the three beasts, or back the other way, toward the two we'd just escaped from.

The roars of the beasts behind us grew louder, making the decision easier. We knew there was no escape that way, but inside this new cave there might be.

We tumbled inside, just as the other two caught up. The three already in the room seemed startled at first, but then quickly sent open mouth snarls our way.

All five moved toward us now, and we huddled together ready to fight it out. One roared loudly, and I used my telekinesis and started ripping off arms, legs, and hands.

Blood splattered everywhere, as they fell hard to the ground, still yelling and screaming. Once they were down, it was easy to see what had been behind them. Nico, sitting in a large ice cage, arms around herself, shaking from the cold.

I let out a sigh of relief and threw the doors open. Toma and Glone helped her out, and together we took off.

Since none of the beasts were behind us now, I opened a portal, and we all jumped through. I didn't want to go straight to Crimson, just in case. So instead I took us to a barren, empty, spot in the first world I could think of.

It only took a moment to realize that the beasts hadn't followed, and we could finally breathe again. Away from the freezing cold, we all began to remove our facial gear.

Nico didn't say a word, just threw herself into her brother's arms and held on tight. "I thought you were dead." I finally heard her whisper. "I thought you were dead." She squeezed him tightly before breaking down completely in his arms. He held her close, kissing the top of her head, and whispering softly in her ear.

Tears stung my eyes, and I turned away trying to get control of my own emotions.

The world I'd picked was cold, and I shivered just a bit. I didn't think it wise to land us into intense heat, not until our bodies had a better chance to regulate.

"Is everyone alright?" I finally asked, after a couple of minutes of silence.

Nico nodded. "Where are the boys from Crimson?"

Clink cleared his throat. "Kirk got hurt bad. Rekia sent him back. Chaz followed."

Her eyes turned to slits, and her whole body went frighteningly still as if she was preparing herself for the answer. "How bad?" Her voice seemed to be holding back a million emotions.

"My sister's with him." I figured that was enough to convey the seriousness of his condition.

I think she literally stopped breathing for a second. Then she found her resolve, hardened her features, and squared her shoulders.

"We can go see him. See how he's doing," Clink offered. The wistful look on his face was enough to let me know that he needed to be close to Chaz right now. Whether Kirk was alive or not, Chaz needed him.

Glone ran a hand over his face. "Did you see my sister while you were there? Is she worried about me?"

We needed to get back because Cherry was as worried as Rowan. They needed to know their brothers were safe, and we needed to make sure Kirk was okay.

A lump formed in my throat as I thought about my clients. They wouldn't be in this mess if not for me. No doubt they were waiting for me to come and save them. I couldn't let them down. I just couldn't. "I won't stay for long. I have to get to my clients."

Glone nodded. "Just want to let my sister know I'm okay, love. Then I'm all yours." His willingness to keep his word earned him my respect. Even at a time like this, he was sticking to it, and I had to admire that.

Clink smiled at him, and I realized that maybe his eagerness to help had nothing to do with me at all.

"Let's go," I said, holding out my hand and opening a portal.

Chapter 18

We arrived at the sick room, and our eyes immediately strayed to the lengthy figure laying still on one of the beds. He seemed to be in an easy sleep and Cherry and Rowan each sat by his side. Rowan had his hand in hers, and she wiped her eyes every few seconds. Cherry lay with her head on the bed, looking completely worn out.

Glone cleared his throat, and her head snapped in his direction, a look of pure relief on her face. She jumped up and launched herself into his arms. Then, after making sure he was okay, she smacked him upside the head. "Ouch," he said, rubbing the spot she'd just hit.

The rest of us laughed, giving the tension in the air, a much-needed break.

"Jerk," she said fondly, and pulled him into another hug.

He held on tight, burying his face in her hair. "I'm sorry I scared you."

She stepped back and wiped her eyes. "I'm proud of you." She finally croaked out. "I'm proud to be your sister, proud that you're taking a stand, so I won't lecture." She wiped her eyes again. "Just be careful."

While she'd been talking, Rowan had walked over. She hugged both Clink and Glone, then updated us on Kirk's condition. "She took blood from me to heal him, then left." Talking about my sister.

Clink's eyes went to the prone figure on the bed. "Why's he lying around like that? Nico was up the moment your sister healed her."

Glone's voice sounded weary, but he seemed to be trying to keep us upbeat. "Like to meet this sister of yours who brings people back from the dead. How many more sisters do you have? Any brothers?"

Knowing that he was just trying to lighten the mood, I couldn't even get mad. "I have two brothers and my sister does not bring people back from the dead. She just saves them when they're two steps away from death."

He didn't look convinced. "Nice try, but I'm not buying it."

I threw my hands up. "I don't have to lie to you, Glone."

"Uh huh. So, when do we get to meet this sister, it's just the one right?"

I nodded.

"An actual necromancer," Glone mused. "This should be interesting."

"She's not—" I started, but Clink cut me off.

"She really does bring people back from the dead, Glone. I've seen her do it. She uses blood magic and all."

Glone shot me a look that said, he knew I'd been lying the whole time, because of course, Clink was telling the truth.

"Where'd she get the blood from?" Glone asked, his voice filled with wonderment.

Clink put a hand on the other man's shoulder. "This part, you'll love. She bit Toma's face off!"

Glone burst out laughing. "She did not! I saw Toma's face a few minutes ago. It was perfectly intact."

Clink nodded somberly. "It grew back fast. That was her blood magic too."

The two men shared an amused look, then both fell over laughing. It took me a second, but I finally got it. They were doing what they could to distract from the shock of what we'd just been through.

"Guess I missed the joke," Chaz said, coming around the corner. I couldn't tell if he was serious or not. He shook his head and ran a tired hand down his face. "Had Rowan check on Fina. She's fine for now, but you two need to talk to her at some point."

Glone and Clink both sobered, neither looking too happy at this, but it was Clink who spoke. "Hard conversation to have. The possibility that she could lose Glone and me. Not sure how to do that."

I thought back for a second as I knew I'd heard that name before. Then it hit me. Clink's heart had almost stopping beating when Glone and Cherry had spoken of her earlier. "Who's Fina?" I asked, as all three men seemed genuinely concerned about her.

"She's Clink and Glone's daughter," Chaz answered.

I blinked, "Uhh, what?" Though that did explain some things when it came to Clink and Glone, I still hadn't seen that coming.

Clink shot Chaz a heated look. "She has a mother and father." He looked at me. "Her father was my best friend. He died before she was born, so Glone and I stepped in." He took a breath, and I could tell he wanted to be talking about anything besides this. "We try to protect her from all of this. Always have. She lives up top with her mother, good woman.

Glone rocked back on his feet. "Only fathers she's ever known is me and Clink, but we keep the memory of her dad alive for her, would never try to take his place."

Clink nodded and Chaz rolled his eyes. "Still need to talk to her while you can."

Clink sighed and pulled Chaz into a hug, trying, I thought, to change the direction of the conversation. He kissed the top of Chaz's head. "Your brother's okay," he said, stating the obvious.

Chaz looked to where Kirk lay on the bed, Nico in one of the empty chairs by his side. "Lazy fucker won't get up though. He's okay. They say he damn near jumped to the sky after your sister healed him. Now he's just trying to get all the pretty girls to come by and kiss him on the cheek. Cherry's been with him the whole time and look at Nico."

Leave it to Chaz to cut straight to the point. "Maybe he's just tired," I offered.

Chaz rolled his eyes. "Nah, just an attention hound. He'll get out of bed once he's had enough."

"How soon until he's ready to go?"

Chaz looked at me as if I hadn't heard a word he'd just said. "He's ready now! I just told you, this is all a part of his game. Didn't you understand what I meant, Love? "

I laughed and couldn't help from pulling him into a hug. He detangled himself from me and tried to look offended, which only made me laugh more.

We decided to stay on Crimson for a while longer, in order to eat and heat up. We also needed to come up with some type of game plan.

I knew the people of Synex to be peaceful, so where did these underground creatures come into play?

I had to find out more, and the only way to do that was to go back there.

AFTER A COUPLE OF HOURS of getting our thoughts together and our bodies adjusted, we once again stood in snow up to our thighs. All seven of us had come, and though we'd agreed it would be better if we spread out, we knew it was just too dangerous. Ice and snow rained down on us, and I wondered if we could make it out of here before it was at our waist.

Each step was a struggle, as the cold went through all our protective gear and chilled us to the bone. We could barely see two feet in front of us and had to keep tapping each other to make sure we were all still together.

We walked for a while before the snow cleared, and visibility became better. We seemed to be downtown, as people milled around, going in and out of shops and cafes.

Every building we saw was made of black or white ice. Even the people, who walked around with short sleeves, dresses, and shorts, seemed to be made completely of ice. A lady walked by in a bikini, talking to another in a bathing suit, both complaining about how hot it was today.

I blinked and remembered that the natives here were impervious to the weather, which is why it was often said that they had ice in their veins. If I remembered correctly, it was summertime here. A shiver went through me as I thought of what would have happened had we actually come in the dead of winter.

Delightful cries rang out as kids skidded up and down the street, throwing snowballs and playing other games. Many went without shirts or shoes, yet it didn't seem to affect them in the least.

Finally, we'd walked until the Synexes faded away and we came to open land, where nobody but a Clamor man stood. A familiar Clamor man. My fists clenched at my sides, as I remember this man kicking me repeatedly in the face, then knocking me out after Kirk and I had already surrendered.

The cold didn't bother him either. He wore no coat, no gloves, and no hat. He had a long, thin, silver weather ring around his neck, which kept his body temperature at its normal level.

I'd heard of them, and seen them in pictures, but never had one of my own. They were hard to come by, and only sold to certain people, and on certain worlds. I think the danger was that one could set themselves on fire or freeze to death if they used the device improperly.

He looked at us as if we were dirt on his shoe. "Did you have any trouble finding the place?" The irony in his words told me he knew exactly what we'd been through.

I wouldn't rise to the bait, though. No matter how much I wanted to smash his face in, this was about so much more than that. "Where are they?" I asked through gritted teeth.

He wanted to play games, but the moment he took my people we went way beyond passing barbs. We were not friends, and I wouldn't engage in schoolyard banter with him.

His smile was crooked and slimy, and for a minute he reminded me of Jerry and Clerry, the prison overlords. That thought stopped me for a minute, and I remembered Clerry saying that he had a big family.

The Clamor continued to smile, and the only thing it did was piss me off. "I didn't come here to play games. Give me my people back. That's why we're here, remember?"

He raised an eyebrow. "Really? I thought we were here for an exchange." He rose to his full height and pointed his finger at Toma and Nico. "Hand over the murderers, and we have a deal. Not that it will save you, of course."

My back stiffened because that sure as hell wasn't about to happen. We would leave with Toma, Nico, and my clients. I would have it no other way.

He walked toward us. His whole body shaking with anger. "You came illegally into our world and killed thousands of our citizens. It was the worst massacre... Never in our history has such a mass genocide taken place! You will answer for that, and we will watch you burn." His voice was hot and heavy, and it was the most emotion I'd seen from any Clamor to date.

Chaz stood beside me, his anger so visceral that he trembled from the force of it. "You tried to kill a man." He grabbed Clink's hand and placed it in his shaking and unsteady one, "For the merriment of your countrymen, and you expect us not to defend ourselves?"

By now the Clamor had gotten himself back under control. His voice was once again bland and devoid. "That man made a choice. No one forced him to take the bid."

Chaz started to speak again, but I held up my hand to stop him. We needed to get back on track because this wasn't getting us anywhere. "So why should we give up anyone then? If it's only going to be a fight to the death for us all?"

He smiled as if this was the moment he'd been waiting for. A feeling of complete and utter dread washed over me, and I knew I wouldn't like what came next. "Because of them." He pointed up and slightly to the right. "I will allow you to open a portal and let them go home."

I followed his hand and nearly fell to my knees when I saw what was making him so cocky. Ten of my people. People who'd trusted me and had paid me to find them a better life. People who had believed me when I'd told them that I had.

All ten were strung up on a platform floating in the air. The Clamor held a small device in his hand. He clicked one of the multiple buttons on it, and the platform lowered to the ground.

I swallowed in sickening horror as I realized they were all naked, their hands tied to an ice pole behind their backs. They all had weather collars around their necks, so at least their body temperatures remained at an acceptable level. Their mouths were taped shut, their eyes tearing holes into my soul.

Toma put his hand on my shoulder, and I didn't move it off, too thankful for the comfort. Sharon was there, as was

Larry. Her brown hair was in disarray and her chocolate eyes bored into mine. She looked so scared, frightened, and I felt my blood boil, because there wasn't a damn thing I could do about it.

She'd already been through hell. She'd left her whole world behind to live in a place where she didn't know a soul, and I'd promised her peace. I'd promised her, and her children, a happy life, but now I had no clue if the kids were even still alive.

I tried to convey with my eyes everything I wanted her to know. That it would be okay. That I would do what I could to protect her and the others.

Larry too looked afraid. These two were my most recent clients, and I'd failed them both. Hell, I'd failed all ten of the people on that platform.

The Clamor motioned to someone off to the side, and a horde of Clamors emerged from the shadows. I tensed involuntarily, and my body immediately took on a fighting stance. The rest of my crew did the same.

One of these new Clamor's held a small device in his hand as well. He pointed it toward my people on the platform and clicked it. I could literally see the moment the cold hit them and knew that he'd turned down the temperature on their weather collars.

They shook uncontrollably as the cold ripped through them. I could only watch for a second before I had to do something. "Stop!" I could feel the moisture on my face, but had no way to wipe it. "Just stop." My knees buckled, and the only thing holding me upright was Toma's strong grip around my waist.

The Clamor turned the dial again, and my client at the beginning of the line, Tony was his name, sagged, his face frozen in horror. "Turned his down a little more and I will continue to do so until he's dead. Then I'll go to the next, and the next, until you hand over the murderers Toma and Nico. We will not shed your blood here. You will be at your full health when you face our justice. No one can say we didn't give you ample opportunity to defend yourselves. Even if you don't deserve it." That last bit he spat out.

Tony's lip turned blue, and I made a decision. I started to rise in the air, but Toma pulled me down. He shook his head sadly and turned to his sister. She squared her shoulders, and I could see the steel in her spine as she nodded.

Toma exhaled slowly as if to say, 'we tried, but...' He held out a hand to his sister, and she grabbed it without hesitation. They turned to the Clamor. "You got your prize. Now let them go," Toma said.

No. I looked to Chaz. We had a deal. A deal we'd made in an alley back on my homeworld. We all stood together, or none of us stood at all. My eyes pleaded with him, begging him to do something.

He moved the same time as his brother did, and soon Clink and Glone followed. They gathered around the siblings, enclosing them in a protective shell. Chaz's hands flexed by his side, and I knew he was ready to suss out their power.

The Clamor in charge tensed and looked at the Clamor holding the torture device. The other man's eyes blinked rapidly as he stared at Chaz in horror.

My eyes widened, as I realized what was really going on here. They were scared. Scared of Chaz and what he could do. Well they should be. He'd single-handedly killed thousands of Clamors, and they hadn't been able to do a thing to stop him.

That's why they didn't want to engage, why they wanted us to come along willingly, they were terrified of what would happen if they openly challenged us. My hope rose, because I knew there had to be some way we could use this to our advantage.

Their numbers had been great when they'd sent us to Kalem and Tieden's world, but even then they hadn't wanted to fight, which is why they'd sent us there in the first place I realized.

Chaz's hand started to shake. "I guess you got a fight then, mate, 'cause they ain't going nowhere."

Yes! I looked at Sharon and tried to show her that it would be okay. Her stare was blank, her eyes vacant. A cold hand gripped my heart, as I realized that she'd already made up her mind to die.

Uncertain fear washed over me, and I wondered about her kids. Did she think she no longer had anything to live for? Had they been hurt? Had the Clamors... I couldn't even finish that thought. Not right now anyway.

The Clamor with the device, put his hand on the dial as if to turn the temperature down even more.

Toma's voice rose through the crowd. "I said we give ourselves up!" He and Nico pushed Chaz and the others out of the way and walked toward the Clamors. "We give ourselves up! Now let them go."

Panic hit me in the throat, making my voice break. "Chaz, please." I wanted him to do something, anything. He was the only one I trusted to fix this, and I just knew he'd do something.

There'd been just four of us at one time. He, Toma, Nico, and I had stood in that alley and made a pact. We'd agreed to stand together. We'd agreed to stand up for each other.

He hung his head low, then he looked up at me. "Oh, love, I don't know what to do."

All the air went out of me after that, and I deflated like a popped balloon. I started a slow descent to the ground, but his arms around me stopped my fall. "We can't just let them go," I choked out.

"Shhh." He kissed the side of my head. "Don't let them see you break, love. Later. We'll break later, but not in front of them. Never in front of them, love."

I hung on to him for dear life, his strength the only thing keeping me upright. Toma's and Nico's hands were tied behind their backs. Toma locked eyes with me and nodded, probably trying to offer me what comfort he could. I appreciated the effort, but it didn't work. I felt like someone had sucker punched me with a steel pipe, and I wasn't sure I could come back from this.

With Toma and Nico now detained. My clients' hands were untied. They fell to the platform, none able to stand on their own. Chaz and the others immediately helped them up. I opened a portal, my mind in a haze of confusion and disbelief.

Chaz put an arm around my shoulder and whispered in my ear. "Come on, love, we have to go." My eyes strayed to

Nico and Toma. Both stood tall, heads held high, resolved to whatever happened next.

They were being so brave and here I was a freaking wreck. I nodded, at them, throwing one last look over my shoulder, knowing this could be the very last time I saw either of them again.

Chapter 19

The portal I opened was to a nonviolent world. I landed us inside a skilled hospital that I'd used a time or two in my travels. All ten of my clients were immediately taken back, as Clink explained what they'd been through.

I watched them go, wanting to say so many things, but also wanting to make sure they were okay before I said anything at all.

Seats lined the waiting room, and I sunk down into one, handing my phone to Chaz. "Robin."

He sat down beside me, looked up her number, and put the phone to his ear. "You need to get here now, love," was all he said before handing it back to me. I told her where we were, praying she'd get here soon. Chaz stayed by my side, arm around me, my head on his shoulder.

Kirk hadn't said a word. He looked furious, but he hadn't uttered a sound. Clink sat on one side of him, Glone on the other. Both men repeatedly cast worried glances his way as if scared that he would explode at any moment.

Robin appeared, her face softening the moment she saw me. She squatted on the floor in front of me and waited for me to speak.

Seeing her gave me the safe space I needed to fall apart completely. I screamed out my pain, thinking of the ten clients that had been hurt and the horror of having to say goodbye to Toma and Nico.

"Oh, wow, babe." She gathered me in her arms and began to rock. "What happened? Why are we in a hospital? Did Toma and Nico get hurt? They're the only ones not here."

I sniffed and sat up in the chair. "No, but they'll be dead soon. They got taken. The Clamors have them."

"What?"

Yeah, it was hard for me to believe as well. "They gave themselves up to save those ten clients you told Chanel about."

She put a hand over her mouth and gasped. "Rekia..."

I bowed my head. "We need to get my clients home. Then we'll talk. For now, though, we need to get them home."

She squeezed my hand. "I'll go check, okay."

Kirk got up, kicked the door open, and walked out of the room. Chaz was up immediately. "I got him."

Chaz walked back in alone a second later. He didn't say anything, just sat heavily in his chair, a defeated look on his face. Clink laced their hands together, and Chaz seemed to take comfort from that small contact.

Robin came in about an hour after that and gave me the thumbs up sign. "All ten are cleared to go."

I swallowed hard. "Are they stable?"

She nodded. "Might need some extra TLC, but they're okay. The Clamors didn't hurt them and they were never really exposed to the cold because of the weather collars."

We decided that she would take half of them back and I would take the other half. Together we made sure they were safely placed back where they belonged. Sharon still hadn't uttered a word, which made me even more scared for the safety of her children. "How are the kids? Did the Clamors hurt them?"

She wouldn't look at me, just shook her head. "They weren't home, thank Goodness. Probably wondering where I am. Probably thinks that my husband somehow..." She gasped, unable to continue, a horrified look on her face.

My heart sank deeper than I'd ever thought possible. I'd done this to her. I'd caused this. I'd promised her and her family protection, and all I'd delivered was misery. "Sharon, I... don't... I don't know what to say. I'm sorry this happened. Sorry, you got caught up in something that had nothing to do with you."

Robin had called Chanel, who'd gone about setting up protection for all my clients until this mess blew over. I started to tell Sharon this, to reassure her, but she shook her head, not letting me speak. "Anything you're about to say, just don't. I'm used to living in fear. I guess I just thought this time would be different. I just want to be with my kids now, please."

My heart heavy, I slowly opened the portal that would take her back to Trent's world. "But Sharon you don't have to be afraid anymore. We've set up protec—"

She stepped inside the portal and disappeared before I even had a chance to finish the sentence. I had wanted to send her to a few different worlds before landing her back home, just for precaution, yet something told me that wouldn't have gone over well.

She'd been hurt when she'd come to me, and I'd somehow managed to hurt her even more. Shit! I kicked over a chair, and walked toward the last client on my list, not sure what to do with him.

My phone rang before I could decide and I picked it up to see my sister's number. She told me that she was with Sharon's kids at this very moment. Relief flowed through me. They were safe, and Sharon had just appeared back in her living room.

I released a breath of air, and knew that Chanel would set them up with effective protection.

That done, I closed my phone and turned to Larry, the last one on my list. "I'm going to find you somewhere safe to go," I promised him.

He shook his head. "Take me home."

My shoulders slumped. "Larry, why would you want to go back to Sentra? That's where all this trouble began."

He seemed nonplussed. "You have to protect me then. Sentra is everything I've ever dreamed of. I'm not going to some lesser world. Send an army to protect me, and I shall be fine. I don't want to see them, though. So, tell them to use stealth. I don't want this interrupting my life any more than it has to."

"Okay." I nodded. I didn't have the strength to argue with him, and Chanel was always thorough in anything she did. But just to be sure, I called her and alerted her where he'd be coming in, so that she could put some people on it.

Then I opened a portal, taking him to five different worlds, stopping on a sixth to recharge with food before sending him back to Sentra. He nodded a thank you, then pushed up his glasses and slipped through.

I covered my tracks by speeding through five more worlds. Once again stopping to refuel, before heading back to the hospital.

Robin stood off to the side, hands in her pockets being uncharacteristically quiet. Kirk had come back, he sat beside Chaz, head bowed, looking at the ground. Chaz wasn't talking, but he didn't seem to be moving from his brother's side either.

Clink and Glone sat on either side of them. No one uttered a word, and no one talked about the two that were missing. The two we were going to get back, no matter what it took.

Not able to look anyone in the eye, I mumbled instead. "Glone can we go to your world and rest?"

He nodded, and I opened a portal and watched them all go through. Once the last one was in, I closed it and turned to my cousin. "Why are you so quiet?"

A serious look on Robin's face almost seemed like an oxymoron, so the fact that she wore one now made me anxious.

She shook her head sadly. "You're going to get yourself killed, Rekia. These people are serious. This is not a game. Why does it have to be you? Why can't you pass this off to someone else?" Her voice choked with emotion, and it hurt like hell knowing that I was the cause of it. Hell, I was just messing up everybody's life today.

"What would you have me do?" I asked, my hands outstretched. I had to see this to the end. Surely she understood that.

She snatched me into an ironclad bear hug. "Be careful," she said, before pulling away. She gave me one last worried look, before opening a portal and disappearing.

I was all alone now, and part of me felt as if I deserved it, deserved the isolation. Yet, another part of me knew there was only one place I wanted to be.

I TRANSPORTED TO MY cottage on my father's home world. The living room was empty, but I could hear sounds coming from the television in my bedroom. "Trent?" I called out, letting him know it was me before I felt the burn of his lovely lasso again.

He sat on the edge of the bed, hands clasped together, a worried look on his face. One glance at me, and he sat up straighter and held his arms out. "Tell me what happened."

All the air left me then. Just seeing him there offering his comfort was all it took to start the water works again. I climbed into the bed, and he wrapped himself around me, pulling me close, and whispering in my ear. "You don't have to talk. But I'm here if you want to."

I unloaded on him, telling him every single step we'd made since I'd last seen him. Ending with me standing alone in that hospital waiting room.

He held me tighter. "You did the best you knew how. Like always." I sniffled, and he continued. "You didn't cause any of this. This was dumped in your lap, yet you've gone out of your way to help Toma, Nico, and the others."

"But I haven't helped," I cried, not willing to accept his kind words.

He kissed the top of my head. "It's not always easy doing the right thing, and the results are not always as we wish them to be, but you tried. You did your best, and no one can fault you for that."

He gently lifted my head, his fingers warm and comforting on my skin. His expression was serious, his eyes searching mine for something. "Besides, it's not over. Because the Rekia I know never goes down without a fight."

I stared at him, wondering what I'd ever done to make him believe in me so much. "I'm not what you make me out to be."

He shook his head, placing a tender kiss on my cheek. "You are so much more than I give you credit for. Don't ever doubt that."

Not really believing him, but willing to take the compliment anyway, I settled into his arms and stayed there for the rest of the night.

I awoke the next morning to the smell of coffee brewing. I followed my nose down the hall to see Trent sitting at the kitchen table, reading the paper, and drinking a cup.

He looked up when he saw me. "Some interesting stories they publish in this thing." He set the paper aside and got up to pour me a cup of coffee. He had a stack of pop tarts in front of him, and he offered the plate over while sitting back down.

I took a frosted one off the top. "Thanks," I said, nibbling on it, but not really liking the taste.

He smiled. "You don't have to eat it you know."

"I know," I said, my tone subdued.

He pushed his food away and turned to me, taking my hands in his own. "You can't blame yourself for doing the right thing. It doesn't work that way. You helped Toma and Nico, free of charge, knowing that you could be hurt or killed in the process. There was no malice there, Rekia. Now, you have to pull yourself out of this slump and go save them.

"They don't need your tears. They need your help. That is unless the Clamors and Sentras have already defeated you. They hurt your clients and your team. You really going to let them get away with it?" He raised a brow.

I pulled him to me for a kiss. He tasted like strawberry pop tarts and bitter black coffee. An excellent combo, I thought, leaning in for a little more. "You know me better than anyone," I said, running my fingers through his hair.

He smiled and leaned back in his seat. "Great. So, when do we leave?"

I stiffened and shook my head. I should have known this was coming. "You're not going anywhere. We talked about this."

His jaw tightened. "I'm not your boy, Rekia."

"I know that."

"Then stop treating me like I am. I'm not defenseless."

Why wouldn't he just drop this? Why couldn't he understand? I took a moment to collect my thoughts and search for the right words.

He sat rigid, eyes locked on mine, waiting for me to speak. "You make me vulnerable," I finally said. His face softened, and I reached out to run light fingers across his jaw. "I need you here, and I need you safe. Can you agree to that please?"

He pulled my fingers from his face and held them in his hands. He stared at me for a good thirty seconds before he spoke. I swallowed hard, not sure I was ready for his response. "You know where I am if you need me." His tone was low and grainy, and his eyes held something I didn't quite understand.

He let me go and stood. He didn't utter another word, nor did he look back, as he walked down the hall and closed the bedroom door.

I nodded because I knew that was as good as I was going to get from him. I'd hurt his pride, and for some reason, men lived and died by that thing. Silently vowing to make it up to him later, I opened a portal to Crimson and stepped through.

Chaz and the others were outside at the swing set watching the kids play. Kirk sat, eyes closed, Rowan right beside him. Clink and Chaz sat on the opposite side of him, caught up in conversation with a woman I didn't recognize. Glone was eating a piece of chicken and licking his fingers. He pointed to the plate on the table, knowing I needed to recharge after my portal hop. I snatched up a piece and wolfed it down, nodding him a thanks.

Chaz's eyes widened when he saw me. He jumped up and ran my way. "Don't do that again, love. You can't keep appearing and disappearing like that. Especially not now with so much going on."

I didn't want to fight. "I'm sorry. I should have told you I was going to see Trent."

He nodded. "Well, I guess that's all right. Just let us know next time, yeah?" His words were serious, but his tone playful.

By that time Glone and the others had walked up as well. We talked a little about our next move but didn't get far, before a portal opened and a lone figure stepped out.

I immediately went on guard until I saw who it was, then I went on guard even more.

Saylor stood before us, chest rising and falling. She was covered in blood. Her hair was in disarray. She had a knife in her hand, and a wild look in her eyes.

"Saylor, what the hell?" I asked, not wanting to get too close. She looked deranged, and I didn't know how she would react to sudden movement.

"I had to torture a few people to get their locations." She sounded like she was breathing through her words.

Kirk's big hands flexed at his side. "So, you know where they are?" he asked roughly.

She nodded. "They're on two separate worlds, but we have to get to them soon. Word has it that they're transporting them both tonight, after that, I don't know."

I didn't trust this lady. Maybe she really was here to help, but she'd done so much fucked up shit, that with her it was hard to tell where her loyalties lay. Not with us. I knew that, even if I didn't know anything else. "Why do you care?"

The hand holding the knife shook as she looked up at me. "None of your business. Now are you going to help me or not?"

Kirk stepped forward, a menacing look on his face. His voice came out hard and biting. "I'll help you, but if you're lying, if this is a trap, I'll break your neck."

In a blink, she had him on his back, knife pressed against his throat. "Don't threaten me, boy. My husband and my... She stopped herself and stood, letting him up as well. She looked frightened and furious at the same time. "Will you help me get them back?" Her voice actually broke on that last part.

I was stunned at the extent of her emotions, as I'd never seen such from her. There was something else going on here. Now, whether that was good for us or bad, I didn't know. I intended to find out, though. "I'll help you, but I can't speak for the rest of my team."

Chaz hit me with an, 'are you kidding me?' look. "Oh, love, you're not getting rid of us that easily, now."

I turned to Clink and Glone. Clink took Chaz's hand. "I go where he goes."

Glone stared hard at Clink, and I could see those same words written across his face, yet he dared not speak them. Instead, he cleared his throat and nodded.

Well, now that that was settled, I needed a little information. "We can't go in blind," I said to Saylor. "Tell us what you know."

She looked at me, eyes unhinged and unfocused. This was all so strange. I'd never gotten the impression that there were any lingering feelings between her and Toma. Not on her part anyway, so why the outpouring of emotions. I didn't understand.

Saylor wiped a few strands of hair away from her eyes, as her knife twisted and turned at her side. "Toma is being held on Rydie. It's a dark world, with hardly any light. We can come in through an abandoned part of town. He's not with criminals. Rydie doesn't take criminals, but if the money is right, they'll cage any being you bring them."

I shook my head. It was always about the money it seemed. "So, what are we up against?"

She nodded as if she understood I had to ask, but she was still anxious to go. "Rydie only wants the money. They're not going to fight. They won't risk their lives getting involved in another world's problems. No. The only thing we're up against is more Clamor and Sentra." She wiped more hair out of her face. "I don't know how many."

Good enough, I guessed. "So, the name of the world is Rydie, and it's a prison world of sorts?" I asked, trying to get a feel for the place before I attempted to make a portal there.

"Not prison. Every person there was kidnapped or captured."

"Got it."

MY FRIEND, PEPE, SOLD infrared contact lenses and would assist with putting them in correctly. We stopped in his world first, so that I could purchase a few. Saylor had said the world was dark and devoid of light. We were already going in blind, so we needed every advantage we could get. We didn't have time to send home every person in the prison, but we could at least send them to a neutral world until this thing was over.

"Why so many?" Glone asked.

"The other captives, we may need their help to make it out alive."

He nodded, blinking his eyes a couple of times now that the lenses were in place. "Always thinking ahead, huh?"

My shoulder slumped at his words. "If I were, then we wouldn't be in this mess. Sharon and Larry would have been safe in their new lives, and Toma and Nico would be with us now."

He gave me a frank look. "Can't carry the world on your shoulders, Rekia. Eventually, they'll break and then you won't be able to carry anything."

I gave him a small smile and turned to the others. "You ready?"

Clink cracked his neck. "Let's do this."

I opened the portal and we stepped into what I assumed was supposed to be straight darkness, but with our contacts, it looked no different than midday.

"I guess they really work then," Chaz said, pointing to his eyes. "I can see everything."

We were in the woods, and the rustle of scurrying animals sounded all around us making me go even more on guard. The air was fresh at first, but as we walked, the smell of rot and unwashed bodies made its way to my nostrils.

I put my hand over my nose, trying to stifle the scent because, to be honest, it was starting to take my breath away. "Do you know which way to go?" I asked Saylor, who we all followed behind.

Her tone was short and biting. "I know what I was told."

I rolled my eyes, suddenly missing Nico more than ever. Not that she was all that nicer, but at least with her, I knew there was some affection there.

We'd only walked about ten minutes when we noticed a large outdoor cell that seemed to run the length of the forest.

We could hear voices, lots of them. There were guards walking back and forth, and I cursed because somehow, I'd gotten it into my head that this one would be easy.

"If we can see them, it won't be long before they notice us. We need to think up a game plan."

Chaz closed his eyes and appeared to be concentrating. After a moment, he opened them and shook his head. "Something's blocking the power inside the cells. I can't get a signal from anyone." He tried again, with the same results.

"What about the guards?" I asked.

"Them either, love. It's like the prison on Clamor."

Great. I ran a hand down my face, trying to figure out our next move.

Saylor held up a small device. "I don't play to lose." She clicked the button. "Now let's get my husband and get out of here."

The air crackled, and Chaz let out the biggest smile I'd seen on him in a while. "Power," he said, and suddenly he began to glow, as it lifted him in the air.

A large boom sounded from the direction of the cell, and I looked over to see the whole thing had been knocked over. The prisoners must have realized they had control again and all hell had broken lose.

There had to be over three hundred men here. All power-ful, rowdy, and out of control. One man opened his mouth, and a hail of fire came out, and took out the three guards in front of him. After that, chaos.

I decided they needed a world with a containment cen-ter on it. There was no way we could get them all sorted to-day. Not with Nico still waiting.

Clink started to blink in and out, a clear sign that he was about to astral project. Instead, he made five of himself. "Let's spread out, see if we can find him. Rekia, you can go ahead and open the portal and start trying to get them through." With that, he disappeared.

I stood for a moment mouth opened. How the hell did he expect me to convince all these men to go through a por-tal when the last time they'd done it, they'd been put in a cell.

Chaz and Kirk set out through the forest looking as well. Saylor turned to me. "As soon as we find Toma, open the por-tal and I'll send them through."

I shook my head. "I'm not sending them through with-out telling them where they're going."

She was on me in an instant. One moment I was stand-ing, the next I was on my back, knife pressed against my throat. I tried to use my TK to throw her off, but it barely had an effect. She shuddered, but never lost her grip on the knife. "We have to get to Nico. Now as soon as we have Toma. Open a fucking portal. Unless you want her death on your hands."

She jumped off me and by the time I stood she was more than five feet away. I decided to let it go for now and wiped my clothes down. "I won't—" a whirl of miniature sand bullets flew into the tree to our right, and we both took off running in that direction.

Toma and two other prisoners were surrounded by three guards. Toma's clothes were torn off him, he was dirty, and his face was bruised and swollen. I used telekinesis to smack the guards against nearby trees. They hit with a thump, and blood splattered everywhere as they dropped to the ground.

Toma looked up shocked. "Rekia? Saylor?" Oh, I forgot they couldn't really see. I handed contacts to him and the two men who stood beside him. Once in place, Toma glared at us. "What are you doing here? I thought we had a deal. What about your clients, what happens to them now?"

Saylor, who was more unhinged than I'd ever seen her, leaped into his arms and whispered something in his ear.

He seemed surprised at first but then wrapped his arms around her as if he welcomed the embrace. He listened closely to what she had to say, his face going hard. He squeezed her tighter, then whispered something back to her.

I wasn't sure what was going on, as last I'd known they hated each other, so this was certainly unexpected and a little disconcerting as well. I didn't know who to trust now, and that was a problem.

Chaz and the others walked up a few minutes later.

"We gave lenses to everyone we saw. We took most of the guards out, but I'm sure more will be coming," Clink said.

I nodded, still not sure what the hell was going on with Saylor and Toma. I opened a portal that would lead the prisoners to a containment center, hoping it wouldn't be too much of a problem.

Surprisingly we didn't have to argue with them to go, which probably meant that any place was better than this one.

They all rushed through, knocking each other back, each fighting to be the first one inside. It was toward the end that we heard shouts and footsteps coming our way.

"On it," Clink said, blinking out. He came back, a sense of urgency on his face. "More guards. They're almost here."

After the last one went through, I quickly closed the portal. There could have been stragglers out there, but there was no way to be sure.

With the footsteps of the guards getting closer, I hurriedly opened a portal to the least confrontational place I could think of. Somewhere we could squat for just a minute and recharge.

I called my sister once there, telling her to get Robin and check on the prisoners in the containment world. After they were cleared, I needed them to make sure they got home safely. She agreed, and I hung up the phone, glad that was out of the way, but feeling a little guilty about putting so much on her.

She did have a family to take care of after all.

After we'd loaded up on carbs and calories, I opened another portal immediately, not wanting to waste any time getting to Nico. Who knew what was happening to her. I only hoped she was still alive.

Chapter 20

Darkness surrounded us again, but this time it was just nightfall. We had on our contacts, so it wasn't a problem.

We were in the woods again, and fallen branches along with hard ground crunched lightly under our feet. We heard owls hooting and crickets chirping, as other nighttime animals scurried by, going on with their regular routine. The air was chilly here, making me wish I'd worn a sweater instead of a simple T-shirt.

Thick trees, filled with green and brown leaves stretched out for miles, making it difficult to see anything else. The scent of pine and forest floated through the air, giving the place a woodfresh scent.

Glone took an interested look around. "Never thought of outside blockers. They'd never do that on Crimson. We'd dig a hole in the ground and escape the second their backs were turned. Aye, Clink."

Clink smiled. "Hey, remember that time—"

"Hey," I said, cutting them off. "We're not here for that. We're here for Nico. Remember her?"

They didn't answer, but Kirk burst through in front of everybody.

Saylor and Toma both moved as if they had fire under their feet and I wondered just what was going on with them.

We walked until we came to a clearing, where the trees thinned and we could see a small patch of grass and rock. I looked around but saw nothing in either direction so we kept going straight.

We'd probably been bumbling for around about fifteen minutes when we finally stumbled upon something. A group of guards dragging something or someone down a well-beaten path.

"What do you think that is?" Chaz whispered to me.

I shrugged. "I don't know, but if it can lead us to Nico, I'm all for following."

The others agreed, and we cautiously traced the guards' footsteps, keeping behind trees and out of the way.

We eventually came to another clearing. A huge empty space, beaten down by grass and dirt. It was easy to see footprints, many different sizes and it was clear that it was used often. A cell sat in the middle of the man-made space, a single occupant inside. Nico.

Toma and Saylor shared a worried glance when they saw her. Neither looked happy, in fact, they both looked a bit disappointed.

I blinked, not sure I was seeing correctly. I would have thought Toma would be overjoyed to find his sister unharmed. He wasn't, though, that much was clear.

Before I could think on it more, the guards opened her cell and tossed whatever they'd been dragging inside.

A young girl no more than sixteen or seventeen hit the ground hard. Her face was bruised and swollen, and her hair was a mess. Her clothes had been ripped, and she was favoring her right arm. There was steel in her eyes though, and I knew from just one look that she would not be giving up without a fight.

Saylor's breath hitched, and Toma's hands clenched at his side. Nico looked down at the girl, a reassuring smile on her face, though her eyes glistened with tears. "It's okay, Lala. Just stay down, and they won't hurt you."

One of the guards grabbed the girl by the hair and yanked her head back. Her cheeks puffed with anger, but she never cried out. "Never thought we'd see a Sentra around these parts, much less two." He looked straight at Nico. "Now get on your knees and beg for her life or watch me take her head off her shoulders."

Toma and Saylor charged just as Nico was lowering herself to the ground. The girl pulled a knife from her hair and jabbed it into the leg of the man who was holding her.

He fell to the ground, and she hopped on top of him, and tore his throat and esophagus out with her bare hands.

Damn. I stepped back, both amazed and horrified by her power. The other guards tried to attack, but by that time Saylor and Toma had reached the cell. Toma choked them by shooting sand into their mouths and ears, while Saylor's whole body hummed and buzzed with blue and gray energy. She focused on the guards closest to the girl, Lala. Her eyes sparkled with wild energy and when she held up her hands, the guards disintegrated to dust.

The girl jumped fully into the fight, tearing out hearts, and splitting bodies in two. It was a strength like I'd never seen, and I turned to Glone curious. "Can you do that?"

He nodded. "Could probably teach her a thing or two given the chance."

If he thought so. I turned back to the fight to see that Nico had joined as well. The whole cage was ablaze now, and Nico, Lala, Toma, and Saylor slipped out and came to where we stood.

Chaz and the rest of us hadn't joined the fight, and the truth was, we hadn't needed to. "Any more prisoners here?" I asked Lala and Nico.

They both shook their heads, which was good enough for me. We portaled to three different worlds, before I felt satisfied that we weren't being followed.

On the fourth world I stopped, so that we could all recharge with some food, then I took us to Yunge. I had a large home there with multiple baths and bedrooms. We landed in the living room. "I know there's a lot to discuss. But first, let's get cleaned up and let me introduce you to the first aid kit." I took the large white case down and sat it on the table.

The girl, Lala, had been so strong before, but now she just collapsed into Toma and Saylor's arms. "Mom, Dad, what the Sentra is going on?"

I stepped back stunned. Daughter... This girl was Toma and Saylor's daughter. When the hell had they had a daughter? I shook my head. That was a stupid question. But why hadn't they said anything? I took a closer look at her. Her skin was the same brown as her mother's, but her features were definitely in the like of Toma and Nico.

To be honest, I really didn't know where to put this. Maybe they'd just been trying to protect her. All three of them. Nico, who was almost her twin, walked up behind her and wrapped her arms around the girl's neck. She straightened and turned to Saylor, a savage look on her face. "Why didn't you tell us she was missing? You had no right to keep that from us."

Saylor seemed completely unconcerned. "What were you going to do? My daughter was dragged through the woods while you sat in a cage, useless as usual."

Nico lunged for her, but Toma stopped her in her tracks. "Don't," he said in a voice that left no room for argument.

Nico shook her head. "Toma, look, I know you... I know we... She had no right to keep this from us!"

He wouldn't look at his sister, but his words spoke volumes. "She did what she had to, to protect our daughter."

Nico gave off a chuckle of disbelief. "You're so blind when it comes to her. You always have been."

Toma put a hand on his daughter's shoulder. "What matters most is standing right here."

Saylor took a seat on the couch and hit Nico with a death glare. "You stupid, little girl. Do you really think I would risk my baby's life just to get at you? Just to get one over on you. Egotistical bitch. Everything I've done since the moment Kolo died has been in protection of my child."

Nico threw her hands in the air. Her whole demeanor said she thought that to be a steaming pile of horse shit. "Lala was fine when you murdered Kolo."

"I didn't murder him. I put him out of his misery. He was going to die either way. I just made sure he didn't suffer."

"What does that have to do with my niece?"

"Remus and Welvina... killing them wouldn't have saved Lala. They have friends in high places. They threatened her, all of them did. If I didn't go along with their plan to kill Ko-lo, they would have killed her."

Nico's eyes narrowed. "You really expect us to believe that?"

Saylor sat back in her chair. Hands clasped in front of her. "What you believe matters less than the dirt on the bottom of my shoe." She turned to Toma. "But when have I ever lied where our daughter was concerned? When?"

Toma laid eyes on his sister. "It does explain a lot."

Nico's brows rose to the ceiling. "Like what?" I sat up a little more in my seat because I was interested in hearing the answer to that myself.

Saylor held out her hand and pulled her daughter closer. "Why don't you go get cleaned up. Wash your hair, put some fresh clothes on. Rekia, could you help her with that?"

I pointed down the hall. "There are several bedrooms, each with their own baths. You're welcome to any of them, except the first one on the left, that's mine. Clothes are scattered throughout the rooms. You just have to find your size."

Lala stood and looked from her mom to her dad to her aunt. "Promise you won't kill each other while I'm gone. I mean you can maim, I'm not taking that off the table. But I would like you all to be alive when I get back."

I laughed, and she scurried out of the room with no backward glance. Once she'd been gone long enough to be out of hearing range, Nico turned back to Saylor. "Explain yourself."

Toma spoke instead. "Why did you think following us around would help Lala?"

She thought what? I looked to Clink and the others, who all wore blank faces. How do we know that she thought that? I looked to Toma.

He shrugged. "I know her. Know how her mind works. Saylor?"

She stared at him hard, seeming almost pissed that he would speak so intimately about her. "Lala was taken the moment you found out who really killed Kolo. To use as leverage against me in case my feet once again caught a chill."

She looked from Toma to Nico. "Also, to bring you two to heel, if need be. They thought to use her as a last resort. Keep your mouths shut about who really killed Kolo, or they would kill what you, what we all, loved the most."

Toma looked horrified, while Nico's hands trembled at her side. "I would never have... You should have told us! We would have turned ourselves in immediately!"

Saylor leaped from her chair like a lion going in for the kill. She landed inches from Nico. Her face a storm of emotions. "And just how would that have helped my daughter, you stupid little girl? As long as you and Toma were free, her life still had value. What would happen to her if they killed you or had you captured? The only reason she was kept alive was to use against you and your brother when the time came. If they already had you, then they didn't need her."

She looked from one sibling to the other. "Why do you think I helped rescue you from that Clamor jail? Why do you think I've gone out of my way to keep you alive?"

Her eyes landed on Toma, and for the first time, I actually saw shock play across her face. She sounded as if she almost couldn't believe the words as she spoke them. "You thought I did it because I loved you?" She shook her head and chuckled, but it was hollow and dry. "Silly boy." She went back to her seat, still shaking her head. "Silly boy."

I rubbed my eyes, which were heavy with sleep. I'd had enough. I stood and stretched out my arms and legs. "We pull out first thing in the morning." Toma tried to catch my eye, but I really didn't have the stomach to look at him or anyone else in that room.

I sunk down in my bath that night, going over everything I'd learned. Toma and Saylor had a daughter, and no one had thought to mention her. Apparently, said daughter, was as strong as a fucking ox.

I soaped up my rag and washed across my chest and down my legs. The water was hot, just the way I liked it, and the tub was more a Jacuzzi than anything else.

I'd brought Trent here once, and the memory of being in this very tub with him floated across my mind and made me hungry for his touch.

I didn't have time to think about that though. What I needed was to figure out what to do about this whole Lala situation.

She couldn't fight with us. As much as we could use her, her parents and auntie would never agree.

I dipped my head under the water then came back up wiping my eyes. Even if they did agree, all three would be too distracted to be of any real use. Not that Saylor was much of an ally anyway. I stood and got out of the tub, wondering whose side the other lady was really on.

Chapter 21

I opened a portal to Crimson about six that next morning. We landed in the hideaway room that Chaz had once thought to be his private spot.

Lala looked around, her eyes big and her smile wide. "This," she said, taking in the cramped space and dingy furniture. "Now this is the way to live."

I looked at her in surprise, as she took a seat on the couch. "This way, I don't have to worry about messing up some bougie ass house that costs way more than it should."

She kicked her feet up on the table, and Glone knocked them off. "Not going to have that, girl. Show some respect for other people's stuff, or didn't your ma teach you any better?"

I shot Saylor a look, but she seemed more amused than anything.

Lala tucked her feet under her, giving Glone a sour look. "Okay then, old man."

Glone's lips quirked up in a smile. "Got some stuff I can teach you, if you're willing to learn."

She played with a loose string on the couch. "What did I do wrong?"

"Huh?" he asked, looking around the room at the rest of us for clarity.

She exhaled as if she thought he should already know the answer to this question. "I fought, you saw me, yet you still think I need help. So, what did I do wrong?" She stood, her eyes on him alone. "I'm willing to learn. You don't have to twist my arm, yeah."

Saylor stared at her daughter, her face unreadable, while Toma just looked like he'd rather his child be anywhere but here.

Glone pointed at the door. "Good. Let's go."

I watched them exit, wondering just what the hell he was about to teach her. She seemed to be doing fine, from what I'd seen.

"So, she'll stay here until we end this," Toma said, once Lala was far enough away that we could no longer hear her asking Glone a million questions.

Saylor took a glance around. "It's okay, I guess. The Crimsons are powerful people. If they're willing to protect her, that is."

Chaz stood a little taller, looking offended at the suggestion that the Crimsons wouldn't do all they could to protect a young girl in need. "I'll settle her with our Rowan and Cherry. She'll be protected alright."

Saylor gave a small nod. It looked as if it hurt her neck to do so, but she still did it nonetheless.

She sat in a single chair, while Nico, Kirk, and Toma sat on the couch. I sat on one of the bar stools, while Chaz leaned up against the bar, Clink right beside him.

Nico was the first to speak. "So, what now?"

Saylor eyed everyone in the room. "Well, I don't know what your plan is, but I'm not going down for Kolo's murder." She crossed one leg over the other, her face not threatening, but not all that friendly either. "I'll do whatever it takes to keep my hands clean of this whole mess." It sounded like a threat to me, but I wasn't sure if anyone else saw it that way.

Nico stiffened, so maybe she did. "The dirtiest hands in the world, yet you expect us to wipe them clean." She shook her head. "I don't think so. Kolo died, and you could have stopped it. Instead you joined."

"Would you rather a dead niece then? Is that the price you'd have been willing to pay to keep Kolo alive? I take no chances when it comes to my daughter. Keep talking, and I'll slit your throat, making sure you die a little faster than he did."

Nico bristled, but Toma put a hand on her shoulder to calm her down. "No one's slitting anyone's throat." He gave Saylor a pointed look, then turned to his sister. "I don't like what happen to Kolo and those involved need to pay, but..."

"But he'd take a dead Kolo over a dead Lala any day," Saylor finished for him.

Nico's jaw tightened. "You're loving this, aren't you?" she sneered.

Saylor uncrossed her legs, then thought better of it, and recrossed them. "Yes, seeing my daughter dragged through the woods really brightens my day. I blame you for that, by the way."

"Saylor," Toma said, stopping either of the two from responding. "Whose idea was it to frame Nico for Kolo's murder?"

"Welvina. Nico was the closest person to Kolo. I didn't particularly like it, but they'd already threatened Lala, so..."

Toma shook his head, a defeated look on his face. "You didn't even warn us."

Saylor blinked hard, but the rest of her face stayed impassive. "Have you listened to a word I've said? No, as usual, you think you've got it all figured out."

Not able to take any more, I stood and cleared my throat. "Bicker on your own time. Bottom line is, we need to figure out our next move. Saylor, Lala is safe here, so are you ready to turn on Remus and Welvina? We need to clear Toma and Nico's name so that they can go home again."

She thought about it a moment, her eyes narrowing as they stared at me. "What are you asking, Rekia? That I implicate myself in wrongdoing?" She shook her head. "That's not going to happen."

"Then implicate Welvina and Remus and leave yourself out of it."

She tilted her head to the side, a complacent look on her face. "I'll see what I can do, but I make no promises."

I stared at her, not even sure why I was surprised. I turned to the others in the room. "Right, so we can't depend on her, so we go along with the original plan. Go to Sentra, and show them that all three senators took part in killing Kolo, then wait for the fallout."

If I'd thought that would rattle her, it didn't work. "Well, you do what you must. I will as well."

Nico sat up a little in her seat. "We're not ready to fight. If we go up against the Sentras and Clamors now, we'll be crushed."

Saylor sighed as if this was all beneath her. "You act as if all of Sentra are aware of Welvina and Remus' plans? Were you?"

Nico shook her head like she didn't understand where this was going.

Saylor smiled at her. "Sentras are not sheep. Neither are Clamors. They will not blindly follow Welvina, just because he thinks they should. The team he has working for him is just that, his team. The normal everyday Sentra, though? Not a chance, especially when they find out what he's planning."

"So, what do you suggest?" Nico asked.

"Half-truths and lies. Both the Clamor and Sentra will want to know what's going on. Especially if it affects their dollar amount."

Well, I had thought they would all blindly follow along, so there was that. I'd seen all Clamor and Sentra as one big like-minded entity and forgot that they were actual living, self-thinking, individuals underneath all that gold and glitter. "What's your plan?" I asked, not really believing I was turning to her for advice.

Saylor put her focus on Nico. "You lied. When you were first arrested, and banished to the sewer, you claimed that you didn't know what had happened to Kolo and that you'd had no knowledge of his death. That was untrue. You and I actually witnessed Welvina and Remus murder him."

Nico's face stayed neutral. "Go on."

"We were told, if we talked, they'd kill our whole family. So, you took to the sewer, and I suffered in silence, still forced to work side by side with my tormenters. The people will think I'm a martyr, Welvina and Remus will be banished or hopefully killed, and then I'll be the head senator in charge, and you two can come back to do, whatever it is that you do."

Nico looked disgusted. "While you get away scot-free."

Saylor seemed nonplussed. "What exactly is it that you think I've done wrong? I didn't kill Kolo, I ended his misery. I went along with Welvina's plan to save Lala's life, unless you think I should have let her die instead?"

"I never..."

"I'm not done talking," Saylor said, cutting Nico off with a little more force than necessary. "The only thing I've done since this whole thing started is keep you and your brother out of harm's way. I didn't have to save you from the Clamors, but I did."

"You did that to keep Lala alive, not for us."

"No matter my reasons, I did it, and you wouldn't be sitting here right now if I hadn't. How do you think you stayed alive all those months' underground? You found food, and bottles of water in all the dumpsters that you frequented and you thought what? That it was a coincidence? I protected you while you were down there. Looked out for you. So stop acting like I owe you something and realize that it's us against them. That's the only way this is going to end. The only way that it can."

I hated working with her. Hated the look that crossed Toma's face as he stared at her, half in awe and half in anguish. She spared him a brief glance and blinked her eyes slowly. I had no idea what that meant, but whatever it was, it brought a small smile to his face, so I guessed it was okay.

"We still need help," Nico said. "What we've got is not enough, and I don't trust Clamor or Sentra not to hire out trained fighters."

I thought back to Kalem and Tieden. They'd been powerful enough to close my portal, and disable us one-handed. If we could convince them to fight with us, them and a couple of their people, that could be enough to turn things our way. "I'm going to go talk with Robin and Chanel. Be back soon." I opened a portal before anyone could question me further.

ROBIN SAT IN MY KITCHEN, playing a game of checkers with Trent. They both looked up when they heard me enter. Robin jumped from her chair and engulfed me in a hug. "You're alive."

I pushed her away and raised an eyebrow. "Why? Did you think I wasn't?"

She waved her hand as if it was a moot question. "With you I never know. Toma and Nico?"

I nodded. "We got them, along with Saylor... and her and Toma's daughter."

Robin's eyes went wide. "Her and Toma's what?"

Trent looked at me. I shrugged, not knowing what else to do. "It's what happened." I pulled out my phone and sent a message to my sister. "A lot has happened. I only want to say it once, so wait until Chanel's here, then I'll tell you everything."

Chanel arrived about ten minutes later, my brothers Kevin and Greg on either side of her. I squinted my eyes in frustration. Why the hell had she brought them? What did they have to do with anything?

Robin, the complete opposite of me, jumped up and gave each of them a hug. "Hey, I got those tickets you wanted," she said, giving Greg a punch in the arm.

He smiled. "Good. Haven't been to Bajo in a while." He pointed to Trent. "Told you I could score."

Trent nodded. "So, when are we going?"

Chanel took a seat at the table. "It's in two months, but Robin was supposed to get tickets for all seven of us." She pointed at me. "Except for her of course. Who knows where she'll be."

I only counted five of them. "Who else is going? Rusty and Blake?"

Our cousin, Rusty was best friends with Greg, while Blake and Robin were close.

Robin nodded. "Yup."

I looked to Trent. "Really? And you didn't tell me?"

Greg let out an exasperated sigh. "The only time you let us know what's going on with you is when you're in trouble. Case in point, the reason we're here now."

No, the reason you're here now is because Chanel, Robin, and apparently, Trent couldn't keep their big mouths shut. I made sure to give each of them a hardened look as I spoke.

Even though I was irritated, I went ahead and brought everyone up to speed.

No one spoke for about three seconds then everyone started talking at once. I could only make out a few words, like, idiot, reckless, dangerous, and criminals. "Stop!" I said before they could go any deeper. Five sets of eyes snapped my way. "Just stop. What's done is done. Can't change that. What we need to do now is focus on what happens next."

Greg ran a hand down his face. "If we can't beat them with power, we can try to beat them with brains." He pointed to his right temple.

I shook my head. "I don't want you involved. None of you. You have kids to take care of and stuff. This, this right here, is no good for you."

Kevin leveled me with that same stare that used to make me wither when we were kids. "If you didn't want us involved then you shouldn't have called us here."

I cut a pissed off eye at Chanel and Robin before I answered. "Who asked you to be here in the first place? It certainly wasn't me, so go. Go home and do whatever it is you do when you're there."

He looked at me as if I was still a three-year-old child, which is what he made me feel like most of the time. "Leave your pride at the door, Rekia. There's no space for it in this room."

"I won't be able to concentrate if you're around! I never have been. You'll get us all killed. I can't fight if I'm worried about one of you. So just go, and let me do my thing. I'll come back. I always do."

Chanel opened a portal. "Not going to argue with your stubborn ass, but I will be telling dad." She stepped through and disappeared. She wouldn't tell him, but even if she did, hopefully, it would be all over before he could do anything.

Kevin looked at me and shook his head. "You're just determined to get yourself killed, aren't you? Well, go ahead. It'll sure be a load off my back if you do."

I resisted the urge to stick my tongue out as only a three-year-old would. "And you're determined not to trust me, or my judgment, but what else is new?" I shot back.

He opened a portal. "I'll tell the kids you said, hi." Then he was gone.

That left me, Robin, Greg, and Trent in the room. "You going to make your dramatic exit too?" I asked, looking at Greg.

He sighed like he just didn't know what to say, then used one arm to pull me to his chest. "Be careful, and tell Chaz and the others, thanks for keeping you safe this long." He fist bumped with Trent, two finger waved at Robin, then opened his own portal and stepped through.

I sat stock-still for a moment. Picking up on the signatures they'd left behind. I knew that Chanel had gone home. Kevin had gone to Aze. A world filled with fast games and faster race cars. I guess he needed to blow off some steam.

Greg, on the other hand, had gone to a world, from what I was sensing, named Blown. I didn't know this world and had no idea what he was doing there. It seemed kind of sexual to me, so I definitely didn't want to know more.

Robin smiled at the spot that Greg had just exited. "Ah, Blown. Love to go there. Fun times."

What? I looked at her, but it was the amused look on Trent's face that really caught my eye. "Don't tell me you go there too?"

"Only when Greg needs a wingman." He flipped his hand backward as if to say it meant nothing. "Now back to the plan. What do we do from this point forward?"

I steeled my nerves before I spoke. "There is no we. I told you, I won't be able to focus if the two of you are there." I was tired of having this conversation.

Robin stood and grabbed a bottle of water out the fridge. "That's just stupid, Rekia, but okay we'll play things your way."

I didn't believe her for one second. "I mean it, Robin. I don't want to see either of you there."

She sat back down and raised one leg in her chair, wrapping her arms around it. "You won't."

"I mean it," I said, a little more forcibly this time, hoping she'd get the point and leave it alone.

She held her hands up in front of her. "I said okay. I want you alive and well, so I'll stay out of it, okay."

I still didn't believe her, but realized it was the best I was going to get. Trent's chair faced me, so I leaned over, putting my hands on either side of the thing. "Can I have a kiss? You may never see me again."

He didn't laugh. "That's not funny."

"Can I have a kiss?"

His eyes said he wanted to choke and kiss me at the same time, but he leaned forward, and our lips met in a sweet soft caress that quickly turned frantic and desperate.

Robin cleared her throat, making us both pull away.

I licked my lips and sighed softly, loving the feel of him. Then I turned serious. "I'll get in touch as soon as this is over. You probably won't hear from me until then."

"Okay," Robin said, a little too casually for my liking. She picked up her water and took a big gulp, ignoring the intense stare I was leveling her way.

"Trent?" she asked, as if she expected him to speak up on her behalf or something.

He shook his head. "Hey, I don't control her, and neither do you, so..."

Sensing that there was nothing more I could do to convince them, I opened a portal. "Just sit tight until you hear from me. I'll be in touch as soon as I can." I gave them one last look, trying to memorize their faces before I disappeared back to Crimson.

My only thought was getting to Glone.

I found him outside at the picnic tables. He and Lala were eating red hots and cabbage, talking over fight moves.

"When you jump up, then bring a closed fist down on their jaw, that right there, they ain't never getting up again."

Lala took a bite of her red hot and nodded like this was the type of thing she liked to hear. "Yeah, but when you hit 'em with an uppercut though..."

He laughed, and they knocked water bottles before going back to their food.

"Good to see you're setting such a good example," I said, standing in front of them.

He shoved a fork full of cabbage into his mouth, then held up his plate so that I could have one of his red hots. "Her mom did leave her in my care."

I ate my food in three bites. "If her mom left her with anybody it was her dad and aunt. Where is her mom anyway?" Knowing her, she'd probably called one of those mysterious portal openers she had and disappeared.

Lala shrugged. "Said she was going back to Sentra."

Stunned, I looked to Glone for confirmation. Jaws fat with food, he nodded. "Said there was something she had to take care of, called somebody for a portal and disappeared."

I bit my tongue to keep from saying something I shouldn't. That was the worst piece of news I'd heard all day. We couldn't trust Saylor! Who knew what she was really up to?

This only made the whole situation even more urgent, and I needed Glone to come with me now. "I need you to go somewhere with me."

Glone looked up from his food and pointed to his chest. "You talking to me?"

"No, I'm talking to the bushes," I said exasperatedly. "Of course, I'm talking to you."

He wiped his mouth and stood. "Where we going?"

I swallowed not knowing how he'd take it. "I want to go back and talk to Kalem and Tieden, see if we can get their help."

He came a little closer, eyes narrowed like he'd caught me with my hand in the cookie jar. "And you thought, what? That you'd bring me along to sweeten the deal? Never took you for the pimping out type, Rekia."

Before I could answer, Toma stepped outside looking for his daughter. "Nico wants to talk with you." He raised an eyebrow at me but didn't say a word.

Lala drained the last of her water, then followed her father back inside.

Glone watched them go. "So, I guess you don't want anyone to know then, huh?"

I shrugged. "If it works then we get much-needed help. If not, then they never have to know we tried."

The look on his face said he thought I was full of shit. "Slippery slope that keeping secrets is, Rekia, but yeah I'm down."

Chapter 22

There was a risk coming back here, who knew what kind of mood Tieden and Kalem would be in when they discovered we were there. Still, they had promised us hospitality, so I hoped they'd meant it.

We'd only been there about three seconds when they appeared in front of us. Tieden stood with his shoulders back, eyes intent on both me and Glone. Kalem stood by his side, an amused look on his face, but not at all surprised.

Their eyes raked over Glone as if they'd been starving for days, and he was just in time for dinner.

"We didn't come here for that," I said, speaking before Glone could say a word.

"We know why you're here," Tieden said, floating to one side of Glone, while Kalem came up on his right. Glone seemed to welcome the attention. Lips quirked up in a grin, he loosened his shoulders and made his whole stance more inviting.

Tieden pushed silver locks out of his face and leaned over to whisper in Glone's ear. "Can we touch you now, or are you still enamored with the big one."

Kalem moved in closer as well. "Tieden, dear, he still longs for the big one, but he'd like a night with us as well."

Tieden nodded. "Yes, yes he does. Tell me, Kalem," he said, walking around the back of Glone, checking him over. "What will we do to him first?"

I shot Glone a hasty look, and he reluctantly stepped back from the two. "We didn't come here for that. We need help. Got a big fight coming. Could use all the bodies we can get. The way you two handled yourselves the first time we were here, I'd say you fellows would be good allies."

Kalem looked nothing but disappointed. "Well if we're not too busy we may show up."

I let out a frustrated sigh. That wasn't good enough. I needed to know what we were up against. "Can we depend on you or not?"

"Kalem, dear, why does she expect us to tell her more than we already have?" Tieden asked.

Kalem brought Tieden's left hand to his lips and gave it a short kiss. "Pay no attention to her, darling. We've said all we're going to say. We're hosting a ball tonight, remember? We must be ready. It's going to be dazzling."

"Yes, dear, the cooks have been working overtime on all of our favorite dishes."

Tieden smiled as he and Kalem walked in the other direction. "They've been working on our guest's favorites as well. Tell me, Kalem, why are we such good hosts?"

That's all I heard before they disappeared altogether.

Glone and I stared at each other stunned. "Well that went well," I said, not quite sure what to make of it.

The only thing I did know, was that I couldn't depend on them for help. Even if they came, they were likely to get distracted, by well, anything.

Glone stared after them. "Never met anyone like them before. Maybe I will come back here later. With your assistance, of course."

I sucked my teeth, not ready to get into that right now. "Come on, we need to get back to the others."

We arrived back on Crimson to chaos. All around us, people flew about, putting on armor and strapping on weapons. I turned to Glone. "What's going on?"

He looked at me as if I'd just asked him to break out in song and dance. "How do I know, love? I've been with you the whole time, haven't I?"

I pulled out an energy bar and gave one to Glone. He accepted it with a nod.

Toma's loud voice led me to a room down the hall of the cave. He and Lala stood yelling at each other, while Saylor watched, a peculiar look on her face.

Nico was there as well, hands clenched, taking in every word. Kirk, Chaz, and Clink were all moving around hastily, loading up supplies.

"Ah, there you are, love," Chaz said, once we walked fully into the room. All chatter stopped as everyone's eyes turned on myself and Glone.

"Where have you been?" Toma was the first to speak. He turned away from Lala, but the frustrated look on her face said their conversation was far from over.

"What the hell is going on?" I asked. "I leave for a few minutes and come back to this." I waved my hand around the disarray of the room to better get my point across.

Lala put her hair in a ponytail and gave both her parents a defiant look. "The Clamors are attacking, and my dad won't let me fight."

I gaped at her, then looked around the room for confirmation.

Chaz nodded. "It's our best time to strike, love. We better get on it."

If the Clamor's had attacked, then where were they? "I don't see anybody."

Nico frowned. "Who are you expecting to see, Rekia?"

"The Clamors."

"Why would they be here, when they're off attacking my home world?"

Nothing made sense. "Wait a minute," I said, holding a single finger in the air. "You mean to tell me that the Clamors and the Sentras are fighting each other?"

Chaz stopped what he was doing to stare at me. "That's what we've been saying all along. Do try to keep up, love."

I turned to Saylor because this was her doing. It had to be. "What did you do?"

Saylor stood, but the first thing she did was address her daughter. "Your father lets you get away with way too much. You don't talk to him like that. Ever."

Lala scowled but didn't say anything.

Saylor then turned to me, tapping a light finger to her lips. "Two times now, the Clamors have had you in their control, and you were able to get free. Once at the prison and then again on Synex."

She shrugged. "Maybe the Clamor's were simply letting you go. Maybe you made a secret deal with them, to open profitable new worlds. Worlds that would far surpass anything the Sentra had to offer. In exchange, of course, for the freedom of Toma and Nico, and the promise to never bother you or your crew again."

She took in a breath that looked as if it cleansed her whole soul. "Maybe the Sentra felt as though they'd been betrayed and launched a warning attack against the Clamors. Knowing the Clamors, they didn't take that too kindly, and decided to attack Sentra head on."

I stared at her, stunned at the level of conniving she was capable of. "Something tells me you whispered in a few ears and helped them believe that."

"Would you rather they attack you instead?"

I ignored her and turned to Toma. "If they're killing each other, then why are we trying to stop them?"

He ran a hand through his hair. "We're not stopping them. I'm content to let them fight this whole thing out if need be. But I don't think it'll last long. The Clamor and the Sentra are too smart for that, and once they figure out they've been duped, they're going to come at us full force."

I nodded, as it all began to take shape in front of me. "So, hopefully by the time they figure it out, it'll be too late. They'll already be weak and wounded from the first battle, and their numbers will hopefully be thinned out too."

Kirk smiled. "And there we'll be, on the sidelines ready to pick off the remainders."

I liked it. "So, we just need a good place to hide and watch the battle then?"

Clink didn't seem convinced. "We need more than that." I turned to him waiting for an explanation.

"Who's to say they haven't already figured it out and are lying in wait? I just think we're too optimistic and we don't have all the facts," he said.

I nodded, because he was right, and from the look on their faces everyone in the room knew it. "So, what do you suggest we do then?"

He came to stand in the middle of the room, probably so that he could better address everyone. "We send in three teams. The first team can be kind of like a recon to see what's going on, but they need to be able to fight if they have to. Then the second team is when we launch our attack.

"The third team should be able to do the most damage, and since they've been waiting on the sidelines, they should be fresh for the battle. The third team comes when the Clamors and Sentra least expect it. When they think they've broken us. When they're so tired from battle, they can hardly stand. That's when we hit them with the last bit."

Nico gave Clink an approving look, then focused her attention on me. "That means you'll have to be in the third group. We can't have all three teams hiding out on Sentra, so you'll have to stay behind to open a portal to send a new team in each time."

I'd already figured that part out. "Each team needs to have a mixture of fighters. There will be no sending in the weak while the strongest hang back until the end."

Glone went to the door. "Leave that part to me, alright. I know how to separate them properly."

I WAS IN MY ROOM SUITING up when Toma wondered inside. Everyone seemed to be scurrying about, getting stuff ready for the battle, so we were not alone.

He sat down on the bed beside me, a conflicted look on his face.

"What's up?" I asked, knowing him well enough to realize that something serious was on his mind.

"However this ends, I just want to thank you, for Nico and myself. We never would have made it this far without you believing in us, and Nico knows that. She may never say it, but she knows it."

I nodded, not wanting to get too deep with this. "Are you going to let Lala fight?"

"No." His body went from honest and open to completely closed off in a matter of seconds. "That's one thing Saylor and I agree on."

I picked a few pieces of lint off the blanket laying across my bed. "I don't trust Saylor. Do you?"

He shook his head, but I could see a thousand gears turning, with him trying to find some way to excuse her actions. "She would never do anything to jeopardize Lala. I do know that."

"What if they convinced her that the only way to keep Lala safe is to lure us into a trap?"

He stood, a distant look in his eyes. "My daughter is smart. She'd figure it out. Saylor wouldn't risk Lala never speaking to her again. She just wouldn't."

He seemed so sure, and I sighed, thinking that he had a lot more trust in her, than I did. "I went back to that world," I said as he started toward the door.

"What world?" he asked, turning back around.

"Tieden and Kalem. I asked them to help us fight."

His face registered surprise, but I didn't see any objection there. "What did they say?"

I thought about Kalem and Tieden's weird response and shrugged. "Who knows with those two? The only thing we can do is give this thing our all. Even if we don't succeed, at least we know we tried."

He gave me a tight smile and walked out the door, neither of us saying what was blatantly obvious. We were headed into a hailstorm of danger, and at this point, it was probably already too late for any of us to walk away.

I went up the hall and saw that Glone had assembled three teams and sectioned them off, to the chagrin of Chaz. Their loud voices hit me the minute I rounded the corner.

"What's the problem?" I asked.

Chaz and Glone stood toe-to-toe, nostrils flaring, and fists clenched. Clink stood off to the side, leaning against a row of boxes, head down, a hand over his face as if trying to block it all out.

Chaz whipped my way, finger pointing at Glone. "This here wanker is trying to separate me and Clink in battle. He put himself with Clink on the third team and wants to toss me out on the second."

A few people walked by, but none paid us any mind. Which meant that Glone really had excellent control of his people, or they'd already seen so much in their lives, that a screaming match barely registered.

Glone spoke before I could. "It only makes sense, Rekia. Clink and I have to show what happened that day, remember? We can't do that if we're dead in the first or second round. Chaz is a power stealer. He can hold things off until the final team arrives. That's all this is. Nothing more."

"Chaz," I said on an exhale. Not liking what I had to say, but knowing it needed to be said. "Now is not the time to let the personal get in the way. This is bigger than that, and Glone's plan does make sense."

He started to protest, then settled for sending me a glare that said I'd betrayed him for life.

I looked to Clink for help, and he finally walked over.

He put a hand on either side of Chaz's face, softly cradling it. "There is nothing and no one that can keep me from you." He kissed the other man lightly on the lips, causing some of Chaz's anger to dissipate. His shoulders loosened, and his expression became vulnerable and open as he looked into Clink's eyes. "We need to do this, you know that. So, let it go, and let's focus on the fight, Okay?"

Chaz lowered his head, but Clink put two curled fingers under his chin and lifted it until they were eye to eye. "Okay, Chaz?"

Chaz nodded and went in for another kiss.

Glone watched for a second, then rolled his eyes upward. "Good. Now that that's settled, can we get on with this, please?"

WE DECIDED IT WAS BEST for each team to be positioned on a different world. I picked the three most deserted and nonthreatening places I could find and stationed everyone per Glone's directions.

None of my crew were on the first team, but Glone had assured me it was made up of competent fighters who could hold their own.

Team two had both Kirk and Chaz on it, their sister Rowan staying behind just in case she needed to tell their parents and other siblings what had happened.

Glone had also sent Lala up to the top with Rowan so that Saylor and Toma could leave without her causing a big scene. Unlike her brothers, Rowan had never been arrested and could come and go from up top to bottom as she pleased.

Glone and Clink were on the third team, as were Nico, Toma, and Saylor. All five of them played a part in ending this, so that's the way it had to be.

Glone and Clink had talked to their daughter Fina and from the defeated look on their faces when they'd returned, I didn't think it had gone well. It was a hard thing to tell a child, and there was really no way to make it easy.

As for me, I needed to be able to open the portals for all teams. "I'll keep a check on the fight. That way I'll know when to send in the next group."

I looked at all the determined faces around the room. "We've got this. All we have to do is stick to the plan, and everything will be fine."

I did a check of each team, just trying to make sure spirits were up, before flexing my hand and opening a portal to Clamor.

Chapter 23

I opened the portal a short distance away from where I sensed the battle was taking place, then levitated in the air to watch.

I wanted to see just what we were getting into before I sent anyone in.

Even from a distance, the air smelled of blood and human feces. The scent was so strong that I put a hand over my mouth to keep from vomiting. Never had I smelled anything so vile in my life.

That scent alone made things real and tangible in a way they hadn't been before. We could all die here today. We could walk out into battle and never walk away again. That thought sent a shudder through me, and I took a moment to let it pass, before seeing what we were up against.

The streets were a mess of blood and bodies. Sentra and Clamor alike lay stretched out, some moving, but many more not. Buildings had been torn apart. Trees sat on their roots, store signs had been torn down and ripped to pieces.

This once beautiful city now looked like a hollowed-out war zone. The fighting had stopped, but anxious Clamor and Sentra lumbered about, apparently not sure what to do as their leaders talked off to the side.

Welvina and Remus stood in front of a platinum building where the windows were busted out, and a whole side had been ripped away. It had probably been dazzling once, but now it looked no different than any other worn out and abandoned place.

The two senators were talking to three Clamors. I was too far away to hear anything that was said, but going by the way Welvina kept walking back and forward, and the angry way the Clamors kept pointing at the destruction, I'd say it was heated.

I hurriedly opened a portal and went through to get the first team. The Clamor and Sentra both had people laying in the field. We needed to strike now before they had a chance to regroup.

Stopping for a second, I looked around and wondered how my life had ended up here. How had I ended up fighting a battle that had nothing to do with me, or any of the worlds that I loved?

I'd wanted action, craved it even. Now, I'd do anything to be sitting in my small three-bedroom house, watching TV, playing with my nieces and nephews, having lunch dates with my sister, all the while staying safe and out of harm's way.

I shook my head, dispelling such thoughts. Toma and Nico were friends that needed my help. I had to focus.

I'd left the first team on Yaka. It was a desert world, with nothing but red sand for miles. When I entered, I saw that they stood poised and ready to fight.

Someone must have taken charge because they were all lined up, as if awaiting their next command. Looking at their faces, some eager, some scared, I got a sinking feeling in my gut.

This wasn't their fight. It had nothing to do with them, so why should they die today? "You don't have to do this," I blurted out. "I can take you back home right now if you want to go."

One man, in the third row, stepped forward. "That medicine you brought back saved my son's life. We Crimson pay our debts. After this, we owe you nothing." Murmurs throughout the crowd seemed to agree with him.

I bit my bottom lip, and tried to remember that these were proud men and women. To them, a debt owed, was one to be paid. It was probably the real reason Glone had been so helpful and not gone back on his word once. "Then we have to hurry because the Sentras and Clamors are talking, and that's the last thing we need."

I opened a portal where I'd last seen Welvina and the others. Before I could blink, the crowd of Crimson men and women rushed through, some calling out battle cries, all seeming pumped and ready to fight.

Welvina looked up startled, as did Remus and the three Clamor's they'd been talking with.

Welvina ducked, then shot a Crimson man in the face with crackling red energy. The man screamed and fell to the ground. He put a hand to his face, that quickly turned red with blood.

I stifled a cry, knowing this could be all our fates if we weren't careful. Giving one last look, I hurriedly disappeared before I could be spotted. It was a tricky game this, as I was dipping my toes into a lot of pots at once and I just hoped none of them got burned off.

I delayed about fifteen minutes, which I figured was enough time for the first group of Crimsons to do all they could do. By now they'd be weary and glad to see help arrive.

Chaz and Kirk were deep in conversation when I stepped onto Losote, where I'd stationed the second team. It too, was a desert world, with not a lot of people around.

Chaz saw me the moment I stepped out of the portal, and he and Kirk headed straight for me. Chaz looked resigned, yet determined, as if he knew this could be his last day alive and he'd already made peace with the outcome. "Here, love." He handed me two letters. "These are from Kirk and me to our parents. Do portal them underground to Crimson. Rowan will come by and see that they're delivered."

I nodded, because I wouldn't lie and say that everything would be okay and no one would die today. Someone already had, and he'd been Crimson, and I was sure he wouldn't be the last. I stuffed the letters in my pocket, determined to portal them before I even sent Chaz and the others through.

Chaz gave me a small smile, and this time his eyes went a little misty. He took a deep breath before speaking. "These last two." His voice broke, and he stopped to wipe his eyes. "The last two are for Clink and Fina. In case I... maybe... if they..." His voice broke again, and a few tears slipped out of his eyes. Then he pulled me into a hug, slipping the letters into my pocket in the process. "Just see that they get them, love."

He felt warm and alive in my arms, and I squeezed him tight, realizing that this could be the last time I ever saw him. "Dammit, Chaz," I said, pulling back and ignoring the stinging behind my eyes. "You better fucking stay alive."

He laughed, but it was hollow and empty. "I'll try my best, love. I'll try my best."

Kirk flexed his hands by his side, but he didn't say anything. He didn't seem nervous, just anxious to get things over with. "You try to stay alive too," I said pointing at him. "I want us all to walk away as a team when this is done."

He nodded and kept flexing his hands. Figuring that was the best I was going to get, I turned to face the crowd. There were fewer people here than the first team. They stood in small groups, talking and throwing me looks that said they were ready to get this over with.

I exhaled deeply. "Okay, then. Here we go." Heart beating out of my chest, I raised my hand and opened the portal. "You know what to do."

They filed through, some screaming war cries, but most just grunting and moving fast. I lost sight of both Chaz and Kirk in the shuffle, with so many people going through at once, it was hard to keep track. The smells from the battle were as strong as ever, and I just hoped we'd be able to put an end to this soon.

Once everyone had entered Sentra, I closed that portal and opened another one to Crimson, to send the letters through. I made sure they landed in the room we'd first seen Glone in, so that they would be easy to find. Then I chomped down on an energy bar, praying it would be enough to hold me.

After that, I went back to Sentra and levitated over the city to get a better look at the fight.

Buildings sat on their foundations. Cars were burned out and ripped apart. Body parts lay unclaimed and abandoned in the street. Their owners either dead or dying. I put a hand on my mouth and gasped at the destruction. It was a lot to take in and I wasn't sure what I'd expected, but it hadn't been this. This was a catastrophe, and I felt my heart hammer as I noticed the diamond and gold of the streets now ran red with blood.

I blinked rapidly as I looked around. This city had been brought to its knees, and not many Sentra stayed standing. I was sure there were plenty around, but many had probably gone into hiding the moment the Clamors had first attacked.

I didn't see Welvina or Remus, and I wondered if they'd already fallen. The Clamor and Sentra forces were wrecked. All it took now was for the third team to come in, and this fight would be over. Toma and Nico could go home. Lala would no longer be in danger. Chaz, Clink, Glone, and Kirk could return to Crimson victorious, and I could finally see my own four walls again.

A warm feeling ran through my chest at the thought, because we'd actually done what we'd set out to do. Soon Toma and Nico would be cleared, and this thing would finally be over. I floated to the ground intending to make a portal to where the last team waited, when one appeared off to my right.

I gasped and turned in time to see a horde of angry Clamors come flying through. Big hands swinging, and faces full of rage, I knew I had to get to the third team quickly, or this whole thing would be turned on its head.

I tried to run in the other direction, but another portal opened before I'd even made it two feet. I stood in open mouth fear as I watched beings at least two feet taller than the Clamors, and twice the size of a gorilla and bear put together, come galloping through, their large feet pounding the ground beneath them.

I'd seen some big beast before, but I'd never seen anything like these, and I wanted to turn and run, but my feet had forgotten how to work, so I stayed rooted to the spot, heart pounding and body shaking.

I had to get back to the others. We weren't prepared to take on beasts such as these. We'd worked together before, against the creatures in the ice cave, but this was a whole different ball game.

Before I could blink, one was in font of me. His face was wide and angry, his eyes beady like a bird. His skin looked to be made of leather and he had on brown armor that only covered the top of his body. He smelled of destruction and rot and his massive chest rose and fell with the heat of his rage.

I stumbled back, eyes wide with fear. He opened his mouth and let out a roar that ripped through me and had me grabbing my ears in pain.

My only thought was getting to the other team. I thought about just running, but knew he'd be on me the second I tried.

Instead, I decided to open a portal right in front of him. I raised my arms, and the beast's meaty hand came down toward my head. I stumbled back, getting out of the way, because I knew if he hit me, he'd probably take half my face off.

I used my hands to back up a little while still on the ground. Five beasts surrounded me now, and I sat shaking, too scared to move. They stood over me, breathing hard and sneering. Something ugly and hard twisted in my gut and I knew, just knew, that this would be the end of me. A tear slipped from my eye, and I refused to wipe it away.

I thought about my family, and wished I'd been a better daughter, auntie, and sister, because this was the end of the line for me. I'd never see my nieces and nephews again, and that stung worse than anything.

I wondered where Chaz and the others were, wondered if they were okay, or if they'd already fallen at the hands of these beasts.

I couldn't think about that now. Team three was still out there, and I had to find a way to get to them. My hands were face down on the street, and I figured I could use that to my advantage and open a small portal to dip through.

"Did you really think you were going to get away with it?" a voice asked.

I looked up to see Welvina pushing his way in between two of the large monsters. He had a smug look on his face as he swaggered up to me like he'd already won. "You really thought you were clever, didn't you? Setting us against each other like that. I guess you thought we would just rip each other apart. Do all your work for you." He bent over so that our eyes were level. "Not feeling too cocky now, are you?"

I could feel the portal starting to form under my hands and knew it would just be a few more seconds until I could make my escape. I swallowed hard, never moving my eyes from his, hoping he'd take that as a challenge and not break contact. That way he wouldn't see what I was doing.

"She's opening a portal right now. Welvina pay attention," one of the Clamors he'd been talking to earlier said, coming to stand beside him. A tall dark-skinned man, who looked down at me with superiority and hatred.

Welvina pointed to one of the beasts and in a second I was flat on my back, the creature's large foot pinning me to the spot. It felt like I was being held down by a two-ton boulder, which made it hard to breathe.

The smell from the beast's skin was of ash and fire, as if he'd bathed in it or was made from the stuff. I swallowed again, knowing that if I let the fear take me, it would all be over. Welvina came to a stand. "You didn't really think we wouldn't have backup, did you? Thought you were smarter than us this whole time, didn't you?"

I tried to focus, but the agonizing screams and cries from the battle were like scratches of pain on my soul. Where were Chaz and Kirk? I hoped they were safe, but what would become of the third team if I was never able to get back to them? Would they be stuck in some unknown world forever?

I shook my head. No. I couldn't think like that. The sounds from the fighting played havoc on my ears, and the smell of blood and body fluids assaulted my nose and made me want to gag. This was horrendous, and I steeled myself for what I knew was about to come.

Welvina smirked my way, but I wouldn't give him the satisfaction of flinching, even if something in that smile curdled my blood and made my stomach drop. He turned to the beast holding me down. "Kill them all." He pointed to me, that sly grin still planted firmly on his face. "Make it especially slow and painful for this one. I have no interest in seeing her die quickly."

The beast roared his obedience, then looked at me and smiled. It was the creepiest thing I'd ever seen, but I refused to shrink back from it. Instead, I kept eye contact with it, trying to suss out any weaknesses I could find.

As the cries around us grew louder, my heart beat so loud that I thought it would come out of my chest. My body trembled with fear, but I wouldn't beg for my life. No way would I give Welvina and the others the satisfaction of seeing that.

I scanned the chaos around me, hoping to catch sight of Chaz, hoping and praying that he was okay. Then the ground rumbled, and I felt myself go sideways.

The beast swayed too, but his large meaty foot never left my chest. It was getting harder to breathe, the more he pressed down on me, the tougher it was. At this rate, I didn't know how much longer I could last.

I tried to use my TK to throw him off, but the pressure was too much, and I couldn't focus it.

The ground shook again, and I knew it had to be Kirk. Light lit up the sky, and those around me began to falter and wane. That was probably Chaz, doing his thing, draining power. Too much would destroy him, and I just hoped he had a handle on it.

A crack started under me, powerful enough to knock the beast away. Without a moment's hesitation, I took the opportunity for what it was. A chance to get free. Turing all my attention on the beast who'd held me down, I put my hands together, then quickly pulled them apart.

He roared an inhuman cry as his body exploded from the inside out. Blood and body parts rained down, but I didn't linger to see where they landed. Now that I was no longer pinned to the ground, I figured it was best not to open a portal where any of the beasts could easily sneak through.

I ran toward an empty spot, hoping I'd make it in time.

I saw Chaz as I went, standing in the center of everything, all power, and energy being directed toward him. It lifted him off the ground, and he glowed, blue, red, and yellow.

I had to get help soon. No way could he sustain this for long.

A few beasts were still on their feet, and they came at me. I had no idea where Welvina was, nor did I care. The only thing on my mind was getting to Toma and the others and putting an end to this.

Without knowing whether Chaz would still be alive when I got back, I opened a portal and fell through.

Chapter 24

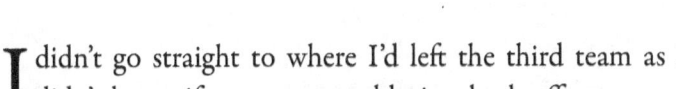

I didn't go straight to where I'd left the third team as I didn't know if someone would piggyback off my portal or not.

Instead, I ate three energy bars, and tumbled through three different worlds. Knowing time was of the essence, I did it as quickly as I could.

Once I was sure I was alone and not being followed, I took a moment to ground myself. I didn't know how I would explain what those monsters were to the rest of my crew.

The only thing I did know, was that Welvina and the others were playing a very dangerous game and for the first time since this thing started, I began to question whether we could really defeat them.

It was a sobering thought, and I leaned against the tree of the barren world I was on and allowed it to develop further.

They'd been one step ahead of us at almost every turn. Saylor seemed like an ally, but I couldn't trust where she really stood or would stand in the end.

Wiping a moist hand down my face, I cracked my neck, then opened a portal to where the third team was.

A nervous tension filled the air when I portaled in, as they all looked on edge and ready for battle. "We have to go now!" I said, hoping the urgency in my voice wasn't too great.

Nico stood talking to her brother and Clink but snapped to attention at my words. "What's happened?"

"Beasts, skin like leather, eyes like a bird, larger than anything I've ever seen. They'll rip everyone apart. We have to get back to them now!"

"Dugons!" Saylor said, looking a little shocked at her own words. "Didn't see that coming. The cost alone, to employ them is more than I ever thought Welvina would be willing to spend."

I looked at her in disbelief. Leave it to a Sentra to think about money at a time like this. "Who are they? Where are they from?"

Toma shook his head. "No one really knows what they are. They seem to be half beast, half man, and highly intelligent. They only have one known weakness that we know of, the eyes." He raised his voice so that all around could hear. "These beast, these Dugons, go for their eyes. Anything else will just bounce right off their skin."

Satisfied that we all knew what we were dealing with, I turned to open a portal, only to stop and give Clink a slight nod, letting him know that Chaz had still been alive last I'd seen him.

WE ENTERED BACK ONTO Sentra to a scene of chaos and confusion. Corpses littered the streets. Some with broken limbs, some had gaping wounds with blood spilling out. We walked by one man, a Sentra, I think, he held out his hand to us, gasping as he took his last breath, his eyes filimg over, and his hand falling back to his side as he did so.

The stench of death and rot was so strong that I had to cover my mouth and nose to keep from gagging. We couldn't walk two feet without stepping over bones and bodies. Rubble from once great buildings lay in tatters all around us.

Looking out, the scene stretched for miles, nothing but blood, death and decay. Even the air seemed oppressive and suffocating as smoke and fumes floated freely, making our eyes burn and giving the place a slight gray tint.

"This is..." Nico looked around, eyes wide and tortured, and I had to remember that this was still her home.

Toma put his hand on her shoulder, his voice sounded as choked up as her own. "We'll deal with that later, for now, we fight."

Clink made his way to Chaz, who was on his knees, bleeding, the power he'd stolen seeping out of him, probably as quickly as he'd absorbed it.

He'd didn't look good and neither did Kirk, who had a gash on his forehead and one across his stomach. His bloodied and bruised fist repeatedly beat the ground but had little effect due to his weakened state.

They wouldn't last long like this, and I tried to go to them, but before I could make a move, one of the beasts snatched me up by my hair and slammed me into the ground. I hit hard, my back scraping against the street and sending shots of pain from my head to my toes.

The beast loomed over me, it's hot, nasty breath roaring down at me and making me shiver.

Off to the side, I could see Toma and Nico circling Welvina and Remus. Though the body language of all four seemed alert and ready, there was no fighting going on yet. Right now, they seemed to be more or less taunting each other.

Everywhere I looked I saw Clink, who'd separated himself into too many pieces for me to count.

I saw Glone jump up and with a single punch to the eye take a Dugon's whole head off. The beast twisted and twitched for a moment, before falling to the ground unmoving. Glone was strong, I knew that, but I didn't think I'd realized how strong.

A Dugon grabbed me by the throat and raised me in the air. I went limp in his grip, hoping that would buy me some time to calculate my next move. He peered at me, pulling me closely, as if checking to see if I was still alive. I used that opportunity to direct my telekinesis straight into his eyes and rip them out.

He screamed, then stumbled back, loosening his grip on me in the process. His face now held two empty sockets where his eyes used to be. It looked disgusting, but I fought down my revulsion and ripped him apart until there were only pieces of him left.

Then I levitated in the air, to get a better look at what was going on.

I saw a Sentra and a Clamor both attacking a man that I'd seen many times on Crimson. He was fighting for us, with us, and I floated down aiming to lend my aid.

The man was barely breathing, and the Sentra had energy flowing from his finger. He wrapped it around the man's neck, choking him.

The Clamor had energy coming out of his hand as well and was squeezing the man's middle, making him look like a balloon ready to pop.

I raised my hands, tearing them both to pieces and allowing the man to break free. He got clumsily to his feet, took a big breath of air, nodded a thank you to me, then jumped back into the fight.

I started a slow descent to the ground, aiming to get back in the fight as well, when I saw that I was surrounded by both Sentras and Clamors, five of them. Two men and three women.

I dropped down hard, ripping the legs off two of them as I did so. The other three dove toward me, and I rolled out of the way, then used my telekinesis to rip their teeth out of their mouths and pull their ears from their heads.

They fell to the ground screaming, and I jumped up, satisfied that they'd been properly disposed of. I walked through the fight now, pulling out lungs, throats, teeth and eyes as I went. It wasn't until I heard Saylor's voice raised in anger that I veered off my deadly course.

Toma, Saylor, and Nico stood before Welvina, Remus, and two of the Clamors from before.

Saylor was encased in blue energy, looking deadlier than I'd ever seen her. "You touched my daughter, Welvina, caused her pain, frightened her. I cannot let that pass. I think you kno—" she stopped talking and suddenly she was on him.

In seconds, she had him on the ground, her shimmering blue hand moving almost too fast for the eye to see. "You shouldn't have touched her!" She reached her hand down his throat, his eyes bugged, and blood seeped from his lips and eyes. "And you shouldn't have killed Kolo," she said, stepping back and giving a small head nod to Nico.

Nico nodded back and walked forward. Her whole body radiated rage and vengeance. "He was your brother. He loved you, and you killed him for money?"

Welvina wiped sweat and blood from his face, his body shaking, probably from the pain. "He was weak! No Sentra in his right mind would turn down that type of cash. You wouldn't have, and you know it."

Nico pointed her finger and a fiery rope wrapped around his neck constricting his throat and causing the smell of burnt flesh to fill the air. "See that's where you're wrong. I'm not that girl anymore." She squeezed tighter and more blood poured from his mouth.

He let out a small laugh that quickly turned into a grimace as more blood squirted out. "Kolo killed himself. All he had to do was join us. You would have reaped the benefits as well, and none of this would have happened."

"I'd rather live in the gutter than drain the people of Clamor the way you tried to."

He attempted another laugh, but just ended up spitting up more blood. "You... are... all... just like me..."

Nico shook her head. "No. We are nothing like you." Then she turned, and raised her hands, while Saylor raised hers. Together they lit him up with fire and blue energy until he exploded right before us.

Remus tried to run, but Toma held out both palms and wrapped sand around his back, pulling him back and slamming him to the ground. He then shot sand into the other man's mouth, causing him to choke and gag until he stopped moving altogether.

Kirk joined us, along with a limping Chaz, who was holding onto Clink for support, Glone walking right behind them. Though I was glad my whole crew was okay, it added small comfort for the hundreds who'd lost their lives here today in a cause that was not their own.

I looked out at the others and saw that same sentiment reflected on some of their faces as well. I swallowed hard and turned to Chaz. "I'll open a portal to Crimson. Let's start to collect your dead. Get them home."

He nodded, face weary, breathing hard. "Was ready to ask you, love. Can't have this be their final resting place, yeah."

I nodded, and along with the Crimsons still standing, we went about the streets gathering up the dead. Some were in so many pieces that it took multiple trips just for a single leg or arm.

Everyone helped, and though there were some Sentra and Clamors still alive, or barely so, we ignored them in favor of gathering up everyone we'd come with.

Once we had them all in one place, I opened a portal, and we began to take them through. We put them in one of the rooms in the tunnels reserved for this type of thing. Glone called on others once we got there and put readying the bodies in their hands.

The last one accounted for, we went back to Sentra to finish what we'd started. We still had to prove to the people that Toma and Nico were innocent.

We were all weary and tired, and it seemed almost impossible to believe that after this last little step we'd be able to go home again.

Clink and Chaz stood holding hands, leaning on one another for support. Kirk stood in front of Nico rubbing his hands up and down her arms as she shuddered. Her face held devastation as she took in the wreckage that was her home.

Glone stood off to the side, looking from Clink to Chaz to the ground, as if not sure what he should be doing at the moment. Or maybe he was just waiting for Clink, so they could do this last little bit and go home.

Toma stood talking to Saylor, and I heard the name Lala being mentioned more than once, so I knew to stay out of that conversation.

It seemed like Glone and I were the odd ones out. Not knowing what else to do, I walked over to him, just to see how he was holding up.

"You okay?" I asked, nudging him a bit on the shoulder.

He looked at me with a sad smile, his face covered and bruises and scratches. "Aye, love, home's calling me, no place I'd rather be, yeah."

I nodded, thinking the same thing. "Yeah." We talked for a bit, all of us working out how to complete this last step, when a portal opened, and a voice I thought we'd left back on Synex called out to us.

I turned to see the man from Clamor who'd held us captive on Synex. The man who'd tortured my clients in front of me, the man who'd kicked me repeatedly in the face on Clamor.

My fists swelled at my sides, but I stopped cold once I saw what was coming out of the portal behind him.

Men and women of slightly lower than average height, who all looked like they'd done nothing for the past hundred years except lift weights, do sit ups, and excel at leg curls. They looked like fucking brick houses.

They all seemed to have shoulder-length black hair, and their eyes were like their faces, hard and alert.

I almost cursed myself for letting the still standing Crimson go. It was only my crew of eight here now, and the Hercules people were still coming out of the portal.

There was so many of them, that I took a few involuntary steps back. "So, we fight," I said, my voice sounding as fatigued as I felt.

Toma came to stand beside me, Nico on the other side, "So we fight," they said in unison.

I focused on one of the extremely well-built men and raised my hand as if to choke him with my telekinesis. He spurted for a bit, but didn't fall like I'd expected him to.

Shocked, I tilted my head to the side and extorted more pressure. Still, he held on. I went down to one knee, using every bit of strength I had.

Finally, I heard bones pop, and his neck dangled to the side, as he fell over, unmoving.

Exhausted now, I stood and swallowed hard. I turned to the others and saw my feelings reflected in their eyes. This was it. The end. No way could we beat these super-powered beings.

Nico took one of my hands, and Toma took the other. She put her other hand into Kirk's, who joined hands with

Chaz, who in turned took Clink's hand. Toma took Saylor's hand, who in turned took Glone's.

Toma was the first to speak. "Don't make it easy for them."

I stood, back straight, head high. "I wouldn't dream of it."

Saylor broke the chain and stepped a few feet in front of us. "If we wait for them to attack, we give them the advantage. Let's charge them, take the upper hand. Let the chips fall where they may."

We broke apart. "To the last breath, then!" I yelled, not feeling in the least bit cheesy.

"To the last breath!" the others repeated, as we all ran toward what we knew would be our doom.

They ran too, right toward us, and out of the corner of my eye, I could see another portal opening and more people coming out.

I gulped hard and almost fell to my knees in surrender. This was too much, we were going to lose, but dammit, no. I wouldn't give up without a fight.

It wasn't until I heard that familiar hiss, and saw that black sizzling lasso sail through the air that I allowed myself to have hope.

They were here, or Trent was at least. I turned to the side and saw them all, Robin, Trent, Chanel, Rusty, Blake, Greg, Kevin, and even my father. My father!

I stopped my steps and ran up to him. "What are you doing here?" I asked, not pleased, but at the same time relieved. Still, I didn't really want him here. Didn't want to see his lifeless body staring up at me from the street.

He gave me a frank look. "Rekia, you didn't think we'd let you face this alone." He talked faster, as the Hercules people were getting closer. "Those are Razons," my father said. "Go for their solar plexus, it's as easy as punching jelly, and they won't get up again. Not if you hit them there."

I nodded and looked to Robin. "How could you? I told you I didn't want them here!"

She didn't have time to answer before the Razons were on us.

"Solar plexus!" I yelled to Toma and the others. "Go for their solar plexus."

One grabbed for Saylor, and she sent out blue and gray energy, slicing him straight through, right where his solar plexus was. He fell to the side, then all hell broke loose.

I now knew where to focus my power, and every Razon I saw, I took apart right through the middle. There were still more of them than us, though, and they just kept coming.

Their only power seemed to be their strength and resilience, so Chaz took what he could and used their own power against them, hitting them in the middle, and laying them out.

Glone, for his part, seemed to be having a blast, using his strength and speed to punch fist sized holes in every Razon he saw.

Toma used his sand to wrap around their middle and Nico used her fire. Clink made many of himself, using sticks and branches to tear through their stomachs.

Kirk combined his hands together to make one large fist, then hit them with everything he had. Chaz soon joined him in doing the same.

Robin, Chanel, my fathers, brothers, and cousins all used their respective powers, not only on the Razons, but on the remaining Clamor and Sentra as well. Trent used his lasso to squeeze them right in their sensitive spot until their bodies separated completely.

The Clamor who'd kicked me and held my people captive on that ice world smiled at me. "Never think you can—"

I put my hands together then used my telekinesis to rip him in half. His eyes, bulged in disbelief, before his body separated, and he fell to the ground unmoving.

I let out a satisfied grunt then rose in the air, cursing as I did so. There were so many of them, and they still kept coming. I put all my attention on their middles, even though I knew it was probably futile.

We'd already had one fight and were worn out and tired. I didn't know how much longer we could last, but I knew it wasn't long. I also knew that as soon as we fell, they'd take us over completely and damn near everyone I loved would die here today.

We were putting up a good fight, but it didn't have staying power. They swarmed us, came at us all at once. From my spot in the air, I saw my family and crew get taken over, as hundreds of Razons, Sentra, and Clamors took them under.

"No!" I screamed, my heart in my throat as I floated back to the ground, fighting my way to someone, anyone. Even though my legs were weak and my powers had all but waned, I fought my way through. My crew, my family, were all in a tight circle, holding off the Razons as best they could.

Trent threw out his lasso, wrapping it around one of the Razon's waist, but before he could command it to squeeze, the Razon pulled him forward, and along with three others began tearing into his stomach and guts.

The scream that ripped from my lips was inhuman. "Trent!" His eyes rolled back into his head, and the only thing I could see was blood as he was steadily torn apart.

Tears blinded my eyes as I ran. No! It wouldn't end like this, he could never end like this. Not with me here. They'd have to take my life too. I tore through the four that were on him and along with my crew took out any that came close.

I fell to my knees and snatched him from them. I wrapped his arms around my neck, though they fell lifelessly back to his side.

I choked on a sob and tried not to panic. "Chanel!" I screamed as I cradled him in my arms. "Chanel, I need you to help me right now!"

The others held the circle, fighting off anyone that came close. Trent's eyes were closed, and he had blood coming from his mouth and eyes. I wiped hair out of his face and kissed his pale sweat-soaked forehead. "Chanel, please! I need you to help me!"

Her face came into view as she scooted down in front of me. I held out my hand. "Take my blood. I give it freely."

She nodded but made no move to do anything, instead she stared at him, still and unmoving in my arms. Her voice was quiet and careful when she spoke. "Rekia, I think that—"

"I don't care what you fucking think! Just save him! I give my blood freely! I give it freely!" I cried out.

"Okay," she said, putting her hand on my shoulder trying to calm me. "Okay, but will it work?"

I looked up at her, knew what she was asking, and didn't understand why she even had to. "Yes. Of course it will, you know that it will, so just do it!"

She sliced down my arm, and I felt everything in me go blank as I watched her perform her work. Something she'd done many times before, but never had it mattered as much as it did in this moment. Trent had to be alright, he just had to.

I stayed with him in my arms. I was unable to move, but I could still see. Glone had done good, was doing good, but three attacked him at once.

They were relentless, delivering blow after blow until they were just punching through him. I heard Clink yell and run his way, saw Chaz do the same.

Clink gathered Glone in his arms, tears spilling from his eyes as he looked at Glone's lifeless form. The two fell to the ground, Chaz falling with them. Clink put tender hands over Glone's face, then turned to Chaz as if begging him to do something.

Chaz turned to Chanel, his voice broken when he spoke. "You can use Clink's blood." He stopped for a minute as if it physically hurt him to speak. "How long until you can help him?

"I'm working as fast as I can," she said, still tending to Trent.

With two of our team down, the Razons took slow deliberate steps, their eyes never leaving us, as their feet brought them closer and closer to where we were. I closed my eyes and waited, Trent still in my arms, him and Glone fighting for their last breath of air.

"No, no, no. This will not do. Tieden, kindly help me take care of these animals who've hurt our friends."

I opened my eyes to see Tieden and Kalem standing in front of me, dressed in silver and gold respectively, hair shining, and bodies alert, they took in the devastating mess around us. "Yes, love, I will help you, but first let's do what we must."

They held up their hands and in an instant, Glone stopped bleeding, and some of the color came back to his face. Tieden sighed unpleased. "Oh, Kalem, this won't do, there is much more that he needs."

The Razon along with the Clamor, Sentra, and Dugons came on us and Tieden and Kalem, only gave a flick of their wrist, and every single one of them dropped to the ground, torn in half and unmoving.

"How?" I asked, my mouth wide with the realization that they'd just taken out hundreds by barely batting an eye.

They ignored me and looked at each other. "I think they have one last thing to do," Kalem said, looking at Tieden. "Do you feel it, love? This last thing they have to do?"

Tieden nodded, then closed his eyes. The streets begin to fill with Sentras, most looking scared, some curious. He turned to Clink. "Do your thing, big one."

Clink wiped his eyes, then laced his hands with Glone's, who was still barely breathing. "This won't show much, but we are too weak to do more."

Clink seemed to draw what strength he could from Glone, and together they projected the image of Kolo being murdered. Except... Clink looked to Glone.

Glone's voice was strained, and he talked between breaths as if every word was an effort to get out. "Lala deserves her mother. Won't throw her to the wolves."

I gritted my teeth, but it was the best we were going to get.

The image lit up the air and showed Welvina killing his brother, but not the part that Saylor and Remus played. If it proved Toma and Nico hadn't committed the murder, then I guessed it was okay.

Saylor's voice rang out to the crowd, and I saw her standing right where the vision had just taken place. "Good people of Sentra, as you can see, Welvina killed his brother and cast my husband and sister-in-law to take the blame.

"I, being the last high senator left, immediately reinstate their rights as full Sentra citizens and all that that entails. May you show them nothing but respect and awe when you pass them on the street. They were wrongly accused and accepted it with nothing but honor and grace. To Toma and Nico!" she yelled, causing the crowd to erupt in cheers.

"Toma and Nico!" they all yelled.

I watched her performance with disbelief. She was laying it on thick, and I had no idea what her real game was. Or maybe this was it, and she'd learned her lesson after all. I looked down at Trent's sleeping face and shook my head. Knowing her, probably not.

Kalem wiped his hands together as if he'd just taking out the trash. He looked at me. "Seems like we helped you after all. Now, if you'd kindly excuse us." I blinked and he, along with Tieden, and Glone were gone.

"What the—" Clink asked looking at his empty arms. Chaz reached for him and pulled him into an embrace. "They can help him, we can't. I don't think they'll hurt him. Do you?"

Clink shook his head. "No, just take me home. I want to go home."

I looked down at Trent. He'd stopped bleeding, and some of the color had returned to his face and I knew they'd helped him as well.

My father reached down and put a hand on my shoulder. "You are too weak, tell me where you want to go, and I'll send you and your friends there."

I had him open a portal to three different worlds, before landing us on Yak, a peaceful world that I kept a home on. Trent and I went through first, with the rest of my crew falling right behind.

Chapter 25

We were all weakened, but I knew that my staff on Yak would take care of us until we got better. Plus, they had some rapid healing herbs here that accelerated the process.

It took over three weeks, but once we were all strong again, it was time to go. We gathered in the living room, Trent beside me, back to his healthy glowing self, and everyone else looking a hundred times better as well.

Clink stood beside Chaz looking subdued and unsure. "I don't know what to tell Cherry and Fina when I get back. We've already been gone so long. I know that they're worried."

Chaz squeezed his hand. "You tell her that Glone was hurt, and is now recuperating. That he'll be home as soon as he's better."

I nodded at Chaz because I couldn't have said it better myself.

We'd gotten Lala, from Rowan, but hadn't told her much about what had happened. The guys would do that when they got back.

Lala stood in between her mom and aunt, her eyes drawn together, her features worried. "So how will we know when Glone's back, and if he's okay?"

Chaz swallowed hard. "We'll keep in touch. Rekia will keep in touch, and you'll know something when we do."

She seemed to accept this, then turned eyes on her father and aunt. "And you two can come back now? No problems?"

Saylor grabbed her daughter by the hand. "Your father and aunt are safe. Their homes, businesses, and income have all been reinstated."

"Then let's go," she said, in a way that seemed to question why they hadn't left already. "Let's go home and help with the rebuilding of Sentra."

I stood, trying to fight the burning behind my eyes. They were leaving me, every one of them, and I hadn't thought it would choke me up as much as it did.

While Kirk and Nico were saying their goodbyes, and making promises to get me to help them meet-up for quickies, I turned to Clink and Chaz. "I don't want you to go," I admitted, tears streaming down my face.

Chaz put my face in his hands. "Oh, love, but you can come see us anytime you like. You will come see us, won't you?"

I grabbed them both into a hug, and they held onto me as tight as I held on to them. "You'll probably get tired of seeing me," I laughed, but it was watery and forced.

"Just make sure you bring them when you come," Chaz said, pointing to the crew from Sentra. "Kirk will want to see Nico, and I'm sure Glone when he gets back, will like more time to train Lala."

I gave him a frank look letting him know he wasn't fooling anybody. "Yeah, because you're not going to miss Toma and Nico."

He shooed me away as Toma, and the others walked over. Trent stayed on the couch simply watching it all unfold. He didn't know them as well as I did, so he probably felt more comfortable there.

Hugs were given all around, and promises were made that we would all soon get together on a nonviolent world, just to party and have a good time. Another round of hugs, and promises and I opened the portal, that would lead them to Crimson.

Chaz gave me one last hug. "Ah, love, if it weren't for you, I'd still be stuck in an alley somewhere on your home world, and Clink and Kirk would still be in the blocker. Thank you."

I fell into his embrace. "You don't ever have to thank me." I wiped my face. "Not ever," I said, as I let him go. I stood and watched until the portal closed, and they'd disappeared.

"Well don't expect me to hug you," Nico said, but I could see the almost playful glint in her eyes. That was strange coming from her, and I didn't know how to respond, so I just nodded and moved on.

"Well, I'll give you a hug," Toma said, engulfing me in his arms. "I can't thank you enough. We can't. I hope you meant it when you said we'd be seeing each other soon?"

Did he even need to ask? "You know I did. We still have to get together and just party, right? Maybe even make it a monthly thing, huh? Hit a different world every time. No two worlds twice, okay?"

Toma smiled. "Sounds good to me. What do you say, Nico?"

She nodded. "Yeah, just give us a chance to get up and running." She looked at her brother. "We have to get Sentra back in order."

Toma took her hand. "Yeah, we do."

Saylor yawned as if she was bored with everything. "Can we go now? I have a city to rebuild."

I gave Toma one last hug, then opened a portal and watched all four of them until they too disappeared.

Trent came up behind me after they were gone and wrapped his arms around my waist. "Like cutting off a leg, huh?"

I fell back into his embrace, grateful for the comfort. "I've still got you," I said, not trying to deny the obvious.

He chuckled softly and whispered in my ear. "That you do, babe. That you do."

He turned me around as I looked at the two spots where I'd opened the portals. "Let's go to bed," he said.

I followed him, excited at what the future might hold.

Author Note

If you read this book and would like to know more about Rekia and Trent check out the novella Crooked Magic here[1], or read for free when you join my mailing list, here.[2]

Do you have questions about Clink and Glone? Chaz and Clink? Then Check out these novellas:

Rebel Magic- The story of Clink and Glone. Buy from Amazon here[3], or read for free when you join my mailing list, here.[4]

Stolen Magic- The story of Chaz and Clink. Buy from Amazon here[5], or read for free when you join my mailing list, here.[6]

Also, be on the lookout for more World Breaker and World Breaker Beginnings stories.

---

1. https://www.amazon.com/dp/B075YF35XX/ref=sr_1_2?s=digital-text&ie=UTF8&qid=1506478708&sr=1-2

2. https://landing.mailerlite.com/webforms/landing/h2l3b2

3. https://www.amazon.com/dp/B075YD3B6V/ref=sr_1_4?s=digital-text&ie=UTF8&qid=1506478708&sr=1-4

4. https://landing.mailerlite.com/webforms/landing/h2l3b2

5. https://www.amazon.com/dp/B075YTLVZK/ref=la_B071SDZRM2_1_3?s=books&ie=UTF8&qid=1506507697&sr=1-3

6. https://landing.mailerlite.com/webforms/landing/h2l3b2

Other Titles by N. R. Hairston

M_agic and Mischief Series_
    A Magical Reckoning,[1] Book One
A Symptom of Magic,[2] Book Two
A Victim of Magic,[3] Book Three
Sun Cursed
Cursed Magic,[4] Book One
Savage Magic[5], Book Two

---

1.   https://www.amazon.com/Magical-Reckoning-Supernatural-Betrayal-Mischief-ebook/dp/B071P7HQVH/ref=as_li_ss_tl?s=digital-text&ie=UTF8&qid=1495929540&sr=1-1&keywords=a+magical+reckoning&linkCode=sl1&tag=fbp02-20&linkId=53cd93b9dc96241660ae8b41ec2bdefe

2.   https://www.amazon.com/gp/product/B07489BQVL/ref=series_rw_dp_sw

3.   https://www.amazon.com/Victim-Magic-Stories-Supernatural-Mischief-ebook/dp/B07H5FHBFB/ref=sr_1_6?ie=UTF8&qid=1536873999&sr=8-6&keywords=n+r+hairston

4.   https://www.amazon.com/dp/B075YDZZ45/ref=sr_1_3?s=digital-text&ie=UTF8&qid=1506478708&sr=1-3

5.   https://www.amazon.com/Savage-Magic-N-R-Hairston-ebook/dp/B094DXP7J1/ref=sr_1_6?crid=2BGRD37EYPF31&dchild=1&keywords=n+r+hairston&qid=1620470219&s=digital-text&sprefix=n+r+%2Cdigital-text%2C148&sr=1-6

Lethal Magic[6], Book Three

World Breaker

Rogue Magic,[7] Book One

Bloody Magic,[8] Book Two

Battle Magic,[9] Book Three

World Breaker Beginnings (Novellas set before the events in Rogue Magic, though you don't have to read one to read the other.) Read this series for free when you join my mailing list, here.[10]

Rebel Magic,[11] Book One

Stolen Magic,[12] Book Two

Crooked Magic,[13] Book Three

Dirty Magic,[14] Book Four

---

6.   https://www.amazon.com/dp/B094DQ663R/ref=sr_1_10?crid=2BGRD37EYPF31&dchild=1&keywords=n+r+hairston&qid=1620470219&s=digital-text&sprefix=n+r+%2Cdigital-text%2C148&sr=1-10

7.   https://www.amazon.com/dp/B075YGLN4P/ref=sr_1_1?s=digital-text&ie=UTF8&qid=1506478708&sr=1-1

8.   https://www.amazon.com/gp/product/B094DR-RQH7?ref_=dbs_m_mng_rwt_calw_tkin_1&storeType=ebooks

9.   https://www.amazon.com/dp/B094DS7WLQ/ref=sr_1_8?crid=2BGRD37EYPF31&dchild=1&keywords=n+r+hairston&qid=1620470219&s=digital-text&sprefix=n+r+%2Cdigital-text%2C148&sr=1-8

10.   https://landing.mailerlite.com/webforms/landing/h2l3b2

11.   https://www.amazon.com/gp/product/B075YD3B6V?notRedirectToS-DP=1&ref_=dbs_mng_calw_0&storeType=ebooks

12.   https://www.amazon.com/gp/product/B075YTLVZK?notRedirectToS-DP=1&ref_=dbs_mng_calw_1&storeType=ebooks

Feral Magic[15], Book Five
Lawless Magic[16], Book Six

Rise of the Dragons

Fire and Ash,[17] Book One
Smoke and Flame,[18] Book Two
Dust and Cinder,[19] Book Three

Atina and Ridge

---

13.   https://www.amazon.com/gp/product/B075YF35XX?notRedirectToS-DP=1&ref_=dbs_mng_calw_2&storeType=ebooks

14.   https://www.amazon.com/dp/B094DSC8ZX/ref=sr_1_5?crid=2BGRD37EYPF31&dchild=1&keywords=n+r+hairston&qid=1620470219&s=digital-text&sprefix=n+r+%2Cdigital-text%2C148&sr=1-5

15.   https://www.amazon.com/dp/B094DQHDHY/ref=sr_1_3?crid=2BGRD37EYPF31&dchild=1&keywords=n+r+hairston&qid=1620470219&s=digital-text&sprefix=n+r+%2Cdigital-text%2C148&sr=1-3

16.   https://www.amazon.com/Lawless-Magic-World-Breaker-Beginnings-ebook/dp/B094DPBVHN/ref=sr_1_11?crid=2BGRD37EYPF31&dchild=1&keywords=n+r+hairston&qid=1620470219&s=digital-text&sprefix=n+r+%2Cdigital-text%2C148&sr=1-11

17.   https://www.amazon.com/Fire-Rise-Dragons-Trilogy-Book-ebook/dp/B076VFSGTZ/ref=sr_1_4?s=digital-text&ie=UTF8&qid=1531259254&sr=1-4&keywords=n+r+hairston

18.   https://www.amazon.com/gp/product/B076V3N5H8/ref=series_rw_dp_sw

19.   https://www.amazon.com/gp/product/B076V14N8H/ref=series_rw_dp_sw

We Got Powers Too,[20] Book One
We Wreak Havoc Too[21], Book Two
We Got Witches Too[22], Book Three

Rebel Writers Anthologies

Street Spells[23]

20.   https://www.amazon.com/gp/product/B07F8D55LL/
        ref=dbs_a_def_rwt_hsch_vapi_taft_p1_i10

21.   https://www.amazon.com/dp/B094DQSMS5/
        ref=sr_1_9?crid=2BGRD37EYPF31&dchild=1&keywords=n+r+hair-
        ston&qid=1620470219&s=digital-text&sprefix=n+r+%2Cdigital-
        text%2C148&sr=1-9

22.   https://www.amazon.com/dp/B094DP9PNQ/
        ref=sr_1_13?crid=2BGRD37EYPF31&dchild=1&keywords=n+r+hair-
        ston&qid=1620470219&s=digital-text&sprefix=n+r+%2Cdigital-
        text%2C148&sr=1-13

23.   https://www.amazon.com/gp/product/B07F6GXSWV/
        ref=dbs_a_def_rwt_hsch_vapi_taft_p1_i11

Acknowledgments

A special thanks to my beta readers, and editors for making this book what it is. Thank You!

If you enjoyed this book, tell me all about it by leaving a review.

Subscribe to N. R. Hairston's newsletter here,[1] to get exclusive short stories, and be the first to hear about deals and promotions.

Join my private Facebook reading group here.[2]

---

1. https://landing.mailerlite.com/webforms/landing/h2l3b2

2. https://www.facebook.com/groups/262478357600840/?fref=mentions

About the Author

N.R. Hairston resides in Southern Virginia with her family. She enjoys writing, reading, cooking, and spending time with her loved ones.

Please be on the lookout for upcoming books by N. R. Hairston.

I hope you enjoyed reading this book. If you'd like to discuss it, join my private Facebook reading group here,[1] or find me on linktree here[2].

---

1.   https://www.facebook.com/groups/262478357600840/?fref=mentions

2.   https://linktr.ee/N.R.Hairston